DOWNFALL

KERRY KAYA

Boldwood

First published in Great Britain in 2024 by Boldwood Books Ltd.

Copyright © Kerry Kaya, 2024

Cover Design by Colin Thomas

Cover Photography: Colin Thomas

A CIP catalogue record for this book is available from the British Library.

Paperback ISBN 978-1-83751-278-2

Large Print ISBN 978-1-83751-279-9

Hardback ISBN 978-1-83751-277-5

Ebook ISBN 978-1-83751-280-5

Kindle ISBN 978-1-83751-281-2

Audio CD ISBN 978-1-83751-272-0

MP3 CD ISBN 978-1-83751-273-7

Digital audio download ISBN 978-1-83751-274-4

Boldwood Books Ltd
23 Bowerdean Street
London SW6 3TN
www.boldwoodbooks.com

For Lucy.

The Carter Family Tree

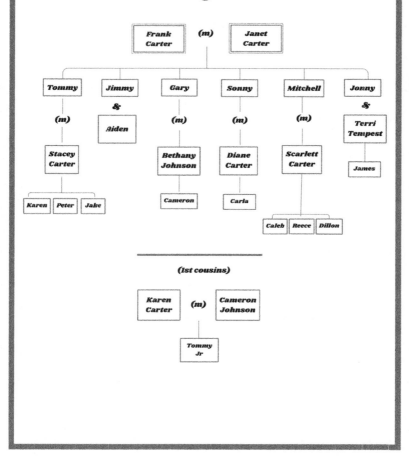

PROLOGUE
2004

A shiver of fear ran down the length of eight-year-old Carla Carter's spine. Never before had she seen her father look so angry. Of course, there had been times when he'd been annoyed, when he would raise his voice or give his wife the look – the one to warn her she was going too far and was starting to make an exhibition of herself. Which, as it just so happened, she liked to do often.

By her own admission, Diane Carter had a big mouth, one that she wasn't afraid to use. She had never been the type of woman to keep her opinions to herself and, as a result, was forever getting into slanging matches. More often than not, if it wasn't her husband on the receiving end of Diane's sharp tongue, then it was his family, or her daughter, or one of their long-suffering neighbours. After one particularly nasty argument, Carla's father, Sonny, had slammed out of the house and not returned home for three days. But never had he been so livid that he'd screamed and hollered blue murder before going on to destroy his and Diane's bedroom.

From her hiding place at the top of the stairs, Carla bit down on her bottom lip, tears spilling down her cheeks. For the first time in her life her daddy was beginning to frighten her. Each and every time she heard a loud thud or the sound of glass breaking, no doubt her mother's expensive perfume bottles being thrown against the wall, she would physically jump out of her skin, afraid that her parents were actually going to kill one another. That this time there would be no kissing and making up, that this time her father really would leave the house and never come back.

As the shouts became even louder and her mother's shrieks for him to get out of the house and leave her alone became more desperate, Carla was in half a mind to run back to her bedroom, screw her eyes shut tight and place her hands over her ears in an attempt to block out the noise. She wanted them to stop, wanted to see her mum smile again and for her dad to do something silly to make them both laugh, just as he used to do in the past when they had been happy. Only it had been a long time since she'd seen her mum smile, at least a genuine one anyway. Although it would be fair to say that she smiled often whenever her dad's friend Bernie Adams popped over, and he'd been coming over a lot recently, especially when her dad wasn't home. Bernie and her mum would spend hours in her parents' bedroom, talking and listening to music, not that they allowed Carla to join in. Her mum would even slide the bolt across the door to keep her locked out.

As the door to her parents' room swung wide open, Carla dug her nails into the palms of her hands and held her breath. Was her daddy still angry? Stepping out of the bedroom she saw that the colour had drained from Sonny Carter's face; the muscles across his shoulder blades taut and his knuckles bloody.

'Daddy.' Swallowing down the large lump in her throat, Carla's voice cracked, terror getting the better of her as she stared down at the holdall in her father's hand. 'Don't go, Daddy, please don't leave,' she cried, running to him and tugging on the bag in a desperate attempt to take it away from him and make him stay.

Sonny gave a loud sigh, and sinking down to his haunches he

pulled his daughter close, the familiar scent of his cologne, combined with body wash and shampoo, bringing her comfort. 'I'm so sorry sweetheart.' He gave a sad smile and kissed the top of his daughter's head. 'I'll only be gone for a little while. Just until things have calmed down a bit between me and your mum.' He glanced over his shoulder, glaring at his wife, his eyes hard, and his expression set like thunder. 'I'll be back soon, you just wait and see, and until then you can come and see me every weekend, how does that sound? You'd like that wouldn't you, you'd be able to spend some time with your cousins?'

Carla began to sob; she didn't want her daddy to go, and she didn't care about spending time with her stupid cousins. It wasn't as though they ever allowed her to play with them and, more often than not, would exclude her from their games, telling her that girls weren't allowed to play football or pretend to shoot guns. Even more than that, she didn't want to stay in the house with just her mum for company. Her mum never wanted to play with her and all she ever wanted to do was talk to Bernie, and Carla didn't like Bernie, at least not any more. She didn't like the way her mum behaved around him, the way she would hang off his every word and bat her eyelashes at him. She even laughed at his stupid jokes. It was all his fault that her daddy was leaving, she knew it was. She'd heard everything that had been said between her parents even if she didn't fully understand the words they had used. Maybe her daddy was mad at her too, mad because she'd told him about the times Bernie had visited. It was supposed to have been a secret, something her daddy was never meant to have found out about.

'That's right.' Amidst the destruction of the bedroom Diane Carter swiped the smeared mascara from underneath her eyes and gave a sarcastic laugh. The crocodile tears she'd put on moments earlier all too quickly evaporated, causing her beautiful face to turn ugly. 'Tell her more lies.' She turned then to look at her daughter with a wicked gleam in her eyes. 'He isn't coming back. In fact,' she crossed her arms over her chest, her lips twisting into a cruel smile, 'you're going to have a new daddy.'

Sonny jumped to his feet so fast that Carla toppled to the floor and as she landed on the thick carpet with a bump she howled from a mixture of both shock and fear. It was so typical of her mum; she was forever goading her dad, forever trying to make him angry. For what reason, Carla didn't know. Her daddy was lovely, the kindest man she had ever known. He would even come home from work early just so that he could read her a bedtime story, something her mum never wanted to do.

'You and that big trap of yours, Di,' Sonny hissed through clenched teeth as he bounded forward. 'You never know when to keep it shut do you. And let me tell you something else for nothing, I'd rather kill the no-good bastard than allow him to step another foot inside my house. My house!' he roared, stabbing a finger into his chest. 'So you'd best tell him that I'm gunning for him and believe me, sooner rather than later, I will end him over this.'

Diane raised her eyebrows, her red painted talons more than ready to lash out at her husband if need be. 'That's right, resort to violence,' she retorted, shaking her head. 'That's all you're good for. At least my Bernie is a real man,' she screamed in his face. 'At least he's more than just a hired lackey.' She gestured around the once immaculate bedroom filled with expensive furniture and sneered. 'My Bernie knows how to treat a woman,' she smirked. 'And unlike you, he's going places. You're nothing but weak; tied to your brothers' apron strings. They say jump and you ask how high; it's been that way ever since the day I met you and if I didn't know any better, I'd say you're scared of them.' She spread open her arms, her sneer intensifying as she pretended to quiver. 'If only people knew the truth, the big Sonny Carter actually terrified of his own family.'

'You know fuck all,' Sonny roared.

'Don't I?' Diane screamed back at him. 'I know that you'll never make anything of yourself, that ten years from now, no, twenty years from now, you'll still be taking orders like the good little foot soldier you are.'

From her position on the floor, Carla watched as her daddy stepped back out of the room, his entire body trembling with rage. Scooping her up from the floor he wrapped his strong arms around her and nuzzled his face into her hair, all the while taking deep breaths in an attempt to keep his temper at bay.

'I'll come and see you soon sweetheart, okay. Be a good girl for your mum.'

Carla could barely bring herself to answer and as her father plonked her back on the floor it took everything inside of her not to chase after him, to beg him to take her with him.

'That's it,' her mother screamed at his retreating back. 'Run away like you always do. Is it any wonder I want a real man in my life?'

Pausing at the top of the stairs, Sonny shook his head, his shoulders sagging. He looked so sad and so defeated that Carla wanted to cry all over again. It was in that instant Carla decided she didn't like her mum very much, at least not when she was screaming and shouting. And as for Bernie, as young as Carla was, she vowed to make him pay for what he'd caused. That one day, when she had grown up, she would make him suffer for tearing her perfect little family apart.

1

2022

As far as family meetings went, the one currently being held at the Carter family's scrapyard didn't disappoint. Not only was it standing room only, but the atmosphere was tense and tempers were beginning to flare.

Sitting behind the desk in the portable cabin that doubled as both an office and meeting area, Jimmy Carter cracked his knuckles, his lips set into a thin line. For more than two hours they had been at a standstill, neither of his brothers willing to budge on the matter at hand and if that wasn't bad enough, he had a flight to Spain booked for 9 p.m., not that it looked as though he was going to make it. Story of his life. He'd lost count of how many times he'd missed a flight over the years. His elder brother, Tommy, had been the worst offender, doing everything in his power to keep Jimmy with him that little bit longer, finding last-minute jobs for Jimmy to do.

In recent years, his youngest brother, Jonny, had become the main cause of him extending his stay. Jonny was reckless, and as much as it pained Jimmy to admit it – if it wasn't for the fact Jonny was family, that he knew how to handle a car, and that he excelled when it came to being the Carter family's getaway driver, then Jimmy would have kicked him to the kerb years ago. In a lot of ways Jonny reminded Jimmy of Tommy. Both were headstrong, not to mention a downright nightmare to work alongside. Yet, despite his flaws, Jonny was also ambitious and knew an opportunity when he saw one and certainly didn't shy away from taking risks. Jimmy allowed himself a small smile wondering how Tommy would have dealt with their youngest brother's antics; he would have had his work cut out for him, that much Jimmy did know.

He took a quick glance at his watch and silently groaned. If he didn't leave within the next five minutes, then he could say goodbye to his flight and the amount of grief that would cause him didn't bear thinking about. His partner, Aiden, was bound to have something to say about the situation, not that Jimmy entirely blamed him. Time and time again he'd left Aiden in the lurch and expected him to run their bar in Spain single-handed whilst he'd jumped on a plane without a moment's notice to sort out whichever latest mess his brothers had got themselves into. Then there were the armed robberies to contend with. The planning of each heist alone could take months, sometimes anything up to a year and that was without the time spent actually staking a venue out. And being the meticulous person he was, Jimmy had insisted on being the one to personally oversee each and every robbery they carried out.

Aware that all eyes had turned towards him, Jimmy leaned back in the chair and chewed thoughtfully on his bottom lip. As he did so, a familiar wave of tiredness washed over him. He was tired of the life, exhausted in fact, and the larger the family grew, the greater the responsibility became. Keeping both himself and his brothers and many nephews one step ahead of the police had finally begun to take its toll on him. He was forever on his guard, forever looking over his shoulder, half expecting the old bill to appear out of nowhere and snap handcuffs upon his wrists. He'd never even wanted to be a part of the criminal underworld, not really. It had been Tommy who'd dragged him along for the ride, Tommy who'd set them on the path as armed robbers. He cast his gaze over his younger brothers, Sonny and Mitchell, and was reminded once again that, like him, they too had been given no other choice but to join the family business – unlike their youngest brother, Jonny, who'd done everything in his power to follow on in his elder brothers' footsteps.

'Well?' Never one to have much patience, Jonny Carter sprang out of his seat barely giving Sonny and Mitchell a second glance. By rights, they should have been the ones to lead the family, now that Jimmy had decided to retire and make a permanent move over to Spain, but Jonny had his eyes on the crown and it was no secret that he wanted to be the one to give out the orders. 'I can do this,' he said, placing his hands on the desk with a determined look in his eyes. 'You know I can.'

Jimmy sighed; he didn't doubt his youngest brother in the least – he took after Tommy after all. But Jonny didn't have the experience of planning out a heist, hence why the meeting had been called in the first place. It was going to be hard enough for Jimmy to hand over the reins and walk away from the only life he'd ever known, without the added pressure of knowing whether or not his younger brothers were capable enough to take over from him. Could he really trust Jonny to keep the family out of prison? He was under no illusions that their good luck was bound to run out at some point, that the slightest wrong move on their part could result in the Carter family receiving a capture and they would more than likely have the book thrown at them and say goodbye to their freedom for the foreseeable future. He cast a glance towards Sonny and Mitchell and couldn't help but take note of the fine lines around their eyes and the faint silver streaks coating their dark hair. His younger brothers were getting old, just as he himself was growing older, which was exactly the reason why he wanted to retire, to leave the family business behind him and live out the remainder of his life in Spain in relative peace. Carrying out armed robberies was a young man's game and seeing as Jonny was their youngest brother it made sense that he should take over, that he should be the one to lead the next generation of Carters.

'You're not seriously considering this are you?' The annoyance in Sonny Carter's voice was more than apparent. Getting to his feet he spread open his arms and looked around him, first to his twin brother Mitchell and then his daughter and nephews who lined the walls of the office. 'Have you lost your mind? You honestly think he can be trusted to keep us, all of us,' he reiterated, jerking his thumb around him, 'out of nick. He's a liability, he'll fuck up, you know he will, it's all he ever does. How many times have we had to bail him out over the years?' he urged, his voice rising. 'How many times have we had to step in and sort him out.'

'I am here you know,' Jonny grumbled, gesturing to himself. 'And since when have you ever planned out a robbery,' he added, his eyes blazing. 'It's me who works out the routes, it's me who's responsible for getting us back here without so much as having a sniff of the old bill on our tail. You and Mitchell haven't got a scooby and you know it. Up until now,' he said, jabbing his finger onto the desktop to emphasise his point, 'you were more than happy to leave the planning to me and Jimmy. The only thing the two of you have ever had to worry about was turning up on time.'

As Sonny began to protest, Jimmy held up his hand in a bid to quieten them down, the soft tick tock that came from the clock on the wall a stark reminder that he should have been on his way to the airport by now. 'Someone has to take over,' he reminded his brothers. He lowered his voice a fraction and gave Sonny a pointed look. 'Do you really want the hag that comes along with running this place, the endless hours spent staking a venue out, the relentless worry that this time something could go wrong?' Just as he'd known he would, Sonny averted his gaze; it may have only been slight, something that the rest of the family would never have picked up on, but it was enough for Jimmy to know that his gut instincts had been right all along. Despite his protests, Sonny didn't want the responsibility of leading the family, and even more than that, he didn't have the necessary drive to propel them forward, had never had it. Even when they had been young men in their prime, Sonny had been more than happy to follow their eldest brother, Tommy's lead. He was a follower, a sheep, much the same as his twin brother Mitchell. And as trustworthy as the two brothers may have been, they had never been hungry for power, a fact that Jimmy and even Tommy himself had been well aware of.

'Come on, Jimmy.' Jonny looked between his brothers, the excitement in his voice more than audible. 'One of us has to take over.' He lifted his eyebrows silently beseeching Jimmy to choose him. 'Who is it going to be?'

Sinking back into the chair Jimmy steepled his fingers leaving the unanswered question thick in the air. The irritated sigh that came from Sonny was all the confirmation Jimmy needed – not that he hadn't known all along that Jonny would be the one to take over from him – that neither Sonny nor Mitchell would fight for the position. In all honesty, the meeting had been nothing more than a farce. He'd needed each of his brothers to understand their standing within the family before he handed over the reins and walked away from them, and the last thing he wanted was for his family to be at loggerheads, yet he knew instinctively that when it came down to it, Jonny wouldn't play fair; that he would scheme and plot his way to the top. Perhaps it would even come to blows between them and seeing as theirs was a large family, it had never taken much to set at least one of them off. They were notorious for their fallouts, and as loyal and protective of one another as they were, they could also be brutal when they needed to be.

Jimmy took a quick glance at his watch then rose to his feet. Digging his hand into his pocket, he took out the keys for the scrapyard and looked down at them. He'd always imagined that he would find it difficult when it came to handing them over, but in truth it wasn't. That wasn't to say, however, that he wasn't worried for his family's future, because he was, how could he not be – he'd looked out for them for so long it had almost become second nature to him. But at the end of the day, he'd done his time; had done his part in keeping the family safe. He tossed the keys across to his youngest brother, eager to be rid of them. 'Don't let me down,' he said in a warning, his expression suddenly becoming menacing.

The triumphant grin that was spread across Jonny's face intensified. 'I won't,' he answered, gripping the keys tightly in his fist.

Jimmy nodded. At the back of his mind, he was still somewhat unsure that Jonny understood exactly what he was taking on, or that any of his brothers truly knew what it meant to be the head of the Carter family. Not that he himself had had any real insight into the sacrifices he would have had to make for the family all those years ago when he'd taken over from Tommy. Only in his case, he'd never been given a choice. There had been no meeting to decide who would take over. After Tommy's murder he had been the next eldest, and so whether he'd wanted the position or not, it had been presumed that he would be the natural successor. And he'd done a good job of it too; the fact they had never so much as ever been brought in for questioning over a robbery had been testament to that fact. He took a moment to study his youngest brother. Already Jonny was eyeing up the desk that until now had belonged to Jimmy. The family's future would fall upon Jonny's shoulders. Every quarrel, disagreement, or feud would now become Jonny's sole responsibility and Jimmy knew from experience that there would always be someone, somewhere, with a grudge to bear. It stood to reason, seeing as theirs was a family that was both notorious and feared in equal measures.

* * *

Carla Carter crossed one shapely leg over the other. Outwardly she appeared impassive, perhaps even bored, as she listened to her father and uncles argue over who would be taking over the business. Inwardly however, her stomach was tied up in knots. As much as she loved her dad, and she really did love him, she wanted her uncle Jonny to become Jimmy's successor. Sonny was too straight-laced, same went for her uncle Mitchell too. They didn't take unnecessary risks, and certainly wouldn't entertain carrying out a robbery in the name of revenge. But her uncle Jonny on the other hand, he was hungry; he wanted to prove that he had what it took to execute the perfect crime. Not only was he ruthless but he also knew an opportunity when he saw one and as it just so happened Carla knew the perfect venue they could rob.

As they filed out of the office Carla watched her father as he headed for his car. The slight tension across his shoulder blades alerted her to the fact he wasn't happy Jonny had been chosen over him. Not that she could say she particularly blamed him; he'd spent his entire life preparing for this moment, knowing that one day Jimmy would retire and that the business, whether he wanted it to or not would fall into his hands. And the fact he'd been bypassed had to have stung, bringing with it further confirmation that Jimmy didn't think he was good enough, that neither he nor Mitchell had what it took to run the business. In that instant, she felt a moment of pity for him. Her dad was too nice for his own good; he would never have argued his case, would never have gone up against Jimmy's decision. When Jimmy said jump her dad asked how high

– not that her dad wasn't able to take care of himself, because he could. Time and time again she'd heard Jimmy state that Sonny had a blinding right hook on him, that out of all his brothers, Sonny was the one he was more wary of. He had a quietness about him, a calmness, that over the years others had mistakenly taken for weakness. It was only when the red mist descended that those who had taken Sonny for a fool realised that beneath the façade, he was a dangerous individual.

'Dad,' she softly called out to him. 'Are you okay?'

Sonny paused, and as he turned around to face Carla, she could see just how weary he was. He'd never remarried after his divorce, unlike her mum, who hadn't been able to walk down the aisle fast enough, much to Carla's disgust. Despite her dad's reluctance to remarry, Carla wasn't naïve enough to think there had never been any other women in his life. He was a good-looking man after all, a catch, not to mention wealthy. Women fell at his feet; she'd even witnessed their shameless flirting with her own two eyes. But to her knowledge there had never been anyone special; perhaps her mum had put him off women for life. Carla knew firsthand just how difficult her mum, Diane, could be. Despite their divorce she'd done everything in her power to make life hard for Sonny; it was almost as though she resented him, as though he were the one who had done wrong and that she wanted to make him suffer for leaving her. At the drop of a hat, she would restrict his visits with his only child and would take great pleasure in watching him beg for contact. Was it any wonder that Carla felt contempt for her mother? And as for Bernie, her mother's husband, Carla despised him, and always had.

Sonny gave a shrug and closing the car door he made his way over to his daughter. 'If you want my opinion, Jimmy has lost the plot. Why else would he have handed the reins over to Jonny? He's going to bring us down,' he warned, glaring at the office. 'Give it six months and it'll be game over. You mark my words, every single last one of us will end up in handcuffs and be carted off to the nearest nick.'

Carla glanced behind her. Maybe her dad was right; Jonny was young after all but in his defence, her uncles had been a lot younger when they'd first set out. Her dad had only been a teenager, barely out of school when he'd robbed his first bank and Jonny was no fool, he'd been taught by the best. She took a deep breath, debating within herself how best to answer. She couldn't let her dad see just how thrilled she was at the prospect of Jonny taking over. 'Jimmy knows what he's doing.'

'Then Jimmy's deluded,' Sonny baulked. 'Jonny can barely rein himself in, what hope does he have with that lot.'

Carla followed her father's gaze to where her cousins loitered on the forecourt. They were a rowdy bunch, some worse than others. Perhaps her dad had a point; would Jonny actually be able to control them? Not that her dad or Uncle Mitchell would have fared any better, especially when it came to Thomas, or Tommy Jr, as he was more commonly known. Technically, Thomas was her cousin's son and her uncle Tommy's grandson, and although he may have gone by the surname Johnson, his genes were strong and he had more Carter blood flowing through his veins then the rest of the family combined, seeing as her cousins Karen and Cameron were Tommy Jr's parents and that both his maternal and paternal grandfathers had been brothers. On more than one occasion she'd heard her dad state that Thomas would need to be watched, that in the wrong hands he could be dangerous. She gave a shudder. She was fond of Tommy Jr; he was a good kid, albeit hard to handle at times.

A short while later, Carla made her way towards the office. For as long as she could remember, all she had ever wanted was to be a part of her family's world, for her father to treat her as he did her male cousins. And after much persuasion on her part her dad had finally relented, giving her a glimpse into what it was that made the Carter family tick.

Growing up she had known that both her father and uncles were notorious, that their reputations made them both feared and respected amongst the local community. But until she'd joined the family business, she hadn't known the exact reason why. Oh, she wasn't daft. Many a time she had questioned just how it was that they had made their money and knew for a fact the vast wealth couldn't have come from the scrapyard alone. How could it when each of her uncles and her father, lived a life of luxury?

Pausing at the door she shook her head. Jonny lounged back on the chair, his hands locked behind his head, his feet up on the desk, and a satisfied expression spread across his face.

'Congratulations.'

Startled, Jonny scrambled to take his feet down, his cheeks flaming red. 'Carla,' he said, pulling a pile of paperwork towards him in an attempt to hide his embarrassment.

Sinking into a chair, Carla couldn't help but laugh out loud. He looked so like her dad – a younger version, of course. All the Carters looked alike, each of them a carbon copy of one another, herself included; there could never be any mistaking that Sonny was her father. 'I see you've already made yourself at home.' She paused for a moment then nodded towards the desk. 'Suits you.'

Jonny narrowed his eyes. 'Is that a sly dig?' he asked, not taking his eyes away from his niece. 'Because if it is, then your dad could have fought for it,' he said, pointing towards the forecourt. 'He had ample opportunity to sway Jimmy's mind.'

Carla shook her head. 'We both know my dad didn't want this place.' She gestured around the cramped space that hadn't changed in all the years she'd been coming to the scrapyard. Even the potted plant tucked into the corner of the office, the leaves brown and dry, and the ceramic pot cracked and chipped in places, had been there for years. Why no one had had the sense to throw it out she didn't know; it wasn't as though a sprinkling of water was going to miraculously bring the plant back to life. 'Not really, not deep down in here,' she said, tapping her chest.

Jonny gave a carefree shrug. If he felt any form of remorse then he didn't show it, not that Carla had actually expected him to. 'What can I do for you then Carla, because I have a feeling you didn't come in here just to congratulate me.'

Carla flashed a smile and leaning slightly forward, her long dark hair fell around her shoulders. 'I have a proposition for you.'

'Let me guess,' Jonny grinned, 'it's one that I won't be able to refuse.'

'Something like that.' Straightening up, Carla looked her uncle in the eyes. 'It's the one thing that will really cement that crown on your head. The one thing no one in our family has ever been able to achieve.'

Almost immediately Carla could see the wheels turning in Jonny's head. He was more than a little intrigued, and as he sat back in the chair, she mirrored his stance, her expression becoming serious, businesslike.

'Diamonds,' she said, watching his reaction closely. 'I just so happen to know where to find some, and if that wasn't enough,' she said with a wicked gleam in her eyes, 'they've got our names written all over them.'

2

Stacey McKay pulled her dressing gown tighter around her and shook her head. She wasn't entirely surprised to see her former brother-in-law back on her doorstep only hours after he'd said his goodbyes. All along she should have known he would miss his flight, just as he'd missed countless flights before now.

'Get yourself in,' she chuckled. 'The spare bedroom is still made up for you.'

Jimmy smiled his thanks. 'I'll be out of your hair first thing in the morning,' he promised.

'Oh, get away with you.' Stacey flapped her hand. 'You know we love having you over to stay and who knows how long it will be until your next visit.'

As he followed Stacey through to the sitting room Jimmy rolled his eyes. 'Somehow I've got a feeling that I'll be back a lot sooner than I'd anticipated.'

With a frown upon her face Stacey spun around. 'What do you mean by that?'

Jimmy shrugged and taking a seat on the sofa he offered a small smile. 'I handed the reins over to Jonny.'

Wearily, Stacey closed her eyes. 'And I bet that went down like a lead balloon?' she sighed. 'Me and Danny,' she said, nodding towards her second husband as he entered the room, 'were convinced that you'd choose Sonny and Mitchell to take over from you.'

'It went down exactly as I expected it would,' Jimmy answered. 'Sonny and Mitchell didn't put up a fight and until the boys...' His voice trailed off and he nodded towards the portraits of Stacey's sons that lined the mantlepiece. 'Well, if the time ever comes and Peter or Jake want to take over the reins then it's theirs, goes without saying.'

Stacey gasped. 'Over my dead bloody body, they will. Have you lost your mind?' she hissed. 'That you think I'd ever let my boys run the business.'

Stacey's husband cleared his throat. 'It is their business, Stace,' he reminded his wife. 'The scrapyard belonged to Tommy and as his sons, whether you like it or not, they have rights.'

'What rights?' Stacey scoffed with a shake of her head. She pointed a stiff finger towards Jimmy. 'It's bad enough that they work for the business, let alone run it. And you're a fine one to talk,' she said, turning her attention back to her husband, her lips pursed. 'You didn't want your Logan to follow on in your footsteps,' she said, referring to Danny's son. 'In fact, you did everything in your power to push him into college, for him to make a legitimate career for himself.'

Danny sighed and holding up his hands he settled himself into the armchair. 'Fair point,' he conceded, not that his son was as far away from the criminal underworld as he would have liked.

Her earlier anger somewhat subsiding, Stacey joined Jimmy on the sofa. 'Jonny's not daft. He's had his moments, admittedly, and let's face it plenty of them over the years, but he isn't stupid, he wouldn't take any unnecessary risks – especially not now, not when he's about to become a father, he'd have too much to lose.'

Jimmy sighed and as he looked between Stacey and Danny he lifted his shoulders, his expression one of concern. 'I hope you're right, Stace, because up here,' he said, tapping his temple, 'I can't help but think I fucked up, that maybe I should have chosen Sonny and Mitchell.' He gave a shake of his head, his forehead furrowing. 'They'd play it safe. You know that as well as I do.'

Stacey clutched Jimmy's hand. She understood his worry and as her gaze drifted back to the photographs of her sons, a feeling of dread swept over her. Both her sons' and grandsons' futures rested in Jonny's hands. All it would take was one mistake and it could very well be game over; they would more than likely spend the rest of their lives behind bars.

As much as she hated to admit it, perhaps she was partly to blame that her sons had followed in their father's footsteps. It had been far easier on her part to turn a blind eye when it came to her first husband's chosen occupation; for her to pretend that the money Tommy Carter had accumulated over the years had come from legal sources rather than armed robberies. Her heart began to race.

'Maybe you're right,' she said, giving Jimmy's hand a tight squeeze, her voice a lot higher than she'd intended.

* * *

'Go on you've got my attention.'

Carla smiled. Of course, she had Jonny's attention – she'd known that from the very moment the word diamond had slipped out of her mouth. 'Bernie...' she began.

Jonny screwed up his face. 'You mean your stepdad?'

The smile slipped from Carla's face. 'He's not my stepdad,' she snapped.

'Listen,' Jonny gave a gentle smile, 'admittedly, I'd be the first to hold up my hands and agree that Bernie is a first-class prick. But when him and your old man used to knock about together as kids, he was actually alright. He could be a bit flash at times, a bit cocky I suppose,' he shrugged, 'but that was about it. I liked him, we all did. And whether you like it or not,' he said, stabbing his finger forward. 'He's married to your mum and in my book that makes him your stepdad.'

Carla shook her head. In her eyes Bernie Adams was nothing more than her mother's husband and to think of him as anything else was the equivalent of betraying her dad, and she'd already betrayed Sonny enough by secretly rooting for Jonny to take control of the business. 'It doesn't matter what he is or isn't,' she spat through clenched teeth. 'My point is he has diamonds in his possession.'

Jonny laughed out loud. 'Give over Carls. Do you honestly think I'm going to put myself out and rob him of a few measly diamond rings, I'd become a laughing stock.'

Crossing her arms over her chest Carla's expression could only be described as smug. 'Who said anything about rings?' She sat forward in the chair and lifted her eyebrows. 'I'm talking about diamonds. Lots and lots of diamonds.'

* * *

On a daily basis, Bernie Adams liked to give others the impression that he was loaded, that he could afford to buy whatever his heart desired. On his wrist he wore a flashy timepiece that had cost thousands of pounds and, wherever possible, he made a point of only dining out at the most expensive of restaurants. In truth, however, his vast fortune had all but dwindled down to nothing. Oh, he still owned a large mock Tudor mansion on the outskirts of Essex, or at least he did until his debts finally caught up with him and bailiffs turned up at the property, promptly turfing him and his wife out on their ears. In fact, it was only because of the second and then subsequent third mortgage he'd taken out on the property, not forgetting the various credit cards he'd secretly taken out in both his and his wife, Diane's, names, that he was still able to drive a car that was guaranteed to turn heads, and could also afford to splash out on bottles of champagne that cost more than what most men earned in a week. In his line of work, it was all about image. He had to be seen as doing well for himself, and even more than that, he had to keep up the pretence that life was on the up. But when it came down to what he actually had in his bank account, he had very little to his name; something that neither Diane nor his business associates were aware of.

Was it any wonder that he'd found himself becoming embroiled with the Tucker family? They'd presented him with an opportunity he couldn't resist, and being desperate for a solution to his money troubles, he'd taken it with both hands. Not only that, but being associated with the Tuckers was bound to open other doors, which as far as he was concerned could only be a bonus. He needed more cash, needed a way to dig himself out of the hole he found himself in.

Weaving his way through a private members club a few streets away from Kings Cross station, a wide smile was plastered across Bernie's face. Despite the fact it was still early evening, the scent of cigar smoke and expensive aftershave assaulted his nostrils. The club screamed of money and from the very moment Bernie had stepped through the doors he'd felt at home. It was all about show, he decided. It made no difference that he was broke, that he didn't have a proverbial pot to piss in; dressed in a dark suit and a pristine white shirt, the cuffs secured with solid gold cufflinks, he looked the part, and in Bernie's world, that was all that mattered.

Towards the rear of the club, he came to a halt in front of a table, his grin still held firmly in place. 'Ozzie.' He nodded in a greeting before turning to look at the man sitting beside him. 'Lenny.' He didn't bother to address the remaining firm members at the table; why should he, when by their own admission they were nothing more than hired muscle?

'Bernie.' Returning the greeting, Ozzie Tucker flicked his head towards an empty chair. As always, an ever-present scowl was etched across his face, his beady eyes observing everything and everyone around him.

Bernie's grin intensified, and with an air of confidence he pulled out the chair and took a seat, all the while tearing his gaze away from the man sitting upon Ozzie's lap. He would have never said it out loud for fear of repercussions, but the man's presence unnerved him. It was the way the man watched him, the way his hard stare seemed to be able to penetrate into Bernie's skull. It was almost as though he'd been able to suss out the truth, that beneath the façade Bernie liked to put on for those around him, he was nothing more than a fraudster, a man who was so desperate that he'd befriended the Tuckers for his own gain. And let's face it there was no other reason why he would have sought the Tuckers out; they weren't exactly men who could be trusted, they weren't even likeable. In fact, he could barely recall anyone who actually had a good word to say about them.

He watched as the man, who called himself Sadie, whispered something into Ozzie's ear before detangling himself from his embrace and sashaying across the club. It took everything in Bernie's power not to stare after him, his eyes hard. Sadie had to be pushing fifty, if he was a day, and if the rumours were anything to go by, he'd only recently been released from prison after serving a long stretch inside for murder. From the corner of his eye Bernie glanced towards the Tuckers' henchmen. If any of them felt the same sense of unease that he did then they didn't show it. Not that it would have been in any of their best interests to openly show any form of contempt. Out of the two brothers, it was well known that Ozzie was the more unhinged, that at the best of times he could be a paranoid bugger, and as such should be treated with kid gloves or better still, given a wide berth.

'Are the diamonds safe?'

It was Lenny who spoke, and nodding his head furiously, Bernie resisted the urge to swipe the droplets of sweat from his upper lip. Of course, the diamonds were safe, he wasn't stupid. As soon as they had been pushed into his hands, he'd placed them inside the cast-iron safe nestled at the bottom of his wardrobe. He'd never even told his wife the combination code, too afraid that the nosy cow would snoop through his most prized possessions the very moment his back was turned.

'Good.' Lighting a cigarette, Lenny pointed the burning embers in Bernie's direction. 'Make sure it stays that way.'

Bernie swallowed deeply. It would be more than his life was worth to allow anything to happen to the merchandise and he was under no false pretences that if the police were to ever raid his home and find the stolen gems in his possession, that he would be the one to end up doing time, and that was only if the Tuckers didn't find a way to silence him first. He wouldn't put anything past the brothers; they could make him disappear if they so wished and when it came down to it, other than Diane, there was no one else who would actually miss him. He had no other family, didn't even have many friends – at least none who would question his absence. As for Ozzie and Lenny Tucker, they'd made no secret of the fact that they viewed him as dispensable, the weakest link in their firm; it was one of the only reasons they had brought him in to work with them. 'Don't you worry.' He tapped the side of his nose, his voice full of mock bravado. 'Believe me when I say this, they're locked up tighter than the crown jewels.' It was a slight exaggeration considering where he'd stashed the diamonds, but he wasn't about to admit this fact out loud, and certainly not to the Tuckers of all people. 'You know what I'm like,' he said, puffing out his chest with a measure of self-importance. 'I don't mess around when it comes to the goods.'

Lenny Tucker leaned back in the chair, his gaze firmly fixed on Bernie as he continued to smoke his cigarette. 'Talking of messing around,' he said, stroking the grey stubble across his jaw. 'How's that wife of yours doing?'

Instantly, Bernie's spine straightened. The hidden inuendo behind Lenny's words making the men around the table snigger. It would be fair to say that his wife Diane had been around the block more than once and that was before she had even married Sonny Carter. And if she could do the dirty on Sonny then he was more than aware that there was nothing stopping her from doing the same to him too. 'She's okay,' he shrugged in an attempt to brush the question off.

Lenny smirked. 'Nice woman, your Diane,' he said, pointing the cigarette forward again. 'Knows how to have a good time. What was it they used to call her back in the day?' He tilted his head to the side as though thinking the question over. 'Oh yeah, that was it: pass the parcel. I mean that was one of the nicer terms of course, believe me there were plenty of other slurs they used to describe her. Yeah,' he said, looking into the distance, 'your Diane was a girl alright, and always up for it if you know what I mean. And as for us lads, well it would have been rude to say no wouldn't it.' He flashed Bernie a wink. 'Great times they were.'

Nausea made its way up Bernie's throat and as he shifted his weight, his earlier good mood quickly evaporated. At a loss for something to say, he turned his head and beckoned for a waiter. He needed a drink and fast; needed something to distract his attention from the all-too-knowing sneers around him. Moments later he knocked back a measure of whiskey, hoping more than anything else that the alcohol would help erase the sickening images that had entered his mind, mainly of Diane and Lenny Tucker in various stages of undress on his king-sized bed, the crisp cotton sheets crumpled beneath them. A scenario he knew only too well seeing as he and Diane had once been in an all too familiar position. Except back then, the bed had belonged to Sonny Carter, his former childhood friend. Perhaps this was his karma, his punishment for betraying Sonny in one of the worst ways imaginable. The thought was as depressing as it was sobering.

* * *

Jonny Carter narrowed his eyes. 'How the fuck did Bernie manage to get his grubby mitts on a stash of diamonds?'

Leaning forward Carla rested her forearms on the desk that separated them. 'He's looking after them.' She gave a slight shake of her head, her patience beginning to wear thin. 'Does it really matter how he came by them?' she asked.

'Of course it matters.' Jonny threw up his hands. 'This isn't a game we're playing. If – and this is only an if at this point,' he warned, stabbing his finger forward, 'I agree to this, then I need to know where they've come from because I'm going to take a wild guess and say that Bernie wasn't the one who lifted them.' He screwed up his face, his dislike of the man who had all but destroyed his brother's marriage clearly visible. 'He might be a lot of things but to have the gall to carry out a robbery isn't one of them.'

Carla sighed and as she looked down at her hands, she picked at her nail varnish. As much as she hated to admit it, her nerves were beginning to get the better of her. What would happen if Jonny was to turn her down? She couldn't go to her dad or her Uncle Mitchell, they would refuse point blank to even hear her out let alone consider her plan for revenge, especially where diamonds were concerned. 'I overheard him and my mum talking,' she answered, looking up. 'The way he was carrying on you'd think he was some kind of big shot,' her lip curled in disgust as it always did whenever she was forced to speak about her mother's husband. 'He wasn't even involved in the actual robbery. Like I said, he's only looking after them until they can be shipped out.'

'Which brings me back to my original question,' Jonny replied, his voice tight. 'Where did they come from?'

Taking a deep breath Carla raised her eyebrows. Instinctively she knew this would be the moment when Jonny would refuse her request no matter how much his interest might be piqued. 'Lenny and Ozzie Tucker.'

Jonny's eyes widened, his expression one of shock. 'The Tuckers?' he exclaimed.

Carla nodded.

'But...' Deep in thought Jonny shook his head. 'How did they...' He paused and cocked his head to the side. 'You mean to tell me it was them, that they were responsible for that heist over in Hatton Garden?'

Carla nodded again. 'That's what I'm guessing.' She gave a small smile. The Tuckers had only been in the game for a short time and already they had managed to achieve the one thing that her family hadn't. Three times her dad and uncles had attempted to steal a diamond from Hatton Garden and each time their attempt had been thwarted to the point that they had all but given up even trying. They'd often referred to the failed heists as more than just a run of bad luck but as a bad omen, a gut instinct telling them that they needed to stay as far away from the gems as they possibly could.

As she watched the different emotions flicker across Jonny's face, Carla forced herself to relax. The Tucker brothers had been a thorn in her family's side for a number of years, so much so, that at one point a war had been on the cards. It had been Tommy Jr who had taken the initial brunt of their vendetta, the fact his late grandfathers had been brothers had been all the ammunition the Tuckers had needed, and still to this day they openly referred to him as being inbred. And even though the two families had eventually called somewhat of a truce, her dad and uncle's dislike for Lenny and Ozzie Tucker was still so tangible that she could almost taste it. 'What are you thinking?' Crossing her fingers, her breathing became hitched in anticipation of his answer.

'What do you think?' As he cracked his knuckles Jonny flashed a wide grin. 'I'd give anything to see those fuckers brought down.' Leaning back in the chair, he looked into the distance. 'Only problem is though,' he flicked his head towards the forecourt, his expression becoming serious, 'your old man and Mitchell, they'll never agree to it.'

Lifting her eyebrows Carla made sure to keep the hint of a grin that threatened to crease her face at bay. 'And there was me thinking that you were the one in charge now.' She leaned in closer and lowered her voice a fraction. 'You're the head of the Carter family,' she smiled sweetly. 'They take orders from you now.'

3

Diane Adams flounced out of her house in a cloud of overpowering, sweet perfume. Despite the fact it had only just turned 10 a.m., she was dressed up to the nines. Not that Diane would ever be seen dead stepping outside the house without a face full of make-up. As far as she was concerned, she had an image to live up to. She was Bernie Adams' wife and as such, had to look her best at all times. Even Bernie himself had never seen her without her warpaint on, which was just as well considering the thick foundation she applied each morning hid a multitude of sins.

Stepping across the gravelled courtyard, Diane fished her car keys out of her designer handbag and pressed down on the key fob. As she climbed behind the wheel of the car, she gave an involuntary shiver. It wasn't necessarily the sensation of the cool leather beneath her bare legs that made her shudder but more so the fact that she despised the car, which had been a gift from Bernie. She'd had her eye on a particular model, a Mercedes, for what felt like an age and had dropped so many hints in the months leading up to their wedding anniversary that it had taken everything inside of her not to let out an audible gasp of complete and utter shock when on the morning of their anniversary he'd led her out of the house and handed over a set of car keys complete with a red satin bow. He'd bought her a Mercedes alright, just not the car she'd wanted. Parked on the driveway had been an older, used model sporting dots of rust just above the wheel arch, and certainly nowhere near as flashy as the brand-new convertible that she'd had her heart set on.

After two attempts of turning the key in the ignition, the engine spluttered to life and just as she was about to put the car into gear and place her foot on the accelerator, up ahead of her the electronic gates that led out onto the road began to automatically open, causing Diane's forehead to furrow. She forced her expression to relax and looking up at the rearview mirror she studied her reflection, her fingers smoothing out the lines etched across her forehead. She couldn't bear the fact she was growing older; not that she particularly looked her age, thanks to the blonde hair dye that covered her grey roots and the Botox she had injected into her wrinkles on a regular basis. And although she'd thankfully managed to keep her trim figure and was still able to squeeze into the miniskirts she'd worn in her twenties, she couldn't help but wonder if others viewed her as mutton dressed up as lamb. Perhaps she should start toning it down a bit, wear something a little more conservative. The mere thought was enough to make her feel depressed. She liked to show off her legs, liked to dress to impress and even more than that, she enjoyed standing out from the crowd, and if that wasn't enough, she adored anything with a bit of sparkle. Bernie would often joke that she was the human equivalent of a magpie, and he had a point, seeing as the vast majority of her clothes were studded with diamantés and sequins.

As her daughter pulled up beside her and stepped out of the car, Diane switched off the ignition, pushed her sunglasses on top of her head and studied her only child. As wrong and as irrational as it was, jealousy engulfed her. Carla was beautiful; her skin still flawless and without a wrinkle in sight. And as for her daughter's figure, her pert backside, long legs that seemed to go on forever, and firm bust were enough to guarantee that men gave her a second glance – not that Carla appeared to notice. As far back as she could remember Carla had only ever had her sights set on one man, Logan McKay. She'd been so determined to bag him that it had come as no surprise when they finally went on to become a couple. And unless Diane was mistaken, she had a feeling that a marriage proposal could very well be on the cards in the near future.

'What are you doing here?'

Shaking her head Carla laughed. 'Cheers for that Mum,' she said with a hint of sarcasm. 'You always know exactly what to say to make me feel so wanted.'

In an attempt to bite back a retort, Diane bit down on her bottom lip. In her mind Carla had only ever been difficult, not only had she been hostile growing up but she'd also done everything in her power to make both Diane and Bernie's life a living hell. What's more, Carla had always known exactly how to push Diane's buttons, and as a teenager she'd become down right uncontrollable. She had too much of her father inside of her to be anything different. Not only did Carla look like Sonny but she also shared his personality and mannerisms, so much so that at times Diane had to force herself to show her daughter any form of affection. Oh, she loved Carla, of course she did, what kind of mother would she be if she didn't love her only child? But they had never been close, had never had what she would call a healthy mother and daughter relationship. In fact, their bond was virtually non-existent. Never one to hold her hands up and admit that at times she was the one in the wrong, it had become all too easy for Diane to blame Sonny for their estrangement. He'd poisoned Carla's mind; after all, Carla was a real daddy's girl.

As for Sonny, he loved their daughter unconditionally, just as he had once loved her too. In Sonny's eyes Carla could do no wrong, even when she'd been a typical, stroppy teenager Sonny had made excuses for her behaviour. It was laughable now really that Sonny's family had once had their doubts as to her unborn child's parentage. Carla was a Carter through and through, you only had to take one look at her to see that. From her dark hair to her startling blue eyes, she was like the spit out of her father's mouth.

Diane's ex-mother-in-law in particular had been one of the first to ask Diane outright if perhaps she'd made a mistake and calculated her dates wrong, more or less accusing her of spreading her legs for all and sundry. And as for her ex-husband's brothers, she'd seen their faces, and had even caught snippets of their hushed conversations. They didn't trust her as far as they could throw her and had assumed that she'd either played around on Sonny or was lying through her teeth and had already fallen pregnant before she and Sonny had had their first date. And yes, it would be fair to say that in the past she'd been promiscuous – she enjoyed being in the company of men, there was no harm in that, it was only natural after all, human nature. But back then her only goal in life had been to get her claws into a Carter, and as it just so happened, it was Sonny's eyes she'd caught. She'd purposely lied to him too, told him that she was taking the contraceptive pill and that it was virtually impossible for her to get pregnant. In reality she'd thrown the foil packet containing the tiny pills away as soon they'd begun dating. It wasn't so much the fact that she'd wanted a baby; the only thing she'd wanted was the lifestyle Sonny Carter could offer – money in abundance and everything else that came from being married into such a well-known family.

Little had she known just how far down the pecking order her husband really was. Yes, Sonny may have been a Carter, but he had little to no power within the family; that role had been reserved for

Tommy and Jimmy alone. It was them Sonny had looked up to, them he had taken orders from. Was it any wonder that Diane had plotted and schemed her way into Bernie's arms? She'd wanted a real man in her life, someone who was respected in his own right and just look at what Bernie had given her in return, a beautiful home that wouldn't have looked out of place on the cover of a magazine and also a lifestyle that could only be envied by her friends. Fair enough, Bernie was far from perfect. Take the car for example, he'd certainly let her down on that front, and then there were the many other women to contend with, but he had always come back to her no matter which little tart he was shagging on the side.

'That's right,' Diane bristled. 'What are you doing here? You're usually too preoccupied spending time with your father. I barely ever see you and when I do, you're spoiling for a fight.' Even as the words left her mouth Diane knew she was being unreasonable. Carla was a grown woman and could see who she pleased; it wasn't as though Diane actually wanted her daughter tagging along with her everywhere she went; and the last thing she needed was for Carla to steal her limelight, which was bound to happen once others noted just how naturally stunning she was.

Carla gave an irritated sigh, her expression hardening. 'Why does everything have to refer back to my dad?' she snapped, throwing her arms up in the air. 'I don't understand why you're still so hung up on him. It was you who left him not the other way around. So do us all a favour, Mum, and just drop it. Move on with your life, God only knows my dad has.'

Diane lifted her eyebrows. She had moved on; she and Bernie had been married for years. So what if they didn't have what would be considered a conventional marriage by anyone else's standards – in their own way they were happy, albeit stuck in a rut and perhaps bored with one another. As for Sonny, she wasn't even sure why she despised him so much. When they'd been married, he'd only ever been a good husband, and would have given her the earth if she'd asked for it. When it came to fatherhood, he'd taken to it like a duck to water. From the very moment Carla had been placed into his arms he'd been besotted with his little girl, and still was. After their divorce he'd gone above and beyond to fight for access and had even threatened to take Diane to court if need be. And they had been no idle threats; he'd been fully prepared to do whatever it took to maintain contact with his child. Yet despite all of this, Diane was still unable to stop herself from berating her ex-husband. Perhaps her animosity boiled down to nothing other than guilt. She and Bernie hadn't only betrayed Sonny without a moment's hesitation, they had torn his world apart.

At the time she'd assumed she was doing the right thing; she'd even convinced herself that Bernie was the love of her life. But as the old saying went, the grass wasn't necessarily greener on the other side of the fence, and she better than anyone else knew that to be true. Bernie was unable to resist chasing after other women, some of them young enough to be his daughters. Or maybe her resentment was born out of regret. Sonny had done well for himself. Once their divorce had been finalised and the marital home had been sold he'd invested his money wisely and had bought himself a penthouse apartment in Canary Wharf that was worth somewhere in the region of six million pounds, more than double the price of her and Bernie's home. From the outside, the mock Tudor mansion may have had what she liked to call the wow factor, but when it came to the inside, the house left a lot to be desired. Not only was the décor fast on its way to becoming outdated but there were also patches of mould in the bathroom. No matter how often she scrubbed at the dark spots they still found a way of returning with a vengeance. As for the kitchen, the solid oak cabinets that had once been her pride and joy had definitely seen better days, so much so that she couldn't help but think of them as an eyesore. In her opinion, the entire house needed gutting and remodelling to bring it up to her high standards.

Holding up her hands Diane offered a tight smile. 'You're right,' she conceded. 'No more talk about your father.' It was on the tip of her tongue to ask how Sonny was doing, if he was happy, but considering the mood her daughter was in Diane thought better of it. Carla could be a touchy little cow where Sonny was concerned and, not wanting to give her daughter the ammunition to start another argument, Diane decided to keep her lips firmly clamped together.

'Thank you.' Giving a nod of her head Carla leaned back against the car and crossed her arms over her chest. Her stance immediately coming across as defensive, as it often was when the two women were in one another's company. 'I was just passing through and thought I'd pop in and see you. Hardly the crime of the century, is it?'

Choosing to ignore the barbed quip, Diane narrowed her eyes. It had only just turned ten, where on earth could her daughter possibly be going to drive past the house at that time of the morning? It wasn't as though her home was even on the main road; Carla would have had to purposely drive down the winding lane to reach the house and that was another thing – how had Carla managed to open the electronic gates? As far as Diane was aware, Carla had handed over the keys for the property when she'd moved out. 'I was just on my way out, maybe we could do lunch. There's that nice little bistro in town, apparently all the celebrities are raving about it.'

Carla wrinkled her nose. 'No thanks, Mum.'

'Well, how about if we just go for a couple of drinks then. It's about time I showed my face in there...' As the front door to the house opened Diane's voice trailed off and giving a deep sigh, she reached out to grasp hold of Carla's hand. 'Be nice,' she warned as she glanced over her shoulder to see her husband standing on the doorstep. As Bernie lifted his hand in a greeting, a lop-sided grin was plastered across his face. 'You know that Bernie thinks a lot of you, that he loves you like a daughter.'

'He thought a lot of my dad too, once,' Carla answered, her voice hard. 'And no matter how much you might try to sugar coat it,' she added, tearing her gaze away from Bernie, 'I'm not his daughter, and never will be.'

'See,' Diane spat, her face contorting with anger. 'This is why we can't have a relationship. You always have to be so volatile! Bernie has bent over backwards for you, he gave you a home,' she said, gesturing behind her. 'A beautiful home might I add, and you wanted for nothing growing up.'

'I already had a home,' Carla replied. 'The one you ripped me away from, remember? The only thing I wanted growing up was to be with my dad, something else you took great delight in ripping away from me.'

Diane shook her head. Carla was still a young woman; maybe once she became a mother herself, she would understand why she had felt the need to restrict Sonny's visits, why she hadn't wanted to have him anywhere near her. She could hardly be expected to play happy families with both her husband and ex-husband in tow. Back then Sonny had been a loose cannon; he'd even threatened to kill Bernie! How could she have possibly taken the risk and allowed him free access to the house? It was an excuse of course; no matter how angry he might have been, Sonny would never have done anything to jeopardise his relationship with his daughter. As Carla continued to give her a cold stare Diane averted her gaze. 'I did what I thought was best.'

'No, you didn't.' Yanking open the car door Carla slid behind the wheel. 'You did it to hurt my dad. All you've ever done is to try and hurt him, it's like you get some kind of sick kick out of it.'

With those parting words Carla slammed the car door closed, pushed the key into the ignition and sped away from the house leaving Diane to stare helplessly after her. Turning back to look at her husband, Diane lifted her shoulders up into a shrug. In hindsight she should have asked for the house keys back; it wasn't as though Carla needed them and from the look of things, she could safely say that it wasn't likely her daughter was going to drop by for another unexpected visit any time soon.

* * *

By the time Carla had driven to the end of the lane she wanted to kick herself. Not only had she allowed her dislike of Bernie to get the better of her but by throwing a childish tantrum she had also missed out on the opportunity to snoop around her mother's house in search of the stolen diamonds. After all, that was the only reason she'd decided to turn up on her mother's doorstep in the first place. Flicking the indicator, she pulled out onto the main road, all the while thinking through her next move. No matter which way she looked at the situation, the only option left open to her was to swallow her pride and apologise, no matter how much it would hurt her to do so.

Moments later she pulled the car over to the kerb and switched off the engine. Across the road was a florist shop, boasting brightly coloured bouquets of flowers propped up in gold-coloured tubs. Not only did the shop look classy, but from Carla's position she had a feeling the products on display would cost the earth too. A smile etched its way across her face. What better way to offer a peace offering than to buy her mother some flowers? Not that Diane would appreciate them. In fact, if she knew her mum as well as she thought she did then she wouldn't be surprised if Diane promptly threw them in the bin the minute her back was turned. Still, she decided it was worth a try and more than anything Carla needed to get back into her mother's good books and even more than that, she had to get inside the house.

Carla entered the shop and as she studied the flowers on display from out of the corner of her eye she spotted a potted plant, the once green leaves beginning to turn straggly and yellow. Bending down she scooped the plant up and couldn't help but grin. It was perfect, her mum would hate it of course, which if Carla was being honest was as good a reason to buy it. Making her way across the shop, Carla placed the plant on the counter then fished inside her handbag for her purse.

The sales assistant flashed a wide smile then looking down at the plant a frown creased her forehead. 'Are you sure that you want this one?' she asked, lightly tracing her fingers across the drooping leaves. 'I was just about to throw it out.'

Handing over her bank card Carla nodded.

Once again, the sales assistant hesitated then shaking her head she waved Carla's outstretched hand away. 'Take it, no need for payment. Like I said I was about to throw it out anyway.'

Smiling her thanks Carla tucked the pot underneath her arm. At the door she paused. 'Thank you...' She pointed up at gold italic lettering above the door that read 'Suzy's'. 'Are you Suzy?'

'No,' the shop assistant gave a gentle laugh, causing her dark hair to fall across her pretty face, 'I get asked that all the time.' She delicately pushed strands of hair out of her eyes. 'Suzy is my mum,' she answered, looking around her. 'This is her shop, or rather our shop; we run it together.'

'Well thank your mum for me too.' Carla nodded down at the plant. 'This is exactly what I was looking for.'

As she walked back to her car Carla sighed, not for the first time wishing that the circumstances could have been different and that she and Diane had been close just as the shop assistant and her mum appeared to be. Perhaps if it hadn't been for Bernie then she and her mum would have gotten along better. Somehow she highly doubted this would be the case though; if anything, out of the two, Bernie had been the one to make sure that she was safe, that growing up she'd had food and clean clothes, there had even been times when she'd found herself warming to him, or at least she had until she'd remembered what he'd caused, that if it hadn't been for him her parents would have never divorced. Choosing not to dwell on the situation she placed the plant beside her on the passenger seat and turned the key in the ignition. She and her mum may not have had the perfect relationship, but she still had her dad. And she had Logan too. As soon as her boyfriend's name popped into her head Carla swore under her breath. She'd totally forgotten she'd agreed to meet him back at their flat for lunch. He'd made such a big song and dance about it over the past week that it seemed to be the only thing he wanted to talk about.

After taking note of the time she pressed her foot down on the accelerator and eased away from the kerb. She'd pop over to the scrapyard before her lunch date with Logan. With a bit of luck she'd be able to catch Jonny while he was alone. Time was ticking and they still had things to discuss and seeing as he hadn't given her a definite answer as to whether or not he was interested in her plan to rob Bernie of the diamonds, she was feeling restless. Who knew how long the gems would remain in Bernie's possession? For all she knew, arrangements were already being made to ship them out, and once the diamonds were out of her reach so too was her plan for revenge.

* * *

Logan McKay was the image of his father, Danny. Both were handsome with tall muscular builds, but thanks to Danny's persistence that Logan make something of himself, rather than follow on in his father's footsteps, this is where the similarities ended. Unlike his father, Logan had by some miracle managed to keep himself on the right side of the law, not that this meant he hadn't been surrounded by those who dabbled in illegal activities. Some of his earliest memories involved being in the company of men who had participated in crimes, some had even gone as far as to commit murder, his dad included.

Jumping out of his car Logan crossed over the street then made his way inside his father's nightclub. After a quick glance at his watch he quickened his pace, eager to collect what he'd come for before heading back home again.

At the door to Danny's office, Logan straightened out the collar of his jacket then turned the door handle. Just as he'd known he would be, Danny was sitting behind his desk, a stack of paperwork in front of him. From as far back as Logan could remember his dad had been a workaholic, even now when he was supposed to have been semi-retired, he could still be found at the club day in, day out.

'Which part of retired don't you get?' Despite it being a genuine question Logan couldn't help but chuckle. The truth of the matter was that Danny had never had any intentions of slowing down, and the same went for his business partner, Moray Garner, too. Danny had only agreed to take a step back to stop his wife, Stacey, from nagging at him, but if anything he seemed to be spending even more time at the club.

'Are you trying to say I'm getting old?'

Logan lifted his eyebrows. Danny may have been fast approaching his sixtieth birthday, but he could still keep up with the best of them. 'As if, Dad.'

Leaning back in his chair Danny studied his son. 'Are you sure about this?' He gestured towards the safe. 'I mean, what's the rush? You're still both young, you should be out enjoying yourselves. There's plenty of time before you start thinking about settling down and marriage.'

'I'm not a little kid any more, Dad. We live together anyway so what's the big deal. Getting married is the next step and who knows, in the future we might want kids of our own, or at least I do anyway.'

Danny lifted his eyebrows. 'Don't go making me a grandad just yet,' he warned. Getting out of his chair he crossed the office and paused in front of the safe. 'I just don't want to see you making a mistake.'

'And your old man's a fine one to talk about making mistakes.' Walking into the office Moray Garner shot Logan a wink. 'What was the name of that bird you were engaged to?' Turning his attention back to Danny, he clicked his fingers several times as though the action would somehow help to jog his memory. 'You know the one I'm talking about; she was as nutty as a fucking fruitcake. Her and her uncle were plotting to have you wiped out.'

'Maria,' Logan piped up.

'That's it, Maria.' Pointing his finger in Danny's direction Moray suppressed a smile. 'Leave the boy alone. If he's anything like you then he won't listen to a word anyone else has to say anyway. How many times did I warn you that Maria was a wrong'un? But would you listen? Would you fuck.' He took a seat and adjusted his trouser legs all the while ignoring the unease that had fallen over the room. Not only had Maria been the catalyst for Danny's attempted downfall, but she and her uncle, a retired police officer, had also coerced Moray's eldest son into their wicked plan. The aftermath of their actions had almost destroyed Moray and Danny's close friendship that had spanned the best part of thirty-five years. 'Besides, Carla's a nice girl; she's got a good head on her shoulders. He could do a lot worse, and you know it.'

Danny sighed and as he bent down to retrieve the ring box from the safe, he shook his head. 'I'm not disputing the fact that she's a good girl,' he said, straightening up and handing the small velvet box over to his son. 'My issue is that she's a Carter, trouble has a nasty habit of following that lot around.'

Moray burst out laughing. 'Give over, you as good as married a Carter yourself.' He held up his hands as if to ward off Danny's protests. 'Fair enough Stacey may have only been a Carter in name, but she's just as embroiled within the family as both Logan and yourself are.'

Still grumbling, Danny returned to his seat. 'What does your mum have to say about this?' he asked, changing the subject.

Logan shrugged, and giving a sheepish grin he tucked the box deep into his pocket. 'I haven't told her yet. You know what she's like, she'll only try and put a spanner in the works, it's all she ever does.'

Danny knew only too well what his ex-wife, Maxine, was like, she would find fault with Jesus Christ himself. 'Married, eh.' He shook his head. 'It only seems like yesterday that you were kicking a ball about.'

'She hasn't said yes yet,' Logan reminded his father. 'You never know she might turn me down.'

Danny waved his hand through the air dismissing the notion. 'We all know that's not likely, that girl worships the ground you walk on.' Steepling his fingers across his chest he tilted his head to the side. 'Do you need anything, some cash to tide you over?' he motioned towards the outline of the ring box in Logan's pocket. 'That sparkler had to have cost you a fair few bob and I'm going to take a wild guess and say that it didn't come from whichever latest heist the Carters were involved in.'

'Give over.' Logan rolled his eyes. 'I'm hardly going to propose with stolen loot am I?'

Danny raised his eyebrows. 'Nothing would surprise me when it comes to the Carters.' He nodded towards the door. 'Go on, get off with you. Go and do whatever it is you need to do.' He pulled a pile of paperwork towards him then searched around his desk for a pen. 'Oh, and son,' he added, looking up, 'best of luck, not that you're going to need it. She'll say yes, I can feel it in here,' he winked, tapping his finger against his chest.

Logan gave a small smile in return. He only wished that he had his dad's confidence. A niggling voice at the back of his mind told him that there was every possibility Carla could refuse his proposal. She'd seemed preoccupied of late, and he had a nasty feeling that whatever was troubling her could have ramifications for the both of them, and perhaps for everyone they cared about too.

4

'Is he having a bubble?' The incredulity in Sonny's voice was more than apparent and as he turned to look at his twin brother, Mitchell, his expression was one of shock. 'I can't get my head around this,' he stated, with a shake of his head as if to emphasise his point. 'Am I actually hearing this right?' he asked, turning his attention back towards his younger brother. 'You're seriously suggesting that we turn over my ex-wife's house?'

The office chair creaked beneath Jonny's weight and as he shifted his position to make himself more comfortable, he gave a shrug. 'It's Bernie's house an' all,' he said, offering a small grin. 'Think of it as a payback of sorts. That jumped up prick deserves everything he has coming to him. I might have only been a kid at the time, but I still remember everything he put you through. Mum was worried sick. She was too scared to even leave you on your own at one point and it was me,' he said, stabbing a finger into his chest. 'Who was left babysitting you. I should have been out with my mates, having the time of my life doing whatever it is that kids do and instead I had to sit there day in, day out making sure you didn't go off the rails, that you didn't end up as fucked up in the head as that fruitcake Gary was.'

Still shaking his head in disbelief, Sonny's mouth hung slightly open. 'I wasn't that bad. Fucking hell, anyone would think I'd turned into a stark raving lunatic the way you're carrying on.'

Jonny raised his eyebrows and turning his head he gave Mitchell a pointed look. 'You were there, you remember what he was like. He was gone up here.' He tapped his temple. 'It was a case of the lights were on, but no one was home.'

Averting his gaze Mitchell blew out his cheeks. 'I've got to admit it wasn't pretty and you were drinking yourself into a stupor on a nightly basis.'

'There you go.' Jonny spread open his arms. 'And you still reckon that Bernie doesn't deserve this?'

'No matter what Bernie deserves, it's also my daughter's mother's house,' Sonny bellowed. 'What the fuck is wrong with you. We might be a lot of things but we're not petty thieves. Who are you planning to target next? I tell you what, how about we try our luck with the old dear who lives next door to Mum and Dad? You never know,' he added, throwing up his arms, 'she might even have a few bob tucked away under the mattress. That would really set us up for life wouldn't it? If we're really lucky, it might even be enough to buy us a couple of rounds down the pub.'

Jonny rolled his eyes. He should have known that this would be Sonny's response; he and Mitchell liked to play it safe, too safe for his liking. 'Diamonds,' he gritted out. 'A little birdie has told me that Bernie has a stash of diamonds. In fact, I have it on good authority that he's keeping them warm for the Tucker brothers.'

Sonny's eyebrows shot up. 'Please tell me this a wind up.' He pressed his fingertips to his forehead. 'And you've got the audacity to question my sanity. Have you actually lost your mind? What exactly are you trying to do, eh? Start a war? We've already dealt with the Tuckers; Jimmy saw to it that and we've come to an understanding. They stay out of our path, and we stay out of theirs.'

'Try telling that to Tommy Jr,' Jonny snapped back. 'At every available opportunity they get the no-good bastards to take a swipe at him. Last week I had some geezer come up to me in the boozer asking if it was true, that we,' he gestured between them, 'like to keep it in the family, insinuating that we're all fucking inbred. Are we supposed to sit back and do sweet fuck all while those bastards are taking the piss out of us left, right and centre? And as for Jimmy, you know as well as I do,' he spat, 'that in the end all he wanted was a quiet life. He would have agreed to anything if it meant getting the Tuckers off our back.'

'Oi, watch your mouth.' Stabbing his finger forward, Sonny's eyes hardened. 'Jimmy isn't weak and believe me, he would never have agreed to something just for a quiet life. He would have been one of the first to take matters into his own hands, he's done things for our family that you know fuck all about.'

Thoroughly chastised, Jonny looked down at the desk. 'Forget the Tuckers for a moment,' he said, looking back up. 'We can't let this opportunity pass us by. It's not like Bernie would be able to stop us anyway, is it? The man's a clown, an absolute first-class fool.'

'We don't touch diamonds and that's my final word on the matter,' Sonny growled. Cocking his head to the side he pulled out his mobile phone and began scrolling through his contact list. 'Has Jimmy been made aware of this?' he asked, eyeing his brother. 'Have you informed him about this so-called master plan of yours?'

Jonny snapped his head around to look at his elder brother, his chiselled jaw clenched so tight that he was in grave danger of actually breaking a bone. 'Unless it's escaped your notice, Jimmy doesn't run things around here any more.' He poked a stiff finger into his chest, his eyes blazing as if daring his brother to argue the case. 'I do.'

Sonny gave a weary shake of his head. 'Yeah, you've got that much right because I can tell you right now that Jimmy would have shut this shit down long before now. What exactly are you trying to do?' he asked. 'Get us all banged up, because let me tell you now, you're going the right way about it.'

Momentarily, Jonny paused. Despite what his brothers might think of him he wasn't stupid. Fair enough, he may have been reckless in the past, he'd even go as far as to hold his hands up and admit that he'd probably be six feet under if it wasn't for the fact that time and time again his brothers had been there to bail him out. Only recent events in Jonny's life had forced him to see the error of his ways. He was about to become a father and whether he wanted to or not, now was the time to grow up, he owed that to both his unborn child and his partner. He couldn't let them down, not now. 'I say we put it to a vote. Lay all the cards on the table and let the boys decide if they want in. And if they don't, well,' he pulled his shoulders up into a shrug, 'that'll be the end of it.'

Sonny gave an incredulous laugh. 'Don't you think we've got enough on our plates without you adding to our problems? And as for any of that lot out there,' he said, referring to his nephews. 'Do you honestly believe they would understand the magnitude of what they're actually voting for? We're talking about diamonds here for fuck's sake, not knocking off the local fucking bookies.'

Jonny sighed. Ever since Carla had told him about the diamonds that were in Bernie's possession he'd been able to think of little else. And the fact they didn't have a good track record when it came to the stones didn't have to mean it was impossible did it? Perhaps with the right planning, then just maybe this time they would be successful. After all, it wasn't as though they had any trouble when it came to robbing banks, or security vans.

'Jonny.' The anger in Sonny's voice was more than palpable. 'Are you listening to me. The answer is no, and that means...' He began ticking the words off his fingers. 'No vote, no planning, and no fucking heist. Do you understand what I'm telling you, is it actually penetrating through that thick skull of yours? In fact, let me spell it out for you, we do not go after diamonds.'

'And like I said,' Jonny growled, 'we put it to the vote.' He jerked his thumb behind him in the direction of the forecourt. 'They're not kids, they're grown men, they can make their own decisions.'

'What do you mean they're not kids. Tommy Jr is barely out of school, what the fuck does he know? He can just about tie his own shoelaces, let alone pull off an armed robbery.'

Running his tongue over his teeth, Jonny narrowed his eyes. 'He's a lot older than you were when you robbed your first bank. Besides if he's old enough to get into scrapes then he's old enough to know his own mind.'

'I can't believe we're still having this conversation,' Sonny growled. 'The moment you mention the word diamond, all that lot will see is pound note signs flashing before their eyes.' Getting out of his chair he walked across the office and sucked in a breath. 'If you go through with this madness then you're on your own. I mean it,' he warned. 'I'm out.'

Jonny narrowed his eyes. Right from the start he'd known it wouldn't be an easy task getting his brothers on board, but as Carla had stated, he was the one in charge, they took orders from him, not the other way around and the quicker they learnt that the better it would be for all concerned. 'Does that go for you too?' he asked, turning his attention to Mitchell.

Mitchell looked between his two brothers and sitting forward, he rested his forearms on his knees. 'What exactly are you trying to prove, eh? Tommy failed, Jimmy failed, what makes you think it'll be any different this time around? And let me tell you something else for nothing, if you think that you're going to drag my boy into this fucking fiasco of yours then I can tell you right now it's not going to happen.'

The muscle at the side of Jonny's eye twitched. 'Reece is a big boy,' he barked out, referring to Mitchell's son. 'I'm pretty sure that he's capable of thinking for himself, and if he wants in then that's his choice to make, not yours.'

'He's nineteen,' Mitchell spat. 'What the fuck does he know about the life.'

Laughing out loud Jonny shook his head. 'You're a fine one to talk. You and Sonny were barely out of school when you took part in your first bank job.'

'We were nothing but a couple of impressionable kids!' Sonny shouted. 'Tommy should never have dragged us along with him.'

For a few moments Jonny was quiet. They were right, he supposed. If anything, as teenagers, Sonny and Mitchell should have been out with their mates playing football, chatting up birds, or getting into scrapes instead of learning how to carry out an armed robbery, not that their dad would have ever allowed them a free rein to do as they wished. Each and every morning without fail, Frank Carter had had his sons up at the crack of dawn so that they could spar in the gym. 'Tommy obviously thought you were ready,' he shrugged. 'And sooner or later you would have joined the family business. You wanted to knock boxing on the head as much as I did, and you know as well as I do that if it wasn't for Tommy putting his foot down and fighting our corner, Dad would never have allowed us to step away from it.'

Mitchell gave a sad shake of his head. 'Dad didn't have any other choice but to let us go. As for Tommy, as much as he loved boxing, he was sick to the back teeth of living and breathing the sport. Dad was too hard on him, never gave him a moment's peace, why else do you think he quit. I can remember this one time, Tommy must have been, I don't know,' he scratched his chin as he tried to think back, 'maybe fourteen or fifteen. And he was ill, and I mean proper ill: headache, cold shivers, temperature, the fucking lot, and still the old man dragged him down to the gym. Dad didn't care about Tommy's wellbeing, all he cared about was him winning his next belt. And then when Tommy had finally had enough and hung up his gloves the old man could barely even bring himself to look at him, let alone speak to him and do you know why that was?' he growled, stabbing his finger forward.

Jonny shrugged again. 'Because he was disappointed, I suppose.'

Mitchell threw up his arms. 'Because Tommy,' he said through gritted teeth, 'was the only one who was good enough to make it as a professional. If anyone shattered Dad's dreams of raising a boxing champion, then it was Tommy. The rest of us were nothing but his second choice, his backup plan.'

As Jonny's mind wandered to the glass cabinets filled to the brim with trophies and medals that took pride of place in his elderly parents' lounge he screwed up his face. Admittedly, the majority of them had been won by Tommy but a few of them belonged to either himself or his other brothers. 'You're talking bollocks,' he spat. Tommy may have had a natural gift when it came to boxing but that didn't mean the rest of them hadn't inherited at least some of Tommy's talent, that they too couldn't have made it. 'We were good, all of us were.'

'I didn't say we weren't,' Mitchell sighed. 'I'm saying that we wouldn't have made it as professionals. We didn't have the same raw talent that Tommy had and deep down you know it's true.'

'Maybe,' Jonny conceded. He gave a nonchalant shrug. 'Not that it really matters in the grand scheme of things. If anything, armed robbery is what we excel in, not boxing.'

Mitchell shook his head. 'We're not invincible. We were this close to getting our collars felt last time,' he said, placing his thumb and forefinger an inch apart. 'Are you really willing to take the risk for a few poxy stones that are so hot they'll be near impossible to shift?'

Opening his mouth to answer Jonny momentarily paused. Mitchell had just hit the proverbial nail on the head. In the past his two eldest brothers had both come away empty handed from any diamond raids they'd made, but what if this time they were successful? What if he was the one to finally execute the perfect crime and bring home a diamond? The very notion was enough to make the tiny hairs across the back of his neck stand upright. 'We can do this,' he reiterated. 'Listen, it'll be nothing more than a smash and grab. We get in the house, take the diamonds and then have it away on our toes. It will be over and done with so fast that there's fuck all Bernie, or anyone else come to think about it, will be able to do to stop us. I mean, let's face it, I can't quite see Bernie or the Tuckers turning to the filth for help. All we'd be doing is taking the diamonds from the bastards who lifted them in the first place. It's a win-win situation.'

'And that's your logic is it? You really think it's going to be that simple?' Holding his head in his hands, Mitchell sighed. 'Then you're on your own bruv.' He looked up and jerked his head in Sonny's direction. 'We're both out and if you think any of that lot,' he said, pointing towards the door. 'Are going to be able to pull this off then you're even more deluded than I first thought.'

Jonny swallowed deeply and as the door to the office opened, he caught sight of his niece standing at the threshold. Perhaps his and Carla's motives were different but at the end of the day they both wanted the same result, to wrench the diamonds out of both Bernie's and the Tucker brothers' hands. 'Fair enough,' he said, leaning casually back in the chair, his expression hard. 'Looks like I'll be doing this without you then, doesn't it?'

* * *

Carla was on cloud nine. In fact, she was so elated she could barely contain her excitement and as she perched on the edge of a chair, she placed her hands on the desk, more so to stop herself from fidgeting than for any other reason. 'We need to move fast...'

Jonny narrowed his eyes. 'Woah, hold up a minute,' he said, shaking his head. 'What are you talking about?'

Forcing herself to keep her voice even, Carla looked her uncle in the eyes. 'The diamonds,' she exclaimed, throwing her arms up in the air. 'We can't just sit around and do nothing; we need to get them out of my mum's house and pronto.'

Still shaking his head Jonny frowned. 'It doesn't work like that Carls.' He leaned forward in the chair and pulled a sheet of paper towards him. 'These things take time; you can't expect us to go in all guns blazing, that's how rookie mistakes are made, and no matter how much of a prick I happen to think Bernie is, I still need a plan of action. Take your mum's gaff for example, I need to know the comings and goings, what time they go out, what times they're likely to be home, etcetera, etcetera.' He began making a list. 'I'll need to acquire firearms.' He lifted his eyebrows and flashed a grin. 'Just in case Bernie should turn up and start getting lairy. You'd be surprised how easy it is to make someone compliant, especially when they've got a shooter shoved under their nose. And then there's the transport to consider.' He cracked his knuckles. 'It should be fairly easy to find a van, I've got nimble fingers and as it just so happens, I'm an expert when it comes to obtaining getaway vehicles.' He winked. 'And then,' he chewed thoughtfully on the end of a pen, 'this is where things start to become difficult. I'm going to need a buyer for the diamonds.' Resting his chin in his hands he looked into the distance. 'I've got a mate who used to deal in gold, he might have a contact we could use. I dunno,' he shrugged, 'I can't say I'm overly thrilled at the prospect of bringing an outsider in, but in the circumstances what other choice do I have?'

Carla's jaw dropped, her mind reeling. 'You can't be serious, that could take weeks.'

'Maybe even months,' Jonny agreed.

'But we don't have months; we have to act now.'

Jonny looked up, his expression becoming serious. 'Since when did this,' he said, motioning between them, 'become we?'

Taken aback, Carla gripped the edge of the desk so hard that her knuckles turned white. 'It was my idea,' she gasped. 'I was the one who told you about the diamonds. You're not pushing me out. I want in.'

Bursting out laughing, Jonny motioned to the door that Sonny and Mitchell had exited just moments earlier. 'Give over. Do you honestly think your old man would allow that? You know as well as I do that he'd blow a fucking gasket. And it'll be me,' he added, pointing towards himself, 'who'll take the flak for it and let's just say that at this precise moment in time I'm not your dad's favourite person. So you can imagine just how upset he is going to be with me should something happen to his little princess.'

'No.' Two pink spots appeared on Carla's cheeks. 'Don't you dare try to palm me off. You're not doing this without me, I mean it.' Before Jonny could open his mouth to answer, Carla rounded on him. 'Is this because I'm a woman?' she asked, screwing up her face. 'Because if it is, newsflash for you, we're not in the dark ages any more. It's been a long time since women were tied to the kitchen sink, their sole purpose in life to breed children.'

Jonny shifted his position. 'Cut the sarcasm Carla, it really doesn't suit you. Look,' he sighed, 'I know your dad might have given you the go ahead to work in the office, to front the legal side of the business but...'

'I can't believe this. I'd bet any money that you'd be willing to give Tommy Jr the chance to prove himself. Do you really think that you can trust him more than me, that he's got what it takes?' Shaking her head, her lips curled into a snarl. 'And what about Terri?' she said of Jonny's partner. 'She works with her brothers, so what's the big deal?'

'The Tempests aren't armed robbers, are they?' Jonny snapped back.

'Maybe not,' Carla snarled. 'But from what I've heard, they're just as dangerous as our family, maybe even more so.'

'Listen.' Taking a moment to rein his temper in, Jonny held up his hands. 'I admit Tommy Jr can be a liability at times, and believe me, some days I'd love nothing more than to knock some sense into that head of his, but at the end of the day he's family...'

'And so am I,' Carla interrupted, her eyes flashing with anger. 'I'm as much a Carter as Tommy Jr is, as much you are.'

Jonny sighed; she had him on that one he supposed. He held up his hands in defeat. 'Your dad would skin me alive.'

'And?' Carla protested. Swiping a lock of dark hair out of her face she jutted her chin in the air. 'Since when were you scared of my dad?'

Ignoring the comment, Jonny got to his feet. 'I'm sorry Carla, but I can't take the risk.'

Sinking back into the chair Carla crossed her arms over her chest. 'You're forgetting something, Uncle Jonny,' she said, giving him a knowing smile. 'Other than Bernie I'm the only one who knows where those diamonds are.' It was an exaggeration of course, and if the truth be told, she was as clueless as Jonny was. The only thing she knew for certain was that the diamonds were in her mother's and Bernie's house, they had to be, where else would Bernie have stashed them? 'So, without me on board, whether you like it or not, it looks like you're at a standstill.'

For long moments, Jonny and Carla stared at one another, each of them not wanting to give in. 'You're not going to let this drop, are you?' Jonny finally asked, his shoulders drooping in what Carla could only assume was defeat.

'Nope.' Carla shook her head, and breaking out into a triumphant grin, she nodded down at the sheet of paper. 'So, let's stop playing games and start planning this out because without my input, it's highly unlikely that you'll get your hands on those diamonds any time soon.'

* * *

Thirty minutes later, and for the second time in as many days, a meeting was being held at the scrapyard. As they lined the walls of the office, Carla's cousins were restless and, if the excited buzz that filled the air was anything to go by, she had a feeling that they too could sense that something of epic proportions was about to take place.

Leaning back in his seat Jonny let out a loud whistle in an attempt to gain their attention. 'Right, you lot,' he looked at each of his brothers' sons in turn, 'I've got a proposition for you. A job...'

'I knew it,' Tommy Jr interrupted, throwing his father a wide grin. 'Didn't I say a job was on the cards?'

Jonny gave his great-nephew a cold stare. 'Do you think you could let me finish? I know it might be a big ask for you to keep that trap of yours shut for five minutes but come on.'

'Yeah.' Peter, the eldest of Jonny's nephews clipped Tommy Jr around the back of the head. 'For once in your life keep that buttoned.' He motioned to his lips, then nodded towards Jonny. 'Carry on.'

'Right.' Ignoring Tommy Jr as he made a show of rubbing the back of his head all the while muttering a half-hearted apology,

Jonny continued, 'As I was saying, I've got a job in mind.' He cleared his throat and jerked his head in Carla's direction. 'Or rather Carla has brought an opportunity to my attention.'

As all eyes turned to look at her, Carla resisted the urge to squirm in her seat. She could almost see the cogs turning in their heads, each of her cousins wondering why she would have been brought into the meeting. She may not have been a stranger when it came to working in the office, fronting the day-to-day running of what was the legitimate side of the business, such as answering the telephone, filing receipts, and making endless cups of tea, but that was about the extent of her experience of working for the family.

'Diamonds,' Jonny continued.

A deathly silence fell over the office and after what seemed an age Peter spoke, his voice hard. 'Is this a joke?' he asked, his eyes narrowed into mere slits. 'You know as well as I do that we don't touch diamonds.'

'We didn't,' Jonny agreed. 'Or at least we didn't when Jimmy was running things.'

'Now we're talking,' Tommy Jr butted in again. 'You can count me in.' He rubbed his hands together. 'We're gonna be raking it in.'

'Nah, I don't think so.' Peter stabbed his finger in his nephew's direction, warning him for the second time to keep his mouth closed. 'This is madness. Even my dad,' he said, turning back to look at his uncle, 'couldn't lift a diamond, so what makes you think that we would fare any better?'

Steepling his fingers across his chest, Jonny raised his eyebrows. 'Things are different now.'

A nerve at the side of Peter's eye twitched. 'Different how? Because from where I'm standing, other than who's sitting behind that desk, nothing has changed.'

As she looked between her uncle and cousin, Carla bit down on her bottom lip. This hadn't been the reaction she'd been expecting, if anything she would have thought her cousins would jump at the chance to get their hands on a diamond. 'Like Jonny said, this is too good an opportunity to miss out on,' she blurted out, eager for them to agree to the heist.

Cameron narrowed his eyes. 'I'm not being funny, Carla, but this has fuck all to do with you. In fact, what are you even doing here?'

Her back instantly up, two pink spots appeared on Carla's cheeks. 'It was my idea,' she snapped. 'So I think you'll find it has everything to do with me.'

'Yeah, right,' Cameron laughed. 'As if your dad would allow you to go on a job.'

'Enough,' Jonny warned, stabbing his finger towards his nephew. 'Carla is as much a Carter as the rest of us. And let's face it you're a fine one to talk, you're not even a Carter you're a Johnson.'

'Maybe,' Cameron growled as he thought back to his grandfather, Dean Johnson, and the hatred he'd held for the Carter family hence why he'd been given the surname Johnson rather than Carter. 'But my dad was still a Carter.'

'Yeah, when it suited him.' Jonny muttered under his breath, the familiar animosity he felt towards his elder brother and subsequent offspring once again rearing its ugly head.

As he looked around him, Peter's forehead furrowed. 'Hold up a minute – why aren't Sonny and Mitchell here?'

Jonny glanced towards Mitchell's son Reece. 'They've bailed,' he said, turning his attention back to Peter, a steely glint in his eyes. 'They reckon it's too risky.'

'Too right it's risky,' Peter shouted. 'It was me and Jake,' he said, flicking his head in the direction of his younger brother. 'Who were there the last time it all went tits up. And you know as well as I do,' he added, pointing at his uncle, 'that we were headed down a slippery slope. If it wasn't for Jimmy calling everything off, we would have been caught bang to rights. In fact, we'd still more than likely be banged up.'

'Yeah, and we both know why.' Casting a glance towards Cameron, Jonny paused for a moment to allow his words to sink in. 'If Gary hadn't tried to set us up, we would have been home and dry.' He held up his hands. 'I'm sorry Cam,' he continued. 'I know he was your dad, but he was also my brother, and I despised the cunt, we all did. The only reason we put up with him for so long was for your nan's sake.'

Cameron looked down at the floor, his cheeks flaming red. 'It's alright,' he finally answered. 'No offence taken. He was bang out of order for what he did.'

Jonny nodded. 'Which is exactly why I'm telling you that this time things will be different.'

Peter sighed and raising his eyebrows he addressed his brother. 'What do you reckon?'

Thinking the question over, Jake stuffed his hands in his pockets. 'I dunno,' he shrugged. 'Like you said, it's risky.'

'Look.' Sitting forward in the chair, Jonny rested his elbows on the desk. 'Trust me when I say this, the old bill won't even come into it...'

'But...' Throwing his brother a sidelong glance, Jake pulled his hands from out of his pockets and crossed his arms over his chest. 'Why do I sense a but coming?'

Jonny paused. 'But there could be a comeback of sorts and believe me when it comes to those bastards, I wouldn't put anything past them. Carla's stepdad...'

'How many times do I have to tell you,' Carla spat. 'He is not my stepdad.'

Jonny waved his hand through the air and rolling his eyes he began again. 'Bernie, who just so happens to be married to Carla's mum is looking after the diamonds for the Tucker brothers and the plan,' he said, tapping his finger upon the sheet of paper on the desk, 'is to intercept the diamonds before they reach the Tuckers' hands.'

Jake raised his eyebrows and looking from his nephew to his brother a slow grin made its way across his face. 'So basically, we would be stepping on the Tuckers' toes.'

'Step, stamp, whichever way you want to look at it, it'd be safe to say that they won't be happy bunnies.'

Peter laughed out loud. 'Well, that shakes things up a bit,' he grinned. 'I've had it up to here with those fuckers,' he said, pointing to his head. He slung his arm around Tommy Jr's shoulders and pulled him close. 'They've been giving it a bit too much of this,' he said, mimicking a mouth opening and closing. 'And for far too long if you want my opinion. It's about time someone taught them a lesson.'

Grinning, Jonny spread open his arms. 'I had a feeling you might say that. So, who's in?'

As a flurry of hands shot up in the air Carla sank back in her seat, relief flowing through her veins. For one sickening moment she'd actually begun to think that her cousins would refuse, that like her dad and Uncle Mitchell they would think the risk too great. And with all the will in the world it just wasn't possible that Jonny alone would be able to carry out the heist. Not that she thought he'd have any trouble in actually taking the diamonds from underneath Bernie's nose; after all Bernie wasn't exactly someone to be feared. But when it came to the aftermath of the robbery and the Tucker brothers were baying for Jonny's blood, would he have been able to escape their clutches on his own? A cold shiver ran down the length of her spine and for the first time since the idea had sprung to her mind, she had doubts. What if she'd over estimated her family? What if one of them ended up being hurt, or even worse, killed? Pushing the dark thoughts to the back of her mind

Carla inched forward on the chair and listened intently as Jonny began talking her cousins through his plan.

* * *

A short time later Carla jumped back into her car. A quick glance at her watch told her that she was already two hours late for her lunch date with Logan and if the number of missed calls and text messages she'd received from him were anything to go by, she could safely say that he wasn't amused that she'd let him down.

Aware that time was ticking, and she was still none the wiser to where the diamonds were actually being housed, she bit down on her bottom lip and started the ignition, her gaze automatically drifting down to the potted plant on the passenger seat beside her. Surely, once she'd explained the reason for her lateness, Logan would understand, wouldn't he? It wasn't as though he was a stranger when it came to crime; his own father was a criminal. And as for the lunch Logan had arranged, they had ample opportunities to share a meal, they lived together after all.

Her mind made up, Carla sped out of the scrapyard. If she put her foot down, her unexpected trip back to her mother's house should only take a couple of hours, three at the most.

By the time Carla was heading in the direction of Brentwood, Logan was far from her mind and in his place was a determination so strong that it almost took her breath away. She was close, so close to bringing Bernie down. In fact, she wouldn't be surprised if by the time her family had finished with him, Bernie didn't promptly fall to his knees and beg her father for his forgiveness.

5

As the electronic gates that led to her mother's property began to open, Carla glanced nervously around her; not that she had anything to actually be apprehensive of, it wasn't as though she was letting herself into a stranger's house. This was her childhood home, however reluctant she may have been to actually spend any time there. Easing her foot down on the accelerator, she drove through the gates more than a little relieved to see that both her mother's and Bernie's cars were absent from the drive.

Moments later she unclipped her seat belt, pushed open the door, and stepped out of the car. With the plant tucked underneath her arm she took in the house. Everything about the mock Tudor mansion was ostentatious, from the water feature complete with a life-sized Greek goddess stone statue that took centre stage in the middle of the driveway, to the overly large cast-iron lion head that was used as a door knocker.

Making her way forward she took the house keys out of her pocket and paused in front of the entrance door. Nerves were beginning to get the better of her and as she cocked her head to the side, she strained her ears to listen out for any signs of life coming from inside the property. Satisfied that there was indeed no one at home she hastily let herself in and quietly closed the front door behind her.

'Mum?' she cautiously called out as she stepped across the marble hallway, her heels clip clopping as she went. 'Bernie?' When she received no response, Carla took in the vast space. The house was huge, and with six rooms and a staircase leading off the entrance hall alone, she was at a loss as to where to begin her search for the diamonds.

'Think,' she told herself. 'Where would Bernie have hidden the gems?' Her gaze went to the staircase and narrowing her eyes she looked upwards. Tearing up the stairs she made her way to her mother's bedroom and looked around. If her memory served her correctly, Bernie kept a safe at the bottom of his wardrobe. She'd stumbled across it as a child when she'd been snooping for Christmas presents.

In front of the wardrobe Carla took a deep breath then flung open the door. Positioned to one side of the floor was a metal box, it was a lot smaller than she originally remembered and crouching down, she attempted to tug the box towards her. The safe didn't budge and inspecting either side of the box, she took a wild guess that it was bolted to the floor. This had to be where Bernie had stashed the diamonds. She took a moment to think the situation through then reached out to turn the combination dial, lining up the numbers on what she considered to be notable dates, her mother's birthdate, Bernie's birthdate, she even tried the date when they had married and still the safe didn't open.

Getting to her feet, Carla sighed. Up until now she'd always considered Bernie to be predictable and she briefly wondered if her mother knew the combination code. Somehow, she highly doubted it.

A car door slamming closed caught Carla's attention and as her heart began to quicken she momentarily froze, the hairs on the back of her neck standing upright. 'Shit,' she all but squealed. In a wild panic she pushed the wardrobe door closed, tucked the plant back under her arm and raced back out of the room and down the stairs.

By the time she'd reached the bottom step, the front door opened. Smoothing down her hair, she took a deep breath then plastered what she hoped would be an innocent smile across her face.

'Carla.' Tossing his house keys onto the hallway table, Bernie's eyes twinkled as they always did whenever they were in one another's company. 'What are you doing here?' he asked, his voice becoming gentle.

Carla gave a light laugh and gesturing to the plant she stepped forward and placed it beside Bernie's keys. 'A peace offering for Mum.'

Bernie narrowed his eyes. 'It looks half dead,' he chuckled.

'Does it?' Carla's voice came out a lot higher than intended and tracing her fingers lightly over the leaves, she pretended to study the gift. 'All it needs is a drop of water and it'll be as right as rain.'

As they both stared intently at the plant an awkward silence followed.

'I suppose I'd better be off then,' Carla finally announced.

Bernie nodded and bringing out his arm he caught Carla by the wrist as she made to pass him by. 'It was nice to see you. Don't be a stranger and try to pop in a bit more often. This old place isn't the same without you here,' he said, motioning around him. 'I even miss hearing your music blast through the walls,' he laughed. 'And that's something I never thought I'd admit to.'

Carla gave a stilted smile and pulling her arm free, she took a step closer to the front door.

'I'll let your mum know that you stopped by and left her a present.' He motioned to the plant. 'I'm sure that she'll love it.'

It was a lie and they both knew it. Diane would promptly throw the plant in the bin. Nodding, Carla placed her hand on the door handle.

'Oh, and Carla.'

Carla span around, her heart thumping so hard and fast that she wouldn't be surprised if it actually stopped beating altogether. 'Yes.'

'Maybe next time you might want to phone ahead, just to make sure you don't have a wasted journey.'

'Yeah,' she gave a tight smile, her gaze drifting towards the staircase, 'thanks for the tip. I'll make sure to do that.'

* * *

The moment the front door closed after his stepdaughter, Bernie chewed thoughtfully on his bottom lip. As happy as he'd been to see her, Carla must think he was born yesterday if she truly thought that he would believe her cock and bull story about dropping off a gift. Not only were Diane and Carla more often than not at loggerheads, but Diane also loathed plants, flowers, and anything else she had to take responsibility for, her own daughter included.

His forehead furrowed, he stood at the bottom of the stairs, rested his hand on the banister rail and looked upwards. It was in his nature to be suspicious; he didn't trust easily and nor should he when he, better than anyone else, knew just how easy it was to deceive those around him. A sickening sense of dread tore through his body and tearing up the stairs, he raced into his bedroom and made a beeline for the wardrobe. Flinging open the door he let out a cry of relief. From what he could make out the safe remained untouched. He dropped to his knees and took a deep breath in an attempt to stop his hands from shaking, then reaching out he turned the combination dial and lined up the numbers. As far as dates were concerned there weren't many he was able to recall off the top of his head, in fact he would be hard pushed to remember the date he and Diane had taken their wedding vows. But there was one date that was burned into his memory, one that he knew as well as he knew his own, and so he should, considering how they had once been so close that they had been more like brothers than friends. With a final turn of the dial, he entered in Sonny Carter's date of birth and as the door to the safe sprang open with a click he drew in a breath. Sitting at the bottom of the safe, exactly where he had left them, was a stash of jewellery ranging from diamond rings and bracelets, to necklaces and pendants, the price tag on each piece alone coming well into the thousands. And more importantly, sitting beside the haul was a black, velvet drawstring bag, that bulged slightly open to reveal the loose diamonds inside.

Bernie chewed on his thumbnail, paranoia getting the better of him. He needed to be rid of the diamonds and fast. Carla may have been his stepdaughter but she was also a Carter and considering the Carters' track record of carrying out armed robberies could it be possible the family had got wind of the fact he was storing the diamonds for the Tucker brothers? What other possible reason could there have been for Carla to turn up unannounced? The fact he'd caught her descending the staircase was more than enough to prove to him that she was nothing more than their mole, their spy.

Hauling himself to his feet, Bernie darted across the room, dropped to his knees and felt underneath the bed. Pulling out a rucksack he moved back to the safe and scooped the contents into the bag. If the Carters had knowledge of the diamonds, then who else could be aware of the gems? Could the police be onto him, could both he and the house be under surveillance? As the old saying went, loose lips sank ships, and just maybe he hadn't been as tight-lipped as he should have been where the goods were concerned. After all, he'd told Diane that the stones were in his possession, bragged about it, in fact, and God only knew who she'd blabbed her mouth to. It was a sobering thought and as Bernie raced back down the stairs, with the diamonds safely nestled inside the rucksack clasped tightly to his chest, he grabbed his car keys and ran from the house as fast as his feet would carry him.

* * *

Forty minutes later, Carla pushed her key into the lock and opened the front door to the apartment she and Logan shared.

'I'm home,' she called out, pocketing the keys.

Walking through to the lounge she stopped dead in her tracks, her gaze drifting down to the dining table. 'Logan,' she gasped as she took in the laid table complete with candelabra and vases of fresh flowers, the red rose petals a stark contrast to the starched white, linen tablecloth.

'Don't even bother.'

The tone of Logan's voice was enough to make Carla snap her head up to look at him. 'I am so sorry...' she said, about to move forward again.

'I said don't.' With his arms folded over his chest Logan shook his head, his expression one of anger. 'You're five hours late Carla, five fucking hours. You knew exactly how important this was to me,' he said, sweeping his arm in the direction of the table. 'And you couldn't even be bothered to call me back or answer my messages. I was worrying myself sick about you, I thought you'd had an accident, that you were dead in a ditch somewhere.'

Carla's mouth dropped open and as she looked back down at the table she continued to shake her head. 'I thought it was just lunch, how was I supposed to know that you'd gone to all of this trouble.'

'So that makes it alright then, does it?'

'No of course not.' Brushing her hair out of her face Carla's mind whirled. 'I was just... I was working, I was at the scrapyard.' It was a small white lie, not that Logan needed to know the truth. Where would she even begin to find the right words to tell him that she'd purposely ignored his calls in order to search her mother's and Bernie's house?

'There's always something, always an excuse.'

'It's true,' Carla lied again. 'I was with Jonny; he needed my help with something...'

'Needed help with what, cleaning a gun...?'

'Now you're just being a dick,' Carla said, cutting him off.

'Do you know what, forget it.' Pushing himself away from the wall Logan blew out his cheeks. 'It's not like it's the first time you've blown me out, is it?' He made to walk away and then spun back around. 'Do you know what I think the trouble is here?' he said, gesturing between them. 'I'm too straight-laced for you, Carla.'

Carla's eyes widened. 'What are you talking about?' she snapped.

'The fact I have a job, a real job. Maybe if I went out robbing banks, or...' he shook his head grasping to find the right words. 'I don't know... If I was a thug or if I murdered people for a living, then, just maybe then, you might actually have some respect for me, you might even put me first for once.'

'Now you're being ridiculous.'

'Am I?' Logan retorted. He rubbed at his temples. 'You know sometimes I wonder if it was my dad's reputation that actually attracted you to me, because let's face it, those are the kind of people who you like to surround yourself with: villains, thieves, career criminals.'

'I can't help who my family are,' Carla retorted. 'Or the way I was brought up. Just the same as you can't help who your dad is. This is the world we live in; this life is all we've ever known.'

'No, it's not,' Logan shook his head. 'That's not the world I live in, and you know it isn't.'

'Don't be daft, of course it is. You're Danny McKay's son, you're as much a part of the underworld as I am.'

'No, Carla, you're not listening to me!' he shouted. 'I might have spent time around men who would make most normal people want to cross the street just to avoid them, but that's not who I am. I graft for my money, I have mates who work twelve hour shifts just to make ends meet, mates who wouldn't dream of shoving a shotgun into someone's face.'

Shrugging off her jacket, Carla resisted the urge to roll her eyes. 'Look, I'm sorry, okay.' She held up her hands then motioned towards the table. 'I'm here now, so let's stop arguing and...'

'You just don't get it do you?' Logan let out a laugh of disbelief. 'Maybe I'm sick to death of coming last on your list of priorities. And just maybe, Carla, at the end of the day it's not worth fighting for any more. I mean what's the point? We both want different things in life; I want to settle down...'

'And what – this isn't us settling down?' Carla rounded on him. 'We live together for Christ's sake, what more do you want from me?' As soon as the words had left Carla's mouth, she regretted them. 'I'm sorry, I didn't mean it like that, you know I didn't,' she cried, grasping for his hand.

Shrugging Carla away from him, Logan dug his hand into his pocket, pulled out the velvet box, placed it on the table then slid it towards her. 'Just maybe I thought that this would change things between us. I want kids one day, I wanted us to have a family, for us to live like a normal couple. I don't want to spend my life traipsing halfway across the country visiting you in prison twice a month, because that's the road I can see our life taking. And I'm sorry but I can't live like that.'

With those parting words he grabbed his jacket from the arm of the sofa and slammed out of the house.

Carla sucked in a breath and as she tore her eyes away from the front door, she looked down at the velvet box. Her heart in her mouth, she stepped forward, picked the box up and then gingerly prised open the lid. On seeing the two-carat diamond ring glinting up at her, a lone tear slipped down her cheek and biting down on her bottom lip so hard that she could taste blood, she screwed her eyes shut before slumping down on the sofa and holding her head in her hands.

Guilt ate away at her. Had her obsession for revenge pushed away the only man she had ever loved? And he was right, as of late she had become so consumed with Bernie and the diamonds that there was little room for anyone else, least of all Logan. Some days she barely even gave him a second thought. She'd just wrongly assumed that he would always be there; that coming home to him would give her a sense of normality, someone to keep her grounded. And even more than that, she'd fully believed that no matter what, and no matter who their families were, they would find a way to make their relationship work.

As irrational and as wrong as it was, a new level of hatred for Bernie engulfed her. Not only had he torn her parents apart, but he was also now the catalyst for Logan leaving. Determined more than ever to make him pay she jumped to her feet and tore out of the house, her face set like thunder. She was going to put her foot down with Jonny. They didn't have weeks to sit around doing nothing. She wanted those diamonds, sooner rather than later, and if her uncle and cousins didn't want to play ball then she would take matters into her own hands. No matter what, Bernie was finished even if it meant destroying him herself.

6

With her hand placed lightly on her ever-growing bump Terri Tempest heaved herself off the sofa and padded out into the hallway.

'I'll get it...' she shouted. Before she could even finish the sentence Jonny Carter raced down the stairs.

'Hey, what are you doing up and about?' he asked as he placed his hand on the small of her back and attempted to guide her back into the living room.

Terri laughed out loud. The unplanned pregnancy had come as a surprise to the both of them, but once they'd overcome their initial shock they were delighted, albeit apprehensive about what was to come. She herself hadn't exactly had a good role model when it came to motherhood and as for Jonny, well, he was terrified at the prospect of becoming a father, although he did his utmost to try and hide it from her. 'I'm pregnant,' she said, wriggling out of his arms in order to open the front door. 'I'm not sick.'

'Yeah, and,' Jonny protested, 'you still need to rest.'

'I get plenty of rest working at the pub and believe me I use the term "work" loosely, considering you, Rina, and not forgetting my brothers, barely allow me to lift a finger.' She gently swatted Jonny away from her. 'Besides I'm more than capable of opening the door.' Plastering a smile across her face, she slid across the bolt and pulled down on the door handle. 'See, no harm done, I'm still in one piece, and the baby is still happily kicking away at my bladder.'

Jonny sighed and as he turned to see who their visitor was, his forehead furrowed. 'What are you doing here?'

Standing on the doorstep Carla offered a tight smile. 'I know it's late, but I just wanted to go over our plans.'

On taking note of his niece's red-rimmed eyes Jonny pulled himself up to his full height. 'Have you been crying?'

'No, of course not.' Carla shook her head, her cheeks flushing pink.

'Has someone upset you?'

'I'm fine,' Carla barked out. 'Can you just drop it?'

Stepping aside, Jonny ushered Carla into the house. 'If someone's hurt you then tell me who it is, and I'll hunt the fucker down.'

'And he would do too,' Terri smiled as she rested her hand on Jonny's arm. 'Leave her be, if she wants to talk about it then she will do.'

Carla smiled her thanks.

'Yeah, but...'

Terri lifted her eyebrows. 'Just do as she asks,' she said quietly, giving him a knowing look. 'And drop it.'

Holding up his hands again Jonny motioned towards the lounge. 'Don't say I didn't offer,' he grumbled as he followed both women inside.

Once seated on the sofa, Carla shrugged off her jacket. 'I'm not waiting around,' she blurted out. 'I want those diamonds and I'm going to take them with or without your help.'

Jonny cleared his throat and feeling Terri's eyes bore into the side of his head, he squirmed in his seat. 'Maybe now isn't the time.'

'Now is the time,' Terri protested, her hands fluttering protectively down to her tummy. 'You failed to mention the fact you were going after diamonds. You told me it would be an easy job, in fact your exact words were, "it'll be a piece of piss".'

'And it will be,' Jonny insisted, shooting daggers at his niece. 'Everything is under control, isn't that right?'

Carla swallowed deeply. 'Yeah, of course it is,' she lied. 'We'll be in and out within minutes. There's nothing for you to worry about.'

Terri let out a strangled laugh. 'Try telling that to my blood pressure. I want the father of my baby to actually be at the birth, not locked up behind bars.'

'And I will be there.' Shaking his head at his niece, Jonny clasped hold of Terri's hand. 'Come on babe, you knew right from the start that I don't work a nine-to-five job. There's always going to be risk involved, some jobs more than others, that's just the way it is.'

'But diamonds!' Terri exclaimed. 'If something goes wrong, you'll go down for years.'

'I'll be sentenced to years no matter what the job is,' Jonny answered gently. 'That's why,' he said, turning to look at Carla, 'the heist needs to be planned out, and any risk we might come across needs to be minimised.'

Carla averted her gaze and as an emotional Terri left the room, she steeled herself for her uncle's onslaught.

'See what you've caused now,' he hissed. 'Thanks for that, Carla.'

'How was I supposed to know you hadn't told her,' Carla hissed back.

'Common sense maybe.' He slumped back on the sofa and pinched the bridge of his nose. 'Seriously I'm starting to wonder how the fuck Jimmy coped with all of this. If it's not you, it's Tommy Jr pulling shit everywhere he goes, and if that's not bad enough I've got your old man and Mitchell in my ear twenty-four-seven moaning like a couple of old women.'

'I'm sorry,' Carla sighed. 'I didn't mean to...'

'Forget about it,' Jonny groaned. He sat forward and rested his forearms on his knees. 'As much as I can't quite get my head around this hatred you have for Bernie, in a way I do understand where you're coming from, the diamonds aren't going to be kept at your mum's house for the duration.'

Carla frowned. 'You know why I don't like him,' she protested. 'He tore my parents apart. It's because of him they got divorced.'

'Maybe,' Jonny sighed. 'Although if you want my opinion,' he added, holding up his hands. 'I'd say that your mum was equally to blame, maybe even more so. And from what I can remember Bernie was only ever good to you.'

Carla looked down at her lap, the truth behind her uncle's words finally hitting home. As much as she hated to admit it, Bernie had been good to her, he'd stepped up and tried to be a parent, and even more than that, he'd wanted her around, which was a lot more than could be said about her mum.

'Which is why,' Jonny said, 'I've already set up a meeting with McKay for him to get us some guns.'

Carla's eyes widened. 'Logan's dad?'

'How many other McKay's do you know?' he answered with a hint of sarcasm. 'Yes, Logan's dad, that's where we've always obtained our firearms from. And that's another thing,' he said, stabbing his finger forward. 'Make sure you keep schtum around your dad. The last thing I need is for him to get wind of your involvement; he's giving me earache as it is, let alone bringing you into the equation.'

Carla nodded. 'So how soon can we go ahead with the robbery?'

Thinking the question over, Jonny shrugged. 'Maybe three or four days, five at the most, which believe me is a lot sooner than I wanted.' He slumped back on the sofa again. 'I'm not so worried about Peter, Jake, or Cameron, they know the score, they've been around for years and have got some experience behind them. It's the others I'm more concerned about. That mouthy little fucker, Tommy Jr, for starters, then there's Caleb, Reece, Dillon,' he ticked his nephews' names off his fingers. 'This is bigger than anything they've ever been involved in before and one wrong move on their part and that'll be it, curtains, game over, we'll all end up in the clink, you included.'

Shaking her head, Carla picked at her nail polish. 'It's going to be okay, isn't it?' she said, looking up. 'We can do this?'

'Yeah,' Jonny nodded. And as he looked towards the hallway he gave a half smile. 'It has to be okay. I've got too much to lose if this goes wrong.'

* * *

By the time Bernie had reached Lenny Tucker's house he was a sweating mess. Convinced he'd been followed, he glanced nervously around him. 'Come on!' he cried as he banged his fist on the front door. 'Open up.'

'What the fuck do you want...'

Before Lenny could finish the sentence, Bernie pushed his way into the house. 'They're onto me,' he shrieked, looking over his shoulder, his skin ashen.

Lenny Tucker narrowed his eyes and taking a quick peek either side of his house, he closed the door. 'Who's onto you?'

'I don't know.' Bernie wiped sweat from his forehead. 'The old bill, the Carters, take your pick.'

Lenny's eyes narrowed even further and flicking his head towards one of his henchmen he signalled for him to take a look outside. 'Go and have a butchers,' he ordered, his gravelly voice hard. Taking a seat in the lounge he leaned back in the armchair and rested his hands casually over his stomach. 'Let's get something straight,' he said, nodding towards Bernie. 'If you've led the filth to my house, I'll cut you from ear to fucking ear. Are we clear on that?'

Bernie swallowed deeply, the fear inside him rising a notch. 'Where else was I supposed to go?' he pleaded with Lenny's better nature. 'The diamonds have got nothing to do with me.' He made to push the bag onto Lenny's lap. 'I was only looking after them.'

'Woah.' Holding up his hands, Lenny shook his head. 'What do you think you're doing?' he snarled. 'That bag has got your prints all over it. It's fuck all to do with me.'

'Yeah but—'

'No, yeah buts.' Lighting a cigarette, Lenny drew the smoke deep into his lungs. 'We had an arrangement,' he said, exhaling a cloud of smoke above his head. 'Should our friends in blue turn up looking for those diamonds you take the fall for the robbery. And,' he said, his voice beginning to rise, 'don't forget you're being paid a hefty fucking wedge for the privilege of doing business with me and my brother.'

Close to tears, Bernie could scarcely breathe, so acute was his fear. And, if he was being honest with himself, he wasn't so sure which scared him the most: the prospect of eating porridge for the remainder of his life or being on the receiving end of the Tucker brothers' wrath.

'Coast is clear.' Making his way back into the room Lenny Tucker's henchman gave a shake of his head. 'There's no one out there.'

Bernie clutched at his chest, relief flooding through him. 'I could have sworn I was being followed,' he cried. 'I honestly thought my number was up.'

Lenny gave a small smile, showing off a row of even, white teeth. 'Now that we've established the old bill aren't about to burst through my front door, what this about the Carters?'

The blood drained from Bernie's face. He and the Carter brothers may not have been on good terms, but he couldn't hand on heart state that he had any ill feelings towards them per se. He'd thought the world of Sonny Carter once, and if that wasn't enough, he'd practically raised his daughter, not that he'd ever got any thanks for it, least of all from Carla, who for the most part was a stroppy little mare, and most definitely her father's daughter. 'It was nothing.' He waved his hand in the air. 'You know what I'm like,' he said with a light laugh as he looked between Lenny and the henchman. 'I'm paranoid. It's these bleeding diamonds,' he said, speaking so fast he could barely get the words out quick enough. 'They're putting me on edge, making me go a bit cuckoo up here,' he said, pointing to his forehead.

The laugh Lenny emitted was enough to make the tiny hairs on the back of Bernie's neck stand upright. If he wasn't terrified before then he certainly was now.

'Don't give me that old bollocks.' Lenny got to his feet, the smile that seconds earlier had been plastered across his face all too quickly replaced with a look that was bound to terrify the hardest of men. 'There ain't nothing wrong up here,' he said, stabbing his finger none too gently into the side of Bernie's head. 'The only thing wrong with you is that you're a snidey, two-faced, little bastard.'

The punch that landed in the centre of Bernie's abdomen was enough to knock the wind out of him and as he doubled over clutching at his stomach, he braced himself for a second blow.

'I'm going to ask you one more time,' Lenny roared. 'What do the Carters have to do with my diamonds?'

As predicted Bernie didn't have to wait long for the second blow and as Lenny rained down punch after punch, Bernie gasped for breath. 'Alright,' he screamed as he positioned his arms protectively over his head. 'Alright, I'll tell you everything you want to know.'

7

The next morning Danny McKay made his way into the scrapyard office and after shaking Jonny's hand he took a seat on the leather sofa, that by some miracle was still standing. Although it would be fair to say that the arms and cushions were now threadbare and that the outline of the metal springs were clearly visible through the thinning leather, making a rather unpleasant experience for those who had the misfortune to have to sit upon it.

'About time you chucked this old thing out isn't it,' Danny stated, wrinkling his nose.

Jonny chuckled. 'It's on my list of things to do. We should have got rid of it years ago, but, you know what Jimmy is like, he can be a right sentimental old bastard at times.' His voice trailed off and he nodded towards the sofa. 'You know how it is, it belonged to Tommy and...'

Danny held his hands up. 'Say no more.' He let out a sigh and looked Jonny in the eyes. 'So what can I do for you then? Because I've got a feeling you didn't call me over here just for a trip down memory lane.'

'Nah,' Jonny shook his head and leaning back in the chair he got down to business. 'I need some shooters.'

'Okay,' Danny nodded thoughtfully. 'How many are you after?'

'Two, maybe three.'

Danny narrowed his eyes. 'So how many is it?' he asked, spreading open his arms.

Thinking it over, Jonny sighed. 'Three.'

'Shouldn't be a problem. And how soon do you want them?'

Jonny paused a second time before offering a cheeky grin. 'Like today.'

Letting out an incredulous laugh Danny shook his head. 'No pressure then.' He tilted his head to one side, studying Jonny. 'I might be out of line here so feel free to tell me if I am, but I've known you for a long time and, well...' he shook his head, 'whatever the fuck this is that you're planning, Carla's not involved, is she?'

Momentarily taken aback, Jonny glanced out onto the forecourt as though fully expecting his niece to miraculously appear from out of thin air. 'No,' he lied. 'Why would she be?'

'Well,' Danny answered. 'You know me, I'm not one to interfere, but when my son turns up on my doorstep because him and his missus have had a barney it's kind of easy to speculate that something's going down, that maybe she's becoming a bit too involved with the real side of the business.'

Jonny swallowed deeply, and shaking his head, he screwed up his face. 'First I've heard about them having a row.' He gave a shrug. 'She hasn't mentioned anything to me.'

'Right.' Danny flashed a grin. 'Just thought I'd check. So,' he asked, changing the subject, 'you're after three shotguns?'

'That's what I said.' Jonny made to stand up, signalling that the meeting was over and when Danny remained seated he reluctantly sat back down.

'See, this is where we have a bit of a problem,' Danny said, running his hand over his jaw. 'Jimmy, who happens to be a good pal of mine, well I gave him my word that I'd keep my eyes and ears open, that I'd look out for you now that he's decided to retire.' He paused for a moment to allow his words to sink in. 'And I've got to admit I've got some concerns.' He held up his hands. 'Maybe I'm being out of line here, but from where I'm sitting, it doesn't look as though you've thought any of this through. I mean you've only been in charge for a couple of days and already you're after shotguns and I'm going to take a wild guess and say that this heist isn't one that Jimmy had been planning, nor one that he gave his permission to...'

'He doesn't need to give his permission.' Jonny spat. 'I run things around here now.'

Danny continued to shake his head. 'If you want my opinion, it doesn't look like you've planned any of this out. And seeing as my Stace's sons and grandson work for the business,' he said, using his fingers as quotation marks. 'Well, it shouldn't take a genius to tell you that if something should go wrong because you rushed this through, that I'll have no other choice but to come down on you like a ton of bricks.'

The nerve at the side of Jonny's eye pulsated. 'Cheers for the vote of confidence.'

'I'm just saying it how it is, so that we don't have an issue further down the line.'

'There is no issue,' Jonny growled. 'Either get me the guns or don't: your choice. Or maybe you'd rather I take my custom elsewhere, because I'm pretty sure I could get a shooter just as easily and without any questions being asked from some hood rat on the street.'

Danny shook his head. 'You'll get your guns; in fact, give me an hour and I'll have them ready for you.' He got to his feet and walking across the office he stopped in front of the door and turned around. 'Just remember what I said. I don't like to see my wife upset and believe me when I say this, I'd kill for that woman.'

* * *

As soon as Danny had left the office Jonny banged his fist down on the desk, upsetting an old, chipped mug that they used to store pens in. As the biros rolled across the desk and onto the floor, he fought the urge to kick out at them.

What with Sonny and Mitchell and now Danny McKay questioning his capabilities, he was in a foul mood.

The door barged open and as Tommy Jr traipsed inside, Jonny clenched his fists. 'Don't you know how to knock?'

Tommy Jr screwed up his face. 'What for?' he answered, flopping onto the sofa and pulling his mobile phone out of his pocket.

'Is this what I'm actually paying you for,' Jonny snapped. 'To sit on your arse all day?'

Looking up Tommy Jr frowned. 'What's got into you?'

Jonny shook his head. His great-nephew looked so like his brother Tommy that at times it was unnerving, he even had Tommy's cocky attitude. 'What's got into me?' Jonny bellowed, 'I'll tell you exactly what's got into me, I'm sick to the back teeth of people undermining my authority.'

Screwing up his face again, Tommy Jr continued nonchalantly scrolling through his phone. 'You need to chill out, mate.'

The words were the equivalent of a red rag to a bull and jumping out of his chair Jonny hauled his Tommy Jr up off the sofa and jerked him around to face him so that their noses were almost touching. 'Are you actually taking the piss out of me you cheeky little bastard? First of all,' he bellowed into his Tommy Jr's face, 'I'm not your mate, and secondly,' he continued to holler, as he flung open the door and proceeded to shove Tommy Jr outside, 'it's about time you started showing me some respect. Would you have spoken to Jimmy like this? Like fuck you would have done, and I'll tell you why not shall I? Because he would have beaten ten bells of shit out of you, that's why fucking not.'

As he landed in a crumpled heap on the floor Tommy Jr's expression was a mixture of both confusion and shock. 'Fucking hell,' he shouted. 'What's the matter with you? You could have done me some damage.'

Jonny bounded down the steps, his face set like thunder. 'Carry on creating chaos wherever you go, and you'll soon know what damage is. Three calls I've had about you causing shit, three,' he said, holding up three fingers. 'If I so much as hear another complaint about you, I swear before God I'm going to batter some sense into that skull of yours.' With those parting words he stormed back inside the office, slammed the door shut behind him and then rubbed his hand over his face. It was like history repeating itself all over again. Jonny had been Tommy Jr once, not only had he been wayward in his youth, but he'd also been so out of control that he'd actually thought of himself as untouchable. He'd also been the sole reason his brothers had been roped in to commit the murders of four men, all thanks to a debt he'd owed to Danny McKay, the very same Danny McKay who thought he could question Jonny's judgement.

As he bent down to scoop up the pens, Jonny shook his head. He'd had a gutful; he knew that much and he hadn't even been in charge of the business for more than a week yet.

'Is it safe to come in?'

Jonny looked up and on seeing his niece standing at the threshold he gave a brisk nod.

Carla walked into the office and perched on the edge of the sofa in an attempt to avoid the raised springs. 'I just saw Tommy Jr; he had a few choice words to say about you,' she said, raising her eyebrows.

'Yeah, well I'm not proud of it,' Jonny said, glancing out of the window. 'But I laid into him.'

'I gathered as much,' Carla answered, offering a smile. 'Look do you want me to have a word with him? He listens to me, and he's not a bad kid, not really, not deep down. His heart is in the right place.'

Jonny gave an incredulous laugh. 'Are we talking about the same Tommy Jr here?'

Carla rolled her eyes.

'The thing is,' Jonny said as he took a seat behind the desk. 'I'm a fine one to talk. I used to be just like him. I was a right little toe rag as a kid. I used to wind Tommy Snr, up something chronic. The difference is though, he had Jimmy to back him up, and believe me,' he said, lifting his eyebrows, 'the pair of them together were like something from out of your worst nightmare. And if they were after you,' he laughed, 'then you soon knew about it. If Tommy didn't give me a slap, then Jimmy would, you couldn't escape from them no matter how much you tried.' He gave a sigh. 'Who the fuck have I got backing me? And don't even bother saying your dad and Mitchell, the pair of them are dimmer than an energy saving light bulb, and that's putting it mildly.'

'That's not fair,' Carla retorted. 'My dad has been there for this family, he's loyal, trustworthy...'

'Yeah, I know,' Jonny conceded cutting her off. 'I didn't mean it how it came out.' Resting his chin in his hand he offered a small smile. 'What's this I've been hearing about you and Logan?'

Carla's face fell. 'It's nothing,' she shrugged. 'We're just taking a little break that's all.'

Jonny raised his eyebrows. 'And are you alright about that?'

'Of course I am.' Carla attempted to smile. 'It's not over between us. It was just a silly misunderstanding, that's all. He'll come around.'

Jonny nodded and leaning back in the chair he gestured towards the door. 'Do me a favour then and have a word with Tommy Jr for me. Tell him I'm sorry and that I've got a lot on my mind, what with the diamonds and everything.'

Getting out of her chair Carla walked around the desk, placed her hand on Jonny's shoulder and gave it a reassuring squeeze. 'It's going to be alright you know. You're not an idiot Jonny, you could plan out this robbery with your eyes closed. It's like you always say, you had a good teacher.'

Jonny laughed and straightening up he nodded. 'Yeah, I did.'

Carla winked. 'Besides, you've got me. Maybe I could be your Jimmy.'

Jonny laughed even harder. 'We'll see,' he said, jerking his head in the direction of the door. 'Go on, go and sort him out for me.'

As soon as Carla had closed the door behind her, Jonny dug his hand into his pocket and pulled out the notes he'd been making. Carla had been right about one thing; he may not have had his brother Tommy's acumen when it came to pulling off a heist, but he knew enough. And it wasn't as though he was a complete stranger when it came to carrying out armed robberies. In recent years he'd spent months at a time with Jimmy planning out escape routes, he'd even been responsible for the getaway vehicles themselves, and not once had he ever let his brothers down.

Feeling somewhat happier, Jonny glanced at his watch. He'd give it thirty minutes or so and then go and meet McKay. Getting out of the chair, he walked across the office and opened the door.

'Oi, Tommy,' he called out, keen to build bridges with his great-nephew, 'I've got a little job for you.'

* * *

Within thirty minutes, Jonny and Tommy Jr were heading down the A13 in the direction of Romford, Essex.

'Do you remember my grandad?' Tommy Jr asked out of the blue.

Not taking his eyes of the road ahead of him Jonny flicked the indicator. 'Which one?'

'Gary.' Lighting a joint, the pungent scent of cannabis filled the car and resting his elbow on the open window, Tommy Jr gave Jonny a side long glance.

Snapping his head around to look at his great-nephew, Jonny's eyes were almost bulging out of his head. 'Do you fucking mind,' he growled, his patience once again beginning to wear thin where his great-nephew was concerned. 'Are you seriously trying to get us nicked.'

Tommy Jr shrugged. 'What's the big deal?' he asked, looking down at the spliff. 'Everyone does it, even you.'

'Not in my car I don't,' Jonny retorted as he glanced in the rear-view mirror. 'And certainly not in the days leading up to a job. Get rid of it now and that's an order.'

Rolling his eyes Tommy Jr flicked the joint out of the window. 'Are you happy now?' he mumbled underneath his breath.

The muscle at the side of Jonny's left eye twitched. 'I'll be a lot happier once you start toeing the line.' He shook his head. 'What the fuck is wrong with you, eh? You might pull this shit when you're out with your mates, or your cousins, or even when you're with your old man because from what I've heard, even he's struggling to control you. But you don't do it when you're out with me, do you understand what I'm telling you? You're a Carter for fuck's sake and it's about time you started acting like one.'

'Johnson you mean.' Tommy Jr corrected. 'I'm a Johnson not a Carter.'

Jonny clenched his jaw. 'It's the same thing,' he snapped as he glanced up at the rear-view mirror again on the lookout for any signs that the police could be tailing them. 'The last thing I need is an excuse for the filth to pull us over.'

A moment of silence followed and clearing his throat Tommy Jr kicked his legs out in front of him. 'Do you remember him then, I mean my grandad, Gary?'

'Yeah, of course I do, he was my brother.'

'Only I know a lot about my other grandad, Tommy, but no one ever wants to talk about Gary.'

'That's because no one liked him.'

Tommy Jr screwed up his face. 'Yeah, but he was your brother; how could you not have liked him?'

'Because he was a fruit loop,' Jonny spat. Pulling into the car park behind Danny McKay's club, he switched off the ignition and sighed. 'Look, it's a long story,' he finally answered. 'But let's just say he caused a lot of hag amongst the family,' he added with a measure of bitterness. 'It was the only thing he was ever good at, and believe me, I wasn't sorry when he kicked the bucket. It was more of a relief not to have to put up with his shit any more.' Climbing out of the car, he leaned against the door and pulled out his phone.

'Yeah, but what about me?' Tommy Jr asked, shifting his weight from one foot to the other.

Jonny looked up. 'What about you?' he asked, his forehead furrowing.

'Well, seeing as I keep fucking up all of the time...'

'I didn't say it was all the time.' Jonny shook his head. 'Just sometimes, well maybe the majority of the time.'

'Yeah, but what if it's because I take after him – Gary?'

Jonny threw his head back and laughed. 'Leave it out,' he said, ruffling Tommy Jr's hair. 'Who told you that you're anything like Gary? Take it from me, and I should know seeing as I knew the both of them. You're like the spit out of your grandad Tommy's mouth, the two of you are that alike. You've even got his smart mouth,' he grinned. Jerking his head in the direction of the club as Danny McKay made his way towards them, he slipped the phone back into his pocket, leaned into the car and retrieved an envelope filled with cash from the glovebox then tossed the car keys in Tommy Jr's direction. 'Make yourself useful and unlock the boot.'

'Jonny.' After shaking both Jonny's and Tommy Jr's hands Danny handed across a holdall. 'They're clean,' he said, referring to the guns as he pocketed the envelope. 'So whatever you do just watch out for prints.'

Jonny rolled his eyes. 'I have done this before. I'm not exactly new to the life am I?'

Danny's eyes hardened. 'I didn't say that you were. And for the record I wasn't having a dig,' he added before motioning to Tommy Jr. 'It was just a friendly reminder to be careful, and nothing more than that.'

As Jonny made to climb into the car Danny tugged on his arm. 'Listen,' he said, lowering his voice. 'I don't know what you're planning and to be perfectly honest I don't want to know, I'm too old for all that shit, but just be on your guard okay? Keep your wits about you, because going by the speed you're working at, I've got my suspicions about what you're up to, and you and me both know there are a few people out there who would love nothing more than to see you, in fact to see all of you Carters,' he said, nodding towards Tommy Jr, 'brought down a peg or two.'

Jonny narrowed his eyes. 'Have you heard something?'

Danny held up his hands. 'Other than the Tucker brothers were responsible for that raid over in Hatton Garden, no.'

Stepping back out of the car Jonny closed the door behind him. 'How the fuck did they pull that off? You know as well as I do that both Tommy and Jimmy failed when it came to diamonds.'

Danny gave a light laugh. 'How do you think?'

Jonny paused for a moment. 'An inside man?' he asked, cocking his head to the side.

'Bingo,' Danny grinned. 'And I've also heard,' he said, leaning in closer, 'that they already have a buyer lined up to put the stones back onto the market.'

'You're joking.' Jonny's jaw dropped. 'But how? I mean...' he shrugged. 'I assumed that they were going to be shipped out of the country?'

Holding up his hands again, Danny shook his head. 'Not my area of expertise I'm afraid. But,' he said, giving a wink, 'should you need this person's whereabouts later down the line, if you were ever to get your hands on some diamonds, then come and see me and I'll happily pass his details over.'

Jonny laughed and shaking Danny's hand he jumped into the car. 'I might just take you up on that offer.'

'Yeah, that's what I thought.' Danny winked again. Tapping the car roof he gestured towards his wife's grandson. 'Look after him,' he said in a warning. 'Otherwise, it won't be me you have to answer to. You'll have Stacey on your case and trust me, once she gets wind of what you're up to she's gonna go mental.'

'I'm not a kid,' Tommy Jr scowled from the passenger seat. 'It's about time my nan realised that.'

Danny's expression hardened. 'You're still her grandson,' he barked back. 'And if anything, you should be showing her some respect. She's not exactly green around the edges. She lost a brother and a husband to this world; another loss will tip her over the edge.'

As Tommy Jr had the grace to look away, Jonny started the ignition. 'Don't worry, I'll keep my eye on him.'

Satisfied with Jonny's answer, Danny nodded then tapping the car roof again he offered a tight smile. 'Remember what I said. If at any point you need the details for that buyer then let me know.'

Giving a nod, Jonny stepped his foot on the accelerator and eased out of the car park.

Tommy Jr lounged back in the seat, the scowl he'd exhibited moments earlier working its way back across his face. 'I don't know what his problem is,' he remarked nonchalantly, flicking his head behind him to the club.

An incredulous laugh escaped from Jonny's lips. 'Trust me,' he said, glancing up at the rear-view mirror. 'Danny is the last person you'd ever want to make an enemy of.' He shook his head. 'I've been there, done it, got the bloody T-shirt. And if it wasn't for the Carter surname, and the fact Danny and your grandad Tommy had had a lot of respect for one another, I'd be six feet under today.' He cast his great-nephew a glance. 'Let me put it this way he might not be as young as he used to be but believe me, you'd rather him fight your corner than be an enemy.'

'Yeah, I suppose so,' Tommy Jr sighed somewhat reluctantly.

* * *

Sporting a heavily bruised and battered face and still wearing the same crumpled, blood spotted clothes he'd worn the previous day, Bernie reluctantly followed Lenny and his henchmen into Ozzie Tucker's house. Lenny had more or less kept him captive overnight, point blank refusing to allow him to go home. In the end he'd had no other choice but to resign himself to that fact that he'd have to sit it out. And if that wasn't bad enough, he'd even had to switch his phone off. The constant phone calls from Diane had begun to grate on his nerves, and if her irate text messages that followed were anything to go by then it was more than obvious that she thought he was out having fun with some little tart.

In the cold light of day, he was starting to wish that he'd kept his mouth firmly shut and even more than that, he wished that he'd never turned up on Lenny Tucker's doorstep. In hindsight, he should have known that he'd be roped in to their plans considering his history with the Carters.

Once inside the lounge, Bernie glanced around him. If he hadn't thought that Ozzie was unhinged before, then he certainly did now. Amidst the dated flowery wallpaper was an arsenal of weapons tacked to the walls. And as his gaze took in a series of boning knives, handguns and other paraphernalia that looked better suited to an armoury than a house in East London a feeling of cold dread swept over him.

'What happened to your boat race?'

As Bernie tore his gaze away from the weapons, he resembled a rabbit caught in the headlights of a car. 'It's nothing.' Breathing deeply, he wrapped one arm across his ribs before gingerly prodding the blood encrusted split in his lip. 'I bumped into a door that's all,' he wheezed.

Ozzie gave a hearty chuckle. 'Must have been some fucking door if it was able to do that much damage.'

Fear radiated out of Bernie and giving a painful nod of his head he gave Lenny a sidelong glance before hastily averting his gaze. More than ever, he wished that he was anywhere but at Ozzie Tucker's house surrounded by what could only be described as bona fide nutcases, not that he had anyone to blame other than himself for the predicament he found himself to be in.

'So what's this I've been hearing about our old friends, the Carters?'

The humour was gone from Ozzie's voice and as he sank into an armchair, he clicked his fingers in order to beckon Sadie towards him. 'Don't mind my Sadie,' he added with a maniacal grin as he pulled the man roughly onto his lap. 'You can talk in front of her.'

Bernie kept his head down low, too afraid that his expression would give his true thoughts away. He didn't trust Sadie as far as he could throw him, and considering Sadie had some muscle behind him, that was saying something. Not only had the man spent a great number of years behind bars but he was also a convicted murderer. And that fact alone should have been enough to alert not only the most foolish of people, but also all of the do-gooders out there in the world that the man was a danger to society.

'I'm not being funny Oz,' Lenny barked out, breaking the silence. 'But this is a private matter.'

Ozzie's eyes hardened. 'And like I said,' he growled, 'you can talk in front of Sadie; she knows how to keep her trap shut, ain't that right,' he said, running his thumb down the length of Sadie's arm.

Sadie nodded his head, his light brown hair dancing around his shoulders. 'Ozzie's right, it would be more than my life is worth to open my mouth.'

'See, she knows the score,' Ozzie chuckled. Sweeping his arm out in front of him he turned his attention back to his brother. 'So, answer my question. What's the low-down on the Carters?'

A second silence followed and throwing up his arms in defeat, Lenny's voice dripped with venom. 'The bastards have been sniffing around.' He motioned for Bernie to pass the rucksack across to one of the Tuckers' henchmen. 'They're onto the diamonds.'

'I didn't say that for definite,' Bernie all but squeaked out, feeling a moment of relief to be free of the bag and with it any incriminating evidence that linked him to the robbery.

As Ozzie turned his hard stare towards him, Bernie swallowed deeply, fear once again getting the better of him.

'I caught my stepdaughter at the house,' he explained, his voice wavering. 'Not only is she a Carter, but she also looked shifty, and me being me, well you know what I'm like, I put two and two together, came up with five, and panicked.' He was talking fast and as he paused for breath, he looked around him. 'I mean, it could have been innocent, I could have made an honest mistake. I mean she did have this plant that she'd bought for Diane, and...'

'Like fuck it was innocent,' Ozzie snarled. Pointing his finger forward, there was a wicked gleam in his eyes. 'I say we do the bastards in, stop playing games and wipe the inbred fuckers off the face of the earth once and for all.'

A shard of fear shot down the length of Bernie's spine and as he opened his mouth to protest Lenny laughed.

'Or better still, we could wait for the bastards to turn up looking for the diamonds and then give them a welcoming committee they won't forget in a hurry.' He mimicked shooting a gun. 'It'd be one way of getting rid of them and you've got a lot of land around that house of yours,' he said, turning to look at Bernie. 'We can dig a couple of six-foot holes,' he shrugged. 'Throw the cunts in and Bob's your uncle, no one would be any the wiser. Problem solved.'

Horrified, Bernie's jaw dropped. 'But...' he began.

Lenny laughed even harder. 'I'm joking,' he said, slapping Bernie non too gently on the back. 'Nah,' he grinned. 'We'll feed them to the pigs and as it just so happens,' he winked, 'I know a pig farmer who owes me a favour or two.'

Bernie closed his eyes in distress. This had to be a nightmare, one that he was bound to wake up from at any given moment. By his own admission he was a lot of things: a liar, a braggart, and a man of few morals, to name but a few. But when it came to murder, he knew for a fact that he didn't have the stomach for it. He'd rather shoot himself than look someone in the eye, take aim, and pull the trigger. 'Maybe we could just talk to them,' he suggested. 'Scare them off.'

'Why don't we throw them a tea party while we're at it?' Ozzie narrowed his eyes until they were nothing but mere slits. 'Anyone would think that you and the Carters are the best of pals the way you're carrying on.' He stabbed his finger forward again. 'Is there something going on here that we don't know about. Are you and the Carters in cahoots?'

'No.' Shaking his head, Bernie's eyes were wide open. 'On my mother's grave the Carters mean nothing to me,' he said, holding up his hands.

'He's lying.' Shoving Sadie off his lap, spittle flew out of Ozzie's mouth. 'This little fucker has been playing us for fools,' he roared, jumping to his feet.

Clasping his hands in front of him, Bernie shook his head, the fear in his eyes intensifying. 'I swear to you,' he cried, 'I'm telling the truth.' Of course it was a lie, one that he had more than just a feeling Ozzie was able to see right through. He had no beef with the Carters, if anything it was the other way around. He'd done them wrong, or rather he'd done Sonny wrong. He raised one arm protectively over his head and slammed his eyes shut. 'Lenny,' he all but screamed. 'Tell him will you. Tell him that I'm on your side.'

'Ozzie,' Lenny said with a measure of caution. 'Just calm down.' Holding out his arms he took a step towards his brother. 'Like I told you on the phone. Everything is under control.'

'I don't trust him,' Ozzie continued to protest. 'I told you right from the start that he's a snidey cunt, that he'd try to have us over.'

'Yeah,' Lenny agreed as he threw Bernie a glance over his shoulder. 'I admit he looks like a weasel, but he hasn't got the gall to betray us.'

Still grumbling, Ozzie returned to his seat. 'If I find out that you're lying to me,' he warned, stabbing his finger in Bernie's direction. 'I'll bury you beside the Carters.'

'There won't be anything left to bury,' Lenny grinned. 'Not once the pigs have finished with them.' He rubbed his hands together. 'From the look of things, it's safe to say that the Carters days are well and truly over. And I can't say,' he grinned, 'that I'll be sorry to see the fuckers go.'

Yes, Bernie decided, it was definitely a nightmare of epic proportions. And as he was frogmarched back out of the house and into Lenny's waiting car, not for the first time did he wish that he'd never laid eyes upon the Tucker brothers. Greed had always been one of his biggest downfalls; even as a kid he'd wanted to have more than those around him, hence the reason why he and Sonny Carter had become firm friends to begin with. As young as he'd been, he'd sensed that Sonny was going places and so he'd latched on to him wanting a piece of the action. And now all these years later he was to have a hand in Sonny's downfall, not content in destroying his former best friend's marriage and subsequent life, he was also to become the catalyst for Sonny's demise. If the situation wasn't so dire, Bernie would never have believed himself capable of such treachery. Fair enough he may have shagged Sonny's wife, he'd even gone on to marry her, but he would never have willingly harmed a hair on his head.

Feeling thoroughly depressed he stared out of the car window. By the time the car was speeding through the East London streets Bernie had resigned himself to the fact that there was nothing he could do to help Sonny, nor any of the Carters come to think of it. Sadness washed over him. Not in a million years did he ever think that his involvement with the Tucker brothers would lead to his former best friend's death, the mere thought was incomprehensible to him. He'd loved Sonny once, a part of him still did, they hadn't only been friends, they'd been more like brothers. They'd looked out for one another, and even more than that, they'd trusted one another with their lives – or at least they had until Bernie had committed the ultimate betrayal.

8

Sonny Carter shook his head. A large part of him had hoped that his youngest brother would realise what a grave mistake he was making. That given their track record concerning diamonds he would not only change his mind regarding the heist but that he would also push all thoughts of the Tucker brothers and the gems far from his mind.

'What else was I supposed to do?' Danny McKay said. 'If he didn't buy the shooters from me then he would have bought them off the street, and fuck knows what kind of condition they would have been in then. If it's any consolation to you at least the guns are clean, nothing will come back to him. I also reminded him to make sure he's careful when it comes to leaving any prints behind.'

Raising his eyebrows, Sonny sighed. 'At least that's something, I suppose.' He looked towards his twin brother. 'I still can't get my head around this.' He blew out his cheeks. 'What is he playing at? It's not as if he needs the cash, he's loaded.'

'You know what he's like,' Mitchell growled. 'This is nothing to do with money, all he wants to do is act the Billy big bollocks in front of the boys; even when he was a kid, he was the same. When has he ever listened to a word anyone had to say? From the minute he was born he's been a law unto himself. We've got no one else to blame for how he's turned out other than ourselves,' he sighed. 'Being the baby of the family we've been way too easy on him and not only that, but we've also let him get away with far too much. If it had been me or you pulling the shit he's pulled, then Tommy or Jimmy would have kicked us from here to kingdom come.'

'True,' Sonny answered, giving a shake of his head. 'And what about the boys,' he asked, turning his attention back to Danny. 'Are they toeing the line.'

Danny shrugged. 'I can't answer that. But he did have Tommy Jr with him.'

'That'll be a no then.' Mitchell rolled his eyes. 'That kid is even worse than Jonny was at the same age and not in a million years did I ever imagine that could be possible.'

Letting out an exasperated sigh, Sonny took a swift glance at his watch then got to his feet. 'I take it they'll be down the Fiddlers,' he said, referring to the pub Jonny's partner, Terri, ran with her brothers, Ricky and Jamie Tempest.

'More than likely,' Danny answered. Leaning back in his chair he slipped his hand into his pocket and pulled out his mobile phone. 'Do you want me to get on the blower to Jimmy,' he asked, nodding down at the device. 'And fill him in on what's been going on?'

After giving the question a moment's thought Sonny shook his head, and shrugging on his jacket he made his way across Danny's office. 'Cheers for the heads-up.' He lifted his eyebrows towards Mitchell. 'But we'll take it from here. The last thing we need is for Jimmy to get wind of this. Because I can tell you right now that at the first sign of trouble, nothing you or I say will stop him from wanting to jump back on a plane. And if I'm being honest, I'd much rather he stays where he is, otherwise, the minute that plane hits down on the tarmac all hell will break loose. As for Jonny,' he said, shaking his head again, 'one way or another he's going to be the fucking death of me.'

'You and me both,' Mitchell agreed.

After saying their goodbyes, the brothers made their way through the club and exited the venue by the back entrance that led out to the car park.

'I'm going to nip over to the boozer,' Sonny stated as he unlocked his car. 'I have to try and get through to him, if for no other reason than for peace of mind. At least then I'll know I've done everything I can to make him see sense.'

'Do you want me to come with you?'

'Nah you're alright.' Sonny shook his head and as he climbed behind the wheel his shoulders were slumped. 'What would be the point, I don't even know why I'm bothering if I'm being honest, we both know it's not going to change anything. He's too fucking head-strong for a start and if we both turn up at the pub, he'll only think we're having a pop at him.'

'Yeah you've got a point,' Mitchell said as he made his way over to his own car. 'But should he start kicking off, give me a call.'

Sonny nodded and as he started the ignition he ran his hand over his face, stepped his foot on the accelerator and then eased out of the car park. As he drove in the direction of Dagenham, he couldn't help but feel as though he had a dark cloud hanging over his head, a feeling of dread that wouldn't go away no matter how much he willed it to. He had a bad feeling about the whole situation, and as the days passed, the niggling thought at the back of his mind grew even stronger. Whether he would ever admit it or not, Jonny was in over his head, and with just their nephews behind him, the majority of whom had never so much as held a gun, let alone actually fired one, Sonny couldn't help but wonder if Jonny was leading them down a slippery slope of no return.

* * *

The Merry Fiddlers, or the Fiddlers as it was more commonly known, was a hive of activity by the time Sonny made his way inside. Making a beeline for the landlady, Rina Taylor, he flashed a wide grin.

Returning the smile, Rina leaned her forearms on the bar. 'I wasn't expecting to see you in here tonight.'

'Can't seem to stay away from the place,' Sonny chuckled as he dug his hand into his pocket and pulled out his wallet. 'How long have they been in here?' he asked, motioning across the pub to where his brother and nephews were standing.

Rina looked up at the clock. 'It's got to be at least an hour or two,' she answered, giving the men a surreptitious glance.

Sonny groaned. Fuelled with booze, he highly doubted his brother, nor any of his nephews, for that matter would be in the mood to listen to reason. Not that they were likely to have listened to a word he had to say if they were sober either.

'At least they're behaving themselves,' Rina remarked with a lift of her eyebrows as she pushed herself away from the bar and straightened up. 'Then again, I can't say that they've ever given me much trouble. Archie would have never stood for it.' She turned to look at the framed portrait of her late husband that took pride of place on the bar and sighed. 'You know what Archie was like. He might have let a lot of things slide when it came to this lot,' she said, nodding around the pub. 'But overstep the mark and he'd not only turf you out on your ear, but more than likely bar you for life.'

Tearing his gaze away from the photograph, Sonny nodded. He'd had a lot of respect for Archie Taylor as had the vast majority of his customers. As far as landlords went, Archie had been one of the best; firm but fair, and seeing as many of the locals were what could only be described as colourful characters, some considerably shadier than others, the pub had needed a guvnor who wasn't afraid to put them in their place. 'Well at least that's something,' he said, nodding towards his nephews. 'But if they should start getting lairy let me know and I'll sort them out.'

Rina gave a light laugh and nodding towards the entrance door as Ricky and Jamie Tempest walked inside, she leaned slightly forward. 'They wouldn't dare play up,' she smiled. 'Do you honestly think those two,' she said, gesturing to Ricky and Jamie again, 'would put up with any nonsense?'

A hint of a smile tugged at the corner of Sonny's lips. 'Yeah, you've got a point,' he winked. 'But if they do, you know exactly where to find me.'

After ordering a drink, Sonny pocketed his change and as Rina placed the filled glass in front of him, he smiled his thanks then made his way towards his family. 'I thought this is where I might find you.'

Jonny spun around and offering a wide smile he clasped his brother by the hand. 'What are you doing here?'

'I would have thought it was self-explanatory.' Sonny nodded down at his drink and as he took a sip of the whisky he eyed his nephews over the rim of the glass, his heart automatically sinking as he did so. With the exception of Peter, Jake, and Cameron, the rest were nothing but kids. 'Listen,' he moved in closer towards Jonny and bent his head slightly so that he could speak privately in his ear, 'are you sure that I can't change your mind. I mean there has to be somewhere else you can target, a bank, or a post office even, at least until this lot have got some experience behind them.'

'What and let the diamonds slip through our fingers?'

As Sonny nodded, he already knew what Jonny's answer was going to be. But he had to try, he reasoned; he would never be able to live with himself if he didn't.

'Leave it out.' Tipping back his glass Jonny drained his drink and as he turned around to face the bar he gave his brother a side-long glance. 'You've got to be deluded if you think I'm going to let this go. It's like Tommy always used to say, if it's got our names on it, then...'

Sonny held up his hand cutting his youngest brother off. 'I already know the family motto,' he pointed out. 'So no need to preach it to me. And if you think that Tommy would have given his blessing to this madness then you're the deluded one.'

'Yeah, well.' Jonny's expression hardened. 'Maybe you didn't know him as well as you think you did,' he said, tilting his head to the side. 'I'd even go as far to say that you've got a short memory, because the Tommy I remember would have been all over this like a rash and you fucking know it. Didn't he have a beef with Freddie Smith years back?' he said, referring to a local villain that Danny McKay had once worked for. 'In fact, correct me if I'm wrong, but didn't Tommy rob him of some gold bars?'

Sonny averted his gaze. 'That was different, and you know it,' he barked out. 'It wasn't until we'd got inside the club that we even knew Freddie had the gold in his possession.'

'Maybe,' Jonny shrugged. 'But Tommy still intended to rob him, didn't he? That's the difference between us,' he said, wagging his finger between them. 'I'm more like Tommy than you and Mitchell could ever be. I'm not afraid to step on anyone's toes, whereas you...' He gave his brother a pointed look. 'Let's just say that you and Mitchell don't like taking risks.'

Giving an agitated sigh, Sonny ran his hand through his hair. Jonny couldn't have been any further from the truth if he tried. And as much as it would be fair to say that he and Mitchell approached each job with caution, to say that they didn't like to take risks was wrong. At the end of the day, they weren't exactly choir boys; they had spent their teenage years and then their entire adulthood as armed robbers. It was the only career they had ever known, well, that and debt collecting. But when you looked at the two side by side, the robberies were definitely the more risky of the two. 'I take it nothing I or Mitchell say will change your mind then?'

'Nope.' Jonny gave a nonchalant shake of his head. 'So if you want my advice don't waste your breath.'

It was the exact answer Sonny had been expecting and acknowledging the fact he could do nothing to sway his brother's mind he turned back to look at his nephews. Jonny may have been the one in charge, the one to give out the orders, but their nephews still held him and Mitchell in high regard, and so they should considering they had more armed robberies behind them than the boys had had hot dinners. 'You'd better be listening to what your uncle says,' he said in a warning as he looked at each of his nephews in turn. 'Because believe me, it's only him,' he said, jerking his thumb in Jonny's direction, 'who stands between you and prison, so make sure that you follow his instructions to the letter. Don't go getting cocksure of yourself, especially you,' he said, giving Tommy Jr, his great-nephew, a knowing look. 'Because all it will take is one wrong move on your part and it'll be game over.'

At the sudden turnaround of his brother, Jonny's jaw almost hit the floor. 'Cheers for that Sonny,' he said, beaming from ear to ear.

'Yeah well,' Sonny shrugged. 'I still don't like it,' he said, pointing his finger forward. 'And I still think it's a big risk you're taking but seeing as you're hell bent on seeing this through I want to make sure that this lot take it seriously, that they understand this isn't some game they're playing. And if it means I have to put the fear of God into them to make sure they behave themselves, then so be it.' Pulling out his wallet he waved it above his head. 'Who wants another drink?'

As his nephews' hands shot up in the air, Sonny's forehead furrowed. 'Jake,' he called out to the youngest of his brother Tommy's sons. 'What are you having?'

Looking up from his mobile phone the colour had drained from Jake Carter's face and as he glanced back down at the device he shook his head. 'I'll be back in a bit,' he said, backing away. 'I have to take care of something.'

* * *

In a night cafe in East Ham, Newham, Sadie ever so carefully placed two mugs of steaming hot tea on a table, then pulling out a chair, he took a seat. Wiping away a series of crumbs left from the previous occupant, he placed his elbow on the table, rested his chin in his hand and glanced in the direction of the window. Thankful for the condensation that covered the glass, making it near impossible for those passing by to see inside, he allowed himself to relax. Not that he actually believed the Tucker brothers, nor any of their henchmen for that matter, were likely to dine out at the greasy spoon. No, the brothers' tastes were slightly more upmarket. They had an image to maintain and so were much better suited to a five-star restaurant in the West End of London rather than a poky little cafe on the high street. Hence the reason why the eatery made the perfect venue for Sadie to set up a meeting with someone in private.

From the speakers situated above the shop counter, Sadie recognised a UB40 song being played and as he hummed along to the music the door opened, bringing with it a blast of cold air, causing Sadie to inadvertently sit up a little straighter. A hesitant smile etched its way across his face and as the man he'd arranged to meet walked towards him, Sadie looked him over. As far as first impressions went, he had to admit that he looked a darn sight better than the last time they had been in one another's company. Feeling a little self-conscious, Sadie reached up to smooth down his hair. He only wished that he could say the same about himself. Still his skin had the look of prison pallor about it, and as for his hair, it was in need of a good colour and cut. Tucking his hands under the table in an attempt to hide his fingernails that were bitten down to the quick, Sadie nodded towards the empty chair opposite him.

'You look well,' he smiled, keen to break the ice between them.

Jake Carter nodded and taking a quick glance around the cafe he pulled out a chair.

Picking up his mug, Sadie was about to take a sip when he gestured to the mug in front of Jake. 'I wasn't sure if you took sugar?' He made to push back the chair. 'I could get you some.'

'How did you get my phone number?' Jake growled, ignoring the question.

'It doesn't matter how.' Swallowing deeply, Sadie eased himself back onto the chair. 'The Tuckers,' he said, his gaze darting once more from Jake to the window. 'They can't know that I was here. Promise me,' he said, grasping hold of Jake's hand, 'that you won't breathe a word of this to anyone.'

Jake pulled his hand free, his expression hardening. 'What's this about?' he jerked his head towards the door. 'Is this a trap?'

'No. They know nothing about this. I swear to you that they've no idea I'm here. And say what you will about them, but Ozzie has been good to me. I don't want him to know that I've broken his trust.'

Jake screwed up his face. 'He's a nutcase.'

'Maybe,' Sadie nodded. 'But he looked after me when we were banged up, he showed me the ropes. Without him, I don't think I would have survived.'

'Yeah, I bet he showed you the ropes.' Jake's lips curled in disgust. 'Doesn't disguise the fact he's got a screw loose up here though, does it,' he said, tapping his temple.

'No matter what he is or isn't,' Sadie interrupted. 'And I'd be one of the first to admit that he does have his faults, but I'm also very fond of him.'

Raising his eyebrows, Jake leaned back in the chair and crossed his arms over his chest. 'I'm going to take a wild guess and say you didn't call me over here just to tell me how wonderful the Tuckers are?'

'No.' As Sadie continued to study Jake, he gave a small smile and motioned between them. 'You were nothing more than a frightened little boy the last time I saw you. And I see that you've cut your hair short too.' He hesitantly lifted his hand in the air as though he were debating whether or not to reach out and touch Jake's dark strands. 'It suits you, and you look even more like your dad than you did before, if that's even possible.' His smile broadened. 'I still can't believe it took me so long to realise that you're a Carter. I mean I should have clocked it straight away; runaways don't walk about in designer clobber, especially not the brands you used to wear.'

'Stop with the chit chat.' Slapping Sadie's hand away from him, Jake narrowed his eyes and, making sure to keep his voice low so as not to arouse any suspicion towards them, he leaned in closer. 'What the fuck do you want from me?'

Sadie shook his head. 'I don't want anything from you Jake.' He took a sip of his tea as if trying to compose himself. 'I took the rap for you,' he said, his eyes searching Jake's face for a reaction, perhaps some form of recognition for what he'd done in order to save Jake from being incarcerated. 'I spent the best part of my life banged up for a murder you committed.'

Jake had the grace to look away.

'And I'd do it all over again and without a second's hesitation and we both know why,' he said, giving a sad smile. 'You were only a kid; you had your whole life ahead of you. And as for that dirty nonce Ronald Browning,' he screwed up his face, the disgust he felt more than apparent, 'he deserved everything he had coming to him; believe me, death was the easy way out. If it had been left down to me, I would have made the bastard suffer. He should have been punished for what he did, not only to you, but to me, and all the other boys who had the misfortune to come into his orbit.'

Jake squirmed in his seat. 'I don't want to talk about that,' he snarled, his cheeks turning red. 'I don't...' He took a moment to collect his thoughts and glancing around him to make sure they weren't being overheard, he lowered his voice even further. 'I don't want anyone to know about that part of my life, what happened to me, what Ronald did. It's over, done with. I'm not that same person any more. I've got a girlfriend, I've got two kids.' His voice took on a desperate tone. 'You can't fuck any of that up for me,' he said, his hands curling into fists. 'No matter what you did for me I'd rather kill you stone dead than allow you to ruin my life, to ruin my kids' lives.'

Wrapping his hands around the mug, Sadie swallowed down the hard lump in his throat. 'It isn't my intention to cause you any trouble,' he said quietly, emotion getting the better of him. 'Which is why,' he said, wiping away a tear from the corner of his eye, 'I can't sit by and watch you and your family become the latest victims of Ozzie and Lenny Tucker. I didn't go to prison just to stand back and do nothing while both you and your family are decimated.'

'What?' Jake snapped his head up, his eyes widening. 'What did you just say?'

'You heard me,' Sadie retorted. 'The Tuckers are on to you and from what I've heard, they don't plan on playing fair.'

As Jake scraped back the chair and jumped to his feet, Sadie reached out to grab his wrist with a strength that surprised both of them. 'The diamonds,' he said, looking up. 'If you go looking for them at Bernie Adams' house then you'll come away empty handed. In fact, the only thing you'll be likely to find is Ozzie and Lenny Tucker waiting for you, and believe me they will be tooled up.' He lifted his eyebrows and attempted to smile. 'Try searching

Ozzie's house for the gems instead.' He held up his hands, and knowing that he'd already said too much, he pretended to pull a zip across his lips. 'Just maybe you'll have better luck there,' he winked.

As Sadie went back to sipping at his tea he watched from the corner of his eye as Jake bolted from the cafe. In a way he still felt responsible for Jake Carter. Oh, he knew that he could never have a place in the man's life, nor did he actually want to if truth be told. After all, what was done was done, he'd taken the fall for the murder of Ronald Browning, he'd done his part in keeping Jake safe. And as he'd already stated, he hadn't spent a large chunk of his life in prison just to watch Jake's existence come to a grisly end at the hands of the Tucker brothers.

Draining his drink, Sadie stood up and weaving his way through the cafe he paused in front of the counter. 'That was a smashing cuppa,' he grinned, placing a crisp ten-pound note beside the till. 'And keep the change,' he winked. He made to exit the premises and pausing he span back around. 'Should anyone,' he said, flashing the waiter a wide smile, 'ask if I was in here tonight,' he slipped a fifty-pound note out of his pocket and placed it into the man's hand, the smile instantly slipping from his face as he pulled himself up to his full height, the muscles across his shoulders becoming rigid, 'you've never seen me before and that goes for the man I was with too, do you understand?'

He waited for the waiter to nod in agreement, then pulling up the collar of his coat, Sadie made his way outside. A quick glance in either direction was enough to tell him that Jake Carter had already left the area, not that he'd truly expected him to stick around. After all what more was there for them to say to one another that hadn't already been said, other than perhaps a thank you for what Sadie had sacrificed in order to keep Jake out of the prison system. It was more than clear that Jake Carter had moved on with his life. Sadie was heartened to hear that he had a partner and children, and even more than that, he was relieved to know that he'd been able to move on from the trauma he'd suffered at Ronald Brown's hands. As for Sadie, well, he was doing his best to readjust to life on the outside, however hard that may be.

Having done what he'd set out to do, Sadie made his way to the bus stop, not only with a smile upon his face but also with his conscience clear. All he could do now was hope and pray that Jake took heed of his warning, because if he didn't, the consequences didn't bear thinking about.

9

Jonny Carter's eyes sprang open as he glanced around the darkened bedroom, his fingers automatically reached down beside the bed for the claw hammer that he kept there. Something had woken him, but what that was he had no idea. A moment later there was another loud knock on the front door, and releasing the hammer he inwardly groaned, his gaze darting across to Terri as she slept soundly beside him. Sitting up he swung his legs over the side of the bed and scooped up his mobile phone.

Noting the time, he swore under his breath, got to his feet, then pulling on a T-shirt and a pair of jogging bottoms he padded barefoot out of the room and down the stairs.

'Do you know what the time is?' he snapped as he pulled open the front door to see his nephew standing on the doorstep.

Jake Carter's face was drained of all colour and without acknowledging his uncle he pushed his way into the house and headed down the hallway.

Once they were in the lounge, Jake's eyes were wide. 'You have to call everything off,' he said, his voice rising several decibels.

Jonny narrowed his eyes and holding up a finger he warned Jake to keep his voice down. Stepping back out into the hallway he cocked his head to the side and looked upwards, his ears straining to hear any sound of movement coming from the bedroom.

'What the fuck is going on?' he asked, coming back into the room and closing the door firmly behind him.

'We can't go after those diamonds,' Jake warned.

Confusion swept over Jonny's face. 'But...'

'I mean it,' Jake said as he wiped his hand over his face. 'I was told something... by a source. Someone who knows a lot more than we do.' Speaking fast the words tumbled out of his mouth. 'Someone who is in the Tuckers' circle.'

'What are you talking about?' Taken aback, Jonny crossed his arms over his chest. 'You'd best start explaining yourself Jake because you're not making any sense to me. Why the fuck would you have a source... and more to the point what fucking source?'

Jake paused. 'I can't...' He shook his head and began again. 'I can't reveal who they are. I gave them my word that I'd keep their name out of it and if nothing else I owe them that, it's the least I can do after what they did for me.'

As he scrutinised his nephew, Jonny tilted his head to the side. 'Is that why you bolted out of the boozer tonight?'

Giving a nod, Jake stepped forward. 'The Tuckers are on to us; they know that we're coming for the diamonds.'

'Nah, that's impossible.' Still unable to get his head around what his nephew was telling him, Jonny screwed up his face. 'I mean how could they know?' He rubbed at his temples. 'And as for this so-called source of yours,' he spat. 'Who are they, and why the fuck would they even warn you about the diamonds?'

Becoming more and more agitated Jake grasped Jonny by the shoulders. 'Listen to what I'm telling you,' he implored. 'I can't tell you who he is.' Taking a step back he rubbed at the nape of his neck and closed his eyes, his breath coming out in short, sharp, ragged puffs. 'Other than it's someone from my past,' he said, raising his eyebrows. 'Someone I thought I'd never have to clap my eyes on again.' Close to tears he shook his head. 'If this gets out...' As the enormity of the situation finally sank in, Jake's expression was one of panic, and pressing his fist to his lips in an attempt to stop himself from vomiting, he swallowed deeply. 'This will ruin me.'

Jonny's mind reeled, and as he stared at his nephew, a memory, or rather a secret known to less than a handful of people flashed through his mind. 'Oh, you mean Sadie,' he sighed. 'I did hear that he'd been released from nick.'

Jake's eyes widened and as he staggered back, he clutched a hand to his forehead. 'Cheers for the heads-up,' he snapped. 'You could have at least warned me that he was out, that he might come looking for me.'

Ignoring the comment, Jonny sank onto the sofa and wiped his hand over the dark stubble covering his jaw. 'So, the past has come back to bite you, eh?'

'Bite me,' Jake hissed. 'It'll do more than bite me. If this gets out,' he said, referring to the abuse he'd suffered at Ronald Browning's hands, 'it'll destroy me.'

Confusion was etched across Jonny's face. 'You were a kid,' he protested. 'It wasn't your fault, none of it was. You were groomed, threatened, blackmailed, or whatever the fuck else you want to call it.'

Jake looked down at the floor. 'I could have told my dad.' Tears sprang to his eyes, and he angrily swiped them away. 'Come on.' He gave a half laugh and shook his head. 'My dad was Tommy Carter; he would have killed Browning with his bare hands if he'd known what was going on. Only I didn't tell him, did I? I didn't tell anyone. So yeah,' he said, jerking his thumb towards himself. 'It was my fault.'

'Jake.' Shaking his head, Jonny's mind whirled. 'No matter who your old man was you were still a kid.'

'I was eighteen,' Jake snapped. 'I was hardly a kid. I knew right from wrong.'

'And what about all of the other poor little fuckers,' Jonny remarked. 'Was it their fault too?'

Without even needing to think the question over Jake shook his head. 'Of course it wasn't, they were victims,' he said, screwing up his face, his anger more than palpable.

'Yeah, that's what I thought. Look,' taking a deep breath, Jonny got to his feet, 'there's nothing for you to be ashamed of...'

Jake gave another incredulous laugh. 'What and you reckon that they'll see it like that?' he said of his elder brother and cousins. 'That my missus will see it like that. If she finds out about my past...' He swallowed down acrid bile. 'She could leave me,' he cried. 'She'll take the kids with her and that'll be it, my life will be as good as over.'

Holding up his hands, Jonny shook his head. 'You're worrying over nothing. I'm not going to say anything, you're not going to say anything, and as for Sadie, I'm guessing that he's going to keep his trap shut an' all.'

'And if he doesn't?'

Jonny sighed. 'If he doesn't,' he gave a shrug, 'then we'll cross that bridge when we come to it, okay?' He placed his hand on Jake's shoulder. 'Do you honestly think that I'd let something like this become public knowledge, that I wouldn't protect you? Come on, you should know me better than that, you're my nephew, we're family and if I have to kill the fucker just to keep him quiet then I'm more than prepared to do just that.'

Jake nodded, albeit reluctantly.

'Right.' Giving his nephew a reassuring smile, Jonny spread

open his arms. 'Now that that's sorted out what's all this about the diamonds?'

'Like I said, the Tuckers are on to us, don't ask me how they know,' Jake said, shaking his head. 'Because I haven't got a scooby how they could have found out. All I know is that the diamonds have been moved.'

Jonny's heart sank. Time and time again Carla had told him that they needed to move fast and he hadn't wanted to listen. And as for the Tuckers, how was it possible that they could be onto them when the diamonds had only been discussed amongst the family. Had one of his nephews opened their mouth and let slip about the planned heist?

'Sadie told me that they're being stored at Ozzie Tucker's house.'

'Do what?' Jonny snapped his head up. 'As if that fucker would be able to stop us.'

Jake's expression became serious. 'Not only will they be waiting for us,' he pointed out, 'but they'll also be tooled up.' He gave a shake of his head. 'It might not be quite as easy as you first thought.'

Jonny opened his mouth to answer and quickly closing it again, he nodded. At times he almost forgot that he would be carrying out the robbery with his nephews and not his brothers. With Jimmy, Sonny and Mitchell on board, the heist would have been a piece of piss, they would have been in and out so fast that before the Tuckers had even known what had hit them, he and his brothers would have been safely tucked away back at the scrapyard. 'Well, that might change things,' he said, pinching the bridge of his nose. 'I need to think this through.'

Jake gestured towards the door. 'I'll see myself out.' He gave a small smile. 'If it's any consolation, I really did believe that we could pull this off. That this time we would bring home a diamond.'

'Yeah, you and me both,' Jonny muttered under his breath, the disappointment in his voice more than audible.

* * *

Thirty minutes later, Terri rolled over in bed and snaking out her arm her fingers came into contact with the cold sheet. Her eyes snapped open and reaching out for her phone she blinked several times in order to make sense of the numbers on the screen. It had just gone 2 a.m., and as she looked around the darkened room, she narrowed her eyes. Where the hell was Jonny? Sitting up, she threw the duvet away from her, climbed out of bed, pulled on her dressing gown then made her way down the stairs.

'Hey,' she said as she entered the lounge and flicked on the light. 'What are you doing sitting in the dark?'

Blinking his eyes in rapid succession as they readjusted to the sudden change of light, Jonny sighed and opening out his arms, he beckoned Terri towards him. 'Come here.'

As she walked across the room, Terri studied him. 'What's wrong?'

'It's nothing,' Jonny lied, pulling her onto his lap. 'I couldn't sleep that's all.'

Terri's forehead furrowed, and as she turned to face him, concern creased her face. 'Something's obviously on your mind?' she said, rubbing her thumb over the back of his hand. 'I'm not stupid Jonny, I know you, and I know when something is troubling you.'

Jonny sighed again. 'It's just…' He shook his head, debating just how much he should divulge. The last thing he wanted to do was worry her any more than was necessary. 'Things are not working out quite as I planned.'

Alarm engulfed Terri and tilting her head to the side, she narrowed her eyes. 'What do you mean?'

Giving a shrug, Jonny attempted to smile. 'The diamonds have been moved and...' He blew out his cheeks. 'Let's just say that the new location comes with more risk.'

A cold shiver ran down the length of Terri's spine. 'Don't do anything reckless,' she begged of him. 'I need you to come back, we both do,' she said, rubbing her hand over her bump.

'No pressure then, eh,' Jonny gave a light laugh. 'Of course I'm going to come back, you've got a Carter growing in there,' he said, gesturing to her swollen stomach. 'Do you honestly think that I'd purposely do something to fuck everything up.'

Despite the seriousness of his voice Terri smiled. 'She's a half-Tempest too, you know.'

'She?' Jonny looked from Terri's face down to her tummy and then back up again. 'You just said she,' he grinned, his blue eyes twinkling. 'Does that mean we're having a girl?'

Terri's cheeks flushed red. 'It's just a feeling,' she said, waving her hand dismissively. 'Intuition I suppose.'

Still grinning, Jonny nuzzled his face in Terri's hair. 'That's good enough for me; if you reckon it's a girl then it's a girl.'

Pulling away slightly Terri turned to look at him, her expression becoming serious. 'I meant what I said Jonny. I need you.' She nodded down to her bump. 'I can't do this without you.'

'Of course you can,' Jonny reassured her. 'You're going to be a natural.'

Averting her gaze Terri shook her head.

'Hey.' Placing a finger under Terri's chin, Jonny lifted her face up to meet his. 'What's going on, babe?'

'It's just...' Biting down on her lower lip, Terri looked away. 'I didn't exactly have a good role model growing up. I rarely saw my mum and on the odd occasion that I did visit her in prison she was more interested in any gossip my grandparents might have had than paying me any attention. What if I don't know how to be a mother, what if I take after my mum?'

She was being so ridiculous that Jonny stifled the urge to laugh. 'Of course, you won't be like your mum! Like I said you're going to be a natural.'

Terri sighed, her eyes brimming with tears. 'Even now my mum isn't interested in the baby,' she sniffed. 'She couldn't care less that I'm carrying her first grandchild.'

'Yeah, well maybe that's a good thing.' Jonny's voice hardened as it always did whenever Terri's mother, Bianca Murphy, was brought into the conversation. Brushing away the tears from under Terri's eyes, it took everything inside of him to keep his temper at bay. 'You know better than anyone what that mother of yours is like,' he said. 'She's trouble, a skank, always has been. And let's face it, she's also added aggravation that neither of us want or need for that matter. Would you really want her to get her grubby mitts on our baby?' He wrinkled his nose. 'She's not exactly the most hygienic of people is she, darling?' He made a gagging sound, and pressing his hand to his mouth, he shook his head. 'I dread to think what that grime is under her fingernails.'

'I suppose not.' As shame washed over her, Terri's cheeks flushed red and then giving an involuntary shudder as an image of her mother sprang to her mind, she screwed up her face. Jonny was right: at the best of times Bianca was a mess, she didn't wash from one week to the next and the smell that radiated from her was enough to make those unfortunate enough to be around her feel nauseous. And as for her lifestyle, it was the equivalent of a car crash just waiting to happen. She was volatile, violent, and not content until she'd riled someone up. 'You're right,' she sighed. 'I definitely don't want my mum around the baby. The only thing I wanted was for her to care about me for once, to know that I actually mean something to her.'

Pulling Terri even closer, Jonny kissed the top of her head. 'See, you're already a good mum,' he said, rubbing his hand over her bump. 'And besides, you'll have Rina to help you out, that woman loves you like a daughter.'

Terri's face lit up, her heart swelling with love. Not only was she close to Rina, but she was also the only motherly figure Terri had known. Every day she thanked her lucky stars that she had Rina in her life and God only knew where she would have ended up if Rina and her late husband, Archie, hadn't taken her in and put a roof over her head. There was no disputing the fact that they had saved her life stepping in and offering her a means to escape from the Murphy family. Terri couldn't bear to think about what could have happened to her otherwise. She would more than likely have been murdered if her uncle Michael had had his way. If it hadn't been for her surrogate parents, she would have never met Jonny either, nor would she have formed a close relationship with her half-brothers Ricky and Jamie.

'And as for coming home,' breaking Terri's thoughts, Jonny gently squeezed her hand, 'of course I will. I always have in the past, haven't I?'

It was true, Terri conceded. In the two years that they had been together he had always come back to her. Only this time, things were different. Not only was he in charge of the business, meaning that the planning of any up-and-coming heists would now fall upon his shoulders, but he was also going after diamonds, the one thing he'd told her he and his family would never attempt to lift, especially seeing as they had had so much bad luck with the gemstone in the past. Climbing off his lap, she held out her hand. 'Let's go back to bed,' she said with a yawn. And as Jonny nodded and got to his feet, she gripped onto his hand for dear life almost as though she was afraid to let him go for fear that she would never see him again.

As they made their way up the stairs Terri glanced down at their entwined hands. As much as she told herself to get a grip, and that perhaps it was just the pregnancy hormones making her feel more on edge than usual, she couldn't help but take note of the icy cold shiver that tore through her body. It was the 'what ifs', that concerned her the most and there were plenty of them. What if Jonny and his nephews were caught bang to rights, what if Jonny was sent to prison for the remainder of his life? And what if, she swallowed deeply as if trying to push the sickening thought away, what if he was hurt, maimed or even worse, killed during the heist? No matter how much Jonny told her everything would be plain sailing, the niggling thought at the back of her mind told her otherwise. At times, he was too cocksure of himself, a trait that all of the Carters appeared to inhibit, even the females of the family.

Climbing back into bed Terri snuggled up beside Jonny, and as he wrapped his arm around her, she closed her eyes. No matter how much she tried to drift off, sleep evaded her and as she lay there just staring into space, her thoughts were plagued with the up-and-coming robbery. It was in that instant that she wondered if she would ever get used to the lifestyle of a gangster's moll. It wasn't as though her own family were perfect, and as the offspring of a Tempest and a Murphy, perhaps some would say that she was a fine one to even question the Carters' chosen occupation. Take her half-brothers Ricky and Jamie for example, they were hardly law-abiding citizens. The only difference between the two families was that she'd never had to question whether or not her brothers would return home after a day's work.

As the baby kicked inside of her, Terri forced herself to relax. Working herself up into a state of heightened panic wasn't going to help anyone, least of all herself or her unborn child and as she turned her head to look across at Jonny, she let out a gentle sigh. Whether she wanted it to or not, the robbery would go ahead as planned and nothing she or anyone else said was going to change that fact. As she drifted off to sleep an idea sprang to her mind. She was no longer the naïve woman she'd been when she'd first met Jonny, and with Rina's support and guidance she'd learned how to toughen up. She was a Tempest, not some wilting wallflower. A sleepy smile creased her face. She knew exactly what she needed to do; the hard part, however, might be convincing Jonny, not that she was prepared to let him change her mind. After all, if anyone should know just how stubborn she was then it was him.

* * *

By the time Bernie wearily slipped his key into the lock and let himself into his house he was not only dog-tired and in a great deal of pain, but he also stank to high heaven. His shirt was peppered with dried blood and sweat had stained the cotton material underneath his arms, turning it yellow. For more than twenty-four hours Lenny Tucker had kept him prisoner, and it was only after the threat of both torture and then the most painful death known to man should he open his mouth and inform the Carters of their impending fate, that he had finally been released.

He looked and felt like a wreck, and tossing his keys onto the hallway table he stood for a moment contemplating what his life had become. Once upon a time he'd had everything he could ever want: a beautiful home, a flashy motor, money in abundance. Life had well and truly been on the up. And now, he gave a great sigh, feeling a wave of sorrow wash over him, he had nothing. Or at least nothing he could be proud of.

Tugging on the shirt he pulled it from his body and as the buttons flew off in all directions before proceeding to roll across the marble floor, he brought his hands up to his face and fought down the urge to sob his heart out. His torso was black and blue, the bruises left from Lenny's heavy fists and equally heavy feet, painful to the touch. His entire body ached and as for his face, the blackened eye, split lip, and torn eyebrow made him look as though he'd just gone ten rounds with Mike Tyson; he felt as though he had too.

With caution, he made his way towards the lounge, one arm still clutched across his ribs. He was no doctor, but he'd take a wild guess and state that they were fractured. They had to be if the excruciating pain was anything to go by.

'Where the bloody hell have you been—' On seeing the condition of her husband, the words died in Diane's throat and bringing her hands up to her mouth she gasped. 'Oh, my Christ,' she shrieked. 'What on earth has happened to you?'

Swallowing down his embarrassment, Bernie attempted to shake his head. 'It's nothing,' he groaned.

'What do you mean, it's nothing?' Diane's voice rose even further, her eyes narrowed with confusion. 'Have you been in an accident?'

Not bothering to answer, Bernie slumped on the sofa. 'I don't want to talk about it, Di,' he mumbled. 'I just want to sleep.' Leaning his head back on the plump cushions he closed his eyes.

Diane stepped closer, her gaze raking over her husband's battered and broken body. 'Please,' she begged him. 'Tell me what happened. I was worried sick about you when you didn't come home.'

Bernie opened one eye to look at her. That hadn't been the impression she'd given him. In fact, if the messages he'd received from her were an indication to her true thoughts she'd automatically, and wrongly might he add, assumed that he'd spent the evening with a woman.

'I ran into a spot of bother,' he said in the way of a vague explanation. As he began to cough, he rolled onto his side and screwed his eyes shut tight. The pain that tore through his chest and abdomen enough to make him want to scream out loud.

Sinking to her knees, tears sprang to Diane's eyes. 'Who did this to you?' she implored.

Bernie's breath caught in the back of his throat and reaching out his hand he sighed. 'It was Lenny Tucker.'

'What?' Ignoring her husband's outstretched arm, Diane sank back on her haunches. 'No,' she shook her head. 'No, Lenny would never do something like this. You must have made a mistake.'

'It's no mistake.' Bernie groaned. 'He did this.'

'But why?' Unable to get her head around what her husband was telling her Diane studied him, her eyes narrowed into slits.

'He wanted some information from me.' He gave a hollow laugh at the memory of the beating. 'It's not like I had any other choice in the matter but to give him what he wanted. Once he'd started laying into me, I would have sung louder than a canary if needs be just to put an end to it.'

Tentatively Diane lifted a lock of damp hair from out of Bernie's eyes and biting down on her bottom lip she shook her head. 'I don't understand,' she cried. 'I thought that you and the Tucker brothers were like this,' she crossed two fingers to emphasise her point. 'You've been looking after the diamonds for them.'

Bernie averted his gaze. It was because of the diamonds that he was in this mess. Not that he could say he was sorry to see the back of them; they'd brought him nothing but anguish, and if he hadn't known any better, he would have sworn they were cursed. 'The diamonds are gone,' he sighed. 'I handed them back.'

Diane was thoughtful for a moment. 'But you have been paid, haven't you?'

For the second time in as many minutes Bernie turned his face away. He hadn't been paid for his part in the heist nor was he likely to be, he conceded. 'They've done me over like a fucking kipper,' he answered bitterly.

'Well, that's not right,' Diane huffed. 'You did your part. Those bastards have no right not to see their end of the bargain through.'

'We're finished,' he croaked out as he blinked away his tears. 'I'm broke. Haven't got a proverbial pot to piss in. I was counting on that money to keep a roof over our heads.' He gestured around him. 'It's only a matter of time until the bailiffs turn up and repossess the house.'

Diane gasped and bringing her hands up to her face, she shook her head. 'No,' she cried as she looked around her, her gaze taking in the beautiful home that she had been so proud of. 'No, you're lying to me,' she shrieked. 'This is our home; where are we supposed to go?'

Giving his wife a shrewd glance Bernie lifted his shoulders. 'A doss house most likely. I can't afford much else. If I was to sell the cars, well, that's if they don't end up repossessed too, then perhaps,' he gave another little shrug and closed his eyes bracing himself for his wife's shrieks to fill the house, 'I might be able to stretch to a used caravan.'

Tears slipped down Diane's face. 'I can't live in a caravan,' she screamed, her nose turning up in disgust. 'I'd never live it down.' Jumping to her feet she began to pace the lounge. 'You know what that lot are like,' she said, referring to her friends, or rather the wives of her husband's business associates, seeing as Diane didn't have any close friends per se. 'They'll be loving this; they'll get a kick out of seeing me, seeing us,' she corrected, 'brought down a peg or two. I'll never get over the shame,' she protested. 'How can you expect me,' she continued to screech at the top of her lungs as she looked around her in despair, 'to live in some poxy little caravan?'

'What else can we do?' Bernie shrugged. 'I was banking on that money to dig us out of a hole and if it hadn't been for Carla...'

Diane's eyes shot open. 'What do you mean?' she demanded.

Bernie inwardly groaned. Him and his big mouth; he never knew when to keep the bastard thing shut. 'Nothing,' he answered, averting his gaze. 'Forget I even said anything.'

'Don't you dare lie to me,' Diane hissed. 'What has Carla got to do with any of this?'

'I caught her snooping around the house,' Bernie sighed. 'And considering her old man has a penchant for armed robbery, you can't tell me that she wasn't staking the house out, that he didn't send her here to look for the diamonds.'

'No,' Diane gasped, her mind reeling. 'She wouldn't.'

Bernie bowed his head. 'It was because of her I had to act fast,' he said, glancing up in order to gauge his wife's reaction. 'What other option did I have other than to hand the diamonds back. I couldn't take the risk and just sit around and wait for Sonny to break in and rob us while we sleep. That's the reason why the Tuckers haven't paid me; I didn't fulfil my end of the bargain. So let's just hope,' he continued, 'that when the time comes, and we're turfed out onto the street, that Carla's one of the first to dig her hands into her pockets to help us out.'

Clutching at her forehead Diane began to weep. 'I know that she's always been difficult, volatile even,' she sobbed. 'But not in a million years did I ever imagine she would be the cause of me losing my home.'

It was on the tip of Bernie's tongue to tell his wife that she was the only one to blame for her daughter's hostility, that perhaps if she'd cared for Carla as a mother should, then just maybe Carla wouldn't have felt the need to rebel.

'I'm going to bloody kill her,' Diane shrieked as she jumped to her feet. 'The spiteful little bitch. And as for Sonny, he'll pay for this if it's the last thing I ever do...'

'Enough,' Bernie shouted, the tone of his voice more than enough to warn Diane that she'd gone too far.

Diane's mouth dropped open. 'We're going to lose the house,' she screamed back at him. 'Don't you care that we will be homeless, that our lives will be destroyed?'

'I said enough!' Bernie roared. Heaving himself up off the sofa he placed his arm across his fractured ribs. 'Not another word Di, have you got that. Maybe this is what we deserve.' He gestured around the lounge. 'We did Sonny wrong, and this is our comeuppance, our punishment for what we did to him.'

As he limped away from his wife Bernie noted the tears in her eyes, not that he could say he was sorry for upsetting her. Still to this day he was plagued with guilt for what they had done to Sonny, and he had a nasty feeling that he always would. As for losing the house, that was only the tip of the iceberg; Carla's life along with the lives of the remaining Carters hung precariously in the balance. Only he couldn't utter the words out loud, couldn't warn his stepdaughter of what was to come. How could he spill the beans when the Tuckers' threat to cause him harm still rang loudly in his ears. A cold shiver ran down the length of his spine. He couldn't bear the thought of another beating, one that would be so severe it was bound to result in his death.

Instead, Bernie slowly made his way up the stairs and blocking out his wife's continued shouts he pushed all thoughts of the Tuckers and the Carters far from his mind. Collapsing onto the bed he closed his eyes and prayed for sleep to envelope him as quickly as was humanly possible. With a bit of luck, when he awoke the whole debacle would be nothing more than a distant nightmare.

10

The next morning Carla perched on the edge of a chair and as her cousins filed into the office, she could barely stop her knees from bouncing up and down she was that excited. The fact Jonny had summoned them all to a meeting, insisting that they drop everything they were doing just to be there was more than enough to tell her that something was going down. And unless she was very much mistaken, she had more than just an inkling that it concerned the diamonds.

Clearing his throat Jonny rested his forearms on the desk. 'There has been a development.'

Carla strained her ears to listen and as her cousins continued to chat amongst themselves patience got the better of her. 'Oi, you lot, shut up a minute,' she shouted. Turning her attention back to Jonny, she spread open her arms. 'What's going on?'

Sinking back in his chair Jonny raised his eyebrows. 'Like I just said, there have been some developments,' he repeated, now that he had his nephews' full attention. 'The diamonds have been moved.'

Nausea washed over Carla and as her heartbeat began to quicken, she wanted to scream out loud at the injustice of it all. Not only had her obsession with Bernie driven a wedge between herself and Logan, but the fact Bernie was once again in the position to walk away unscathed was more than she could bear. 'No,' she began to shake her head, despair flooding through her veins. If it was true and the diamonds had been moved then her plan for revenge was in tatters. 'But...' At a loss for something to say she stared at her uncle. 'What does that mean for us?' she asked, finally finding her voice.

'It means,' Jonny said, 'that even though it's still doable, the risk has just increased tenfold.'

'So where's the problem?' Peter asked. 'I mean,' he said, nodding towards his brother and Cameron, 'it's not like we haven't come up against risk before. You know yourself that every job we've undertaken comes with a risk of some sorts, it goes with the territory.'

Jonny sighed. 'True... But...' he lifted his eyebrows making sure to keep his gaze from drifting towards Jake. 'When we've held up a bank or,' he clicked his fingers several times, 'I don't know, a security van for example, the risk to ourselves was minimal.'

'So what are you saying?' Peter asked. 'That it's too dangerous, that we forget about the whole thing?'

Toying with his mobile phone, Jonny was thoughtful. 'The diamonds have been moved to Ozzie Tucker's gaff. That means should we target Ozzie's yard and they happen to be waiting for us – which for the record I don't actually think will be the case – but on the off chance that they are waiting to ambush us, well it shouldn't take a genius to tell you what could happen.'

Still barely able to get her head around the fact the diamonds had been moved, Carla dug her fingernails into the palm of her hand. 'And what about Bernie,' she snarled. 'Are we supposed to let him get off scot-free?'

Jonny turned to look at his niece. 'This was never about

Bernie. And for the life of me, I can't understand your obsession with him. Just let it go Carla and grow the fuck up. You're not a kid any more, if your dad can move on then surely to fuck, so can you.'

'Of course it's about Bernie,' Carla snapped, her eyes blazing with fury as she attempted to swallow down her humiliation. 'He did my dad wrong, and he needs to pay for that.'

Peter's forehead furrowed. 'Since when was this about revenge?' he asked, looking around him. 'I thought this was about us getting our hands on the diamonds.'

'It is,' Jonny confirmed with a nod.

Carla sprang to her feet. 'I don't believe this,' she cried. 'You,' she said, stabbing her finger in Jonny's direction, 'knew exactly what this was about.' She threw her arms up into the air. 'I can't believe what I'm hearing, that you could betray me like this.'

'Carla.' Jerking his head towards the chair, Jonny's eyes were hard. 'Sit down.'

Still standing, Carla placed her hands on her hips, her nostrils flaring. 'So much for family,' she said bitterly. 'If it hadn't been for me, you would never have even known about the diamonds. You lied to me, Jonny.'

'I didn't lie to you,' Jonny barked out. 'And I'm not going to tell you again, either sit down or get the fuck out of here because I'm really not in the mood to listen to your dramatics.'

Swallowing down a retort, Carla's cheeks flamed red and huffing out a breath, she reluctantly returned to her seat.

'Right, can we just all calm down a bit,' Jonny asked as he gave Carla a pointed look. 'Screaming and shouting at one another really isn't going to help matters is it?'

Once they had quietened down again, Jonny raised his eyebrows. 'Seeing as Bernie was the last person to have the diamonds in his possession before they were moved, then who do you think is going to take the flak for them going on the missing list?'

Carla shrugged and as she looked up at her cousins, she saw the same confusion she felt mirrored back on their faces.

Placing his elbows on the desk, Jonny massaged his temples. 'Correct me if I'm wrong,' he said, looking up, 'but Bernie is one of the few people who knows where the diamonds are. Do you see what I'm getting at?' he asked as he looked between Carla and his nephews. 'No matter where the diamonds are being held Bernie is somehow involved.'

'And?' Carla spat.

'So,' Jonny cocked his head to the side, 'seeing just how paranoid that fucker Ozzie is, do you really think he wouldn't suspect Bernie's involvement if the diamonds went for a walkabout? That in that twisted fucking mind of his,' he said, tapping his forehead, 'that he won't lay the blame at Bernie's door?'

Carla opened her mouth to answer and quickly closed it again, her eyes widening. 'But...'

'Listen,' Jonny added, 'one thing I know about the Tuckers is that they don't trust easily, not that that's a bad trait, mind. I myself don't trust outsiders,' he said, giving his nephew Cameron a surreptitious glance. 'At least not 100 per cent anyway. But the point I'm trying to make is, seeing as it's no secret that Bernie is a sly bastard, I'm going to take a wild guess and say that he'll be at the top of the list when it comes to suspects.'

'I still don't get it,' Carla remarked, convinced that her uncle was clutching at straws. 'None of this is making any sense to me. Bernie doesn't have the diamonds any more so why would they even suspect him.'

Jonny paused, and moving his head from side to side in an attempt to ease the tension out of his neck he gave an irritated sigh. 'Because the Tuckers are not right up here are they?' he growled, pointing to his temple. 'They'll want to blame someone and who better to blame than Bernie? And when we turn up at Ozzie's house and grab the diamonds, they'll be none the wiser as to who really took them.'

Peter screwed up his face. 'Sounds like we'd be taking a big risk if you want my opinion.'

'Peter's right,' Cameron agreed. 'For all we know, the Tuckers could be lying in wait for us. Do you really think they wouldn't expect us to go looking for the diamonds at Ozzie's house?'

Thinking it over, Jonny shook his head. 'They haven't got as much as two brain cells to rub together between them, and seeing as they haven't got a clue that we're aware the diamonds have been moved, I can't see them covering both properties on the off chance that we might turn up.'

Still unsure, Cameron shook his head. 'I can't say that I like the sound of this,' he said, digging his hands into his pockets. 'What if we turn up and the Tuckers have a welcome committee waiting for us?' He glanced towards his son. 'Some of us have more to lose than others.'

Jonny's eyebrows knotted together. 'You're not the only father here Cam,' he barked out.

'Maybe not,' Cameron retorted, screwing up his face. 'But if this goes tits up it'll be my boy's neck that's on the line.'

'I'm not a kid, Dad,' Tommy Jr protested, his cheeks flushing red. 'It's about time you lot started to realise that. My grandads weren't much older than me when they first started out and it didn't do them any harm, did it?'

'Other than that they both ended up in early graves,' Cameron said, his voice rising. 'Is that what you want for yourself?' he shouted. 'To have your life cut down just like theirs was – and for what?' he continued to shout. 'For a bit of cash in your back pocket or a so-called reputation that means fuck all in the real world!'

'You've got some fucking front Cameron.' Jonny's voice was like steel and as he looked his nephew over, his lips were curled into a snarl. 'You weren't even a part of this family until your old man had kicked the bucket, but you've done alright for yourself since then, haven't you?'

'Leave it out.' As a stunned silence fell across the office, Mitchell's son, Reece, stepped forward and spread open his arms in an attempt to block his cousin's path. 'There's no need for this,' he said, giving his uncle a cautious glance. 'Cameron's as much a part of this family as the rest of us.'

'He's right,' Peter agreed, stepping forward. 'That was bang out of order and you know it.'

Waving Reece away from him, Cameron's expression hardened. 'Nah,' he said, his eyes blazing. 'He's clearly got some sort of beef with me, and it's about time we had this out for once and for all. So come on,' he shouted, addressing his uncle. 'What do you mean by "I've done well for myself"?'

Lounging back on the chair, Jonny's eyes were equally as hard. 'I don't remember ever hearing you complain when you were handed out your share of the robberies.'

Giving a hard laugh, Cameron shook his head. 'What and you think that I needed that money, that I should have been grateful. My grandfather left me his businesses...'

'Yeah, of course he did,' Jonny interrupted, his expression twisted with disgust. 'Because as much as my brother may have been your father, you're a Johnson first and foremost and always fucking will be. I mean,' he said, lifting his shoulders up into a shrug. 'When you think about it, that's bad enough in itself, considering what a tosser Dean Johnson was,' he said, referring to Cameron's maternal grandfather. 'But add in the fact that you've got a bit too much of Gary in you for my liking, and we've really got a problem on our hands.' he spat. 'You've only ever been interested when it suits you, or more to the point when you don't have to get your hands dirty. And your old man,' he said, stabbing his finger forward, his voice rising even further, 'was exactly the fucking same and I should know, seeing as he was my brother.'

Cameron's nostrils flared and before he could charge forward and start throwing punches, Carla banged her fist down on the desk.

'Will you both just stop,' she pleaded, looking between the two men. 'I know that you clearly have some sort of an issue with one another but whether you like it or not we're family. At the end of the day, it doesn't matter what our surname is,' she said, gesturing towards Cameron and Tommy Jr, 'we still share the same blood. And if anything, Cameron's mum is the one to blame. She was the one who registered Cameron as a Johnson, Gary didn't even know he'd had a son.'

Running his tongue over his teeth, Jonny continued to glare at his nephew.

'Please,' Carla begged. 'Enough of this now. I know that tempers are beginning to flare but this isn't the answer.'

'Fine.' Jonny held up his hands and tearing his gaze away from his nephew he shook his head. 'If it makes you happy, I'll keep my opinions to myself.'

Carla nodded and as she turned to look at Cameron, she tilted her head to the side, her eyes silently beseeching her cousin to let bygones be bygones and put his feud with their uncle to rest. 'Cam?'

Cameron shook his head. 'I'm sick to the back teeth of him treating me like I'm an outsider, like I'm some sort of mug,' he continued to grumble. 'Especially when I've done fuck all wrong.'

'Yeah, well if the shoe fits,' Jonny mumbled under his breath.

For the second time in as many minutes Carla shot her uncle a glare. 'You're not helping matters,' she snapped.

Jonny held up his hands and as he glanced towards Tommy Jr his expression ever so slightly softened. 'Maybe I overreacted.'

'You think,' Cameron muttered back.

'For crying out loud,' Carla shouted before Jonny could retaliate and start throwing insults again. 'Will the pair of you just grow up. How the hell are you going to be able to work together when you can't even spend five minutes in the same room without at least one of you kicking off?'

An awkward silence followed, and giving both her uncle and cousin a pointed look Carla lifted her hand in the air. 'I mean it,' she warned. 'This feud of yours needs to end and the quicker the better.' She turned to look at her remaining cousins and lifted her eyebrows. 'I can't be the only one who is sick to the back teeth of listening to this day in, day out.'

As her cousins nodded their agreement, Carla took a deep breath and turned her attention back to her uncle in an attempt to hastily change the subject. 'Do you honestly believe that this could work, that we still have a chance of getting our hands on the diamonds?'

For a split-second Jonny hesitated, and shifting his weight in the chair, he nodded. 'Like I've already said, the Tuckers are expecting us to turn up at Bernie's house. That means if my assumption is right then there will be no one to stop us.'

'So, the job is still going ahead?' Peter asked.

Jonny nodded. 'We need to strike while the iron is hot, and the last thing we want is for those diamonds to be moved from Ozzie's gaff because once they do, they will be gone forever and I'm not prepared to let that happen.' He cocked his head to the side, his eyes remaining hard. 'We're going after them tonight.'

Peter blew out his cheeks as he made eye contact with his brother.

'And what if you're wrong about this,' Jake piped up. 'What if the Tuckers are not as stupid as you think?'

Jonny gave a hollow laugh. 'Leave it out. Do you honestly think they would be able to suss us out? They've only been in this game for five minutes, and the fact they entrusted the diamonds into Bernie's care in the first place is more than enough to prove my point. They're fuck all for us to worry about.'

'I hope you're right,' Peter muttered.

'I am.' Getting to his feet Jonny glanced at his watch. 'Right, you lot, meet back here at 5 p.m. and don't be late,' he warned. 'We still need to finalise the plans.'

As everyone filed back out of the office, Carla remained seated. 'I'm sorry if I was out of line,' she said, offering a small smile. 'It's just,' she pressed her lips together and shook her head, 'I don't like the fact you and Cameron are at loggerheads.'

Jonny groaned. 'I know,' he begrudgingly answered. 'Maybe I was the one out of line, but I can't help myself, he riles me up. Every time I look at him all I can see is Gary staring back at me and there's nothing I'd like more than to be able to smash my fists into Gary's face.' He held up his hand as if to stop Carla's protests. 'I know he might be six feet under, but he was still a complete and utter arsehole. I wouldn't have pissed on the cunt if he'd been on fire, none of us would have.'

Carla nodded. In a roundabout way, she could understand where Jonny was coming from. It was no secret that Gary had been disliked by his brothers. Even her dad spoke about his elder brother with a measure of pure hatred, and she had a feeling that her uncle's contempt for Gary went a lot further than any of them could ever imagine.

'I'm telling you now,' Jonny continued as he jabbed his finger in Carla's direction. 'That snidey bastard,' he said, referring to Cameron, 'is the weakest link in this family.'

Lifting her eyebrows Carla gave her uncle a pointed look.

'I don't trust him,' Jonny continued, his eyes flashing danger-ously. 'Never have done. He's got too much of my brother in him and as for Cameron's mother, Bethany Johnson, she was a complete and utter nut job an' all. You wouldn't believe the amount of shit she caused the family. You can't tell me that Cameron hasn't inher-ited at least some of those traits, he's bound to have, that's how it works.'

'I hope not,' Carla grinned in an attempt to lighten the mood. 'I'd hate to think that I'm anything like my mum.'

'Nah,' Jonny chuckled. 'You take after your dad. You're a Carter through and through.'

'And so is Cameron,' Carla protested. 'Fair enough, he might not be a Carter by name but in here,' she said, pointing to her chest, 'he is one of us. And he does have his good points, he's loyal for a start, which from what I've heard is a lot more than can be said about Gary.'

'Yeah, I suppose so.' Jonny blew out his cheeks.

Carla sighed and as she stood up and made to leave the office, she paused in front of the door. 'Will you talk to him, or at least try and clear the air before things end up getting out of hand and it comes to blows between you?'

Jonny burst out laughing. 'Do you honestly think he'd stand a chance against me. I'd wipe the floor with him and not even break out in a sweat.'

Carla pursed her lips. 'He's not a stranger. And no matter who his dad was, he's still your nephew. We all share the same blood.'

'Fair point.' Jonny conceded, holding up his hands. 'I'll try and speak to him but I'm not promising anything,' he groaned. 'At the best of times he can be a tetchy little bastard.'

'It might help if you stopped antagonising him. Every time he opens his mouth you jump down his throat.'

'I said I'll try,' Jonny reiterated, his voice slightly rising. 'I can't be any fairer than that.'

Feeling somewhat satisfied with her uncle's answer, Carla rested her hand on the door handle. 'Be honest with me,' she begged of him. 'In regards to the heist, just how dangerous is this plan of yours likely to be? I mean getting into my mum's house was always going to be easy, I've got a key for a start,' she said with a laugh. 'And it isn't as though my mum – or even Bernie for that matter – would have been able to stop us. But if we're targeting Ozzie's house,' she bit down on her bottom lip, her expression one of concern, 'what if something goes wrong, what if they turn up and catch us in the act? I know that you keep saying they're as thick as pig shit, but you know as well as I do that they're no pushovers, they've got a lot of muscle behind them. And the amount of bad blood between them and our family is enough to guarantee that someone could end up getting hurt.'

As he thought the question over Jonny was quiet for a moment. 'I don't know,' he finally answered with a shrug.

Not prepared to let the matter drop, Carla probed a little deeper. 'But you must have a plan. What are we going to do if they turn up? We need to be prepared for every scenario, and even more than that, they need to be prepared,' she said, referring to her cousins as she pointed towards the forecourt.

Jonny cocked his head to the side, his eyes twinkling. 'Years ago, your dad and uncles planned to rob this bloke called Freddie Smith. Amongst other things, Smith used to run the doors for a few nightclubs, in fact Danny McKay and Moray Garner, used to work for him when they first started out.'

Carla nodded, and as an image of Logan sprang to her mind, she hastily pushed it away in an attempt to stop her heart from breaking all over again. As it was, Logan was never far from her thoughts. He just needed the space to calm down, she told herself over and over like a mantra. Their relationship wasn't over, it couldn't be, they were made for one another.

'Well,' Jonny continued, oblivious to the turmoil running through his niece's mind, 'Tommy couldn't stand Smith and there was a lot of bad blood between the two of them, so much so that it almost came to blows on numerous occasions.'

Carla forced herself to smile. She loved hearing stories about her dad when he was young. 'So what happened?'

'Well,' Jonny continued, 'I was only a kid at the time, so I wasn't actually there but I do remember beforehand just how cocky my brothers were, how easy they thought the job was going to be, and it should have been considering the experience they had. All they had to do was get into the club, clear out the safe, have it away on their toes, and Bob's your uncle, job done.'

'I can feel a but coming.' Enthralled, Carla took a step closer. 'Did something go wrong?'

Jonny chuckled. 'Yeah, you could say that. They managed to get into the club easily enough but imagine their shock when they found themselves surrounded by Smith's henchmen.'

Carla's eyes widened and as she walked back across the office, she took a seat. 'What happened?'

'Well,' Jonny leaned closer, his eyes twinkling as he retold the story, 'Tommy being the kind of person he was, had a feeling in his gut that something wasn't right about the situation. I mean you have to remember they were expecting the club to be empty, so the fact Smith's firm were even on the property spoke volumes. As it turned out, they were looking after a stash of gold bullion that Smith had been minding for an armed robber called Mark Hopper who believe me was one of the biggest nutcases this side of the water.' He momentarily paused and rubbed his hand over his jaw. 'I don't know what ever happened to him,' he shrugged. 'He more or less dropped off the face of the earth.'

'No way.' Carla's mouth fell open and as she shook her head she screwed up her face. 'Why has my dad has never mentioned any of this?'

'Why do you think?' Jonny laughed. 'The less people who know about it the better. As it is, the old bill are still looking for the gold, not that they're likely to ever find it,' he winked. 'Believe me it's gone, or rather it was melted down and put back into the market. I wouldn't be surprised if the majority of the population own a piece of gold from that robbery.'

Stunned, Carla lightly tugged on the gold locket hanging from her neck. The necklace had been a gift from her dad for her sixteenth birthday. And she briefly wondered if it had crossed his mind when purchasing it that there could be a possibility it contained traces of the stolen gold. 'How did they manage to escape?'

Jonny grinned. And lifting his hand in the air he pretended to fire a gun. 'They were armed, of course. When it came down to it, Smith's men didn't stand a chance against them. It was a case of they either hand over the gold or have a bullet embedded into their skulls.'

The mere thought that her dad and uncles could be so ruthless was enough to make Carla shudder. Oh, she knew for a fact that they had reputations, but not for a single moment had she imagined that they could resort to murder. 'And what if the same thing happens tonight?' she asked with a measure of caution. 'What do we do if the Tuckers are waiting for us?'

'Then we do exactly the same thing,' Jonny answered, his voice hard. 'We shoot at the fuckers, grab the diamonds and then get out of there as fast as we can.'

* * *

A short time later, as Carla made her way across the forecourt to where her car was parked, her stomach was tied up in knots. It was all well and good Jonny saying that they would shoot at the Tuckers but what would happen if they were to shoot back? One of her cousins could be hurt in the crossfire, perhaps more than one. Her heart heavy, she unlocked the car and climbed behind the wheel and as she turned the ignition she glanced back towards the office. Not for the first time, a cold shiver ran through her body: it was an omen of what was to come; it had to be. And as she drove out of the scrapyard Carla felt the urge to speak to her dad, to tell him everything, to tell him how the heist had been her idea. And perhaps even more than that, how her need to avenge him could very well come at a price for the remainder of her family. There was every possibility that her uncle and cousins could be walking into danger, and as much as they may be prepared for the risks they were undertaking, it would be her conscience that would never be able to forgive or forget her involvement if one of them didn't return home. It was a thought that weighed heavily on Carla's mind and as she reached the end of the road, she automatically flicked the indicator and turned onto the A13 heading towards London. If nothing else, she needed a hug from her dad, for him to tell her that everything was going to be okay, that despite everything she wasn't the one responsible for sending her uncle and cousins into unknown territory like lambs to the slaughter.

* * *

Diane Adams had taken extra care applying her make-up, and with her hair freshly washed and blow dried to within an inch of its life, she knew for a fact that she looked good. If anything, she was a little overdressed considering it wasn't even lunchtime, not that Diane particularly cared. She was on a mission of sorts and was determined to make an impression. Dressed in a skimpy, short skirt that left little to the imagination, she climbed out of her car and adjusted the neckline of her top, making sure that her cleavage was on full display. As an added effect she reapplied some perfume across her wrists and then between her breasts.

Glancing up at the building before her, she made her way forward, her strides confident, and so they should be considering she knew the man she was planning to visit inside and out.

As she stepped into the lift she applied another layer of lip gloss across her lips, pinched her cheeks to give them a rosy glow then fluffed out her hair. As an afterthought she turned to look in the mirrored panel behind her, and practiced what she hoped would look like a coy smile.

Despite her confidence, Diane was unable to stop her stomach from churning. It had been years since she had last seen him, and she briefly wondered if he had changed in that time. Of course, he would look a little older, but from what she could remember of him, he had aged like a fine wine, unlike her husband who had definitely seen better days. Not only was Bernie's hair thinning but add that to the slight pouch that hung over his trousers, and it was a definite turn-off.

Stepping out of the lift, Diane glanced either side of her. She had only been here once before and that had been when she had dropped her daughter off for a visit with her father. She'd thought him crazy at the time for buying the apartment; she'd told him so to his face too, but now all these years later he was the one to have the last laugh. The property was worth millions and as each year passed and the area became more and more sought after and the price increased even further.

Outside his front door she licked her lips then took a deep breath before tentatively lifting her hand and rapping her knuckles on the wooden door.

It seemed to take an age for the door to open, and plastering a smile across her face, Diane took the opportunity to pat down her hair, the smile instantly freezing into place as she took in the tiny woman standing on the opposite side of the door.

'Oh.' Glancing up at the door number to check that she had the correct apartment, Diane's forehead furrowed. 'I'm sorry, I was looking for Sonny.'

Within moments Sonny Carter came into view and after hastily tucking his shirt into his trousers he ran his fingers through his hair in an attempt to tame the dark strands and make them look a little less unruly. 'Diane, what are you doing here?' he asked, screwing up his face as he placed his hand affectionately on the mystery woman's shoulder.

Diane's stomach lurched and as she took in the familiarity between the two, she fought down the urge to cry. She didn't need a genius to tell her what they had been up to, or more to the point, what she had interrupted considering they were both barefooted and that their faces were flushed. Not for one single moment had she expected her ex-husband to have a woman in his life. Carla hadn't said a word on the matter and considering she was her father's greatest champion, the fact she had been so tight-lipped didn't sit right. Why all the secrecy?

'Diane,' Sonny repeated, his expression full of concern, 'has something happened; is it Carla?'

Still too stunned to speak, Diane shook her head and swallowing down the hard lump in her throat she let out a strangled laugh, more so out of shock than for any other reason. She'd obviously got herself dolled up for nothing, and the plan she had so meticulously formed in her mind to seduce Sonny was now up in smoke. She glanced behind her ex-husband into the apartment, the hallway alone was almost as big as her kitchen. If nothing else, she would have been happy to live here and would certainly have been the envy of her friends; not only would she have had a beautiful home, but also a handsome man hanging off her arm.

'Diane,' inching slightly forward, Sonny raised his voice, panic radiating off him, 'is Carla okay?'

Blinking rapidly, Diane nodded. 'Of course she's okay.'

Confusion swept across Sonny's face and as his shoulders relaxed, he frowned. 'Then what are you doing here?' As he asked the question, he looked down at the woman beside him and pulled her into his body. It was such an intimate, yet at the same time natural moment between the two, that Diane fought the urge to turn her face away from them.

To hide her embarrassment a second laugh escaped from Diane's lips, and finding the strength to compose herself, she shook her head. 'I just wanted to have a little chat with you that's all, but if you're busy...' She made to walk away, all the while cursing her stupidity. She should never have come, should never have assumed that after all these years Sonny would still be single, and even more than that, that he would still want her in the same way that he had when they'd been young. She was an old fool, that was what she was.

'No, wait up a minute.' Stepping out into the communal hallway, Sonny lifted his hand in the air. 'What's going on, Di?'

Diane spun around and wiping away the tears from underneath her eyes, she gave the mystery woman a pointed look. 'I just wanted a word in private.'

'Well.' He gave a small smile. 'You can speak in front of Rina,' he said, gesturing to the woman standing on the doorstep. 'We don't have any secrets between us.'

A hollow laugh escaped from Diane's lips. She could think of nothing worse and certainly wasn't prepared to air her dirty laundry in front of another woman. 'No, it's okay, another time perhaps.' She made to walk away again when Sonny tugged on her arm.

'Come inside,' he insisted. 'Please.'

Diane shook her head. 'I don't want to put you out.'

'I was just about to leave anyway,' Rina blurted out as she looked between Sonny and Diane. 'I have to open up the pub.'

A smug grin etched its way across Diane's face. My God, he had to be desperate if he was slumming it with a barmaid. Just maybe her plan to worm her way back into his life hadn't been so futile after all. Pulling herself up to her full height, she gave a curt nod then followed the couple into the apartment. Making her way into the lounge she looked around her. The expensive furniture and plush cream carpet underneath her feet screamed wealth and as she stepped closer to the sideboard positioned across the far wall her gaze fell across a series of silver photograph frames. The majority of the photographs were of Carla taken at various stages in her life, a few were of Carla and Sonny together and as she picked up one of the frames, she studied both her daughter's and ex-husband's faces. They not only looked happy but also totally at ease in one another's company. It was more than obvious that they shared a close bond, something she and her daughter had never had, nor were likely to have for that matter, seeing as Carla had betrayed her in one of the worst ways imaginable. Not that she wasn't prepared to forgive and forget her daughter's treachery if it meant Diane was once again financially stable, and seeing as Sonny was obviously loaded there was no reason for her to think otherwise. Hearing the front door close, Diane hastily returned the frame to the sideboard then made her way back across the lounge. A few moments later, Sonny joined her.

'She seems nice,' Diane said, nodding towards the door.

'She is,' Sonny answered as he took a seat on the sofa. 'So what is this all about?' he asked, leaning his forearms on his knees. 'I mean, from my understanding I was under the impression that you despised me, so to have you on my doorstep is a little disconcerting, to say the least.'

Diane hesitated, and placing her handbag on the opposite end of the sofa, she shook her head. 'I've never despised you, Sonny.'

Sonny narrowed his eyes. 'You could have fooled me.'

Swallowing deeply Diane shrugged. She couldn't blow it now, not when she was so close to snaring him again. 'It was a difficult time,' she said in the way of explaining her deceit. 'My head wasn't in the right place.'

'Yeah,' Sonny rolled his eyes, 'you can say that again.'

'You don't know what it was like for me,' she cried, her bottom lip trembling as she sniffed back crocodile tears. 'I was suffering from post-natal depression.'

Throwing his head back Sonny burst out laughing. 'Don't give me all of that old bollocks. Carla was eight years old, not a babe in arms, and no matter what you might think of me,' he said, stabbing his finger forward, 'I'm not as stupid as you might think, so do me a favour and stop trying to insult my intelligence.' As he leaned back on the sofa, Sonny narrowed his eyes. 'You put me through hell and back and as for my so-called best mate...' he paused for a moment, then shook his head, his hands involuntarily curling into fists, 'maybe the less said about him the better.'

'It was all Bernie's doing,' Diane was quick to answer. 'He manipulated me. You were never home, and I was stuck in the house, day after day, bringing up our daughter. I was lonely, I just wanted some attention and Bernie took advantage of the situation.' She placed her hand on her heart, her expression sombre. 'But not for one single moment did I ever stop loving you.'

'Cut the crap, Diane.' Sonny's voice was hard. 'I was there, remember? Bernie wasn't the first, and I highly doubt he'll be the last, given your track record. Before the ink was even dry on our wedding certificate you were eyeing up your next conquest.'

Momentarily closing her eyes Diane bowed her head. How was she supposed to even answer. It was all true, within weeks of being married she'd embarked on the first of her many affairs. She hadn't wanted Sonny, not really, the only thing she'd wanted was his surname and the notoriety that came with it. From day one, Bernie had been the one she had her heart set on and if Carla hadn't slipped up and told her father about Bernie's visits then she would have been the one to spill the beans. She would have done just about anything to keep Bernie close; his threats to end their affair had been enough to tip her over the edge. She'd loved him and couldn't bear the thought of seeing him with another woman; the mere thought was incomprehensible to her, if nothing else she would have driven herself mad with jealousy. She'd even lied to Bernie and told him that she was pregnant just so that he would marry her. He'd hit the roof when he'd finally found out that there was no baby and that she'd deceived him. That wasn't to say that she hadn't wanted to carry his children, because she had, but after years of trying for a baby, nothing had happened, not even a sniff of a pregnancy. She'd even arranged for them to see a fertility specialist in Harley Street, hopeful that with the right treatment they would one day have a child of their own, until during a particularly nasty argument Bernie had all but shattered her dreams, and subsequently her heart, when he'd admitted to having a vasectomy out of spite. No amount of treatment was ever going to give her the baby she'd longed for. Bernie didn't want her to bear his children and had refused to even consider reversing the vasectomy. Still to this day Diane's heart broke for what could have been. If nothing else, she would have been a good mother to Bernie's children, would have idolised them, would have given them everything their hearts desired.

'And as for being lonely,' Sonny continued, breaking his ex-wife's thoughts, 'it was me who put Carla to bed every night so don't you dare try to insinuate that I was never around. I gave you everything you could have ever wanted. I would have given you the moon if I could have. That was how much our marriage meant to me.'

'And you still could.' Dropping to her knees Diane flashed a wide smile, and pushing her ample breasts forward she snaked out her arm and tentatively placed her hand on his leg, her fingertips ever so softly caressing his muscular thigh through the material. 'We could pick up where we left off. Think about it, just you and me, we were made for each other, you know we were. We were more than just good together; we were that couple everyone wanted to emulate.' Conveniently she chose to forget the times when they had argued, more often than not because she was bored and loved nothing more than to push his buttons and get a reaction out of him. 'We could be a family again. Think of Carla and how much this would mean to her to have her parents back together again.'

Shrugging Diane's hand away from him, Sonny shook his head. 'It's too late for any of that,' he snapped. 'I'm happy as I am. It might only be early days for me and Rina but she gets me, and I think a lot of her.'

The smile slid from Diane's face. 'You're happy with a barmaid,' she spat, disgust etching across her face. 'Some tart who pulls pints for a living and scrubs out toilets on a daily basis.'

'Yes, I am, and she's not a tart, neither is she just some barmaid. In fact, she's worth ten of you so don't you dare look down your nose at her as if your own shit doesn't stink, because believe me Di, it does. I know you, just you remember that.'

With as much dignity as she could muster Diane got to her feet and snatching up her handbag, she tossed a lock of blonde hair over her shoulder. 'I can see you haven't changed one little bit,' she sneered. 'Even when we were together you were happy to just plod along, to take orders from all and sundry, to be nothing more than your brother's lackey. And this barmaid of yours is more than likely cut from the same cloth.' She gave a bitter laugh and gestured around her. 'She landed on her feet when she met you, didn't she? Must have seen you coming a mile away. You mark my words she'll rinse you of everything you own.'

'And what, you wouldn't, I suppose.' Shaking his head Sonny gave an incredulous laugh. 'We both know what you're like, that you've only ever looked out for number one. As long as you're alright then fuck everyone else, that was always your motto wasn't it.'

Undeterred Diane continued. 'You know what your trouble is, don't you,' she smirked. 'You're too gullible for your own good, is it any wonder that I sought comfort in the arms of another man.'

Sonny stiffened, and as he glared at Diane his eyes resembled hard flints. 'Have you finished? Let's get one thing straight, my personal life is fuck all to do with you. Now I'm not going to ask you again – what the fuck do you want?'

Diane gave a deep sigh and as she averted her gaze, genuine tears filled her eyes. 'It's Bernie,' she finally admitted, throwing up her hands. 'He's got himself into a spot of bother. We're going to lose the house. We'll be homeless, in fact we'll be lucky if we get to walk away with the clothes on our backs.'

As he processed the information Sonny scratched at his jaw. 'And what, you thought you'd turn up on my doorstep and try to have another crack at me, I mean,' he gestured around the lounge, 'this has got to be better than living on the streets hasn't it, even if it means being stuck with me for the considerable future, and those were your exact words. What was it you'd said?' he asked, tilting his head to the side as though thinking back. 'Oh yeah, that was it, you'd rather die than have to live out the remainder of your life with someone as weak as me?'

'No,' Diane lied, her eyes widening as though she were scandalised. 'The thought never even crossed my mind. And no matter what you might think of me I meant what I said, I do still love you. I'm not afraid to admit that I made a mistake, that I thought the grass would be greener and that Bernie...' She momentarily paused, and placing her hand behind her back in an attempt to hide her gold wedding band, she shook her head. Perhaps Sonny was right and the less said about her husband, the better. 'If I could turn back time, don't you think that I would? I'd give anything to go back to when it was just me and you against the world.'

'You've got to be living in cuckoo land,' Sonny retorted, pointing to his head, 'if you think that I'd ever take you back,' he screwed up his face, 'that I would want you in my life again. Even when we were together you caused me nothing but aggro and as for it being "you and me against the world",' he said, using his fingers as quotation marks, 'that's a complete and utter lie. The only person you ever cared about was yourself, you barely even gave Carla any attention, you viewed her as nothing more than an inconvenience.'

'That's not true,' Diane gasped. 'Carla means a lot to me.'

Sonny laughed again. 'She means a lot to you.' He shook his head. 'You're something else, do you know that? Carla should be the centre of your world, your everything.'

Diane groaned, frustration getting the better of her. Anyone would think that Carla was still a child the way he was carrying on. 'She's a grown woman, for Christ's sake,' she said, waving her hand dismissively. 'I brought her up, fed and clothed her, what more do you want?'

'Makes no difference,' Sonny retorted. 'No matter how old she is I'm still her dad. I would still lay my life on the line for her without a moment's hesitation.'

Huffing out a breath, Diane looked away. The plan that she had so callously devised was all but dissolving before her eyes. 'Then what about Bernie?' she pleaded. 'You loved him like a brother once, would have done anything for him. Are you really prepared to sit back and watch him lose everything?'

The nerve at the side of Sonny's jaw twitched. 'Is this some kind of joke?' he asked, his voice rising. 'Do you honestly think that I'd go out of my way to make that bastard's life easier? He was my mate,' he yelled. 'Which part of that don't you understand? I would have fucking died for him.'

Diane swallowed deeply. 'Sonny, please,' she cried. 'As the mother of your only child, I'm begging you to help us.' In a last-ditch attempt to sway his mind she sank down to her knees and steepled her hands in front of her. 'If not for my sake, then for Carla's. How do you think she's going to feel when I've lost everything, and she finds out that you stood by and did nothing to help me.'

'I stopped caring a long time ago,' Sonny answered. 'So if you don't mind,' he motioned towards the door, 'I think that we're done here. You can see yourself out.'

Stunned, Diane's mouth dropped open. 'Is that it?' she shrieked as she pulled herself up from the floor, her cheeks burning with humiliation. 'You're actually going to throw me out.'

Sonny gave a nonchalant shrug. 'What else do you want me to say? As the old saying goes, you made your bed, now lie in it. And let's face it, you couldn't have given two shits about me or my feelings when you and Bernie were shagging behind my back, so why should I give a flying fuck about you now?'

Lifting her chin in the air Diane's eyes blazed with fury. 'You really don't care, do you?'

'Nope,' he replied, accentuating the word. 'Like I've already said, I stopped caring a long time ago.'

'I see.' Running her tongue over her teeth Diane pushed her

chin in the air. 'And how about your daughter, do you care about her?'

'Of course I fucking do!' Sonny shouted back, his eyes flashing dangerously.

'Well.' Crossing her arms over her ample chest Diane gave him a pointed look. 'If that's the case, then why did you send her to the house looking for those diamonds? It's because of you that I'm going to lose my home, because of you that my Bernie was beaten to within an inch of his life. Whether you like it or not you owe me, Sonny,' she smirked.

Sonny's forehead furrowed and as he jumped to his feet he strode across the room. 'What are you talking about?'

Diane gave a shrill laugh. 'Don't play the innocent with me. You know exactly what I'm talking about. You sent Carla to the house as your mole. Bernie caught her in the act.'

The colour drained from Sonny's face, and grabbing Diane by the elbow, he dragged her through the apartment. 'Get out,' he said, pushing her across the threshold. 'And don't ever show your face here again. Have you got that?'

Staggering across the landing, Diane rubbed at the indentions his fingers had left on her arm and as the front door was slammed shut in her face, she fought down the urge to scream out loud. The Sonny she remembered from old, had idolised her, some would even say that he had worshipped the ground she walked on. Even when she had betrayed him, all it would have taken was a click of her fingers and he would have come running back to her, he'd been that besotted.

Slowly, she made her way across the hallway and with her head held high, she pressed the button to activate the lift. The fact Sonny had snubbed her stung, and as fresh tears sprang to her eyes, she used the sleeve of her top to wipe them away, not caring one iota if she smeared her mascara in the process. Her entire world was crumbling before her. She couldn't live in a caravan; she'd never get over the shame of it.

As the door to the lift sprang open, Diane's eyes widened, and pulling herself up to her full height the anger that spread across her face was more than apparent. 'I hope that you're happy with yourself,' she spat as she locked eyes with her daughter.

Carla's jaw dropped and stepping out of the lift, her nervous gaze went from her mother to her father's front door and then back again. 'What are you doing here, Mum?'

Diane gave a nasty laugh. 'What do you think I'm doing here,' she said, jerking her thumb in the direction of Sonny's flat. 'Giving that bastard you have the misfortune to call a dad a piece of my mind.' She took a step closer to her daughter, pulled back her arm and then delivered a slap to Carla's cheek. 'You thought you were so clever, didn't you? That my Bernie wouldn't clock what you were up to. You're a Carter, for crying out loud,' she spat, looking Carla up and down with disgust. 'And considering their livelihood you couldn't have been more blatant if you tried.'

With her hand clutched to her cheek, confusion was etched across Carla's face. 'I...' she began.

'I don't want to hear your excuses,' Diane screeched. 'And as for him,' she said, flicking her head back towards the door. 'The fact he sent you to do his dirty work speaks volumes.' She looked her daughter up and down and sneered. 'I wash my hands of you, you're no longer a daughter of mine. All thanks to you and that bastard back there,' she said, nodding towards Sonny's flat again. 'Me and Bernie have got nothing. We were relying on that money from the Tuckers to keep a roof over our heads. How could you be so spiteful, so vindictive? I'm your mother for Christ's sake, I gave birth to you, I felt as though I was being split in two just to bring you into the world and this is how you repay me.' She moved closer, her entire body trembling with rage. 'Do you despise me that much, that you would be happy to see me out on the street?'

Still at a loss for words, Carla shook her head. 'No, of course not.'

'You're your father's daughter, alright,' Diane hissed. 'Not a single care for anyone else other than yourselves.'

Carla's mouth dropped open. Diane was a fine one to talk about being selfish. Not once had she ever put her daughter first. As Diane shoved Carla out of the way and stepped into the lift, she jabbed at the control button. 'I will never forgive you for this,' she remarked as the door closed on her.

'It could be a lot worse,' Carla mumbled under her breath. 'I could take after you.' Turning away from the lift, she stepped across the communal hallway and as the front door to her father's apartment was flung open with such force that it banged heavily against the wall, it took everything inside of Carla to stop herself from physically jumping out of her skin.

'Get yourself in here,' Sonny growled, his voice brooking no arguments. 'And believe me when I say this: you had best start talking and fast before I end up doing someone some serious damage.'

A shard of ice-cold fear shot down the length of Carla's spine, and for the first time in her life she could honestly say that felt wary of her dad. The very notion was so ludicrous that if she hadn't been so afraid, she would have laughed out loud. Her dad may have had a reputation as a hard man, someone who should be feared on the street, but in her presence, he had only ever been kind and gentle.

Closing the front door, Carla took a deep breath then crossing her fingers, she made her way towards the lounge. Just maybe, once she'd explained the situation, her dad would understand her actions, perhaps he would even agree with her that it was about time Bernie received his comeuppance. Somehow, she highly doubted that this would be the case, but still, she had to try, she reasoned. Her dad may have seemingly forgiven Bernie for what he'd caused, but she hadn't, nor was she ever likely to.

11

From across the bar, Terri Tempest eyed Rina with a level of suspicion. It hadn't escaped her notice that over the past few weeks Rina had become more and more secretive, when under any normal circumstances she was an open book. Not only was her head forever in her phone but she would also disappear for hours on end, supposedly visiting friends.

Tossing a towel onto the bar Terri made her way towards the woman she viewed as her surrogate mother. 'Are you okay?' she asked.

Rina looked up from her phone, and hastily pushing the device back into her pocket, she gave a light laugh. 'Of course, I am. Why wouldn't I be?'

'I don't know.' Terri's forehead furrowed. 'Only you look as though something is troubling you?'

Rina bit down on her bottom lip.

'What is it?' Terri asked, concerned. 'Has something happened?'

'No, nothing like that,' Rina sighed. 'I've met someone.' She gave an unsure smile and as her gaze drifted up to the portrait of her late husband that sat behind the bar, the smile slid from her face. 'Well not just met him as such,' she said, flapping her hand. 'I've known him for years, but in recent months we've become close.'

Terri's eyebrows shot up and clasping Rina's hand she offered a bright smile. 'You're a dark horse. Why didn't you say anything?'

Rina glanced back to the photograph and sighed. 'No one could ever replace my Archie...'

As she followed Rina's gaze Terri nodded. She too had loved Archie and just like Rina, she had been left devastated when he'd been murdered by her uncle, Michael Murphy. 'But...?'

Lifting her shoulders into a shrug, Rina's cheeks flushed red. 'I do like him. I suppose I always have really, not that I would have ever played around on my Archie, mind. I'm not that type of woman,' she was quick to add, her expression becoming serious as she clasped Terri's hand even tighter. 'I would never have even entertained the notion of having another man in my life, let alone go that one step further and actually see it through. I could never have betrayed Archie; our marriage was rock solid; he was my everything.'

'I know.' Terri frowned. 'You don't need to explain yourself to me. I know how much you loved him.'

Rina nodded. 'I just don't want anyone to think badly of me.' She motioned around the pub. 'I don't want any of this lot to assume that I'm some kind of harlot or that I didn't waste much time when it came to replacing Archie.'

'They won't,' Terri answered. 'It's been more than two years since he...' She gave a sad smile. 'Well, you know, since he was taken from us. And if I did hear anyone bad-mouthing you, I'd soon put them in their place, we all would.'

'Oh, I know that,' Rina giggled as she gave Terri's hand a squeeze. 'You've been an absolute godsend to me. I would never have survived if it hadn't been for you helping me through the grief.'

As she continued to study Rina, Terri narrowed her eyes. 'So why do you look as though you have the weight of the world on your shoulders?'

Pulling out her mobile phone again, Rina looked down at the screen. 'Oh, it's nothing,' she lied with a wave of her hand.

'Rina,' Terri warned.

Rina sighed again. 'Something happened and it just...' She shook her head. 'Ignore me, I'm being silly,' she attempted to laugh. 'It's nothing for you to worry your pretty little head over. You've got enough to think about what with this little one,' she said, placing her hand on Terri's bump.

Terri lifted her eyebrows. 'Stop trying to change the subject. Is something bothering you?' She lowered her voice a fraction. 'This man of yours, he hasn't done something to hurt you has he?'

'No, of course not,' Rina scolded. 'He's a gentleman. It would never enter his head to harm a woman.'

Heaving a sigh of relief, Terri's shoulders visibly relaxed. 'But something is troubling you?'

'I suppose you could say that,' Rina admitted. She nodded down at her phone. 'His ex-wife turned up on the doorstep this morning and I've not heard from him since then.' She lowered her voice slightly. 'As much as I do trust him, I can't help but wonder if...' Her eyes filled with anguish. 'What if they've decided to rekindle their relationship. What other reason could there be for him to not contact me? I mean.' She frowned, 'This isn't like him; he usually checks that I've got home safely. Only today he didn't. What if he is too busy with the ex-wife?'

Terri tilted her head to the side and before she could open her mouth to answer, Rina continued. 'You should have seen her, stunning she was. How could I possibly compete with a woman like that. I mean look at me,' she said, opening out her arms, her expression sombre. 'I'm hardly a catch, am I?'

Squashing her lips together Terri suppressed the urge to laugh out loud. 'Have you actually seen yourself,' she chastised. 'You're beautiful. Men fall over themselves just to talk to you.'

Rina waved Terri's words away. 'Stop it,' she pleaded, her cheeks turning a darker shade of scarlet.

'It's true,' Terri argued. 'I've noticed the attention you get. Last week Sonny Carter could barely take his eyes off you.'

At the mention of Sonny, Rina averted her gaze.

'Oh my God.' Terri clamped her hand across her mouth. 'It's Sonny isn't it? He's your mystery man.'

'Keep your voice down.' As she glanced around her, Rina cast her gaze over the customers, hoping that none of them had heard Terri's squeal. At the best of times they were a nosy lot, they loved a drama and would more often than not embellish the stories they heard or witnessed to make the situation even more dramatic.

'Is it true?' Terri persisted. 'Is it Sonny?'

After giving the question a moment's thought, Rina nodded.

'I knew it,' Terri shrieked as she hugged Rina to her.

Releasing herself from Terri's embrace, Rina once again gestured towards her phone. 'What do you think?' she asked. 'I mean, why would his ex-wife even need to visit him? As far as I was aware, they weren't even in contact.'

Terri thought the question over. 'I don't know,' she finally answered. 'But I do think you're worrying over nothing and Sonny would be a fool to let you go.'

Rina bit down on her lip. 'I hope that you're right,' she said, still somewhat unsure.

'I am,' Terri replied with a level of confidence. 'That reminds me,' she said as her gaze fell on her nephew Mason, 'I wanted to ask for a favour.'

'Go on,' Rina asked as she turned back to the customers. 'Fire away.'

Terri hesitated. 'Would it be okay if I take the rest of the day off? I need to sort a few things out with Jonny.'

It was Rina's turn to narrow her eyes, and as she looked Terri over, she lifted her eyebrows. 'Is everything okay. It's not the baby, is it?'

'No, of course not,' Terri smiled as she lightly traced her fingers over her swollen tummy. 'I just need to speak to him about something that's all and he got home so late last night that we didn't get the chance to talk.'

'Well off you go then,' Rina said as she took a customer's order and began pouring out a drink. 'It's not as if I'm rushed off my feet, is it? And even if we were busy, you should be at home with your feet up. You've only got a few more weeks to go before the baby arrives, you should be resting.'

'I've still got a few months to go,' Terri protested.

'Seven weeks,' Rina corrected. 'Before you know it the baby will be here.'

'I know you mean well,' Terri sighed. 'But as I keep reminding Jonny, I'm pregnant not an invalid. I'm quite capable of working behind the bar. It's not like I lift anything heavy is it.'

Rina huffed out a breath. 'What about that box I caught you carrying last week.'

Terri rolled her eyes. 'It was only the bar towels. I was hardly going to do myself some damage.'

Rina lifted her eyebrows and throwing Terri a disapproving look she shook her head. 'You can be a stubborn mare when you want to be.'

Terri giggled. 'Must be that Tempest blood I have in me,' she winked.

'Well, just don't go overdoing it, okay?' Rina warned. 'Otherwise, you'll end up wearing yourself out before the baby's even born.' She placed the customer's money into the till then scooped up her handbag. 'Do you need a lift?' she asked, fishing out her car keys.

Terri shook her head and as she looked towards her nephew again, she grabbed her coat from behind the bar. 'I was going to ask Mase if he wouldn't mind dropping me off.'

On hearing his name being mentioned, Mason Tempest looked up.

'Would you mind driving me over to the scrapyard?' she asked as she made her way around the bar.

'You know that I'd do anything for you Auntie Terri,' Mason teased.

'Behave,' Terri chastised. With only a few years between them they were more like siblings than aunt and nephew and as they made their way outside, she slipped her arm through his, her gaze automatically drifting down to the buckle shaped scar on his forearm, a lasting reminder of his encounter with both her uncle Michael and Raymond Cole, the half-brother of her, Ricky and Jamie.

Sensing her stare, Mason tugged the sleeve of his shirt down. 'I forget sometimes,' he said, referring to the scars that crisscrossed the entire length of his body. 'Well until I look in the mirror that is, would be a bit hard to miss the scars then.'

Despite the small smile Mason gave, Terri noted a sense of bitterness in his voice. He was still a good-looking man, the image of her father and brothers, only the scars made him feel self-conscious. She rarely, if ever, saw him wear anything that meant the scars were on full display. Not that she could say she blamed him for covering up. She'd seen firsthand the damage that had been inflicted, and it was only by some miracle that Mason had survived at all, the injuries he'd sustained had been that horrific. As she thought back to the day when she, Jonny, and her brothers had discovered Mason's lifeless body, tears filled her eyes.

'Hey,' Mason soothed. 'I'm alright. I'm a lot tougher than I look,' he winked. 'I survived and that's the main thing.'

'I know.' Terri smiled through her tears. As much as Mason may have recovered from the ordeal he'd been put through, the experience had definitely changed him to a certain degree. If nothing else he was certainly a lot more cautious than he'd been previously. Sometimes she couldn't help but worry about him, he'd lost the sparkle in his eyes that he'd once had, and as much as he may still laugh and joke around, she couldn't help but wonder if it was all an act, that deep down he was merely masking just how unhappy he really was. 'Ignore me, it's my hormones,' she cried. 'They're turning me into a blubbering mess.'

'Yeah, well,' he motioned down to Terri's bump, 'as long as you don't give birth in my car you can cry as much as you want.'

Terri couldn't help but laugh. Mason's obsession with his car was on a par with Jonny's fascination for anything with four wheels. 'I don't think that's likely to happen,' she said as she heaved herself into the car. 'I've still got a few months to go yet.'

'I hope not,' Mason answered as he eyed Terri. 'Because believe me I'd make a hopeless midwife.'

Still chuckling, Terri pulled across the seat belt. 'The quicker you get me to the scrapyard then the better, eh?'

Not needing to be told twice, Mason started the ignition and as he drove out of the car park and headed in the direction of Barking, he couldn't help but throw Terri a surreptitious glance. 'I heard that they're going after diamonds.'

Terri snapped her head around. 'How do you know that?'

Mason laughed. 'How do you think? Tommy Jr told me.'

Terri shook her head. 'He wasn't supposed to tell anyone,' she fumed. 'And if he's told you then who else has he opened his mouth to?'

'Relax,' Mason reassured her. 'He hasn't told anyone else. He trusts me and seeing as we're pretty much family, no harm was done.'

'That's not the point,' Terri protested. Crossing her arms over her chest she continued to shake her head. 'Jonny won't be happy about this...' she began before Mason interrupted her.

'They're going after them tonight,' he said, giving her a sidelong glance. 'Did you know?'

Terri's mouth dropped open. She'd known that Jonny had been making plans, but she hadn't realised the heist would be so soon, not when some of the past robberies the family had committed had taken months and months to plan out. 'No,' she choked out. 'He can't be, not this quick. I mean, I knew he wanted to act fast, but I thought we'd have at least a few months before that time comes, that the baby would have been born by then. I was hoping that once he'd become a father, he'd realise that he had too much to lose, that he'd put all thoughts of the robbery on the back burner.'

Turning his head to look at her again, Mason gave a sad smile. 'It's tonight, Tel', I just thought you should know. I know that I was pretty much out of it at the time,' he said, referring to the attack upon himself, 'but I do remember you helping me. I'm hardly likely to forget something like that am I? It was you and Jonny who helped me out of the house.'

Terri nodded. It had all but broken her heart to hear Mason's pain-filled whimpers as she'd guided him out of the house and into Jonny's car. He'd been in so much pain that she'd had to remind him to put one foot in front of the other, and with each step he'd taken, the blood encrusted welts across his torso and arms had begun to weep. Patting his arm she returned the smile. 'It isn't something I'll ever forget either.'

Mason cleared his throat and shifting his weight slightly in an attempt to hide his embarrassment, he gave a shrug. 'Plus, you're my favourite aunt,' he added, in a bid to lighten the mood.

'I'm your only aunt,' Terri laughed.

Mason smiled. 'Just be careful,' he warned, his voice suddenly becoming serious. 'We're talking about some heavy shit here and if the Tuckers are involved it won't take much for things to escalate. And the last thing I'd ever want is for you to be caught in the crossfire.'

'You're starting to sound like your dad,' Terri laughed. 'I'm sure that he goes out of his way just to give me the big brother speech at any given opportunity.'

'Only because we care,' Mason retorted.

'Yeah, I know. And I will be careful,' Terri promised. As she stared ahead out of the car windscreen she sighed knowing full well that she'd just made an empty promise. No matter what Ricky, Jamie, Mason, or even Jonny himself said, she didn't intend to stay away. How could she when in the blink of an eye both her and Jonny's lives could be forever changed. Jonny wasn't only the father of her unborn child, she loved him, he was her world, her everything. Not only did he make her feel safe, protected, but she also trusted him with her life, and not only her life but also her freedom. Together they shared a secret, or rather several secrets, that if ever discovered could result in them spending the remainder of their lives behind bars.

Alongside her brothers and nephew, both she and Jonny had participated in the murders of three men, one of them being her uncle Michael, another her half-brother Raymond Cole. The fact they both had blood on their hands bound them together, and in the aftermath of the gruesome murders Jonny had been there for her, he'd been her rock. Over and over again, he'd promised to protect her even if that meant taking the rap himself to keep her out of prison, and she believed him too. Was it any wonder that she wanted to be there waiting for him when he returned from the heist? She needed to see for herself that he was safe, that her worst fears hadn't come true and that he hadn't been carted off to the nearest police station in handcuffs or even worse, seriously maimed. She couldn't lose him, not after everything they had been through together. Her mind made up, she forced herself to relax and as the baby began to kick, she allowed herself to smile, albeit one that didn't quite reach her eyes. If truth be told she felt sick to her stomach and she had a feeling that she would continue to do so until the heist was over and done with, until Jonny and his nephews had returned safely home.

* * *

The muscles across Sonny Carter's shoulders were taut. 'Did he coerce you into this?' he shouted.

Carla screwed up her face, the anger that radiated from her father making her inwardly shudder. She had never been on the receiving end of her father's rage before. Oh, she knew he had a temper, they all did, herself included, but for her dad to actually direct his anger towards her was a first and one that she couldn't say she particularly liked. 'Who?'

'Don't try playing games with me,' Sonny, roared stabbing his finger forward. 'You know full well who I'm talking about. That bastard brother of mine, Jonny.' He pulled out his mobile phone and began scrolling through his contact list, the muscles across his shoulder blades taut. 'I'm going to kill him over this,' he continued to shout. 'He might be hell bent on fucking up his own life but if he thinks he's going to drag my daughter down with him then he's got another think coming.'

'Dad,' Carla protested.

Bringing the device up to his ear, Sonny's face was set like thunder and as the call rang off, he jabbed at the redial button a second time. 'Fuck this,' he snarled when once again his younger brother didn't pick up. Grabbing his car keys he gestured towards Carla. 'I'm seriously going to hurt him,' he exclaimed. 'He's pushed me too far this time.'

'No, Dad,' Carla cried as she tugged on her father's arm. 'It isn't his fault. Uncle Jonny didn't coerce me into anything.'

Sonny narrowed his eyes. 'Of course he did, he manipulated you. What other reason would there be for you to search your mum's house?' He pointed in the direction of the front door. 'Your mum has told me everything, how Bernie caught you in the act.'

Carla groaned. She should have known that Bernie would have sussed her out. Instead of confronting her he'd gone running to her mum telling tales, not that she should have expected any different from him, the man was a spineless weasel, a rat. Her cheeks flamed pink. In truth, Bernie was none of those things, he'd only ever been kind to her, not that she actually deserved his kindness, if anything she'd done her utmost to make his life a living hell. The only person she had to blame for the diamond's being moved was herself. She should have been more careful. As easy as it had been to blame Jonny for not acting sooner, it was because of her the diamonds had been moved. She'd inadvertently forced Bernie's hand. 'No Dad, he didn't.' She took a deep breath then lifted her chin in the air, defiance flashing in her eyes. 'It was my idea. Jonny didn't even know about the diamonds until I told him. It was me,' she said, giving a nonchalant shrug. 'I was the one who wanted to steal them.'

Sonny's forehead furrowed and giving an incredulous laugh he shook his head. 'No,' he said. 'You're lying. You're covering for him; you have to be. He's fucked up yet again and has forced you to take the blame for him.'

'No, he didn't.' Carla shook her head, her expression serious. 'No matter what you might think of him he's my uncle, he loves me, he'd never force me into anything.'

'Then he bribed you,' Sonny declared, giving an exasperated sigh. 'He has something over you and he's using it as a leverage.'

'No, Dad,' Carla shouted. 'You're not listening to me.' She took a deep breath and looked her father in the eyes. 'It was my idea, all of it. So if you want to blame someone, then blame me.'

'But...' Still shaking his head Sonny looked aimlessly around him, 'That's not possible,' he cried. 'Why would you even want to do something like this?'

'For you.' Carla screwed up her face. She would have thought the reason was obvious. Surely her dad knew how much she despised her mother's husband, that she blamed Bernie for tearing her family apart. 'For what Bernie did to our family.'

Rubbing at the nape of his neck Sonny stared at his daughter. 'I can't get my head around this,' he exclaimed. 'I mean, Jonny, yeah. We all know that he's an accident waiting to happen, but you,' he cried. 'I just...' He shook his head, disbelief flashing across his face. 'Surely to fucking God you're not this stupid, that I didn't raise you to be so mindless.'

'I want Bernie to pay for what he did,' Carla blurted out.

Sonny narrowed his eyes, the earlier anger he'd felt once again rushing to the fore. 'What are you talking about?' he shouted. 'Pay for what?'

'He destroyed our family. He was the cause of you and Mum divorcing.'

Sonny's mouth fell open and as he took a series of deep breaths in order to keep his temper in check he shook his head. 'Carla, our marriage was doomed from the start. We should never have been together in the first place, let alone got married.'

'But...' Carla's face fell. That wasn't how she remembered her parents' marriage. They had been happy once; she was sure of it. One of her earliest memories was watching her dad sneak up on her mum and then proceed to twirl her around the kitchen, their arms wrapped around one another as they danced and sang along to the music being played. They had laughed and smiled so often that it couldn't have all been an act, the mere thought was incomprehensible to her. 'No,' she cried. 'You loved Mum, idolised her. If it hadn't been for Bernie...'

'Bernie wasn't the problem,' Sonny interrupted as he rubbed at his forehead. 'Not really. Time and time again my brothers had warned me that she was up to no good, Mitchell had even caught her in the act once, only I didn't want to listen, didn't want to admit that my marriage was in tatters and that your mother was screwing around behind my back.' He gave a bitter laugh. 'Diane did her utmost to persuade me that it was all lies, that they had it in for her, that they were jealous of what we had, and she was so convincing that for a while I actually believed her. It caused ructions amongst the family I can tell you that much, almost came to blows between me and your uncle Tommy, and probably would have done if your Uncle Jimmy hadn't stepped in and calmed the situation down.' He gave a small smile and shook his head. 'Tommy would have annihilated me, but at the time I didn't care, Diane was my wife, the mother of my daughter. I overlooked her flaws, even made excuses for her behaviour, but in here,' he said, tapping his chest, 'I knew it was all true. There was nothing your mum liked more than to remind me of my failures. She'd married into the Carter family, only I was too far down the pecking order for her liking, I was never going to head the family, not when I had three elder brothers. And as for your uncles, they were looking out for me, they had nothing to gain from lying, they had their own lives to contend with, their own families to look after.' He gave a great sigh. 'Bernie was nothing more than the straw that broke the camel's back. He wasn't some stranger, some meaningless bloke she'd met down the pub, he was my best mate, the last person on earth I thought would ever betray me. How could I forgive and forget after that?'

Sickness washed over Carla. Had she orchestrated the theft of the diamonds for nothing? She'd wanted to avenge her dad, had wanted to ruin Bernie, had wanted him to know how it felt to lose everything he held dear just as her dad had done all those years ago. And all the while her parents' marriage had been nothing but a sham. If anyone was to blame then it was her mum. Diane was the one who had betrayed her husband without a second's thought for him or for anyone else. 'I...' she swallowed deeply then began again. 'I thought Bernie was to blame, that if it hadn't been for him leading Mum astray then the two of you would have still been together.'

'Then you thought wrong,' Sonny growled. 'Your mum fucked up our marriage long before she and Bernie got together.' Moving across the room he gripped Carla by the arms and shook her. 'Do you understand what you've caused?' he asked through gritted teeth. 'What you've done?'

Carla nodded, her mind reeling. Had she set Bernie up to take a fall for no other reason than her own stupidity, her own stubbornness? Could it be possible that Bernie was as much a victim of her mother's selfishness as both she and her father were?

'I said do you understand?' Sonny repeated, his voice becoming even louder.

Pulling herself free Carla breathed heavily. 'Of course I do,' she screamed back at him. 'It's because of me that they're going to break into Ozzie Tucker's house.'

Sonny's eyes widened and as he rocked back on his heels, he took a large, shuddering intake of breath. 'What did you just say?'

The anger in Sonny's voice was enough to make Carla tremble and digging her fingernails into the palm of her hand in an attempt to stop her hands from shaking she swallowed deeply before summoning up the courage to answer him. 'The diamonds were moved from Mum's house and returned to Ozzie Tucker.' Her shoulders slumped downwards and as she studied her father's reaction, she reached out for him again, concern etched across her face. 'They're going after them tonight.'

As the enormity of the situation hit home Sonny pinched the bridge of his nose. 'Has he got some kind of death wish?' he asked, referring to his younger brother, his voice so low that Carla had to strain her ears to hear him. 'Surely he knows what this will cause, that the Tuckers are not going to take this lying down.'

'He seems to think that he's got it all sussed out.'

Sonny gave an incredulous laugh. 'He's got nothing all sussed out. I knew this would happen,' he seethed. 'He's a liability and always had been. He hasn't got the first clue of what he's doing. He's going to destroy this family.' He pulled out his phone again and sucking in his bottom lip, his finger hovered over his eldest brother Jimmy's contact number.

'It's no different to the risk you and my uncles took when you stole the gold,' Carla argued.

Sonny looked up, his body becoming rigid. 'That was different,' he snapped, returning the phone back to his pocket. 'We were lucky to walk away from that robbery with our lives still intact.'

Carla opened her mouth to answer before hastily snapping her lips closed again. Despite the heist not working out quite as her dad and uncles had planned, Jonny had made it all sound so easy, exciting even. 'But...'

'There are no buts,' Sonny continued. 'If it hadn't been for the fact Tommy and Danny McKay were on friendly terms, we would have all been murdered, and Jonny would have been one of the first to have had his life extinguished. He might have only been a kid at the time, but Freddie Smith was still willing to use him as a bartering tool in exchange for the gold.'

In that instant Carla's blood ran cold. Her uncle Jonny had been right when he'd said that they weren't playing a game. All she could do was hope and pray that it was her family who emerged as the victors.

12

As he perched on the edge of the desk, Jonny Carter shook his head so vigorously that he was in grave danger of giving himself whiplash. 'I said no,' he repeated, his voice stern. 'I can't get my head around the fact that you're even suggesting it.' He motioned to Terri's swollen tummy. 'Unless it's escaped your notice, you're pregnant.'

'Am I?' Terri rolled her eyes. 'I've been wondering what this bump is or why I need to get up every ten minutes during the night to go to the toilet.'

Jonny shook his head, his forehead furrowing. 'Don't try to be funny Tel', I'm being deadly serious.'

'And so am I,' Terri implored. Coming forward she placed her hand upon his forearm. 'I want to be here for when you get back.'

'No.' Shaking his head again, Jonny crossed his arms over his chest. She had to be delusional if she thought that he would ever agree to her having an involvement in the heist. 'It's too dangerous.'

'How?' Terri let out a laugh. 'What difference does it make if I wait for you here or at home. I can just as well make myself comfortable in the office.' She nodded down to the sofa then shook her head as she took note of the metal springs poking through the fabric. 'Or I'll just sit here.' Walking around the desk she took a seat in Jonny's chair then spread open her arms. 'See I'll be fine. I've got everything I could possibly need, a kettle, a heater,' she said, motioning to a small portable heater that had been dumped in the corner of the office.

Jonny turned his head and as he followed her gaze, he screwed up his face. The heater was so old that it was covered in a thick layer of dust. He highly doubted that it even worked and to his recollection they had never used it. 'And what if the old bill turn up, eh, what then? You'll be charged as an accessory. You could be sent down, is that what you want, to have the baby while handcuffed to a bed in Holloway prison?'

Terri's heart plummeted. 'You told me it wasn't dangerous, that everything was under control.'

'It is under control,' Jonny answered, barely able to look her in the eyes. For a few moments he was quiet. 'Look,' he finally said, his voice becoming gentle, 'you knew right from the start that in my line of work there was always going to be risk. I could be here one day and banged up the next.' He gave a shrug and moving his head from side to side, he forced Terri to look at him. 'I haven't got a crystal ball; I can't predict the future any more than you can.'

Terri's face fell and as she opened her mouth to answer, Jonny pulled her as close as her bump would allow then kissed the top of her head, the familiar scent of her shampoo assaulting his nostrils.

'That doesn't mean I'm planning on getting nicked any time soon,' he said with a light laugh. 'You know what I'm like,' he winked. 'I'm a Carter, we're lucky thieves. The old bill have never so much as had a sniff let alone an actual lead to arrest any of us. And as for you staying on your own in this place.' He gestured around the office then shook his head. 'I need to be able to concentrate darling. I need to be able to keep focused and I can't do that if I'm worrying myself sick about you, can I?'

'But I need to be here,' Terri reiterated, her voice catching as she tried in vain to swallow down the hard lump in her throat. 'I'll go out of my mind with worry if I'm stuck at home not knowing what's going on.'

Jonny shook his head. 'I'm sorry babe,' he sighed. 'But it's not gonna happen.'

As Terri was about to protest, the door to the office slammed open and as Sonny, followed by Carla, stormed inside Terri grasped hold of Jonny's hand, alarm resonating across her face.

'I'm this close,' Sonny shouted, placing his thumb and forefinger an inch apart, 'from punching some sense into that skull of yours. What do you think you're playing at?'

Jonny's jaw clenched, and as Terri stepped out of his arms he straightened up, his hard stare going from his brother to his niece. 'What have you been telling him?' he asked Carla, his tone accusing.

'It wasn't me; it was my mum.' Taking a deep breath as if preparing herself to take the brunt of her uncle's rage, Carla looked down at her feet. 'She paid my dad a visit and told him everything.'

'How the fuck would your mum know about the heist?' Jonny barked out.

Still looking down at the floor Carla lifted her shoulders into a shrug.

'Answer me,' Jonny shouted, his temper getting the better of him. 'How does Diane know anything about this?'

'Bernie caught me at the house,' Carla admitted, the words tumbling out of her mouth in a rush. 'I needed to know where he was stashing the diamonds. I was trying to help.'

Anger flashed across Jonny's face. 'Why is this the first time I'm hearing about any of this?' he snapped. Pushing himself away from the desk he pointed to his head. 'Have you lost your mind?' he shouted. 'It's because of you the diamonds were moved.' He rubbed at his temples, the conversation he'd had with Jake at the forefront of his mind. If it hadn't been for Sadie giving them the heads-up on the situation, they would have unknowingly walked into a trap, one that they wouldn't have been able to escape from. 'You could have got us all killed.'

'I'm sorry.' Carla gave an involuntary shiver.

'You're sorry.' Jonny threw his arms up in the air and gave an incredulous laugh. 'A fat lot of good that would have done us when we had shooters pointing at our heads.'

A lone tear slipped down Carla's cheek. 'I messed up,' she apologised, clasping her hands in front of her. 'How was I to know that Bernie would turn up, or that he would suss me out.'

'A bit of common sense, maybe,' Jonny retorted, still barely able to get his head around what he was hearing. 'How could you have been so stupid?'

'Carla's not the one to blame for this,' Sonny interrupted before his daughter had the chance to open her mouth and answer. 'This plan of yours was always going to fail.' He shook his head. 'Jimmy must have lost his fucking mind to even consider putting you in charge.' He pointed towards the door. 'You're leading them down a slippery slope,' he roared, referring to their nephews. 'You're going to be the sole cause of their downfall.'

A laugh escaped from Jonny's lips and as he tore his hard stare away from his niece he focused on his brother. 'And I suppose you think you could do better?'

Glaring at his brother, Sonny shook his head in a warning. 'Don't test me,' he spat. Pulling out his mobile phone, he gestured down to the device. 'One phone call and it's all over. Jimmy will wipe the floor with you and believe me, it's been a long time coming. It's about time someone taught you a lesson that you won't forget in a hurry. We've been too soft on you that's the problem, we've let you get away with too much for far too long.'

Jonny warily eyed the phone. 'Yeah, and you would love that wouldn't you,' he said through gritted teeth. 'This isn't even about the job, you're just pissed off that Jimmy chose me over you and Mitchell. Instead of having a pop at me maybe you should be asking yourself why he didn't trust you and Mitch to take over from him.' His lips curled into a snarl and as he leaned slightly forward, the tone of his voice became menacing. 'Perhaps it's because he knew that you and Mitchell have no backbone, that if it was left down to the two of you, we'd end up with nothing better to do other than pinch penny sweets from the corner shop.'

As Sonny's finger hovered over the call button, he looked up, his eyes hard. 'You are seriously not right up here,' he said, pointing to his forehead. 'And the fact you've dragged my daughter into this fiasco is more than enough to prove my point.'

'Dad,' Carla protested. 'I've already told you Jonny had nothing to do with this,' she said, giving her uncle a nervous glance. 'It was my idea.'

Ignoring his daughter, Sonny continued to glare at his brother. 'You've pushed me too far this time.' He stabbed a stiff finger forward. 'I'll be one of the first to hold my hands up and admit that in the past I've let a lot of your shit slide. Every single time you fucked up I was one of the first to say, "give him another chance, that maybe this time he'll have actually learnt his lesson and start toeing the line." But you never do. Time and time again you prove yourself to be nothing more than a liability. You can't be trusted to head the family. And if that wasn't bad enough you've now got it into your head that you can take on the Tucker brothers. If anyone's going to fuck everything up, it'll be you. Jimmy worked his bollocks off to make sure a truce had been called between our families, that we stayed out of one another's path.'

A snort of laughter escaped from Jonny's lips and as he shook his head, he crossed his arms over his chest. 'Cheers for that Sonny. It's nice to know what you really think of me. And as for the Tuckers,' he added with a snarl. 'Somehow I don't think they got the same memo because those cocky bastards are still walking around giving it all this,' using his fingers he mimicked a mouth opening and closing. 'The way you're carrying on, anyone would think we're scared of them. We're becoming a laughing stock, only you're too blind to see it. The same goes for Jimmy, too, he only heard what he wanted to hear. There is no truce.' He gave another incredulous laugh. 'They pulled the wool over your eyes and you, Mitch and Jimmy fell for it hook, line and sinker.'

Sonny threw up his arms. 'This is exactly what I'm talking about.' He gave an exasperated sigh. 'Even now you're acting like this is all one big joke to you.'

Snaking his tongue across his teeth the muscles across Jonny's shoulders tensed. 'Believe me, it's no joke.'

'Too fucking right it's not.' Curling his hand into a fist, Sonny moved forward. 'I'm so done with you and your antics that I could seriously lay into you. Maybe then it would actually sink into that brain of yours that you're playing a dangerous game.'

Jonny lifted his chin in the air, his eyes silently daring his brother to follow through with his threat. 'So what are you waiting for?' he goaded. 'If you want to take a shot at me then go for it.'

'Jonny don't,' Terri pleaded, her eyes wide with fear.

As Sonny lunged forward, Carla screamed at her father to stop, and as she tugged on his shirt, she shouted for Terri to help her.

It was in that instant that Jonny took his eyes away from his brother, and as he put out his arm in an attempt to block Terri from coming close, Sonny pulled back his fist, swung out his arm and threw a punch.

Staggering several paces back, Jonny's eyes flashed dangerously.

'And you reckon I've got problems,' he shouted as he regained his balance. 'I'm not the one throwing punches am I?'

Sonny snarled, his stance more than ready to lash out at his brother a second time. 'Did you honestly think that I was just going to let this go. Are you that deluded that you thought I would allow you to drag my daughter down with you, that I'd give this fiasco of yours my blessing?'

'For crying out loud,' Carla continued to scream. 'Will you just stop; it had nothing to do with him. It was my idea, Dad, I keep telling you that.'

Rubbing at his jaw, Jonny gave Terri's hand a squeeze and giving a slight shake of his head to reassure her that no real harm had been done, he opened and closed his mouth several times to make sure that his jaw was still in working order and that no lasting damage had been caused. As it was, Sonny had a blinding right hook on him and the fact Jonny was still standing was more than enough to tell him that perhaps Sonny hadn't hit out quite as hard as he could have done, or maybe had even wanted to for that matter. 'I don't know what you're having a dig at me for,' Jonny grumbled as he dabbed at the corner of his lip. On seeing traces of blood smeared across his fingertips he cursed under his breath. 'I know I might be a lot of things, but I'm not entirely clueless. I've been in this game long enough to know what I'm doing.' He jerked his head towards his niece. 'Neither Carla nor Tommy Jr will be coming with us tonight.'

'What?' Carla's eyes almost popped out of her head. 'What do you mean I'm not coming,' she demanded. 'It was my idea. You can't push me out.'

Jonny sighed and as he lifted his shoulders into a shrug he gave his brother a wary glance, his body still tense as though he was anticipating Sonny to start swinging for him again. 'You're staying here. And as for Tommy Jr the same goes for him too. You were the one who told me to make amends with Cameron. Well,' he shrugged, 'this is me trying to put things right between us, I can't do any more than that.'

'I can't believe this,' Carla seethed.

'Well, you'd best start to believe it,' Jonny stated, his voice brooking no arguments.

As he shook out the tension in his fist, Sonny shook his head. 'You're still in way over your head,' he said, his temper slowly dissipating. 'Even if you manage to get your hands on those diamonds, do you honestly think that the Tuckers will let you walk away from this unscathed. You'll be on their territory; they'll see it as a piss-take of the highest order.'

'Probably,' Jonny agreed. 'It's more than likely going to kick off.'

'You reckon?' Sonny replied with a hint of sarcasm. 'And I suppose you think that you can handle that, do you?' he asked.

Jonny gave a nonchalant shrug. 'Probably.'

The nerve at the side of Sonny's jaw pulsated. 'Probably isn't good enough!' he roared. Rubbing the palm of his hand over his face, he momentarily closed his eyes. 'Call it off,' he pleaded. 'For once in your life do the right thing. Get on the blower and tell them it's not worth the hassle. Find another target, anything but this.'

'No.' Jonny shook his head and as his tongue darted out, he licked at his bleeding lip then shoved a hand into his pocket and leaned casually against the desk. 'It's not gonna happen. I've had it up to here with the Tuckers,' he said, motioning to his head with his free hand. 'If anyone is going down it'll be them.'

'So you reckon you've got all of this sussed out then, do you?'

Jonny nodded.

Sonny narrowed his eyes and motioning towards the forecourt, his gaze raked over the cars parked there. 'What about transport?'

'What about it?'

His patience wearing thin, Sonny motioned outside. 'Where's the getaway car?'

Glancing towards Terri, Jonny shrugged again. 'We'll take my car.'

'And that's your masterplan is it?' shaking his head, Sonny gave an incredulous laugh. 'For someone who was supposedly our "get-away driver",' he said, using his fingers as quotation marks. 'I would have thought obtaining a vehicle would have been high up on your list of priorities.'

Jonny gave an irritated sigh. 'I'm not a miracle worker. And unless it's escaped your notice, I've not exactly had any help planning this job out, have I?' He ran his hand through his hair and shook his head. 'It will have to do. I haven't got the time to get us anything else.'

Sonny's lips curled into a snarl. 'Come on,' he growled, tapping his temple. 'Surely you're not this stupid. What are you trying to do, lead the Tuckers – not to mention the filth – back to us?'

Crossing his arms over his chest, Jonny was thoughtful. As much as he hated to admit it, Sonny was right. It had always been an unspoken rule that they didn't use their own cars on a job, the risk of being caught was too great, especially if the getaway vehicle could be traced back to one of them. 'Maybe I could send Tommy Jr out,' he said, pulling out his phone as though he were contemplating the idea. 'Knowing that lairy little bastard, he'll more than likely come back with a Porsche and draw even more attention to ourselves.'

Closing his eyes in distress, Sonny rubbed at the nape of his neck. 'You're not seriously considering this, are you?'

Jonny gave a calculated smile. 'You can bet your life I am. I taught that kid everything he knows,' he said as he wandered across to the other side of the office to make a call.

Moments later he switched off his phone and shoved the device back into his pocket. 'Sorted,' he grinned, turning back to look at his brother. 'Is there anything else you want to have a dig at me about?'

Defeated, Sonny shook his head.

'Right then.' Jonny rubbed his hands together. 'If you don't mind,' he jerked his head towards the door, the smile instantly slipping from his face, 'looks like I've got a job to get ready for.'

Running his tongue across his teeth Sonny looked between his daughter and Terri. 'You're going to regret this,' he stated.

Jonny gave a chilling laugh. 'We'll see,' he winked. 'When I come back with those diamonds then we'll see which one of us regrets it because I can tell you right now it sure as hell isn't going to be me.'

13

Switching off his mobile phone, Tommy Jr drained his drink, then placing the empty glass on the bar, he slipped off the bar stool. 'Cheers Rina,' he called out as he set off across the pub.

From behind the bar, Rina waved her hand in acknowledgement and as the door to the pub opened and Lenny Tucker followed by several of his firm members sauntered inside, she snapped her head around to look at her business partners, Ricky and Jamie Tempest.

'Fuck me, Rina.' Lenny exclaimed loud enough so that the patrons could hear. 'Standards are slipping.' He focused his hard gaze upon Tommy Jr. 'From what I've heard, this lot will shag just about anything, including their own family. Ain't that right you fucking notright.'

'Who are you calling a notright?' Tommy Jr snapped, his back instantly up as it always was whenever he found himself within the Tuckers' close proximity. Aware that the entire pub had heard what had been said about him, his cheeks flamed red, and shame coursed through his veins. As much as it was true that his parents were first cousins, how the Tuckers had come by the information he had no idea, it certainly wasn't something they broadcast to those outside of the family.

'Hey, enough of that,' Rina called out, her voice strained. 'We don't want any trouble in here.'

Lenny spread open his arms. 'Who said anything about trouble.' He turned to look back at Tommy Jr and gave a calculated smirk. 'I was only stating facts. If I'm being honest, I'm more surprised that the inbred bastard hasn't got two heads.'

'Oi,' pushing himself away from the bar Ricky Tempest made his way forward, his eyes as equally hard, 'you heard what Rina said. We don't want any trouble in here, so either watch your mouth or get the fuck out of my pub.'

Giving a light laugh Lenny held up his hands. 'There's no need for that.' Stepping aside he allowed Tommy Jr to pass him by. 'I'm all for helping out the waifs and strays,' he grinned. 'And from the look of things, this numpty here is more like a fucking mongrel.'

'You bastard.' Spinning back around, Tommy Jr charged forward and before his fist could make contact with Lenny's face, he was slammed heavily into the wall by one of Lenny's henchmen.

Lenny chuckled. 'Kids today,' he smirked, glancing around him as though he were talking to a captive audience. 'They haven't got the first fucking clue, have they?' He took a step closer his eyes flashing dangerously. 'By rights, I should smash you into oblivion.'

Tommy Jr snarled and as he struggled to free himself from the heavy's vice-like grips his efforts proved to be futile. 'Yeah, and you'd probably like that, you dirty cunt. I know all about you, and what you and your brother get up to.'

As a deathly silence fell over the pub, Lenny's eyes hardened and without warning he pulled back his arm then smashed his fist into Tommy Jr's gut before proceeding to grab the younger man by the front of his shirt and yank him roughly towards him. 'You know fuck all about me,' he roared, spraying him in spittle as he did so.

Winded by the punch, Tommy Jr groaned. 'I know enough,' he choked out as fought to catch his breath. 'Everyone does.'

As Lenny made to lash out a second time Ricky charged forward, using his considerable strength to haul Lenny several feet away. He stabbed his finger into the man's face. 'I've already warned you once,' he spat, his eyes flashing dangerously. 'Now get out of my boozer and take these muppets with you,' he said, nodding towards the Tuckers' firm.

Pulling himself free, Lenny straightened out his shirt. 'I'm going to have you for this,' he continued to shout, jabbing his forefinger in Tommy Jr's direction. 'You'd best watch your back boy because believe me your days are well and truly numbered, same goes for that family of yours too. The whole fucking lot of you are no better than scum.'

'He told you to get out.' As he casually made his way across the pub Jamie Tempest eyed Lenny with contempt. 'And trust me, we won't be telling you a second time.'

As he looked between the two brothers, Lenny puffed out his chest. 'I'm not some mug,' he shouted.

Jamie laughed. 'Yeah, if you say so.' He nodded towards the door. 'Off you go. Fuck off.'

Making no attempt to move, Lenny glanced around him, and rubbing at the nape of his neck in a bid to hide his humiliation, his lips curled into a snarl.

As Jamie narrowed his eyes, the muscles across his shoulder blades tensed and his hands involuntarily curled into fists. 'Don't make me tell you a second time, because you really won't like the outcome.'

Lenny swallowed deeply, and knowing instinctively that without his brother to back him up he was way out of his depth, his cheeks flamed red. Flicking his head towards the exit indicating for his firm to follow him, he gave Tommy Jr a final glare. 'I'm coming for you,' he warned. 'And believe me, you little prick, you're gonna pay for this.'

Once Lenny and his firm had left the pub, Ricky shook his head, and throwing his arm around Tommy Jr's shoulders he smiled to take the edge off his words. 'What are you playing at, eh? I'm not denying that you're a hard little fucker but sometimes you have to swallow your knob and let it go over your head. Getting into a scrap with Tucker isn't worth the aggro, do you get what I'm saying? For a start he's all mouth and no trousers. Why else do you think he has his so-called firm following him everywhere he goes? He wouldn't know how to have a straightener if it leapt up and bit him on the arse.'

'Yeah, I know.' Tommy Jr groaned and rubbing his hand across his abdomen, he screwed up his face. 'I hate that muggy ponce,' he spat out.

Ricky laughed. 'You're not the only one. He's a tosser, both him and his brother. Everyone knows that.' He motioned towards the door. 'If I were you, I'd give it ten minutes or so before going out there. Just to make sure the bastard has actually fucked off. Or better still, get on the blower and get one of your cousins or uncles to come and back you up.'

Tommy Jr shook his head. 'I can fight my own battles,' he declared with a hint of bravado. 'I'm not scared of that pussy.'

'I didn't say you were,' Ricky argued as he glanced back to the door. 'But next time you might not be so lucky. Tucker was spoiling for a fight, and he had you in his sights. And let's face it, we both know that he won't fight fair. For a start you're heavily outnumbered and he'd use that to his advantage.'

'He's always had it in for me,' Tommy Jr complained. 'He's never made it a secret that he has a problem with me.'

'More of a reason to stay out of his way then,' Ricky answered with a rise of his eyebrows.

'I suppose so.' Not that Tommy Jr actually believed Lenny would have been able to get the better of him, at least not one-on-one, anyway. But that was the Tuckers all over, they needed their firm to back them up, without them they were nothing but cowards. Resigning himself to the fact that he wouldn't be going anywhere for the time being, he took a seat at the bar and rested his chin in his hand.

'Here you go darling.' Rina placed a drink in front of him. 'On the house,' she winked.

'Cheers, Rina.' Taking a sip of the drink, Tommy Jr jerked his thumb behind him. 'I'm sorry about that...'

'Don't be.' Rina flapped her hand, and motioning towards Ricky and Jamie, she flashed a grin. 'You've more than likely made their day. They've been itching for a reason to throw the Tuckers out.' She momentarily paused, and leaning her forearms on the bar she lowered her voice. 'Just be careful okay. I wouldn't want to see you get hurt.'

Tommy Jr sniggered. 'I'm alright, it was a lucky punch, that's all,' he answered, ignoring the ache in his stomach as he shifted his weight to make himself more comfortable. 'I can take care of myself.'

Rina nodded. 'I don't doubt that sweetheart, not in the slightest,' she said, straightening back up. 'You're a Carter, well, a Johnson,' she corrected, waving her hand dismissively. 'And I know your family well enough to know that you're no pushovers. But even so, it doesn't hurt to be on your guard, to keep your wits about you.' She glanced towards the door and as Ricky's son, Mason, walked into the pub, she lifted her eyebrows and gave a sad smile, the hidden meaning behind her words more than apparent.

Taking the warning on board, Tommy Jr sucked in his bottom lip and nodded. He'd caught glimpses of the scars that covered Mason's arms and he had a sinking feeling that the rest of his body was covered in the same buckle shaped marks. As he wiped away the beads of condensation from his glass, Tommy Jr couldn't help but shoot a glance in Mason's direction. Rumour had it that it had been Mason's own uncle who had inflicted the damage. Whether there was any truth to the gossip, Tommy Jr had no idea, it certainly wasn't a question he was prepared to ask Mason. He thought of his own uncles, Peter and Jake, thankful that his was a close-knit family. They may have their fall outs from time to time, but they still looked out for one another and had each other's backs.

Twenty minutes later he slipped off the bar stool and said his goodbyes. As he made his way outside, he took a cautious glance around him, fully expecting Lenny Tucker to appear out of nowhere and attempt to finish off what he'd started. With no sign of Lenny, nor any of his firm loitering in the car park, Tommy Jr made his way over to where he'd parked his car, eager to get on with the job his uncle had asked him to carry out. Climbing behind the wheel, he cracked his knuckles. He may have been a Johnson, but he took after Jonny when it came to stealing cars. Like Jonny, he had nimble fingers and as of yet he hadn't come across a motor that he couldn't get into. Turning the key in the ignition, he stepped his foot on the accelerator and drove away from the pub, his watchful gaze on the lookout for a target, something inconspicuous so that they wouldn't stand out like a sore thumb and even more than that, something that didn't look as though it would let them down while making their getaway.

* * *

Lenny Tucker was seething. In fact, he was so livid that the colour had drained from his face. Sitting inside his car across the street from the pub he drummed his fingers on the steering wheel, his jaw clenched tight and his beady eyes remaining focused on the entrance. The fact he'd been thrown out of the boozer as though he were a no one grated heavily on his nerves. Both he and his brother had reputations as hard men; they were known to be ruthless, and the fear they instilled amongst the local community was enough to guarantee that they were afforded respect from those around them. And for Ricky and Jamie Tempest to have the audacity to speak to him as though he were the shit beneath their shoe was a piss-take of the highest order. Not that he should have expected anything different in all fairness. From his understanding, the Tempests were so far up the Carter brothers' arses that they would need to be surgically removed and that was the understatement of the century.

He narrowed his eyes and as Tommy Jr exited the pub Lenny's expression became murderous. 'Follow the bastard,' he instructed one of his henchman. 'And make sure to keep me updated.'

A wicked gleam twinkled in the heavy's eyes and straightening up, he tapped the car roof. 'I'm on it, boss,' he answered in a gruff voice before making his way over to where his own car was parked.

As he lit a cigarette Lenny took long, hard drags in quick succession, all the while resisting the urge to lash out at something, or to be more precise, someone. And there was nothing he would like better than to be able to pummel his fists into Tommy Johnson's face. The kid was a mouthy little bastard, and the same went for the rest of his family. Lenny's lips curled into a snarl and as he exhaled two plumes of smoke through his nostrils, he forced himself to calm down. The Carters had had their day, everyone knew that. They were has-beens, their so called reputations nothing more than a distant memory.

Flicking the cigarette butt out of the open window, he started the ignition and drove away, his anger so tangible that he could almost taste it. As he sped through the streets heading in the direction of his brother, Ozzie's house, there was only one thing on his mind and that was revenge. It was about time the Carters realised who they were dealing with. He and Ozzie were no mugs and the quicker the Carters learnt their place, the better it would be for all concerned.

* * *

Sitting in Ozzie Tucker's kitchen, Sadie rested his elbows on the table. In front of him was a magazine, and as he flicked through the articles, eagerly awaiting a headline to catch his attention, he lifted a mug to his lips and took a long sip of tea. He loved nothing more than to lose himself within the pages of a magazine, he'd even go as far as to say that it was one of his favourite pastimes. Before being incarcerated he and his old mum would spend many an evening pouring over the stories, often chuckling at how absurd some of them were. He smiled at the memory, albeit was tinged with sadness. He missed his mum, and he had a feeling that he always would. He would give anything to have her sitting opposite him again, her lips pursed, and her forehead furrowed as she concentrated on the story unravelling before her. Not that she could of course, she barely even knew who he was these days, which considering the circumstances may have been a blessing in disguise. She would have disapproved of Ozzie, he knew that much, and knowing the sharp tongue his mother had once possessed, she wouldn't have been afraid to tell him so to his face too.

On hearing a loud knock at the front door, he looked up, and closing the magazine, he pushed back the chair and got to his feet.

'I'll get it,' he called out to Ozzie as he made his way into the hallway. At the front door he patted down his hair then flung open the door, the smile plastered across his face instantly freezing into place. 'Hello, Lenny,' he said with a measure of apprehension.

'Where's Ozzie?' Barging Sadie out of his way, Lenny's lips were curled into a snarl, his hard stare looking Sadie up and down with disgust.

Taken aback, Sadie pointed towards the lounge, his mind reeling. He was under no illusions that Lenny disliked him. The look of disdain he gave whenever they were in one another's company said it all, so much so that Sadie did everything in his power to stay out of Lenny's way, which was no mean feat seeing as he chose to visit his brother on a daily basis.

As Lenny entered the lounge, Sadie held back slightly, eavesdropping. It would be a lie to say that he wasn't a little intrigued to know what was going on.

'I'm going to kill the bastards,' Lenny roared as soon as he entered the lounge.

Sadie's eyes widened and taking a step closer to the door he rested his hand upon his chest, his heart beating ten to the dozen.

'Who?' Ozzie asked, his voice holding a note of confusion.

'Who do you think?' Lenny spat. 'The fucking Carters.'

Through the crack in the door Sadie watched as Lenny stabbed his finger forward, the anger across his face more than enough to make the hairs across Sadie's arms stand upright.

'And that trappy cunt Tommy Johnson is the first on my list.' He began to pace the floor, his expression becoming more and more murderous with each and every step he took. 'The cocky little fucker mugged me off. Made me look like some muppet in front of the entire boozer. And as for the Tempests.' He shook his head, his eyes blazing with fury. 'Those bastards,' he seethed, 'need to be taught a lesson an' all. They need to be reminded of who they're dealing with.' He stopped pacing and turned to look at his brother. 'I want them brought down. All of them, the Carters, the Tempests, the whole fucking caboodle. We run this manor, not those fucking muppets.'

Ozzie flashed a sadistic grin, and pausing to light a cigarette, he exhaled a cloud of smoke above his head. 'What are you getting yourself worked up for.' He pointed the cigarette forward. 'Sooner or later, they're going to get what's coming to them.' He stood up and clasped his brother by the shoulder. 'In fact, by this time tomorrow the Carters will be nothing more than a distant memory.' He gave a wide grin and pulled his brother close. 'As soon as the no-good bastards enter Bernie's gaff they're not going to know what's hit them. And as for that little prick Tommy Johnson, or whatever the fuck his name is, we'll save him for last,' he winked. 'Let him bear witness to the rest of his family getting topped and then you,' he grinned even wider, 'can be the one to do the honours. Make the bastard really suffer, before blowing his head clean off his shoulders. You could even make him dig his own grave first,' he added with a chilling laugh.

As Sadie bit down on his bottom lip, fear gripped at his heart. He was only thankful that the Carters had no intentions of entering Bernie's home. Why would they, when they knew the diamonds were now in Ozzie's possession? Where exactly the jewels were being stored, however, Sadie had no idea. The gems were in the house somewhere, he knew that much but it wasn't in his best interests to be caught snooping or asking too many questions. The last thing he wanted to do was rock the boat and give Ozzie a reason to turn on him. For the most part they had a good relationship, and as unpredictable as Ozzie could be, Sadie knew how to handle him, or rather he knew when to make himself scarce and stay out of his way. He'd had plenty of practice after all, and considering they had once shared a prison cell, he viewed himself to be an expert when it came to Ozzie's mood swings. He had a vicious temper on him and could be laughing one moment, then as if a red mist had descended, he could be screaming, hollering, and threatening all kinds of violence the next. But despite their closeness, Sadie was under no pretence that Ozzie viewed him as disposable. Ozzie had made that fact more than clear to him on numerous occasions and Sadie believed every veiled threat that spilled out of his mouth. If nothing else, Ozzie demanded loyalty and until now Sadie had been more than happy to give it. He catered to Ozzie's every whim and in return was given stability, a home, and the kind of lifestyle that would make most people envious. It was imperative that he did his utmost to make sure that Ozzie had no need to disregard him. As an ex-con and a convicted murderer to boot, he wasn't in the position to start his life over. Who in their right mind would even consider giving him employment. Neither was he as young as he used to be, and other than go back to dancing in a seedy strip club, he had no hope of finding a decent job.

Wandering back to the kitchen he pulled out a chair, sank down onto the seat, then held his head in his hands. As fond of Ozzie as he was, Sadie was unable to condone violence, the mere thought was abhorrent to him. Oh, he knew in a roundabout way that that made him a hypocrite, take Ronald Browning for example. Browning had ruined countless boys' lives – his and Jake Carter's to name but a few, and if Jake hadn't been the one to finally end Browning's life then Sadie would have been more than happy to do the honours. As he picked up his mug and sipped at his tea he began to once again flick through the magazine, all the while keeping one ear out so that he could continue to listen to Ozzie and Lenny's conversation. The only consolation he took from the situation was that any plans the brothers were making would prove to be fruitless, and that the Carters would come to no harm. As a cold shiver spread throughout Sadie's body he swallowed deeply. He could only hope and pray that if Ozzie was to ever find out he had betrayed him then the same could be said for himself, that he too would be able to walk away from the situation unscathed.

* * *

Tommy Jr was grinning from ear to ear as his uncle walked around the car he'd acquired for them. He spread open his arms. 'Well. What do you reckon?'

Jonny nodded and as he returned the smile, he ruffled Tommy Jr's hair. 'Yeah, you did well,' he praised.

As he leaned against the car door Tommy Jr shrugged. 'I mean, it's not exactly something I'd choose for myself but at least it won't let us down, or at least it shouldn't do,' he said with a measure of trepidation as he pushed himself away from the car and gave it the once over. 'I got it started easily enough.' He shoved his hands into his pockets. 'And it's got some power behind it I can tell you that much, we're gonna have no trouble making a getaway.'

Clearing his throat, Jonny looked up. 'About that,' he said, giving the office a sidelong glance. 'I know that I...' He momentarily paused then rubbing at the nape of his neck he began again. 'I know I said you would be coming along with us tonight but...'

Tommy Jr's forehead furrowed and crossing his arms over his chest he turned to face his uncle. 'But what?' he asked.

'The thing is,' Jonny said, lowering his voice as he looked towards the office again. 'Terri is hellbent on waiting here for me and well what with her being pregnant and everything I don't want her to stay here alone.'

'And?' Tommy Jr screwed up his face. 'What's that got to do with me?'

Jonny lifted his eyebrows. 'I need someone to stay here with her.' It was an excuse, of course, and in Jonny's opinion the kindest way to let his great-nephew down seeing just how keen he'd been to take part in his first heist. In a roundabout way Jonny could understand where Tommy Jr was coming from. As a youngster he'd practically had to beg his eldest brother to let him join the family business. He'd even thrown away a promising career as a boxer just to prove how much he wanted to work alongside his brothers, and the amount of grief that had caused his dad didn't bear thinking about.

Breaking his thoughts, Tommy Jr let out an incredulous laugh. 'Leave it out,' he said, looking from his uncle to the office. 'You don't mean me, do you? Because I can tell you right now, I'm not babysitting her.'

'You wouldn't be,' Jonny was quick to answer. 'Carla will be here too.'

'So why do I need to be here?' Tommy Jr's face fell and as Cameron walked out of the office he glared at his father. 'Did my dad put you up to this,' he scowled. 'He did, didn't he?'

'Of course he didn't.' Jonny shook his head.

'What's going on?' Cameron asked once he'd reached them.

Jonny sighed and without answering he turned back to look at his great-nephew. 'I'm asking for a favour,' he said, the lie tripping off his tongue with ease. 'It's not like I can ask anyone else is it. I need your dad and uncles with me, they've got years of experience behind them, and even more than that, if this does end up going tits up, they'll know how to handle the situation.'

'Yeah, but...'

'Just in case the Tuckers should turn up here,' Jonny was quick to add. Not that he actually believed this would be the case, but Tommy wasn't to know that. 'You know how to look after yourself and I trust you to keep Terri safe for me.'

'Can't someone else stay behind?' Tommy Jr grumbled. 'What about Reece?' he said of his older cousin. 'He's only a year or two older than me. Why can't he stay here instead?'

As he glanced across the yard towards Mitchell's son, Reece, Jonny shook his head. 'I need him with me,' he hastily explained.

'Yeah, but I was looking forward to putting the Tuckers in their place. That bastard Lenny Tucker swung for me today.'

As he looked his son over for any visible injuries Cameron

frowned. 'When did this happen?' he asked, his voice becoming hard.

'This afternoon in the boozer.' Rubbing his hand over his stomach, Tommy Jr shrugged. 'Just after I got off the phone to you,' he said, nodding towards his uncle. 'The bastard had the front to call me an inbred mongrel. I wouldn't mind,' he laughed, 'but have you seen the state of him, he's hardly an oil painting is he, looks more like the back end of a bus.'

'What and you didn't think to tell any of us?' Jonny asked through gritted teeth.

The smile slipped from Tommy Jr's face and pulling himself up to his full height he shook his head. 'I didn't need to. I sorted it.'

'That's not the point,' Jonny seethed. He blew out his cheeks then grasped his nephew by the shoulders. 'In future make sure that you let one of us know, okay. What if something had happened to you? We would have been none the wiser.'

'As if,' Tommy Jr chuckled. 'Despite what you lot think of me I'm not a kid,' he added, giving his father a pointed look.

'I'm being serious,' Jonny warned. 'There's a lot of bad blood between our families and you know as well as I do that those bastards would do anything to score a point.'

'Yeah, I suppose so.' Nodding his head Tommy Jr gave a sheepish grin and glancing towards the office he sighed. 'I'll stay here,' he said somewhat reluctantly, his shoulders drooping. 'But I'm not happy about it.'

'You don't need to be happy,' Jonny retorted. 'Just make sure that you keep an eye on Terri for me.'

As he watched his son head into the office Cameron sighed. 'Thanks for that,' he said, motioning towards the portable cabin. 'Him staying here is a weight off my mind. He might think otherwise but up here,' he said, tapping his temple, 'he's still a kid, he's nowhere near ready for this. Maybe in a year or two things will be different but right now,' he squashed his lips together and gave a slight shake of his head, 'he's still got a lot to learn.'

Jonny sighed. 'Yeah, well,' he gave a shrug then leant back against the Audi., 'I doubt that he'll see it that way.' He sighed then glanced towards the office. 'But if it's any consolation, he is too young. I know we were all roughly the same age when we started out, but it was different back then. We had a different upbringing I suppose, or at least some of us did,' he said, referring to the fact Cameron had been brought up in Marbella and had spent his younger years living in his grandfather's villa. 'We had no other choice but to claw our way out of the dirt and try to make something of ourselves.'

Cameron nodded and choosing to ignore the barbed quip about his supposedly wonderful upbringing, he nodded towards the car. 'At least he turned up with something practical. I had visions of him coming back with a Lamborghini.'

'There is that,' Jonny chuckled as he made his way towards the office, the feud between the two men temporarily forgotten about. 'Maybe there's hope for him yet,' he winked over his shoulder.

14

Diane Adams was practically frothing at the mouth she was that angry, and as she followed her husband from room to room it took everything inside of her not to lash out at him.

'What do you mean the Tuckers are coming here?' she shouted.

Bernie rolled his eyes. 'Exactly what I said,' he groaned. 'They've got some business to attend to.'

Diane's mouth dropped open. 'In our house?' she shrieked.

'Yes,' Bernie shouted back. 'How many more times do I need to tell you?'

Barely able to get her head around what her husband was saying, Diane placed her hands on her hips. 'This isn't adding up,' she spat at him. 'What aren't you telling me? Just a few days ago, Lenny Tucker beat you black and blue and now you've given him an open invitation to our home.'

Bernie hesitated. How could he even begin to tell her the true meaning of the Tuckers' visit; that her daughter along with her father and the rest of the Carters were about to feel the full force of Lenny and Ozzie's wrath. 'Just stay in the bedroom,' he ordered. 'And no matter what you hear don't come out.'

Diane's jaw dropped a second time. 'What the hell is going on?' she hissed. Goose flesh covered her arms, and she rubbed her hands up and down her limbs in an attempt to bring some warmth back into her body. 'You're starting to scare me now. Are we in danger?'

Rubbing his hand over the greying stubble that covered his jaw, Bernie shook his head.

'Then what is it?' Diane cried. 'Isn't it enough that I'm going to lose my home? Don't lie to me on top of it.'

Bernie averted his gaze. 'I can't,' he said, his eyes pleading with her to understand the predicament he'd been forced into. 'If I could tell you I would, but I can't. I'm sorry.'

Screwing up her face, Diane opened her mouth to answer when the headlights from a car shone through the bedroom window and halted her in her tracks. 'Is it them?' she cried rushing over to the window and peering outside.

On seeing two cars pull onto the drive she turned back to look at her husband, her expression a mixture of both fear and confusion. 'Bernie,' she pleaded with him, 'please will you just tell me what's going on. I know that we've had our differences over the years but I'm still your wife, I deserve to know the truth.'

Bernie shook his head. She could say that again; their marriage wasn't one that he would call a match made in heaven. They'd given up pretending they were happy a long time ago and ever since Carla had moved out of the house, Bernie went out of his way to stay out of his wife's path, preferring not to have to deal with her on a daily basis. Her voice went right through his head, and that was without her constant nagging. He could have given her the moon and it wouldn't have been enough. She'd made it more than clear that she didn't trust him as far as she could throw him and her constant need to be with him was suffocating. He needed space, needed air to breathe and even more than that, he didn't want a constant reminder of how much he'd fucked up his life by marrying her. Giving Diane a look of warning to stay put he closed the bedroom door and made his way wearily down the stairs.

At the front door he momentarily closed his eyes then took a deep breath before pulling the door wide open. 'Ozzie.' He nodded, plastering a false smile across his face.

Ozzie Tucker breezed across the threshold. 'Nice gaff,' he grinned. 'Bit ostentatious for my liking but I can see why someone like you would like it.'

Bernie gave a small smile, unsure if Ozzie was actually complimenting the house or taking the piss out of him. You never could tell with Ozzie, he was the type of man who could slit your throat and smile while doing so.

'Come on in.' He watched as the Tuckers' firm traipsed in behind their boss, his eyebrows ever so slightly knotting together. 'Where's Lenny?' he asked as he looked back to the cars on the drive.

Taking a seat on the sofa, Ozzie made himself at home and pulling out his mobile phone he tapped the screen before giving a calculated smirk. 'He had something else to deal with,' he said, his eyes glinting with amusement. 'Or rather someone,' he chuckled as his henchmen sniggered at the hidden inuendo. 'Let's just say that we're covering all bases.' He glanced back down at the screen, his expression becoming one of glee. 'And from the look of things,' he said, rubbing his hands together with excitement. 'The Carters' scrapyard is a hive of activity. When they turn up here, the bastards won't know what's hit them.'

As he swallowed Bernie nodded, his blood running cold. Giving an involuntary shiver, he was filled with what could only be described as complete and utter horror and as Ozzie and his firm began to take a series of guns out of a holdall, a mixture of both shame and guilt washed over him.

Not only had Sonny Carter been his childhood friend, but he'd been his only friend. It was no secret that the Carter brothers didn't trust outsiders and yet he and Sonny had formed a bond that had been so tight nothing had been able to come between them, or at least it hadn't, until he'd overstepped the mark and laid a finger on Sonny's wife.

A hard lump formed in Bernie's throat that he swallowed down whilst blinking away the tears that threatened to blind his vision. He'd already ruined Sonny's life once and now... he gave an inward shudder and tore his eyes away from the firearms, hating himself for what was to come. Taking Sonny's wife was one thing, but when it came to actually extinguishing his life it was a different ball game altogether, one that he knew for sure he wouldn't be able to bear witness to.

The last thing Bernie had ever meant to do was cause Sonny pain, he'd loved him as a friend, like a brother. Still to this day he could recall the cold shiver that ran down his spine when Sonny had confronted him about the affair. In that instant, he'd known that their friendship was over, that there could be no coming back from something so heinous. And as easy as it would have been to lie and deny that anything untoward had taken place between himself and his best friend's wife, he just couldn't bring himself to do it, he couldn't hurt Sonny any more than he already had. A part of him wondered if Diane had purposely encouraged Carla to tell her father what had been going on as a means of keeping Bernie close, a way for her to dig her claws into him even further. He'd put nothing past her, she'd always been a spiteful, vengeful woman. One thing he did know was that he didn't love her any more, some days he didn't even like her and if it wasn't for Carla, Sonny's daughter, he would have had it away on his toes years ago.

For the most part Carla was the only reason he'd stuck around; he owed Sonny that much. And as hostile as Carla was towards him, he did love her. She wasn't only his stepdaughter, she was also an extension of Sonny, his flesh and blood. And she was so like her father that at times it took Bernie's breath away. He'd give anything to turn back the clock, and one thing he did know for certain was that if he had his time over again, he would never have so much as looked at Diane, let alone touched her.

Retreating into the kitchen, Bernie leant against the kitchen worktop. Pulling out his mobile phone he scrolled down his contact list. Despite his considerable wealth, Sonny wasn't one to flash his money around. He didn't feel the need to own the latest gadgets, even his car was quite modest considering he had the money to splash out on something that was guaranteed to turn heads. As for his home, he may have lived in an up-and-coming area but he'd bought his apartment at a time when the area was still considered undesirable. In the years that followed Sonny had made millions from his investment, and Bernie was happy for him, not that he'd ever had the opportunity to tell him so. They'd not been in one another's company since Carla's twenty-first birthday party and even then, the atmosphere between them had been strained. Sonny had barely even looked at him, let alone allowed himself to be drawn into a civil conversation.

His finger paused over Sonny's number; he wasn't even so sure if the number was still in service, but he had to try and warn him he decided, he owed his former best friend that much. Taking a quick glance in the direction of the lounge he eased open the back door and stepped outside before walking several feet away from the house. Then taking a deep breath, he pressed dial and brought the device up to his ear, hoping more than anything that Sonny would actually answer the call.

* * *

Jonny Carter was quiet and as his nephews chatted amongst themselves the atmosphere in the scrapyard office sizzled from a combination of both nerves and excitement. Chewing on his thumbnail, Jonny went over the robbery, checking that everything was in place, and more importantly, that he hadn't forgotten anything. Unused to this side of the business, Jonny's stomach was tied in knots. In the past, the responsibility for making sure that everything went to plan and that all possible scenarios had been covered would have fallen upon Jimmy's shoulders and until now, Jonny hadn't realised just how stressful the planning of the heists actually were, not that he would have ever admitted that fact out loud. He began to mentally tick off everything they needed. They had the car, the guns, balaclavas, gloves. He looked up. 'Have you all got your gloves?'

He watched as his nephews each pulled out a pair of gloves and nodded. He'd forgotten something, he was sure he had. 'Did you make sure that the car had diesel?' he asked, addressing his nephew.

'Of course I did,' Tommy Jr groaned. 'I'm not stupid.'

Jonny nodded again and as his forehead furrowed, he went back to chewing on his thumbnail before looking up a second time. 'Are your phones switched off?'

He watched as they pulled out their phones, each of them confirming that the devices were indeed switched off.

'Are you okay?'

He turned to look at Terri and as she reached out for his hand, he gave it a gentle squeeze. 'Yeah.' He gave a small smile then cleared his throat. 'Like I said, the job will be a piece of piss.'

It was a lie and they both knew it. She gave him a smile and he nodded across to where Carla was casually chatting with her cousins. 'You'll be alright here, won't you?'

Terri gave a nervous laugh and as she looked in the direction of both Carla and Tommy Jr, she gave a nod. 'We'll be fine. You don't need to worry about me.'

'Yeah I know,' Jonny sighed, although it would be fair to say he would have been a lot less worried if she'd done as he'd asked and stayed at home. He glanced at his watch, then releasing Terri's hand, he got to his feet. 'Right, you lot,' he said as he stuffed his own gloves and balaclava into a rucksack before hauling the bag up onto his shoulder. 'Time to go.'

As his nephews traipsed out of the office, Jonny paused at the door. 'Make sure that you keep this door locked,' he ordered Tommy Jr, then pulling Terri into his arms he kissed the top of her head.

'Be careful,' she whispered in his ear, her voice ever so slightly cracking as she swallowed down her emotion. 'And promise me that you won't take any unnecessary risks. I need you to come back in one piece, and this baby,' she said, placing her hand on her bump, 'needs his or her dad.'

'I thought you said it was a girl,' Jonny teased.

'I mean it,' Terri said as she continued to cling to him. 'We both need you.'

Jonny sighed. 'Don't worry I'll be careful,' he promised, giving Terri a small smile as he tried in vain to prise her arms from around his neck. At the door he paused. 'Don't forget,' he warned his nephew, 'keep this door looked at all times.'

'Yeah, I know.' Tommy Jr rolled his eyes. 'You don't have to keep telling me. I'll make sure that it stays locked.'

Jonny nodded then giving Terri one last look he made his way outside, walked across the forecourt then climbed into the car and turned on the ignition, all the while blissfully unaware of Lenny Tucker's car that was parked less than forty feet away from the scrapyard.

* * *

Sonny Carter was deep in thought and as he sat at the bar in The Merry Fiddlers, he rested his chin in his hand whilst his free hand absentmindedly wiped away the beads of condensation from his glass.

'Penny for them?' Rina said.

Sonny looked up and ever so slightly frowned.

'You were miles away,' Rina said, giving a soft smile.

Wiping his hand across his face, Sonny shrugged. 'It's nothing,' he answered with a sigh. 'I was just thinking.'

Rina rested her forearms upon the bar. 'I gathered as much.' Lowering her voice she raised her eyebrows. 'Do you want to talk about whatever it is that's troubling you? They do say a problem shared is a problem halved.'

Thinking it over, Sonny shook his head. As close as he and Rina were becoming, the last thing he wanted to do was drag her into his family's troubles. He reached out for her hand and gave it a reassuring squeeze. 'Trust me you wouldn't want to know.'

Alarm filtered across Rina's face and straightening up, she wrenched her hand free. 'Is it something to do with your ex-wife paying you a visit.'

Sonny screwed up his face. 'Diane,' he exclaimed. 'Why the fuck would I be thinking about her?'

Rina's cheeks flamed red. 'I don't know,' she snapped. 'You tell me?'

About to open his mouth to answer, Sonny's mobile phone began to ring. Digging his hand into his pocket he pulled out the device, his heart practically beating out of his chest as a wave of nausea washed over him. It had to be Jonny or one of his nephews, he decided as the tiny hairs on the back of his neck stood upright. Something must have gone wrong, just as he'd instinctively known that it would. Had the Tucker brothers caught them in the act, or could the old bill have been staking the property out and caught them red-handed with the diamonds in their possession? But instead of his brothers' or nephews' names flashing across the screen as he'd expected, the name that was displayed was enough to make Sonny involuntarily curl his hand into a fist. 'I have to take this,' he said as he slipped off the bar stool and wandered across to the other side of the pub so that he could speak in private.

Answering the call, he took a deep breath then brought the phone up to his ear. 'What the fuck do you want?' he asked, his voice becoming instantly cold.

* * *

Bernie was practically hyperventilating by the time Sonny answered the call.

'Please,' he cried. 'I'm begging you. Don't put the phone down. Hear me out.'

He took note of the hardness in Sonny's voice and after hastily glancing back towards the house Bernie closed his eyes in distress. 'Don't,' he warned. 'Please, whatever you do, don't come after the diamonds. The Tuckers are waiting for you, they're tooled up. And Lenny...' his voice trailed off as the back door opened and one of Ozzie's henchmen stepped out of the house his eyes narrowed into slits.

'Who are you on the phone to?' he called out his voice hard.

Bernie's blood ran cold. He'd been rumbled and gripping onto the phone even harder, his breath came out in short, sharp puffs, his eyes wide with fear. 'Lenny isn't here,' he stuttered into the phone as the henchman walked across the grass towards him. 'I don't know for sure where he is, but I've got a feeling, an intuition that he's...'

The henchman neared closer; his head tilted to the side as he studied Bernie. 'Who the fuck are you talking to?' he repeated.

'I think he's staking out the scrapyard,' Bernie screamed into the phone as the heavy made a grab for the device.

Having seized the phone, the henchman stared down at the screen. 'Carter,' he spat, jerking his head up to look at Bernie. 'You no good grass,' he began to roar. 'You were on the blower to Carter.'

Bernie swallowed deeply and as he glanced around him desperately searching for an escape route his mind wandered to Diane. He may not love her, but despite his ill feelings towards her she was still his wife. How could he leave her behind, or more to the point how could he leave her alone with a nutcase like Ozzie Tucker? 'I...' he began as looked towards the house and took note of the fact that the heavies shouts had brought Ozzie and the remaining henchmen outside to investigate what all the commotion was about. 'This is wrong,' he said, his tone becoming pleading. 'No matter who they are or what they may have done, the Carters don't deserve this.'

The henchman laughed and in that instant Bernie's insides turned to liquid. He should have known that his pleas would fall upon deaf ears and that the Tuckers' firm were just as barbaric as both Lenny and Ozzie were, and that they revelled in inflicting as much damage as their bosses did.

'This ponce was on the blower to Carter,' he called over his shoulder, his voice holding a note of excitement.

As he snapped his head towards Ozzie, Bernie took the split-second decision to make a run for it, not that he managed to get very far. Before he'd even reached the panelled fence surrounding the property, he'd been rugby tackled to the floor, and as his chin collided with the gravelled ground the impact forced one of his teeth to slice through his bottom lip. Blood filled his mouth and as the iron scent assaulted his nostrils his fingernails raked through the pebbles and mud as he desperately tried in vain to claw himself away from Ozzie.

'You sly fucker,' Ozzie hissed. So intense was his rage that his eyes bulged and the vein at the side of his head looked as though it were in grave danger of bursting. Pulling back his foot, his steel toe capped boot connected with Bernie's already fractured ribs. 'I always said you couldn't be trusted.' He kicked out again even harder, spraying Bernie in spittle as he continued to shout. 'That you'd fucking betray us.'

Barely able to catch his breath, Bernie gasped for air, the pain that ripped through his ribcage rendering him incapacitated. 'No,' he cried as he lifted his hand in the air in an attempt to stop the beating. 'No.' He coughed and as blob of bright red blood landed on the gravel beside him, he closed his eyes. No matter how much he might want to, he had a sinking feeling that this was one situation he wouldn't be able to talk his way out of. He was guilty as charged. He'd given Sonny the heads-up, had warned him that Lenny Tucker was coming for him and as Ozzie kicked out a third and fourth time his last conscious thought before everything turned black was that of his old friend Sonny Carter.

15

In disbelief Sonny stared down at his phone, his mind whirling. Around him revellers chatted and laughed amongst themselves, their voices loud to his ears, and as he looked up and locked eyes with Rina, the colour drained from his face.

Rina tilted her head to the side, her expression one of confusion as she studied him and in that moment, Sonny swallowed deeply, barely able to get his head around what Bernie had just told him.

He glanced back down at the phone and taking note of the dark screen he hastily pushed the device back into his pocket. Then without giving Rina so much as an explanation he ran from the pub.

His daughter and great-nephew, not to mention Terri, were at the scrapyard. Fear engulfed him and as he jumped into his car, he rammed the key into the ignition and sped out of the car park, swerving across the road as he did so to avoid the oncoming traffic.

In a wild panic he thumped his fist upon the steering wheel. 'Get out of my way,' he screamed as he narrowly missed ploughing headfirst into a car that had stopped at the junction. Still, he didn't slow down, how could he when his daughter's life could very well be in danger? Instead, he pressed his foot down even further on the accelerator.

Momentarily taking his eyes off the road he felt inside his jacket pocket, pulled out his phone and then began frantically jabbing at the buttons.

'Danny,' he yelled into the phone once Danny McKay had answered his call. 'Meet me at the scrapyard. It's the Tuckers,' he hastily explained. 'Carla's in danger.'

Ending the call, he made a second call to his twin brother, Mitchell, filling him in on the situation. By the time he flung the phone onto the passenger seat he was beside himself with worry. 'Please let me make it in time,' he repeated over and over like a mantra.

* * *

Switching off his mobile phone Danny McKay ran his hand over his face.

'What's wrong?' her expression one of concern, Danny's wife, Stacey, sat forward on the sofa. 'What's happened?'

Danny shook his head and casting his son a glance, he sighed. 'That was Sonny,' he said, gesturing to his phone. 'There's a problem.'

Looking up from his own mobile phone Logan frowned. 'What kind of problem?'

Without answering Danny shrugged on his jacket and pocketing his car keys, he motioned to the door, 'I have to go.'

'Dad,' Logan reiterated. 'What problem?'

At the lounge door, Danny paused. 'It's Carla,' he answered. 'The Tucker brothers have targeted the scrapyard and Sonny seems to think that she might be there.'

'Oh my God.' Bringing her hand up to her face, Stacey gasped.

'What about my boys,' she cried as she jumped to her feet. 'Are they involved?'

Danny shook his head a second time. 'I don't know, Sonny didn't mention them. As far as I know Carla is the only one at the office.'

'I'm coming with you,' Logan declared, his voice full of panic as he began to pull on his trainers.

'And so am I,' Stacey bristled as she gathered her coat and shoes.

'No,' Danny's voice held a note of authority and holding up his hand as though to keep both his wife and son at bay he shook his head. 'I'm not having you anywhere near the scrapyard. I don't know what I'll be walking into, the Tuckers could be kicking off.' He ran his hand over the stubble covering his jaw. 'For all I know they could be tooled up.'

'I said, I'm coming with you,' Logan protested, standing up to his father. 'If Carla is in danger then I need to be there, she's my...' The words died in his throat as though it had suddenly occurred to him that he'd walked away from her, that he'd given up on their relationship. 'I have to be there,' he argued. 'And nothing you say or do is going to stop me.'

About to argue the case Danny hesitated. If it had been his Stacey at the scrapyard, he would have moved heaven and earth to make sure that she hadn't been harmed. Against his better judgement, he relented. 'Okay, but if this turns into some heavy shit, I want you out of there is that understood?'

Logan nodded, not that he actually intended to take heed of his father's warning. No one and nothing would be able to keep him away. He may not have been a part of his father's world but that didn't mean he was afraid of his own shadow, that he didn't know how to look after himself. It was as exactly as Carla had stated, he was Danny's McKay's son and he had more of his father in him than he liked to admit, sometimes even to himself.

As she made to shove past her husband Stacey's expression was a mixture of both concern and determination.

'No Stace.' Gently pushing Stacey back into the room, Danny shook his head.

'But...' Stacey's jaw dropped. 'My boys,' she blurted out. 'They could be at the scrapyard; they could be in danger.' Her eyes widened even further. 'Tommy Jr,' she said of her grandson. 'What if he's caught up in this?'

'I said no.' Danny's eyes hardened and tossing his car keys across to his son he jerked his head towards the front door indicating for Logan to unlock the car. 'Don't fight me on this,' he begged of her.

Tears sprang to Stacey's eyes. 'But...'

Danny sighed. He could almost taste his wife's fear. If anyone knew the dangers of the underworld then it was her. Not only had she lost her first husband to his world but also a brother. 'If the boys are involved then you'll be the first to know, okay?' he promised her. 'I'll personally come back and get you.'

Stacey nodded as she helplessly watched her husband leave the house before tearing across the room. Snatching up her mobile phone she tapped at the screen then pressed dial. To her dismay, both Peter and Jake's phones were switched off and as concern gnawed in the pit of her stomach, she began to pace the room, knowing full well what it meant. Fear coiled its way around her insides. If her sons were taking part in a heist they wouldn't have taken Tommy Jr with them no matter how much he would have begged them to let him take part. If anything, they would have told him to stay behind and wait for them, and where else would he have waited other than the scrapyard.

Grabbing her car keys Stacey headed for the front door. Danny may have been her husband but that didn't mean she took orders from him. She was a grown woman for Christ's sake, not a child, and when it came to the lives of her sons and grandson, she was more than prepared to fight him tooth and nail.

No matter what he did, Sadie was unable to relax. Even his beloved magazines held no interest for him, and after reading the same sentence more than half a dozen times he finally gave in, closed the magazine and began to busy himself instead. Every surface in Ozzie's kitchen gleamed and filling the sink with hot soapy water he opened the cupboard and began to pull out a series of mugs, not that they were in anyway dirty, he just needed something to do, something to keep his mind occupied.

Rinsing the mugs underneath the tap he gave the heavy, Ozzie had instructed to guard the house, a furtive glance. His presence unnerved Sadie even further, and that, coupled with the fact that at any given moment the Carters could burst through the front door, was enough to send him into a heightened state of panic.

Sadie cleared his throat. 'Would you like a cuppa?' he asked as he lifted the kettle and proceeded to fill it to the brim with cold water.

The heavy looked up from his newspaper and nodded. 'May as well,' he answered as he kicked his legs out in front of him and made himself comfortable.

Sadie gave a small smile, his eyes automatically drifting to the front door. Noticing the action, the heavy pulled in his legs, leaned forward and followed Sadie's gaze.

'I expect Ozzie will be back soon,' Sadie said, in an attempt to diffuse the situation. 'No doubt he'll want feeding.' He opened the fridge and began rummaging around, all the while silently berating himself. He had to get a grip and fast, before he gave the game away and alerted the heavy to the fact that all was not well, or to put a finer point on things, that the Carters were aware the diamonds had been moved and had no intention of turning up at Bernie's home. Pulling out a steak he slammed it onto the kitchen counter then glanced over his shoulder almost sighing with relief to see that the heavy had gone back to reading his newspaper.

Opening the cupboard again Sadie grabbed a jar of seasoning and just as he was about to uncap the lid the sound of wood splintering made him gasp out loud, the glass jar slipping from his fingers and smashing to smithereens on the linoleum floor.

The heavy jumped up from his seat, his mouth falling open as he looked from Sadie, then to the front door. Hindered by his heavy frame, his movements were slow and he'd barely taken a step across the kitchen when several masked gunmen burst inside.

In the chaos that ensued Sadie watched the scenes unfold, his eyes wide and his body trembling. No matter how much he may have been expecting the Carters to put in an appearance, the reality of their arrival was so much more terrifying than anything he could have ever imagined.

'Where are the diamonds?' one of them shouted as he roughly slammed a shotgun into the side of the heavy's head.

'I don't know.' There was a quiver to the heavy's voice, his bloated face becoming pale as he held up his hands in surrender. 'It's the truth. I don't fucking know,' he screamed his expression one of sheer terror.

Despite the tremor that racked Sadie's body he gripped onto the back of the chair, his knuckles turning deathly white. 'Don't hurt us,' he pleaded, his eyes locking with one of the gunmen. He'd recognise the man's eyes anywhere, and so he should, seeing as he'd done time for him. Jake Carter.

Swallowing deeply, he discreetly motioned towards the ceiling knowing for a fact that the diamonds hadn't been hidden in the kitchen or lounge.

With a jerk of his head the gunman who held a firearm to the heavy's head threw across a rucksack and indicated for a search of the upper floor. Three of the men raced from the kitchen, their footsteps were heavy as they scrambled up the stairs and began the process of tearing the bedrooms apart.

Sadie's body ever so slightly sagged and as his fingers relaxed their grip, he cast a nervous glance towards the two remaining men. One he knew for certain was Jake Carter and the other... he took in his height and build: muscular yet toned. He was young too, Sadie decided, perhaps early to mid-thirties. He knew for a fact it wasn't Jimmy Carter. He'd known Jimmy from old and although it would be fair to say they hadn't exactly been what he would describe as friends, they had known one another on a first name basis. He continued to study the man; he had a confidence about him, the type of confidence that could only come from many years of experience, a cockiness that Sadie had a feeling was warranted. Inwardly Sadie smiled. There was no one else it could be other than the youngest of the brothers, Jonny Carter.

A shout from upstairs caused the gunman to stiffen and with a flick of his head he sent Jake to investigate.

'You won't get away with this,' the heavy spat in a moment of bravery. 'The Tuckers will hunt you down.'

The gunman, or rather Jonny Carter as Sadie now knew him to be, laughed, and pressing the firearm even further into the heavy's temple he leaned in closer, his voice when he spoke, low and menacing. 'Unless you want your head blown clean off your shoulders, I'd suggest you shut the fuck up because I'm really not in the mood to listen to your shit.'

The heavy swallowed. And as beads of perspiration coated his forehead and upper lip, he squirmed in his seat, his earlier bravado all too quickly evaporating.

Moments later footsteps could be heard racing back down the

stairs and as one of the men stood in the doorway to the kitchen, he lifted his eyebrows and gave a nod of his head.

Jonny nodded and as he glanced towards Sadie, he gave him a surreptitious wink. 'Looks like that's our cue to leave.' There was a hint of amusement to his voice and shoving the gun roughly into the heavy's head as a warning not to try and be a hero he began backing away. 'I would say it's been a pleasure, but...' he gave a dramatic pause. 'We all know that'd be a lie.'

With those parting words he charged back out of the house leaving Sadie and the heavy with no other choice but to stare help-lessly after him. A matter of minutes was all it had taken for the Carters to locate the gems and then leave as quickly as they'd arrived. For a few moments, Sadie and the heavy were rendered speechless, each of them too stunned to even form words, let alone string a sentence together.

Finally, the heavy swiped his hand across his sweating brow. 'Fucking hell,' he choked out.

Sadie nodded. He could say that again. He lifted his hand out in front of him, and taking note of the tremor that still tore through his body, he glanced down to look at the broken glass at his feet. 'I suppose we'd better let Ozzie know that we've been turned over.'

The heavy's face paled even further, a sight that Sadie would have never believed possible, considering his skin had already taken on a sickly, almost greyish-white pallor; the shock of what had just taken place draining him of his usual flushed complexion.

In a moment of sympathy Sadie nodded down to the broken glass. 'Perhaps we should have a little tidy up first and get rid of this mess. Maybe even have that cup of tea before we give Ozzie a call.'

The heavy nodded and it took all of Sadie's willpower not to smile. Of course, there was a method to his madness – he wanted to give the Carters a head start, wanted them as far away from the house as was humanly possible before Ozzie and Lenny Tucker were informed of what had taken place, and more importantly, that the diamonds were gone.

* * *

'For crying out loud,' Carla snapped, 'you're a nervous wreck. Will you just sit down for five minutes. You're going to end up wearing the poxy carpet out.'

Coming to a halt, Terri span around. 'Of course I'm bloody scared,' she spat back. 'The man I love could be in danger.'

Carla's eyes hardened. 'And they're my family,' she said of her uncle and cousins. 'Getting yourself worked up isn't going to help matters, is it?'

Terri continued pacing. 'I can't sit down,' she protested as she placed a hand upon her lower back in an attempt to ease the niggling ache in her back. 'I'm going out of my mind with worry.' She glanced at her watch. 'What's taking them so long? Shouldn't they be back by now?'

It took everything inside of Carla to stop herself from rolling her eyes. 'They've only been gone twenty minutes,' she answered through gritted teeth. 'They could be hours yet.'

Terri's eyes widened and placing her hand over her heart she resumed pacing. 'I don't know if my nerves can take this,' she proclaimed. 'My blood pressure is bound to be through the roof.'

'Well maybe you should have thought of that before shacking up with my uncle.' Carla retorted, her expression hard. 'You were the one who chased after him, remember, not the other way around.'

As Terri opened her mouth to answer, Tommy Jr shook his head. 'Give it a rest. The pair of you are doing my nut in.' Getting to his feet he pulled out his cigarettes and gave the women a pointed look. 'I'm going outside for a smoke,' he grumbled, ignoring his uncle's warning to stay inside and keep the door locked at all times. 'If for no other reason than to get away from the two of you.'

Once the door had closed after her cousin Carla threw up her arms. 'See what you've caused now,' she hissed. 'Even Tommy Jr has had enough of you and he's only a kid.'

Terri's jaw dropped. 'Me,' she exclaimed, stabbing a finger into her chest. 'I'm not the one complaining every five minutes.'

She was about to continue when Carla put her finger to her lips. 'Did you hear that?' she asked, cocking her head to the side.

'What?' Terri snapped her head towards the window. It was pitch-black outside and she could barely see anything through the grainy glass. 'Is it Jonny?' she asked. 'Are they back?'

Glancing at her watch, Carla shook her head and as she got to her feet her forehead furrowed. 'I heard something.' Snatching up a hammer from the desk, she held onto the makeshift weapon for dear life. 'There,' she whispered, her eyes wide as she nodded towards the door. 'Tell me you heard that too?'

Terri nodded; she'd heard what she thought sounded like a thump followed by a muffled groan, maybe even several thumps. 'It was Tommy Jr,' she said, as a prickle of fear edged its way down her spine. 'He's playing silly beggars, trying to scare us.'

'No.' Carla's back stiffened and as she tentatively inched closer to the door she glanced over her shoulder. 'He wouldn't dare. You know what Jonny's like, he'd go ballistic, especially when it comes to you.'

Moving as far away from the door as she possibly could, Terri's eyes were wide. Carla was right, it was no secret that Jonny was protective of her and as for Tommy Jr it would never even enter his head to try and scare them. He may be young but he wasn't stupid and he certainly didn't have a death wish.

'Someone's out there,' Carla whispered as she gripped onto the hammer even tighter. 'I can hear voices.' She tentatively reached out for the door handle and paused, almost as though she were too afraid to open it for fear of what she might find. 'Are you alright, Tommy?' she called out, her voice loud.

When she received no reply, she turned back to look at Terri and gestured towards the iron poker leaning against the wall.

'Maybe it's your dad, he could have come back,' Terri suggested as she snatched up the heavy iron rod and held it in front of her.

Again, Carla shook her head. 'I would know my dad's voice anywhere and I'm telling you now, that isn't him.'

Terri's eyes widened even further. 'It might be the police.' She placed her hand on her bump, panic beginning to rise inside of her. 'Maybe they know about the diamonds.'

'Don't be ridiculous.' Carla rolled her eyes. 'If it was the old bill they would have been in here by now and we would more than likely be face down on the floor and in handcuffs.'

'Well, who is it then?' Terri hissed back.

Ignoring the question, Carla's fingers curled around the door handle and bracing herself, she gave Terri one final, wary glance before inching the door open a crack. 'Tommy,' she called out as she peered into the darkness. 'Are you okay—'

Before Carla could finish the sentence, the door was smashed open and Tommy Jr was shoved roughly inside, as she gave a startled scream.

'Well, well, well.' Standing at the threshold, Lenny Tucker grinned. 'Not one, but three Carters.' He rubbed his hands together and strolled into the office as though he had every right to be there. 'Nah, that's not quite right though, is it.' He pointed his finger towards Terri and grinned even wider. 'Must be my lucky day we've got a Tempest an' all. Talk about killing two birds with one stone.'

The hairs on the back of Carla's neck stood upright and as she crouched down beside her cousin, she guided him into a sitting position. Already Tommy Jr's face was beginning to swell, and the blood that trickled down from his split eyebrow had seeped into the collar of his shirt. 'What have you done to him?' she shouted.

Lenny laughed out loud and as his henchmen began to ransack the office, his eyes hardened. 'Me and him,' he stated, nodding down at Tommy Jr. 'Have got some unfinished business and this trappy little prick or should I say the mongrel of your family needs to be taught a lesson.'

'Fuck you,' Tommy Jr snarled as he began to pull himself up from the floor.

Lenny narrowed his eyes. 'The fact you're still talking is more than enough to tell me that my lads went a bit too easy on you.' Pulling back his heavy boot he kicked Tommy Jr in the stomach with as much force as he could physically muster and as the sound of Tommy Jr's groans echoed around the office, it was more than Terri could bear. It was like déjà vu all over again only instead of her nephew, Mason, on the receiving end of a vicious assault, it was Jonny's nephew.

'Get out,' she screamed, brandishing the poker above her head, her eyes wild. 'Or my Jonny...'

'Your Jonny what?' Lenny goaded.

'My Jonny will...'

Lenny laughed out loud and making a show of looking at his watch he gave a mock sad smile. 'By my calculation,' he smirked. 'Your Jonny should be as dead as a dodo by now, or at least he will be soon.'

Terri's face paled and lowering the iron poker she shook her head. 'No!' she screamed, her heart shattering into a million pieces. 'You're lying.'

Pulling out a chair, Lenny took a seat; pushing his hand into his pocket he pulled out his cigarettes. 'It's no lie,' he said, lighting up. 'That boyfriend of yours isn't as clever as thinks he is.' He leaned slightly forward and nodded. 'We sussed out his plan and the

minute he steps foot into Bernie's gaff, it'll be a case of game-over.'
He flashed a maniacal grin and nodded towards her bump. 'Looks
like that kid of yours ain't gonna have a daddy.'

Carla and Terri shared a glance. Jonny had no intentions of
entering Bernie's house, it was Ozzie's house they had targeted.
Giving a slight shake of her head in a warning for Terri to keep her
mouth firmly closed, Carla pulled Tommy Jr to his feet.

'You bastard.' Still clutching at his stomach, Tommy Jr's expression was one of loathing. 'Some man you are,' he snarled. 'It took
four of you,' he said, motioning towards Lenny's henchmen, 'to get
the better of me.' He took a step closer, his hands curling into tight
fists. 'I was right all along, you're a pussy, without this lot to back
you up,' he continued flicking his head in the direction of the heavies, 'you're nothing, fuck all.'

'Tommy,' Carla warned as a stunned silence fell over the
office.

'Nah,' his lips curling in disgust, Tommy Jr waved Carla away
from him. 'He wanted this. What was it you called me, an inbred?'
his voice began to rise. 'A fucking mongrel.'

Lenny laughed even harder. 'I should have added in nut job.' He
looked around him, spread open his arms, and smirked. 'After all,
it's no secret that Gary was off his trolley, and they do say that the
apple doesn't fall far from the cart.'

The words were the equivalent of a red rag to a bull and as
Tommy Jr charged forward, Terri let out a shriek of complete and
utter terror.

Punches began to fly and as the chair Lenny had been sitting in
toppled to the floor his face took the brunt of Tommy Jr's pent-up
anger. Stunned by the attack upon himself he held his hands over
his head, he'd clearly well and truly underestimated the boy.

'You cunt,' Tommy Jr continued to shout as his fists flew out so
hard and fast that Lenny could do nothing to block the blows. 'I

should have put you on your arse the first time you opened that big trap of yours.'

'For fuck's sake,' Lenny cried to his henchmen, his voice thick due to blood that oozed from his nose. 'Get him off me.'

Spurned into action, the heavies rushed forward. It took all three of them to wrench Tommy Jr away from their boss and as he continued to kick out with his feet Lenny heaved himself up off the floor.

'You're going to pay for that,' he yelled as he spat out a mouthful of blood, his hair in disarray and his face bright red from a combination of both humiliation and the blood that gushed from his nose.

Struggling to free himself, Tommy Jr shook his head. 'I don't think so.'

A wicked smile creased Lenny's face and the blood that coated his teeth made him look all the more menacing as he pulled back his arm.

Before Lenny could deliver the blow Terri raced forward. 'Stop,' she screamed, tugging on his arm.

Without looking behind him Lenny lashed out, his fist connecting with Terri's swollen stomach, and as her eyes popped open, she doubled over, the scream that tore from her throat so animalistic that for the second time in as many minutes a stunned silence fell over the office.

Dropping to her knees, one hand clutching her stomach, the other resting on the floor, her fingertips digging into the carpet fibres, Terri continued to scream as pain tore through her abdomen.

On seeing a drop of blood slip from between Terri's legs Lenny staggered back, his expression one of shock. 'I didn't know she was there,' he said, his voice full of shock. 'How was I to know she was going to make a grab for me?'

'Fuck this.' One of the henchmen blurted out as he made for the door in an attempt to save his own skin. 'I'm no baby killer.'

Lenny's face paled. The words baby killer whirled through his mind. Killing Tommy Johnson meant nothing to him, in the eyes of the law he was an adult, but an innocent baby that was something else entirely. There was a special place in hell for men who harmed babies and children. And as for prison, the mere thought didn't bear thinking about, the prisoners would tear him apart. Taking one last look at Terri he made for the door. Sweat poured from his face and as the realisation of what he'd caused finally hit him, he bolted out of the office as fast as his feet would carry him.

16

Slamming his foot on the brake, Sonny jumped out of his car and ran across the scrapyard forecourt. Shoving open the door with so much force that it almost came off its hinges, he was met with pandemonium and as his daughter screamed in fright, he took in the scene before him, his eyes widening.

'What the...' At a loss for words, he placed his hand on the wall to steady himself.

'Dad.' Carla's face was pale and as she crouched beside Terri the groans that came from his brother's girlfriend was enough to alert him to the fact she was in need of urgent medical assistance.

'What happened?' he shouted, panic getting the better of him.

'It was Lenny Tucker,' Tommy Jr answered as he gingerly got to his feet, one arm still wrapped around his stomach. 'She was trying to stop him from swinging for me, he caught her instead.' He motioned to his abdomen. 'He punched her right here.'

Sonny screwed up his face, his expression one of shock. Surely Tucker must have seen that she was heavily pregnant.

'Dad. The baby.' Tears filled Carla's eyes. 'I think that something's wrong, really wrong. She's bleeding and I don't know how to stop it.'

As Sonny turned back to look at his daughter, he gave an involuntary shudder. 'Have you phoned for an ambulance?' he urged as he took note of the blood that stained Carla's fingers.

Tommy Jr nodded. 'I called them. It's on its way.'

Sonny blew out his cheeks. 'You need to get out of here,' he ordered his nephew as his gaze raked over the split eyebrow and swelling that covered Tommy Jr's face. 'The old bill would have a fucking field day if they walked in here and saw the state of you.'

Tommy Jr was about to open his mouth to protest when Sonny cut him off. 'Think of how this is going to look,' he said as he knelt on the floor, pulled off his jacket then gently placed it over Terri. Glancing back around the office he yanked the chair upright. 'We'll say that she fell, that she landed awkwardly and that...' His voice trailed off. Even to his own ears it didn't seem plausible that a fall would have caused this much damage. 'Carla,' he demanded as he motioned to the paperwork strewn across the floor, 'start clearing this mess up. And Tommy,' he said, giving his nephew a sidelong glance, 'I told you to get out of here, so for once in your life will you do as you're told and fucking move?'

Carla jumped to her feet and as she wiped her stained hands down the side of her jeans, tears slipped down her cheeks. 'Someone needs to let Jonny know,' she stated, her face still drained of colour. 'He needs to be here with Terri.'

Sonny nodded, not that he was likely to get hold of his brother, his phone would still be switched off as it always was when they carried out a job. 'Tommy, get out!' he roared, his voice brooking no arguments. 'And where's that fucking ambulance?' he continued to shout as he looked over his shoulder in the direction the forecourt.

With his heart in his mouth Sonny turned his attention back to Terri. Her skin was so deathly pale that he had a nasty feeling if she didn't get to the hospital and pronto then there was a high chance that she wasn't going to make it.

* * *

Just moments after her husband's car pulled up outside the scrapyard, Stacey pulled in behind him.

'What the fuck, Stace,' Danny shouted as he slammed his car door closed and stormed towards her. 'I told you to stay at home.'

Her back instantly up, Stacey opened her mouth to answer, when from out of the corner of her eye she caught sight of someone limping out of the office. 'Tommy,' she screamed as she raced across the forecourt. 'Oh my God,' she cried as she pulled her grandson into her arms. 'Are you okay?'

'I'm alright,' Tommy Jr protested as he pulled himself out of his grandmother's embrace. 'It wasn't me who was hurt.'

Logan's face paled. 'Is it Carla?' he shouted as he ran full pelt towards the office.

Cursing under his breath Danny gave his wife a look of warning before charging after his son.

Tearing his gaze away from the portable cabin, Tommy Jr turned to look at his nan, his expression one of terror. 'It's Terri,' he cried as he pulled out his phone. 'We need to get hold of Jonny.'

Stacey's face paled. She was fond of Terri and she'd seen a change in Jonny since the two of them had been together. He wasn't as reckless as he'd been previously. He still had his moments, but in a lot of ways he'd grown up. 'Is it the baby?' she urged her grandson. By her calculation Terri had to be at least seven months into her pregnancy, it was far too early for her to give birth.

Tommy Jr shook his head and as he turned back to look at the office he lifted his shoulders up into a shrug. 'I don't know nan, but there's a lot of claret.'

Stacey's heart was in her mouth and throwing her arm around her grandson's shoulders she led him towards her car. She didn't like the sound of this, not one little bit.

* * *

Jonny, along with his nephews, was in high spirits, in fact he was so elated that he felt giddy with it all. He'd carried out the ultimate job, one that his elder brothers, no matter how much they'd tried over the years, hadn't been able to pull off. Just as he'd known they would, his plans had been a success and tucked safely inside the rucksack that had been placed in the passenger footwell were the diamonds his family had spent decades trying to get their hands on.

'Didn't I tell you,' he grinned as he looked up at the rearview mirror, 'that with the right planning we could do this.'

From the back seat Reece laughed. 'I thought that heavy was going to shit himself when you shoved the gun into his face.'

'He probably did,' Peter butted in with a grin. 'His arsehole was definitely flapping, I know that much.'

The occupants of the car laughed and as Jonny flicked the indicator and pulled into the road where the scrapyard was situated, their laughter abruptly stopped. Illuminating the road ahead of them was an ambulance, the red and blue flashing lights casting shadows across both the pavement and road.

As he brought the car to a skidding halt outside the scrapyard, a shiver of fear shot down the length of Jonny's spine and as he jumped out of the motor and ran towards the office, his earlier euphoria all too quickly evaporated.

'What's going on?' he hollered, his voice filled with panic.

Both Sonny and Danny McKay spun around, holding out their arms in an attempt to stop Jonny from entering the office. Sonny shook his head. 'Don't get in their way,' he begged his brother. 'Give them space to work on her.'

Jonny's eyes widened and shoving Sonny and Danny roughly out of his path, a sense of cold dread swept over him. 'What happened?' he gasped.

Sonny raised his eyebrows and discreetly nodding towards the desk, the drawers bulging with the paperwork Carla had hastily shoved inside, he leaned in towards his brother. 'She had an accident. A fall.'

Screwing up his face Jonny brought his hands up to his head. 'But...' Tearing his gaze away from his brother he moved closer to where the paramedics worked on Terri, the scent of blood filling his nostrils and making him feel nauseous. 'Is she...' barely able to get the words out, his voice wavered.

'She's alive,' Sonny confirmed.

As his shoulders sagged Jonny heaved an audible sigh of relief. 'And the baby?'

Sonny sucked in his bottom lip. 'They won't know for sure until they get her to hospital. But you need to prepare yourself for the worst, it's not looking good.'

There and then, Jonny's world collapsed around him. 'No.' He shook his head in disbelief and as he rubbed at the nape of his neck he had to remind himself to breathe. This couldn't be happening, not now, not when just five minutes earlier he'd felt as though he was on top of the world.

'Jonny, I am so sorry, I...' Carla's voice quivered and pulling herself out of Logan's arms she turned to look at her uncle. 'Tommy Jr called the ambulance straight away,' she said, hastily swiping the tears away from her cheeks. 'I did everything I could to help her,' she said. 'I just didn't know what to do, didn't know how to stop the bleeding.'

Jonny whipped his head around to look at his niece, his expression one of confusion. 'I don't understand,' he said, still shaking his head. 'How could this have happened? How could she have fallen over?' He glanced around him and as though it suddenly occurred to him that his nephew was missing, he narrowed his eyes, his voice becoming hard. 'Where's Tommy Jr?'

'He needed to see a man about a dog,' Sonny answered with a rise of his eyebrows hoping more than anything that his brother would be able to decipher his cryptic answer; in other words that he'd sent Tommy Jr away in the hope that the paramedics wouldn't suspect something untoward had taken place.

His forehead furrowed, Jonny turned back to look at Terri. It was then that he saw the blood smeared across her thighs. 'Jesus fucking Christ,' he muttered under his breath. This was no fall, no accident, it couldn't be. Sinking to his knees his skin was ashen. 'Is she going to be alright?' he urged the paramedics.

Their reluctance to give him a straight answer told Jonny everything he needed to know and as he reached out for Terri's hand he gripped on for dear life. Her skin was cold and clammy to his touch, bringing with it a further sense of dread. 'Come on, babe,' he whispered in her ear. 'Don't do this to me. Don't you dare fucking leave me...'

The groan that came from Terri stopped him midsentence and as he looked up at the paramedics there was hope in his voice. 'That's got to be a good sign, hasn't it?'

Avoiding the question the paramedic gave him a tight smile. 'We need to get her to hospital,' she answered as gently as she could. 'And then we'll know for definite.'

Jonny nodded and getting to his feet he watched helplessly as Terri was lifted onto a stretcher.

'She's going to be alright,' Sonny said, clasping Jonny by the shoulder.

The hard lump in Jonny's throat prevented him from answering and as he followed the paramedics out of the office, he glanced down at a smear of blood on the floor, Terri's blood. It wasn't going to be alright, and he knew that as well as he knew his own name.

* * *

Diane Adams was hysterical and as she crouched down beside her husband's lifeless body, she cradled his head in her hands. 'What have you done to him?' she screamed.

Ignoring the question, Ozzie continued to pace the lounge, his face a mask of anger. 'Where are those fucking Carters?' he roared to his henchmen. 'They should have been here by now.'

Diane's jaw dropped and as she tore her eyes away from the firearm that had been left casually on the armchair, she looked in the direction of the front door. Everything became crystal clear to her. No wonder Bernie had told her to stay in the bedroom, warning her that no matter what she heard she was not to come out. He and the Tucker brothers had planned a massacre. A shiver of fear ran down the length of her spine. She would never have believed it to be possible. Bernie wouldn't hear a bad word said about her ex-husband, let alone voluntarily extinguish his life.

Her heart in her mouth she looked back down at her husband. 'Did you shoot him?' she asked as she glanced up at Ozzie, her bottom lip wobbling.

Ozzie stopped pacing. 'Does he look like he's been fucking shot?' he barked out.

Tears sprang to Diane's eyes. How was she supposed to know what someone who'd been shot looked like. She may have seen it on television but that was fiction not real life. The only thing she knew for certain was that her husband was unconscious, and although his chest rose and fell, indicating that he was still very much alive, his breathing was shallow. And then there was the blood. There was so much of it smeared across his face that she couldn't even tell where it was coming from. 'He needs help,' she croaked out, knowing instinctively that her attempts to help her husband would prove to be futile, that Ozzie wouldn't have given two monkeys if Bernie was dead or alive. 'He needs to go to hospital.'

A loud knock at the front door made Diane physically jump out of her skin and as she pulled her husband's body closer, she began to shake. She was half expecting her ex-husband to walk through the front door and then at any given moment a series of deafening gunshots to ring out. When she saw Lenny Tucker walk into view, she didn't know whether to laugh or cry. It was the tears that won out and as she silently sobbed, she rocked back and forth, her husband's limp body a dead weight in her arms.

'What's happened?' Ozzie took one look at his brother and then ushered him into the kitchen along with their heavies so that they could speak in private. Seeing this as her only chance to save herself, Diane scrambled to her feet, crept across the lounge and then tentatively reached out for the gun. She'd never even held a gun before let alone fired one and as she turned the weapon over in her hand she was surprised by its weight. It wasn't as heavy as she'd imagined it would be and she briefly wondered if it was loaded. Of course it would be, she told herself. Why would the Tuckers have brought an empty gun with them? They weren't the type of men to issue empty threats.

Resuming her position on the floor Diane tucked the gun between herself and her husband, hidden out of sight. And with the weapon now within easy reach Diane kept her gaze firmly fixed on the lounge door, her body on tenterhooks as she readied herself to pull the firearm from out of its hiding place. She had no qualms about using the gun, she'd do just about anything if it meant saving herself, but that was Diane all over. Sonny had been right when he'd stated that she'd only ever looked out for number one. And when it came to the Tuckers, who knew what they were capable of, seeing as they had no obvious problems beating Bernie to within an inch of his life, nor did they seem to have an issue when it came to taking the lives of her ex-husband and his family. Were they planning to kill her too? After all, she was a witness to their crime and they could hardly let her go could they, could hardly risk her giving evidence in court against them. With a new sense of determination, Diane straightened her spine. She'd have one shot at this, just one chance to save herself and like hell was she planning to fail.

* * *

Draining the dregs of his tea, Sadie placed the mug on the table then pushed back his chair. 'I suppose we'd better get it over and done with then and inform Ozzie of what's gone down.'

Reluctantly the heavy nodded.

In that instant Sadie felt a moment of pity for him. If Ozzie was going to blame anyone then it was bound to be the henchman and he had more than just a feeling that the repercussions would be harsh. Ozzie would view the robbery as a personal affront, as a slur on his reputation and the fact the heavy had done zilch to stop the raid was bound to have ramifications. He reached out to pat the heavy's hand then got to his feet and walked across the kitchen to collect his phone.

'Would you like me to be the one to do the honours?' he asked, holding the phone out to the heavy. 'Or do you want to do it?'

The heavy swallowed and giving a shake of his head, he averted his gaze.

Sadie gave a sigh and leaning back against the kitchen worktop, he took a deep breath. He was about to put on the performance of a lifetime, not that that was to say the lies wouldn't tumble out of mouth easily enough, as it was he'd already convinced countless people that he was a murderer, what was one more lie?

Moments later he brought the phone away from his ear and as Ozzie screamed out a torrent of abuse, he tilted his head towards the ceiling and closed his eyes. Perhaps he should have left it to someone else to break the bad news after all.

* * *

Ozzie's eyes were almost bulging out of his head and as a series of expletives spewed out of his mouth, he resisted the urge to throw his mobile phone at the wall in a fit of rage.

Anger tore through his body and barging his brother and subsequent heavies out of his way, he stood at the door to the lounge, his body becoming rigid, so tangible was his fury.

'I'm going to kill him,' he spat as he glowered down at Bernie's unconscious form. 'I'm going to tear the no good, snidey cunt limb from fucking limb.'

Diane let out of a shriek of terror and as Ozzie made to charge towards her, she reached down for the gun.

'Stay back,' she warned as she lifted the firearm in the air, her entire body trembling as she curled her finger around the trigger. 'I'll shoot.'

Momentarily, Ozzie froze and tearing his hard stare away from Bernie he narrowed his eyes. 'You ain't got the fucking bottle,' he goaded.

It took everything within Diane's power not to smirk. Oh, she had the bottle alright, her life was at stake and like fuck was she prepared to become one of the Tucker brothers' latest victims. She steadied her hand and lifting her chin in the air she returned Ozzie's hard stare. 'Take a step closer,' she snarled. 'And then we will see which one of us hasn't got the bottle.'

As though he were debating the idea, Ozzie straightened up and held out his hand. 'Give me a shooter,' he ordered his brother. 'I'm going to blow this mouthy bitch from here to kingdom come.'

Lenny sighed. 'Leave it out, Oz,' he said, giving Diane a wary glance. 'It's bad enough that I killed a baby. We don't need her blood on our hands as well.'

Ozzie gave a menacing chuckle. 'Who gives a fuck about the kid, it's a Carter,' he sneered, referring to Terri and Jonny's unborn child. 'Who would more than likely have grown up to be a bigger bastard than its father. Take it from me, you've done the world a favour.'

'Ozzie,' Lenny reiterated, the anger in his voice more than enough to tell his brother that he was being serious. 'I said leave it.' He turned to walk away, then spinning around, came to an abrupt halt. 'Don't you think we've got enough on our plates without adding to our troubles?' he added, bending his head slightly forward to speak privately in Ozzie's ear. 'And unless it's escaped your notice, the diamonds have been swiped from underneath our noses. We've been made to look like fools.'

'Even more of a reason to kill this grass,' Ozzie spat. 'It was him who told the Carters that the diamonds had been moved.'

Lenny waved his hand through the air and as he glanced in Bernie's direction, he allowed himself a small smile. 'I highly doubt he'll last the hour, let alone live to tell the tale. I mean, come on,' he implored his brother, 'look at the state of him; he's on his last legs. It shouldn't take a genius to tell you that he's gonna kick the bucket.'

Ozzie shrugged. In a roundabout way he could see his brother's point. 'And what about her,' he said, stabbing his forefinger in Diane's direction. 'She'll open her trap and then we'll be done for.'

Narrowing his eyes Lenny screwed up his face. 'She's not that stupid,' he answered. 'She knows when to keep her mouth shut.' He took a cautious step forward, his eyes glued to the firearm in Diane's hand. 'Ain't that right, Di.'

With her finger still curled around the trigger Diane nodded furiously.

'See,' Lenny stated. 'She knows the score.'

Ever so slightly, Ozzie's shoulders relaxed and pointing his finger towards Diane a second time, his steely eyes remained focused on her. 'If I so much as hear a squeak out of you I'll end you. Are we clear on that?'

Again, Diane nodded and as the Tucker brothers and their firm retreated out of the house, she let out a collective sigh of relief. Placing the gun on her lap, she sat as still as a statue, until she heard the distinctive noise of car doors slamming shut, then the sound of gravel underneath tyres. It was only then that she scrambled off the floor, tiptoed across the lounge, and peered out of the window. Once she was satisfied that the driveway was empty and that the Tuckers had indeed left the property, she brought her hands up to her face and promptly sobbed her heart out.

She could so easily have been murdered. In that instant she suddenly wondered if anyone would have actually missed her or even cared for that matter. The thought was as sobering as it was terrifying. Would her daughter have finally, perhaps weeks or even months down the line, stumbled upon both her and Bernie's rotting corpses? With her heart in her mouth she turned her head to look at her husband and as fresh tears sprang to her eyes she raced towards him.

'Bernie,' she cried as she dropped to her knees and tentatively wiped the blood from his face. 'It's going to be okay,' she promised. 'I'm going to get you help.' If nothing else, he had to be okay; Bernie was all that she had, and even more than that, he was all that she'd ever wanted.

17

'I thought I might find you in here.' As she took a cautious step towards the incubator, Rina's heart was in her mouth. 'Oh, look at him,' she cried, tears welling in her eyes. 'He's absolutely perfect.' Dressed in nothing but a pale blue knitted hat and a disposable nappy that was so big that it came up to his chest, the baby slept soundly. 'I popped in on Terri first. She was still sleeping. The midwife said it was more than likely the anaesthetic's still in her system. The poor little cow must be worn out; she's been through the mill and back.'

Jonny nodded. 'She was convinced he was a girl.' As he looked down at his son, Jonny's voice cracked. 'She doesn't even know we've got a boy yet.'

'And you will be the one to tell her,' Rina answered as she gripped hold of Jonny's hand and gave it a reassuring squeeze.

'I still can't believe how tiny he is.' Tearing his gaze away from the infant, Jonny studied the equipment surrounding the incubator and shook his head. He didn't have a clue what any of the machinery meant, nor was he afraid to admit that every time one of the alarms sounded his heartbeat would quicken and a shiver of terror would slam down the length of his spine. 'He's so small,' he said, quietly. 'What if he...?'

'He's going to be okay,' Rina interrupted, her own voice breaking as she fought back her tears.

As Jonny turned to look at her, Rina could see the fear in his eyes, an emotion she would never have believed him capable of if she hadn't seen it with her own two eyes.

'But what if...?' he swallowed and glanced towards the door. 'He's our boy, we can't...' he turned to look back at the baby, cleared his throat then shook his head barely able to get the words out. 'Terri would never get over it. I would never get over it. I'd never forgive myself I know that much. It's all my fault, I should have been there. I should never have left her in the fucking office.'

'Now you stop that,' Rina chastised. She placed one arm around his waist and pulled him close while she rested her free hand lightly on the incubator. 'Blaming yourself isn't going to help matters. How was you to know what would happen? And as for this little boy,' she told him. 'He's a fighter. You can't tell me that he isn't strong. He has Carter, Tempest, and Murphy blood running through his veins. You can't get any stronger than that.'

Jonny nodded and slipping his hand through a circular hole on the side of the incubator he tentatively stroked his son's tiny hand.

'See.' Wiping a stray tear away from her eye as the baby gripped onto his father's finger, she let out a gentle laugh. 'He takes after his dad alright, and his mummy of course. He's absolutely beautiful.'

'I thought I was going to lose them both,' Jonny admitted, his shoulders slumping. 'It all happened so fast. We were barely out of the ambulance, and they were rushing her into the theatre. And the blood Rina.' He sucked in a breath and momentarily closed his eyes. 'I've never seen so much of it. They had this form.' He rubbed his hand over his face. 'They said if they couldn't stop the bleeding, they'd have to give her a hysterectomy. And without a moment's thought or even thinking about the consequences, I signed it. I didn't even need to think about it, just signed along the dotted line. All that mattered to me was that they did everything they could to keep her alive.' He shook his head, his expression that of a haunted man. 'If they'd have gone through with it, she would have never forgiven me.'

'But you didn't lose them,' Rina reassured him. 'You did what you thought was best and if a hysterectomy was going to help save her life, then it would have had to be done. There would have been no other option. Terri would have understood, she would have had no other choice but to accept it.'

Jonny nodded.

'And as for this little one.' rina's eyes sparkled with love for the baby. Terri may not have been her biological daughter but Rina loved her as a mother should and she viewed the infant as her grandchild. 'He is going to be just fine. You just wait and see, my darling. Before you know it, he'll be running rings around the pair of you.'

A small smile creased Jonny's face. 'I hope so.'

Rina returned the smile. 'He will do,' she winked with an air of confidence. As she turned to look back at the baby, she lowered her voice. 'How did this happen?' she asked. 'Terri was fine when I saw her this morning.'

Beside her Jonny stiffened, his expression becoming murderous. 'Lenny fucking Tucker,' he hissed. 'He did this. He swung for her.'

Rina's jaw dropped and as a cold shiver ran down the length of her spine, she momentarily closed her eyes. 'Dear God,' she gasped. 'He could have killed them both.'

Jonny's lips curled into a snarl. 'I'm going to kill him over this,' he spat. 'If it's the last thing I ever do.'

Rina nodded. She didn't doubt him, not for one single second.

* * *

As Ricky, Jamie, and Mason Tempest entered the scrapyard office they were met with complete and utter carnage.

Tempers had already begun to flare and as the occupants raised their voices in a bid to be heard over one another, Ricky could barely hear himself think, let alone get a word in edgeways. Putting two fingers to his lips he let out a loud whistle in an attempt to gain their attention.

Silence fell over the office and as all heads turned to look in their direction, Sonny stepped forward. 'What's the latest? How's Terri doing?' he asked as he shook Ricky's, Jamie's, and Mason's hands.

Ricky sighed and as he went on to shake both Mitchell's and Danny McKay's hands, he nodded a greeting towards the remaining Carters. 'She could be better, but she's alive and that's the main thing.'

'And the baby,' Mitchell asked.

'He's doing okay. Small, but from what Rina said, healthy considering he was born seven weeks early.'

'He's a Carter,' Peter piped up. 'Of course he's okay. He's a fighter like the rest of us.'

'He's a Tempest an' all,' Jamie reminded him, his voice hard.

'Yeah, I know. I didn't mean anything by it, I was just saying that's all.' Thoroughly chastised Peter averted his gaze.

'Any idea of what happened?' Ricky asked. 'I mean a fall wouldn't have caused that much damage, surely.'

'Of course it fucking wouldn't,' Danny answered. 'It was that bastard, Lenny Tucker. He took a swing for her. And from what I can make out it was a punch that had been intended for young Tommy.'

'Do what?' Jamie snapped his head around to look at Tommy Jr and taking note of the injuries clearly visible upon his face, he narrowed his eyes. 'Why is this the first time that we're hearing about any of this?' he gestured between himself, his brother, and nephew. 'She's our sister, we should be one of the first to know what's gone down, so why the fuck did no one have the decency to fill us in on what happened?'

As he rubbed at the nape of his neck Sonny gave a slight shrug. 'We were waiting for Jonny to get back,' he said, by the way of an excuse.

Ricky's nostrils flared and before he could give the Carters a piece of his mind the door to the office opened and Jonny, followed by Rina, walked inside. 'What the fuck are you doing here,' he spat. 'Why ain't you at the hospital with Terri?'

Jonny turned his head and sighed. 'Why do you think?'

Cocking his head to the side the nerve at the side of Ricky's eye pulsated, his temper on the verge of reaching boiling point. 'I don't know,' he growled. 'You tell me?'

Jonny lifted his eyebrows. 'Visiting was over. We were thrown out.' He jerked his head towards Rina as if for confirmation, then rubbed his hand over his face, the trauma of witnessing Terri and his newborn son almost die before his very eyes, taking its toll on him.

As Ricky turned to look at both his brother and son, anger flashed across his face. 'Is that it?' he snapped. 'My sister and her son are fighting for their lives, and you just stand there doing fuck all.' He clenched his fists. 'I warned you,' he spat before Jonny had the chance to answer him. 'Hurt her, and I'll fucking bury you.'

'He's my son, too.' Jonny glared. 'And I didn't hurt her,' he said, screwing up his face as though the notion of laying a hand on Terri was alien to him. 'I could never hurt her.'

Ricky snarled and as he charged forward his fists shot out. 'I said right from the start that you weren't good enough for her,' he roared, as he pummelled his fists into Jonny's face. 'That you'd end up bringing her down.'

'Ricky, stop!' Rina screamed, her voice filled with terror as she looked frantically around her. 'Jamie,' she begged. 'Do something. Can't you see that he'd never willingly harm a hair on Terri's head? Look at him,' she implored as tears sprang to her eyes. 'He's devasted by what happened. He loves her, you know he does.'

Snaking his tongue across his teeth Jamie shoved his hands into his pockets and shrugged. 'He was warned,' he said through gritted teeth. 'And if Ricky doesn't kill him, then I will.'

'Mason,' Rina pleaded. When she received the same response, she turned to Sonny. 'Stop him, please,' she begged of him. 'He's your brother. Isn't it enough that he's already beating himself up over this, that he blames himself for something he had no control over.'

As though Rina had spurned him into action, Sonny bounded forward and as he and Mitchell dragged Ricky away from their younger brother. They blew out their cheeks, their chests heaving from the exertion. 'I get that you're angry,' Sonny said as he threw Jonny a wary glance. 'But if you want to lay into someone then start with the Tuckers, Lenny Tucker in particular, he was the cause of this.'

Breathing heavily, Ricky continued to give Jonny a hard stare, the anger across his face still visible. 'Until the day I die, I will blame you for this,' he spat.

Jonny let out an incredulous laugh, although it would be fair to say it was tinged with hysteria. 'I don't need you to lay the blame at my door,' he said, stabbing a finger into his chest. 'I already blame myself for what happened. Don't you think that if I could turn back time I would? That I'd give anything to make sure that Terri hadn't been here, that she and the baby hadn't been harmed?'

Ricky clenched his fists a second time. The fact Jonny hadn't even attempted to defend himself did nothing to ease the rage that tore through his body.

Slumping into his chair, Jonny shoved the rucksack containing the diamonds roughly out of his way, then resting his elbows on the desk he massaged his temples. No matter how much he tried to push them aside, images of Terri lying in a pool of her own blood flashed through his mind. It was all he could think of and no matter how much he tried he was unable to block them out. Over and over again, the images played out on a loop; he felt sick to his stomach and even more than that, he deserved to be on the receiving end of the Tempests' wrath. He should never have left Terri alone; should never have trusted Tommy Jr to watch over her, he was nothing but a kid himself. What hope did he have against Tucker and three of his heavies?

'Jonny.' Sensing her uncle's pain Carla made to step forward, only for Logan to tug on her arm and pull her back. As she looked up at him, he shook his head. 'Leave him,' he mouthed. Ignoring his request Carla pulled her arm free and as she cautiously inched her way towards the desk, she gingerly placed her hand upon Jonny's shoulder. 'I'm sorry,' she said, swallowing down the hard lump in her throat. 'This is all my fault.' She glanced towards Logan, her expression one of shame. It was all because of her and her obsession for revenge that had driven a wedge between them. For her own selfish reasons, she'd more or less pushed Logan aside, and then there was the situation with Terri and the baby. Both mother and son would have remained safe if she hadn't dragged her uncle into her hairbrained scheme. 'If I hadn't told you about the diamonds then none of this would have happened.'

'The only person to blame is him,' Ricky spat. 'If he hadn't been so greedy, so fucking cocksure of himself, then none of this would have happened.' He threw up his arms. 'What even possessed you to go after the diamonds? Anyone with half a brain cell could have told you it was a bad move, that it would end in disaster.'

Jonny looked up, his lips curled into a snarl. 'Do you honestly think I give two fucks about the diamonds?' Jumping to his feet he snatched up the rucksack and hauled it across the office. 'Do what you want with them,' he snarled. 'I couldn't give a flying fuck.'

As a stunned silence fell over the office, Sonny shot his twin brother a wary glance. 'I think maybe that's enough,' he said as he began to usher the men out of the office. 'It's been a long night and we're not going to get anywhere while tempers are high. Give him a bit of space. And that includes you,' he said, nodding towards his daughter.

Carla hesitated. 'Yeah, but...'

'No yeah buts, I told you to get out,' Sonny reiterated his voice brooking no arguments.

'He's right.' Rina gave a smile and walking across the office, she wrapped her arms around Jonny. 'You take care of yourself sweetheart and don't do anything rash,' she warned him. 'Terri and the baby need you now more than ever.' Straightening up she clasped hold of Sonny's hand and gave it a gentle squeeze. 'Look after him,' she said, lowering her voice. 'He's had a big shock.'

Once they were alone Sonny shot his twin brother another glance as Jonny pulled a bottle of brandy from under the desk, unscrewed the lid, then gulped the alcohol down straight from the bottle.

'Is this wise?' he said, nodding towards the bottle. 'Getting smashed isn't the answer, is it?'

Jonny glared. 'Maybe not,' he answered, swallowing down another mouthful of the brandy. 'But if nothing else, it'll fucking help.'

Sonny sighed and kicking his long legs out in front of him in an attempt to make himself more comfortable, he tried his utmost to ignore the springs that poked into his backside. He hadn't been wrong when he'd said it had been a long night and from the look of things, he had a feeling that they were going to be here for the duration or until Jonny had drunk himself into a stupor and collapsed face first onto the desk. Either way, he had a sneaky suspicion that they wouldn't be going anywhere any time soon.

* * *

To say that Sadie was scared would be an understatement. He'd always known that Ozzie had a temper on him, that he could be both dangerous and violent. But to find himself on the receiving end of Ozzie's fury was new territory and one that he couldn't say he particularly liked. In all the years he'd known him, Ozzie had never once laid a hand on him, nor had he ever made him feel afraid for his life.

Clutching his hand to his face, Sadie's cheek smarted. The punch Ozzie had dished out had not only been out of character, but it had also come as a complete and utter shock. Dazed, Sadie pulled himself into a sitting position and as stars danced before his eyes, he placed one hand on the floor in an attempt to stop himself from toppling over onto his side.

'Ozzie,' he cried. 'How were we supposed to stop them, they had guns.'

Ozzie ran his hand through his unruly hair, his expression the epitome of a stark, raving lunatic as he crouched down and grasped Sadie tightly by his jaw.

If Sadie wasn't afraid before, then he certainly was now, and as he physically cowered away from the man he lived with, he fought down the urge to burst into tears. Sadie had never been a violent man and as he glanced towards the broken body of the heavy who had been blamed for allowing the theft of the diamonds, hot tears slipped unashamedly down his cheeks.

'Ozzie,' he began again, his voice cracking. 'Please,' he begged of him. 'I'm telling the truth, there was nothing we could do.'

As he threw Sadie away from him, Ozzie straightened up and turning to look at his brother, he gave a nonchalant flick of his hand. 'Get rid of him,' he growled, referring to the heavy.

From his position on the floor Sadie watched helplessly as the heavy was dragged from the house and once the front door had been slammed closed after Lenny, Sadie swallowed deeply and as he looked up at Ozzie, his eyes were wide with terror. 'What are you going to do to me?'

Ozzie ignored the question and as he began to pace the room, the anger that radiated off him became all the more tangible.

'Ozzie,' Sadie called out to him again. 'Please stop this.'

Ozzie ceased pacing and spinning around, his lips were curled in a snarl. 'Get out of my sight,' he roared. 'Before I seriously do you some damage.'

Sadie jumped to his feet and as he darted from the room and bolted up the stairs, he could scarcely breathe so acute was his fear. Throwing himself onto the bed Sadie buried his face into the pillow and sobbed. As much as he may have loved Ozzie, he was unable to condone his behaviour and the fact he had shown no remorse over the harm that had been bestowed upon Jonny Carter's unborn baby was not something Sadie was ever likely to forgive or forget. Only a monster, he concluded, would find amusement in the death of an innocent child and as much as he'd known that Ozzie had no scruples, he hadn't believed him to be completely lacking when it came to empathy.

Wiping the tears from his eyes, Sadie sat up and wrapped his arms around his knees. He needed to speak with the Carters, needed to pay his condolences. Perhaps only then would he be able to forgive himself for giving the brothers the heads-up on the situation. Maybe if they hadn't stolen the diamonds from Ozzie's house then the baby would never have come to harm. Not that the alternative would have been any better, he reasoned. If it hadn't been for his input, then the entire Carter family would have been slaughtered.

In a quandary, Sadie bit down on his bottom lip and as he lay back against the pillows, he knew that his mind was already made up. No matter how much he loved Ozzie, his history with the Carters, Jake Carter in particular, would always come first. And if he knew the Carter brothers as well as he thought he did, then he knew for a fact that when it came to dishing out their revenge they wouldn't hold back, that they wouldn't be satisfied until Ozzie and Lenny had paid the price for what they had done to Jonny's baby. Unease spread through Sadie's veins and as a solution to the problem sprang to his mind, he forced himself to relax. He could only hope and pray that when the time came, he would be able to find the courage to see his plan through, because the stark reality of allowing the Carter family the opportunity to carry out their retribution didn't bear thinking about.

18

The next morning as he entered the maternity unit Jonny Carter was all smiles, albeit a smile that didn't quite reach his eyes. Fear engulfed him; what if Terri was unable to recover from the surgery, what if his son's tiny body failed him?

'Hey,' he said when he found Terri sitting up in bed. Despite the fact her skin was a lot less pale then it had been the night before, she still didn't look herself. Her hair was lank, and her lips were dry and chapped and underneath the thin, cotton hospital gown that she wore, a thick padded bandage had been pulled tight across the incision in her abdomen, causing her tummy to look even more distended than it actually was. 'How are you feeling?'

Terri returned the smile and nodding down to the cannula that had been inserted into the back of her hand she gave a small groan. 'I'll feel a lot better once this has been taken out.'

'One step at a time, babe,' Jonny answered as he kissed the top of her head then took a seat beside her. 'You've just had major surgery,' he said, grabbing hold of her free hand. 'You still need to recover.'

Terri's eyes sparkled. 'How's the baby?' she glanced towards the midwives. 'I keep asking if I can see him,' she sighed. 'But they're so busy they haven't got around to it yet.'

Feeling somewhat disappointed, Jonny sucked in his bottom lip. After all that she'd been through, he'd wanted to be the one to tell her they had a son and as he followed her gaze towards the midwife station, he sighed. 'He's doing well,' he said, squeezing her hand. 'He's small, but strong considering he was born premature.'

'I need to see him.' Throwing off the blanket Terri made to climb out of bed.

Alarmed, Jonny shook his head. 'What do you think you're doing? You can't get out of bed.'

'Just you watch me.' Terri's eyes flashed dangerously. 'I want to see my baby,' she demanded. 'So either take me there or I'll find a way of getting to the special care baby unit myself.'

Jonny couldn't help but chuckle and as he wandered off to find a wheelchair he shook his head. It was hard to believe that just days earlier Terri had been afraid that she wouldn't know how to be a good mum. Just as he'd instinctively known she would, she was already proving herself to be a natural.

Ten minutes later, tears filled Terri's eyes and as she studied their tiny son she grasped onto Jonny's hand for dear life. 'He's beautiful.'

'Of course he is,' Jonny smiled. 'He takes after his mum.'

Through her tears a smile creased Terri's face and glancing up she jerked her head towards the baby. 'What do you think of James?' she asked. 'I was thinking we could name him after our brothers: my Jamie and your Jimmy.'

Jonny nodded. 'I like it.' He tilted his head to the side and studied his son's face. 'It suits him.'

Terri continued to smile. 'James Carter,' she whispered, as she pushed her hand through the circular hole on the side of the incubator and stroked the baby's tiny hand. 'It's nice to finally meet you.'

* * *

Just a few floors above the maternity unit, Bernie Adams lay back in the hospital bed. As far as the doctors were concerned, he was lucky to be alive and if anyone knew that to be true then it was Bernie. He'd been convinced that his days on earth were well and truly numbered, and if the beating Ozzie Tucker had dished out had been anything to go by, then it really was a miracle that he was still breathing and still in possession of his faculties.

Several of his ribs and left arm were both broken, and at the side of his head was a lump the size of a golf ball, no doubt caused by Ozzie's heavy feet. As he brought a hand mirror up to his face Bernie grimaced. Both eyes were blackened, and his nose was bent at an unnatural angle, and to top it off his front tooth was chipped, and dissolvable stiches had been administered to his bottom lip.

He looked and felt as though he'd been in a car crash. In fact, this was what he'd actually told the hospital had happened and it was only a matter of time until the police turned up to investigate, not that they were likely to get very much out of him. He had a plan of action and if the time came, he would claim he had amnesia blaming it on the knock to his head. After all, they couldn't get blood from a stone and if he was unable to recall the details of the incident then there was nothing they, nor anyone else for that matter, could do about it.

As she sat beside him Diane's eyes were narrowed into slits and her lips were pursed. Even in his state of helplessness she was convinced he was eyeing up the nurses. Chance would be a fine thing. He wasn't even able to go to the toilet unaided let alone be in any fit state to take a woman to bed.

Still, he was alive, and from his understanding so were Carla, Sonny and the rest of the Carters and in the grand scheme of things that was all that mattered. 'Have you heard from Carla?' he asked as he turned his head to look at his wife.

Diane rolled her eyes. 'What do you think?' she snapped. 'She couldn't give two hoots about me or what I've been through. I could have died,' she hissed, lowering her voice. 'Ozzie Tucker was planning to kill me, and it was no idle threat. He meant business.'

It took all of Bernie's effort to keep the smile from his face. It was so typical of Diane. Not only had he been at death's door but for all intent and purposes the Tuckers had planned to wipe out the entire Carter family. And yet despite all of this, Diane was still unable to think of anyone but herself.

As he made himself more comfortable, Bernie's thoughts turned to the days and months ahead of him. What with his financial difficulties, he had a sinking feeling that he was stuck with Diane for the considerable future. He could barely afford somewhere to live let alone pay for a divorce, not that she would be prepared to let him go without a fight.

He closed his eyes and as he drowned out his wife's voice Bernie, drifted off to sleep, not for the first time wishing that when he awoke his life could be so very different. A life where he had never met Diane, nor betrayed the only person who had ever meant anything to him, Sonny Carter.

* * *

Racked with guilt, Carla felt sick to her stomach as she often did lately, and as she wearily slipped the key into the lock of her and Logan's flat, she fought down the urge to burst into tears. All she wanted to do was hide away from the world, or rather hide away from the mistakes she'd made. As much as they hadn't said anything, she had a sinking feeling that her entire family blamed her for what had happened to Terri. Her dad was angry with her, her cousins had been barely able to look at her, and as for her Aunt Stacey, she'd had some choice words to say on the matter, and so she should, seeing as Tommy Jr was her grandson. Even Logan had appeared somewhat distant towards her and despite her hinting that she wanted him to come home and that she wanted them to rekindle their relationship, he hadn't seemed to want to take her up on the offer.

Dumping her handbag in the hallway, she rubbed her hand over her face then pushed open the door to the lounge. Almost immediately she rocked back on her heels, her mouth falling wide open.

'Logan,' she gasped. 'What are you doing here?'

Logan shoved his hands into his pockets and as he gave a sheepish grin, he glanced around him. 'This is still my home Carls,' he smiled. 'Our rather – our home.'

Carla's gaze went to the holdall that had been placed beside the sofa, and with her heart in her mouth, she turned back to look at him. 'Does this mean that you're coming home?' she asked, her voice tinged with hope.

For the briefest of moments Logan hesitated before giving a nod.

Unable to keep the tears at bay Carla brought her hands up to her face and sobbed. And as her shoulders heaved, the events of the past few weeks finally caught up with her. She'd fully believed that it was over between them, that despite him turning up at the scrap-yard with his dad he didn't want her any more, especially once he'd found out how the heist had been her idea.

'Hey.' Logan pulled her into his arms and stroked her hair. 'Come on babe, stop this.'

Barely able to catch her breath, Carla shook her head. 'I'm so sorry,' she cried. 'I messed everything up.'

Logan gave a gentle smile. 'Of course you didn't.' He gave a sigh. 'In a way you were right, I suppose.'

Carla looked up at him and as she searched his face, she narrowed her eyes.

'Maybe not so much about Bernie and the diamonds,' he hastily explained. 'But what you said about me. Whether I like it or not, I am my dad's son. And as much as I pretend to be nothing like him, if he hadn't pushed me into college I would have more than likely followed in his footsteps. I was ready to kill someone last night when I thought you were in danger, that you'd been hurt.'

Carla began to cry all over again and as she buried her face into Logan's chest she grasped onto him, her fingers clutching at his shirt as though she were afraid to let him go, for fear that he would leave again.

'So,' Logan said as he tilted Carla's chin so that she could look at him, 'maybe I was the one in the wrong. And perhaps in a round-about way I understand what you were trying to achieve. You wanted Bernie to suffer for what he'd done to your dad.'

As she wiped the tears from her eyes Carla nodded. 'Only,' she sniffed between sobs, 'I know now that Bernie wasn't entirely to blame, not really. My mum was the instigator, she was the one who ruined her and my dad's marriage.'

Logan raised his eyebrows, his dislike of Diane rushing to the fore. 'I'm surprised it took you so long to work it all out. And as for Bernie,' he said, his forehead furrowing, 'he does love you.'

Swallowing down her tears Carla nodded. She already knew that. From his hospital bed Bernie had tried to call her and when she hadn't answered, he'd left a voicemail telling her as much. 'What a mess,' she sighed.

'You can say that again.' Logan nodded.

Pulling away from him, Carla walked across the lounge. Opening a drawer, she retrieved the ring box and held it to her chest before walking back across the room.

'When the time is right,' she said, handing over the box. 'I want you to ask me.' She gave him a soft smile. 'I don't mean today or maybe even tomorrow, but one day when you're ready.'

Logan nodded and as he pocketed the box he flashed her a smile. 'Yeah,' he said, pulling her close again. 'One day.'

* * *

Later that afternoon, Jonny returned to the scrapyard and as he lifted a glass filled to the brim with brandy up to his lips, he shook his head. 'Don't say it,' he pleaded, closing his eyes in distress. 'I don't want to hear it, alright? I can't, not yet.'

Sonny sighed and as he glanced over his shoulder to look at Mitchell he shook his head. 'I wasn't going to say anything other than that this has to stop.' He gestured towards the glass. 'Carry on drinking like this and the only place you'll end up is at the bottom of a slippery slope.'

Jonny groaned. 'I'm thinking,' he protested.

'What, and you need a drink to be able to think?' Shaking his head again Sonny blew out his cheeks. 'Look I know it's been a tough couple of days but getting pissed out of your nut every day isn't going to help anyone is it? And as it is, you've—'

'You don't need to say it,' Jonny interrupted, his head bowed. 'I already know what you're going to say – I fucked up. That if it hadn't been for me, Terri and the baby would have...' As he looked up his voice trailed off, and when his gaze automatically drifted towards the office door, his eyes ever so slightly widened. 'What are you doing here?' he asked, screwing up his face.

Jimmy Carter stepped into the portable cabin and, noting the bruising upon his youngest brother's face, he raised his eyebrows slightly. 'Sonny called me. He's worried about you.'

Shaking his head, Jonny glared at his brother. 'Thanks for that, Sonny,' he spat. 'Who needs enemies when they've got a brother like you.'

'I was trying to help,' Sonny protested.

'Yeah, well I need your kind of help like I need a hole in the head.' Jonny retorted. 'Don't you think I've got enough on my plate without you running to Jimmy telling tales.'

Looking from Sonny to Mitchell, Jimmy jerked his head to the door indicating for his brothers to leave the office.

As he and Mitchell shared a wary glance, Sonny hesitated. At the best of times Jimmy could be volatile, and the fact they had called him home after only a few weeks of him supposedly retiring was bound to have ramifications, if not for Jonny, then for themselves. They should have called Jimmy sooner, should have filled him in on what was going on the very moment Jonny had told them about his plan to steal the diamonds.

Jimmy nodded towards the door a second time, his stance enough to tell his younger brothers that it was in their best interests to leave. Once Sonny and Mitchell had reluctantly left the office, he shrugged off his jacket and took a seat on the sofa. After a moment or two of silence he cleared his throat. 'How are they doing?' he asked, referring to Terri and the baby. 'Sonny told me it was touch and go for a while.'

Jonny's body stiffened and rubbing his hand over his face, he shook his head again. 'I don't want to talk about it...' he began.

As he studied his brother, Jimmy sat forward and rested his forearms on his knees. 'It's alright to let it all out, you know,' he said, his voice surprisingly gentle. 'Have a cry if you need to. Your missus and son almost died, that's a lot for any man to get his head around.'

Jonny looked up, anger flashing across his face. 'Don't you think I already know that?' he spat.

'I don't know,' Jimmy shrugged. 'Sonny seems to think that you're trying to block it all out, that you've been drinking yourself into a stupor as a way of not having to deal with the reality, that you almost lost them.'

Smashing his fist down on the arm of the chair, Jonny snarled, his voice coming out as a low growl. 'You think that that's what I'm doing?' he said, stabbing his finger into his temple. 'That I'd be able to block any of this out. Terri almost bled to death. My son had to be resuscitated for fuck's sake, he had tubes sticking out of his tiny body.' He jumped to his feet, his hands curling into fists. 'That's hardly something I'm likely to forget in a hurry!'

Jimmy shook his head and flicking his gaze back to the chair he motioned for his brother to sit back down.

'The question is,' Jimmy sighed once Jonny was once again seated. 'What do we do about this now?'

'We?' Jonny shook his head, his eyes flashing dangerously. 'There is no we. I will deal with this my own way.'

'Yeah, and how are you going to do that?' Steepling his fingers in front of him, Jimmy looked his brother in the eyes.

'How do you think?' Jonny snapped.

'So you're planning to kill them, is that it?' Jimmy probed. 'To have them wiped off the face of the earth?'

Jonny screwed up his face, his expression a combination of both anger and pain. 'It's not like we haven't done it before,' he snapped.

Jimmy nodded. 'I'm well aware of what we've done in the past. But that wasn't my question, was it? I'm talking about the Tuckers. Are you planning to have them wiped out?'

Crossing his arms over his chest Jonny sneered. 'Don't tell me. You think that I should do nothing. That I should let this slide or that we should go back to tiptoeing around them for the sake of the so-called truce you made,' he said, using his fingers as quotation marks.

Jimmy shook his head. 'I didn't say that. And from what I can make out, Terri and the baby weren't the only casualties. Tommy Jr was beaten to within an inch of his life, Carla is racked with guilt. And as for my brother,' he said, gesturing towards Jonny. 'You're on the verge of completely and utterly losing the plot. Either that or you'll end up drinking yourself to death. So I'm going to ask you again. Are you planning to kill them?'

For a few moments Jonny was quiet and when he finally spoke his voice was both cold and hard. 'Let me put it this way: I don't plan on letting them live.'

'Yeah, that's what I thought,' Jimmy sighed. He glanced towards the door and as Sadie came into view, he beckoned the man forward.

Sadie clutched his hand to his chest and as he stepped into the office, he gave a hesitant smile. 'I was so relieved to hear that your son is going to be okay,' he said, wiping the moisture from his eyes. 'It's all I've been able to think about since I heard what had happened.'

Springing up from his seat, Jonny clenched his fists. 'What the fuck is he doing here?' he snapped.

Jimmy held up his hand. 'You know as well as I do that Sadie has been there for this family. He did time for Jake. If it wasn't for him then Jake would have gone down and we both know that he wouldn't have been able to handle that, he was still a kid.'

Jonny narrowed his eyes and as he slowly uncurled his fists, he shook his head. 'Makes no difference,' he protested, stabbing his finger in Sadie's direction. 'He's still involved with the Tuckers.'

Jimmy raised his eyebrows, his expression enough to warn his younger brother not to argue with him. 'Whether you like it or not, we owe him and for that reason alone you'll not only hear him out, but you'll also agree to his request.'

Before Jonny could argue his case, Sadie cleared his throat and as his nervous gaze bounced between the two brothers, he wasn't afraid to admit that their combined presence made him feel intimidated.

'Go on,' Jimmy encouraged. 'Tell him.'

Clearing his throat a second time Sadie glanced down at the floor before looking back up, his body becoming rigid. 'Say what you will about him, but for the most part Ozzie has been good to me.' He gingerly lifted his hand and ran his fingers over the bruise Ozzie's fist had left upon his cheek; he was still unable to comprehend the fact that Ozzie had actually lashed out at him. 'I know he's no angel, but...'

Jonny let out an incredulous laugh. 'Is this some kind of sick joke?' he demanded of his brother as he jumped to his feet again. 'I'm not listening to this bollocks. That bastard was planning to wipe us out, and as for that fucking brother of his he could have killed Terri and my son.'

'Sit down,' Jimmy growled. Then turning his attention back to Sadie, he gave a nod. 'Carry on.'

'As I was saying,' Sadie offered a weak smile, 'I know that he's no angel, and he does deserve to be punished for what he was planning to do to your family. But...' He took a deep breath as though he were trying to compose himself. 'If his life is going to be extinguished then it will be on my terms.'

Jonny narrowed his eyes and before he could answer Sadie continued, the determined glint in his eyes enough to warn the brothers that he meant business.

'It's like Jimmy said, you owe me, you all do. I not only spent the best part of my life banged up, but I also gave up everything to help Jake. So please, I'm begging you to do as I ask.' He clasped his hands in front of him, his eyes silently beseeching them to allow him this one request.

Against his better judgment Jonny nodded. 'Go on?'

Sadie looked to the ceiling, his eyes brimming with fresh tears, and taking a deep breath he lowered his head again and looked Jonny square in the face. 'If anyone is going to end Ozzie's life then it will be me.'

19

Lenny Tucker was seething and as he lifted a cigarette to his lips, he was oblivious to the streaks of blood smeared across his knuckles. The henchman had meant nothing to him, neither had his subsequent death. If anything, his demise was to serve as a stark reminder to his remaining men of what would happen should any of them let him or his brother down. And in his opinion, the deceased heavy hadn't only let them down he'd also made a fuck up of epic proportions. It made no difference to him that both the henchman and Sadie had been outnumbered, nor did it matter that the assailants had had firearms. The only thing that concerned him, was that the diamonds were gone. And as for the Carters, the bastards were bound to be laughing at them, they had to be. They'd not only got one over on them, but they'd also made himself and Ozzie look like complete and utter mugs in the process.

As he looked out across the barren wasteland in Tilbury, Essex, Lenny's expression was hard.

'That should do it,' one of his firm members said as he leant against a shovel, his breath coming out hard and fast from the exertion of digging the hard earth.

Lenny nodded and as he watched his men tumble the heavy's body into a shallow grave, he waited until they had begun shovelling the earth back on top of him before retreating back to his car.

As he climbed behind the wheel, the scowl across Lenny's face deepened and the rage that tore through his veins intensified. It wasn't enough that he'd already rocked Jonny Carter's world and harmed his unborn child. He wanted to kill the Carters stone dead, every single last one of them and he wouldn't rest, wouldn't be able to put an end to the murderous thoughts that raged through his mind until the diamonds had been returned and the Carters had felt the full force of his wrath.

* * *

'Have you lost your mind?' For only the second time in his life, Sonny stood up to his elder brother. 'He can't do this,' he shouted, pointing his finger in Jonny's direction. 'He won't be able to handle it and you know it.'

Cocking an eyebrow, Jimmy shook his head, his expression more than enough to warn Sonny that he was overstepping the mark. Not that Sonny was prepared to take heed of his brother's warning.

'Tell me,' he said, turning to look at Mitchell, 'that I'm not the only one who thinks this is madness.'

Mitchell raised his eyebrows and as he gave Jimmy a surreptitious glance, he blew out his cheeks and shrugged, deciding it was in his best interests to keep schtum on the matter.

'Jimmy,' Sonny tried again. 'He's going to end up getting himself killed. Is that what you want, to have his death on your conscious.'

Before Jimmy could answer Jonny looked up. 'I'm not a fucking idiot, Sonny,' he shouted, his eyes narrowing into slits. 'I do know how to handle myself.'

Throwing up his hands Sonny crossed the floor of the scrapyard office. 'This isn't about you knowing how to handle yourself,' he shouted back. 'The Tuckers mean business. You stole the diamonds from underneath their noses, do you really think they're going to let that slide. That they're not going to come after your blood.'

Jonny snarled. 'And Lenny Tucker could have killed Terri and my son. If anyone's going down, it'll be him. I'm gunning for that bastard and nothing you or anyone else says is going to stop me.'

As Sonny was about to protest, Jimmy held up his hand. 'He's not the only one gunning for them. From my understanding the Tempest brothers are also on the warpath, Terri is their sister after all.'

Shaking his head, Sonny flopped down on the sofa. 'And what about Ozzie? I mean the last time I looked there were two brothers. Do you honestly think that if you top Lenny, Ozzie's gonna take that lying down, that he won't—'

'Ozzie is already being taken care of,' Jimmy interrupted. 'So from my calculation, that only leaves Lenny to deal with.'

Sonny's mouth dropped open and as he glanced back towards his twin brother confusion was etched across his face. 'I can't get my head around this.'

'You don't need to,' Jonny retorted as he got to his feet. 'In fact, Sonny,' he spat, 'you don't have to do fuck all, which let's face it, is nothing out of the ordinary is it.'

The nerve at the side of Sonny's eye twitched and jumping up from his seat his nostrils flared. 'I've been there for you,' he shouted, his temper getting the better of him. 'I've fought your fucking corner, and this is all the thanks I get for it. We warned you,' he said, gesturing towards Mitchell, 'that going after those diamonds wasn't going to end well, but would you listen, would you fuck. You were hellbent on going after them, you couldn't have given two fucks about the consequences. If anyone's to blame for

Terri and your son almost losing their lives, then it's you. It's on your head,' he said, stabbing his finger forward. 'And no one else's.'

Jonny swallowed and as the truth of the matter was finally spoken out loud, he averted his gaze, his shoulders ever so slightly drooping.

'Do I need to carry on?' Sonny continued to shout. 'Do I need to bring up every other fuck up you've made for it to sink into that brain of yours that you haven't got the first clue of what you're doing.'

'Fuck you,' Jonny snapped as he shoved his brother away from him.

Clenching his fists Sonny's face was white with anger and as he made to pull back his arm, Jimmy got to his feet.

'That's enough,' he warned as he looked between his two brothers. 'Tucker's fate has already been sealed and that's the end of it.'

'And that's it, is it?' Sonny growled. 'You're gonna trust him,' he said, nodding towards Jonny. 'To go off and dish out his own form of retribution.'

Thinking the question over Jimmy glanced towards his youngest brother, then nodded. 'He took over the reins from me, so yeah, I do trust him to sort shit out. And as I've already stated, the Tempests are also gunning for Lenny Tucker. Between the four of them I'm pretty sure they can handle it. I mean,' he said, spreading open his arms. 'How hard can it fucking be? Tucker's a spineless rat.'

As Sonny watched his younger brother leave the office, he couldn't help but give a sad shake of his head. 'I hope you know what you're doing,' he remarked to Jimmy. 'Because when this goes tits up and he ends up dead in a ditch somewhere, don't say that I didn't warn you.'

* * *

As well as owning a public house, the Tempest brothers also ran a taxi firm in Dagenham and as Jonny entered the taxi office, he immediately held up his hands as though to stop Terri's family from jumping up and laying into him.

'What do you want?' Ricky growled.

Jonny sighed and as he leaned against the door, he shook his head. 'Look,' he said. 'If anything, we should be working together. Terri is your sister and...'

Lounging back on a chair Mason gave an incredulous laugh. 'Is he having a bubble?' he asked his dad and uncle. Turning back to look at Jonny, his lips curled into a snarl and as he sat forward his eyes were as hard as flints. 'We should fucking bury you.'

Jonny nodded. 'Maybe,' he said, glancing out of the window. 'But that won't achieve anything, will it.'

'Nah, but it would make us feel a lot better,' Jamie chipped in.

As he rubbed his hand across his face Jonny pushed himself away from the door. 'You're angry and I get it...'

'Yeah, he's definitely having a bubble,' Mason interrupted, his expression hard. 'You haven't got a scooby how we feel. Terri's family, she's a Tempest, and for that reason alone, you deserve a kicking.'

Jonny held up his hands again. 'I fucked up,' he admitted. 'I should never have left her at the office and...'

Jamie jumped up from his seat, his face turning bright red as he kicked a chair out of his path in his haste to reach Jonny. 'Keep talking,' he growled. 'You're digging yourself an even deeper hole.'

Standing his ground, the muscles across Jonny's shoulders became rigid and as he looked at each of the Tempests he lifted his eyebrows. 'I'm going after Tucker,' he stated. 'If you want to smash my face in after that then go ahead and do what you need to do, but until then we need to work together to bring that lowlife down.'

Mason sighed. 'He's got a point,' he said, somewhat begrudgingly. Lounging back in the chair he casually toyed with a screw-driver, his weapon of choice. 'What do you reckon Dad?'

As he pondered the question, Ricky gave his brother a sidelong glance. He'd made no secret of the fact he'd disapproved of Terri and Jonny's relationship. Right from the start he'd known that Jonny, or rather his chosen occupation, would become his sister's downfall. 'I take it you've got a plan?' he asked.

'Of course I have,' Jonny answered, his eyes hard. Although to say he had a strategy in place would be a slight exaggeration and other than hunt Lenny Tucker down, he didn't have much else to go on in the way of a plan. The only thing he did know for certain was that Tucker wouldn't be given the opportunity to walk away from him.

'Doesn't look as though we've got any other choice does it?' Ricky said, getting to his feet. 'But believe me,' he added, turning his hard stare towards Jonny. 'This isn't over, and sooner or later you're going to get what's coming to you.'

Jonny sighed. 'I wouldn't expect anything different from you,' he answered, his expression sombre.

* * *

During the drive from Tilbury to his brother's house, Lenny's mood hadn't decreased in the slightest. If anything, he was even angrier than he'd been before – if that was in anyway possible.

By the time he'd climbed out of his car and thumped his fist on his brother's front door he was ready to commit a second murder.

'Why the fuck is he still here?' he asked, jerking his thumb in Sadie's direction.

As he lit a cigarette Ozzie ignored the question. 'Is it done?' he asked, referring to the henchman. 'Is he dead?'

Lenny narrowed his eyes and as he watched Sadie scurry out of the lounge it took everything inside of him not to charge after his brother's lover and then proceed to batter him to death. In his mind, both he and the heavy were equally to blame for the theft of the diamonds. They should have stopped the Carters even if it meant putting their own lives at risk, after all it was better to die a hero than a coward. 'Ozzie,' he hissed. 'Why is he still here?'

Ozzie looked up and blowing out a cloud of smoke, he glanced towards the lounge door. 'Because he lives with me that's why.'

Anger creased Lenny's face and bringing his hands up to his head he stared at his brother. 'I can't believe what I'm hearing. That bastard,' he spat, stabbing his finger towards the door, 'allowed the Carters to walk in here and take the diamonds.'

Stubbing the cigarette out in an overflowing ashtray, Ozzie snaked his tongue over his teeth. 'What do you expect me to do,' he snapped. 'Kill him?'

Lenny threw up his arms. 'It'd be a start. We've been made to look like fools.'

Ozzie's eyes hardened. 'I already know that and certainly don't need reminding.' He crossed his arms over his chest as he studied his brother. 'Why the sudden change of heart? If I remember rightly, you were the one begging me not to top Diane.'

Exasperated, Lenny rubbed at his forehead. 'Bernie's missus had fuck all to do with this, she was innocent.'

Ozzie snorted. 'What are you talking about?' he argued. 'She was threatening to blow my head clean off my shoulders.'

Lenny took a deep breath and as though he were trying to control his temper, he clenched and unclenched his fists in rapid succession. 'I want him gone,' he hissed through gritted teeth. 'And if you don't end him then I will.'

* * *

Sadie's heart was beating so hard and fast that he had to remind himself to breathe. Clutching his hand to his chest, he stood in the kitchen and frantically looked around him for a weapon; something, anything, that he could use should Lenny, or even Ozzie for that matter, decide to kill him.

Yanking open a drawer, he pulled out a bread knife, not that he could say a knife would be his weapon of choice. For a start, it would mean he would need to get close to Lenny, and comparing their strength, he had a feeling that Ozzie's brother would easily be able to overpower him.

No, when it came to defending himself, a gun would be the better option. His gaze drifted to the hallway and for the briefest of moments he wondered if he would have the time to slip past the lounge and make it up the stairs before Lenny was upon him.

Hidden away at the bottom of his wardrobe was a handgun. After his visit with the Carters, he'd swiped the weapon from the holdall where the Tuckers kept their firearms and put it away for safe keeping. He could only hope and pray that when the time came to use it, that he'd be able to see it through, not that he had any other choice on the matter. It was either kill Ozzie himself or leave the task in the Carters' capable hands and if he was to do that, then he knew for a fact Ozzie's death would be brutal, that they would make him suffer, perhaps even torture him if Danny McKay had anything to do with it. And for all of Ozzie's faults, Sadie couldn't allow that to happen. He loved him, cared for him, kept a house for him. He'd even go as far as to say that he felt somewhat responsible for him. His presence somehow seemed to calm Ozzie down, even the red mists that descended over him had become few and far between since they'd been together.

Stuck between a rock and a hard place, Sadie knew it would be just as easy for him to inform Ozzie and Lenny of the Carters' murderous intentions, but how could he do that? For so many years he'd been loyal to the Carters and the fact he'd kept his mouth firmly closed when it came to Jake and Ronald Browning's murder was proof of that fact.

From the lounge Lenny's voice rose even further. 'I mean it Oz,' he roared. 'End him or I will.'

Sadie's heart quickened even further and as footsteps could be heard in the hallway he grasped hold of the knife even tighter, his fingers trembling.

Instead of Lenny bounding into the kitchen the footsteps became more distant and moments later the front door slammed closed. Tentatively Sadie inched forward, his ears pricked, and as he poked his head out of the kitchen he glanced from the front door to the lounge. 'Oz,' he called out, testing the waters. 'Would you like a cup of tea?'

Ozzie grunted in return and heading back into the kitchen, Sadie placed the knife back into the drawer and flicked on the kettle. Unease surrounded him and he knew it was only a matter of time before Ozzie followed through with his brother's request, he was bound to, especially if the truth was to ever come out.

As he waited for the kettle to boil, Sadie gripped onto the kitchen worktop and breathing heavily through his nostrils, he closed his eyes. His entire body shook; the fear of what was to come consuming him. He opened his eyes and as he looked over his shoulder, he knew what he had to do, what had to be done. As though on autopilot he straightened up and as the kettle reached boiling point, he left the kitchen and made his way up the stairs, his movements slow and precise as he made his way into the bedroom, opened the wardrobe door then retrieved the gun from its hiding place.

With the weapon in his hand, he retraced his steps and coming to a halt outside the lounge, he forced himself to enter the room.

He'd have just one chance, he told himself. One chance to give

Ozzie a peaceful ending. Even as the thought popped into his mind, he wasn't so sure it was what Ozzie deserved. After all, Ozzie had lived a life of violence and would have had no qualms when it came to ending the Carters' lives.

Determination spread through Sadie's body and as he swiped the tears from his eyes he lifted the gun in the air, his hand surprisingly steady. Just one chance, he told himself again as he curled his finger around the trigger. One chance.

20

As Ricky Tempest chewed on a piece of nicotine replacement gum he gave an irritated sigh. 'Have you even got any idea where Tucker is?' he snapped.

Momentarily taking his eyes off the road, Jonny turned his head. 'What do you think,' he snapped back. 'I'm not a fucking mind reader.'

Jamie and Mason shared a weary glance and as they went back to staring out of the window on the lookout for the man in question the atmosphere in the car became even heavier.

'Well, he's got to be some—' Mason's voice trailed off and as he turned in the seat he stared out of the back window. 'Was that him?'

Jonny looked up in the rearview mirror as both Ricky and Jamie craned their necks to get a better look.

'It was,' Mason shouted. 'That was him.'

Slamming his foot on the brake, Jonny performed a three-point turn. 'Are you sure?'

'Yeah.' For a split-second Mason hesitated.

'You don't look so certain,' Ricky said as he looked over his shoulder at his son.

'Nah, it was him.' Sitting slightly forward so that he had a better view of the road ahead, Mason nodded. 'It has to be. I've seen his car parked outside the boozer enough times.'

Jonny raised his eyebrows and putting his foot down on the accelerator he overtook the car in front of them. 'I'm gonna kill the bastard,' he stated.

Ricky raised his eyebrows. 'Only if you don't end up killing us first,' he said, gripping onto the grab handle above the door.

A smile spread its way across Jonny's face. 'There's a reason I was the family getaway driver,' he grinned, accelerating even more.

* * *

With one hand gripped to the steering wheel, Lenny Tucker shifted his weight. He was so tense that he likened his body to that of a tightly coiled spring.

Ahead of him, the traffic lights turned amber and as the car in front of him slowed down he thumped his fist on the car horn.

'Come on!' he screamed. 'It's not even red yet.'

A second later, the light turned red, enraging him even further and as he placed his hand on the door handle, he was in a half-mind to jump out of the car, drag the driver out of his motor and beat him to a pulp.

Just as he was about to, both the passenger and rear passenger doors opened and two figures climbed into his car.

Lenny's eyes were like golf balls and as his jaw dropped, the men laughed at his obvious confusion. 'What the...?' he began before snapping his lips closed.

Ricky Tempest's expression was hard and as his hand shot out and grabbed Lenny around the throat he snarled in his ear. 'Drive the fucking motor before I end up doing you in here and now.'

Lenny swallowed and as he glanced up at the rear-view mirror to see Jamie Tempest sitting behind him, his insides turned to liquid. He should have guessed that they wouldn't be happy, that there would be repercussions after he'd lashed out at their sister, not that the silly mare hadn't asked for it. How was he supposed to have known that she was behind him? He didn't have eyes in the back of his head.

The traffic lights turned green and when Lenny made no attempt to move, from behind him Jamie slung his arm around Lenny's neck and yanked him back in the seat, almost cutting off his air supply in the process. 'Move the fucking car otherwise I'm gonna slice you wide open and watch you bleed out like a fucking pig.'

Struggling to free himself, Lenny tugged at Jamie's arm. He could scarcely breathe and as panic began to build inside of him, his face turned bright red and his eyes began to bulge.

'Do you understand what I'm telling you?' Jamie shouted.

Frantically Lenny nodded and as Jamie threw him away from him, he rubbed at his neck gasping for air.

'Now drive,' Ricky ordered.

Despite his predicament Lenny weighed up his options. And just as he was about to open his mouth to tell the brothers to fuck off and get out of his car, the sight of Ricky's hand shooting towards him again made him hastily rethink his choices. 'Alright,' he screamed, pushing his foot down on the accelerator. 'All right, I'm moving.'

Ricky nodded and with his expression still set like thunder, he kissed his teeth. 'You fucked up, Lenny, my old son,' he said, shaking his head. 'Believe me you fucked up big time.'

* * *

Shock resonated across Ozzie's face and as his startled gaze went from Sadie to the gun, he narrowed his eyes.

'What the fuck do you think you're doing?'

Sadie's hand began to shake and as his bottom lip wobbled, he blinked away the tears in his eyes. 'I have to do this Oz,' he told him, his voice thick with emotion. 'It's the only way.'

Ozzie's eyes narrowed even further and as he made to get up Sadie waved the gun towards him.

'It's over,' he said. 'If I don't kill you then the Carters will, and I can't let them do that.'

A sneer spread across Ozzie's face and with one hand gripping onto the arm rest as though he were preparing to use it as a crutch to propel him forward, he began to laugh. 'Those pussies are fuck all. They wouldn't know how to fight their way out of a paper bag.'

Sadie shook his head. 'You know that's not true,' he stated and forcing himself to stand a little straighter he willed himself not to lose his nerve. He couldn't back down, not now, Ozzie would kill him stone dead after the stunt he'd just pulled.

'Put the gun down.' Ozzie stretched out his arm, his eyes not wavering from Sadie's face.

Again, Sadie shook his head. 'I can't,' he whispered. 'I love you Oz. I can't sit around and wait for the Carters to take matters into their own hands. They'll hurt you, they'll...'

'I said put the fucking gun down,' Ozzie shouted, charging forward.

In a blind panic Sadie let out a shrill scream, his body trembling so much so that he was in grave danger of dropping the gun.

In the scuffle that ensued, the gunshot that rang out was deafening to Sadie's ears, and jumping back in fright he stared down at the weapon in his hand as though it were alien to him. His mind and body numb, he stood for several moments not knowing what to do before dropping to his knees and gingerly inching out his hand.

His heart in his mouth he called out to Ozzie, his gaze transfixed on the bright red blood seeping across Ozzie's shirt.

When he received no reply, the tears that had threatened to spill down Sadie's cheeks fell freely. He made no attempt to wipe them away and as he placed his hand on Ozzie's arm, he gently shook him.

There was no response. It was clear to see that Ozzie was gone. Wrapping his arms around himself Sadie rocked back and forth, the enormity of what he'd just done hitting him with the intensity of a sledgehammer. He'd just killed a man, and no matter how much his intentions may have been pure, it still hurt, still broke his heart in two.

After what seemed an age, he got to his feet and wiping the tears from his eyes, he took several deep breaths in an attempt to clear his head. He had to move and fast, had to get as far away from the crime scene as quickly as he possibly could.

With the gun in his hand, he ran up the stairs taking the steps two at a time. He needed to pack a bag and throwing handfuls of clothes onto the bed, he wrapped the firearm in a hand towel then placed it at the bottom of a rucksack before shoving the clothes on top, in an attempt to hide the weapon.

Moments later he was heading back down the stairs. At the front door he paused and turning his head, he looked in the direction of the lounge. Everything inside of him screamed at him to check on Ozzie one last time. What if he wasn't dead, what if he'd only been injured and was in pain?

Swallowing down the lump in his throat, he turned away from the lounge and took a shuddering breath. The blood alone had been enough to tell him that Ozzie was dead. He opened the front door, and hitching the bag onto his shoulder, Sadie ran as though his life depended on it.

* * *

Sonny Carter was feeling shattered and stifling a yawn, he stretched his arms above his head.

'Come on you two,' he said to Tommy Jr and Reece. 'Time to call it a night.'

Ushering his nephews out of the office, Sonny was about to turn off the lights and lock up when two cars pulling onto the forecourt stopped him dead in his tracks. As his eyes adjusted to the darkness, he threw Tommy Jr and Reece a glance then stepped forward.

'What's going on?' he called out when his younger brother jumped out of his car.

When Jonny didn't answer, Sonny turned to look at the second vehicle, his eyes almost bulging out of their sockets as Lenny Tucker was dragged kicking and screaming out of his car.

'Tell me you haven't,' he pleaded, bringing his hands up to his head. 'That you're not that stupid you'd bring him here.'

Jonny's face was white with anger. 'Fuck off, Sonny,' he growled, shoving his brother out of his way.

Too stunned to speak, Sonny's mouth dropped open. 'You can't, not here.'

'I told you to fuck off.'

Sonny snapped his lips closed and as Lenny was hauled past him into the office, he nodded towards his nephews. 'Leave now,' he ordered.

'Yeah but...' Tommy Jr nodded towards the office. 'If he's gonna get what's coming to him,' he said, referring to Lenny, 'then I want to be here. That fucker's had it in for me,' he said, stabbing a finger into his chest.

Bounding forward, Sonny gripped his nephew by the elbow. 'I told you to leave, both of you,' he reiterated, the tone of his voice enough to warn Tommy Jr and Reece to do as he asked. 'And make sure that you keep your mouths shut,' he called after them.

Once his nephews had left the scrapyard, Sonny pushed open the door to the office and as he took in the scene before him, he rocked back on his heels. 'Jonny,' he said in a warning. 'I know that you're angry, but you can't do this, not here in the office.'

Jonny snarled and as he rounded on his brother, he pushed him back onto the forecourt. 'I've already told you once. Fuck off. This is fuck all to do with you.'

At a loss for words Sonny looked helplessly around him. Finally finding his voice, he snapped his gaze back to the portable cabin. 'Does Jimmy know about this, that you've brought Tucker here?'

Enraged, Jonny spun back around, his expression enough to warn Sonny to back off. 'Let's get one thing straight,' he said, stabbing his finger forward. 'I run things now, not Jimmy. So do yourself a favour and fuck off because you're really starting to make me lose my rag. I'm warning you, Sonny,' he shouted. 'Get off my fucking back.'

As he studied his brother, Sonny nodded. From the steely glint in Jonny's eyes, he knew there was no way of changing his mind, and holding up his hands, he sighed, then turned and walked away.

He'd said all along that Jonny was a liability, that his recklessness was going to bring them all down. The only thing he hadn't realised was how stupid his brother really was.

* * *

In a cafe in East Ham, Jake Carter placed two mugs of tea on a table. He couldn't say that he was entirely overjoyed that Jimmy had requested he be the one to meet with Sadie. If anything, he wanted to do everything within his power to stay out of the man's path.

After all, one word from Sadie and his entire world would come crashing down around him.

As the door opened Jake glanced up, and narrowing his eyes, he watched as Sadie made his way towards him. His hair in disarray and his face as white as a ghost.

'Are you okay?' Even as he said the words, Jake realised how stupid he sounded. Of course, Sadie wasn't okay, just one look in his direction was enough to tell him that.

Without answering Sadie took a seat, and lifting the mug to his lips, his hands shook so violently that the liquid spilled over the sides.

Jake averted his gaze and slipping his hand into his pocket he pulled out an envelope. 'Jimmy asked me to give you this.' He slid the envelope across the table. 'It's some money to tide you over and the keys to one of his properties.' He dipped his hand into his pocket again and retrieved a burner phone. 'He also said that if you need to contact him then to use this.' He nodded down at the device. 'His phone number has already been saved to it.'

'I suppose that's it then.' Sadie gave a sad smile. 'It's over.'

For a second time, Jake glanced away. Was it over, could it ever be over? Jake wasn't so sure. Maybe the past would one day rear its ugly head, and when that happened, he had a sinking feeling that their lives would never be the same again.

'You know, you can trust me.' As though reading his thoughts Sadie took another sip of his tea. 'Up here,' he said, tapping his temple, 'are secrets that I will never tell another living soul. Secrets that I intend to take to my grave.'

Jake nodded and as he drank his own tea they fell into a comfortable silence. From an outsider looking in they must have looked an odd couple. Jake, as was typical of the Carters, reeked of money, and his clothes, although casual, were designer brands. And then there was Sadie, his hair in need of a cut and colour, nails bitten down to the quick, and then his outfit that he'd pulled on in a rush to escape from the scene of Ozzie Tucker's murder, a mix match of different styles and colours. Only they were more alike than anyone could have ever guessed. Both had once been victims, and both were now murderers.

21

Despite the shard of fear that ran down the length of Lenny Tucker's spine he couldn't help but scowl at the men who had all but taken him prisoner. 'You won't get away with this,' he smirked. 'You just wait until Ozzie gets wind of this. And you,' he said, pointing towards Jonny, 'will be the first on his list. You thought you were so clever didn't you, that we wouldn't guess it was you and those cunts you call a family who took the diamonds.'

As he began the process of rolling up his sleeves Jonny looked up. 'You mean these diamonds,' he said, nonchalantly flicking his head towards a rucksack that had been slung into the corner of the office. 'I hold my hands up, it was me.' He flashed a wicked grin. 'And as for Ozzie,' he gave a mock sad smile, 'somehow, I've got a feeling he won't be putting in an appearance.'

Lenny's mouth became suddenly dry and as he tore his gaze away from the rucksack, he racked his brain as he tried to decipher the hidden meaning behind Jonny Carter's words. Warily, he glanced towards the Tempests and spreading open his arms he let out a nervous laugh. 'Come on, it was an accident, surely you know that. How was I supposed to know the stupid mare was standing behind me?'

Jamie Tempest narrowed his eyes. 'That's my sister you're talking about.' He clenched his fists. 'You hit her so fucking hard her uterus abrupted. You could have killed her – both her and my nephew.'

Lenny screwed up his face and as he turned to look at Jonny, his heart beat a little faster. Did that mean that the baby was alive, that he wasn't a child killer? Well, that had to change things surely. He backed away and bumping into the wall behind him, he let out a laugh. 'Well seeing as they're both alright there's no need for any of this is there.'

He didn't receive a reply and with his back against the wall, his gaze darted towards the door in an attempt to gauge the distance between himself and his only means of escape. 'When Ozzie—' he began.

'Ozzie's dead,' Jonny barked out. 'Did you honestly think I was going to let him live. In fact, it was Sadie who did the honours.' Momentarily he paused, clicked his fingers then pointed at Lenny. 'You didn't know that Sadie and my family are like this did you.' He crossed two fingers to emphasise his point. 'We go way back, decades in fact.' He leaned in closer. 'It was Sadie who tipped us off. He was the one who told us where the diamonds were, that they'd been moved from Bernie Adams' gaff.'

In that instant, a flurry of different emotions spread through Lenny's body. All along, he'd known that Sadie couldn't be trusted. Was it any wonder that he'd despised him, that he'd wanted Ozzie to get rid of him. And then it hit him. If they'd told him about Sadie's involvement then they had no intentions of allowing him to walk away. He swallowed deeply, his gaze drifting back to the door. He'd never make it in time, they'd be upon him before he'd even taken two steps across the office.

It was then that Lenny knew he was about to die, that no matter what he said or did he wouldn't be walking out of the office anytime soon. And as they advanced towards him, he shook his head, the snarl across his face intensifying. They were going to take him down; he knew that as well as he knew his own name, but if they thought he was going to go down without a fight then they were very much mistaken.

* * *

Clutched in Mason Tempest's fist was his screwdriver and as he glanced between his dad and uncle, a grin spread across his face. 'I've missed this,' he said, nodding down at the makeshift weapon.

Ricky lifted his eyebrows. Like Terri, he too had been worried about his son. After the injuries Mason had received, he'd seemed to retreat into himself. A small part of him had even wondered if Mason had lost his nerve; he certainly didn't appear to be as aggressive as he'd been previously. He cocked an eyebrow. 'Go on then,' he coaxed, jerking his head in Lenny Tucker's direction. 'He's all yours. But,' he winked, 'don't kill him – at least not yet, anyway. I'm pretty sure we're all gonna want a turn.'

Lenny's mouth fell open. 'You're sick,' he spat, his voice high. 'You should all be locked up in a nut house.'

Ricky laughed. 'Coming from you, I don't know whether that's an insult or a compliment. I mean,' he said, laughing even harder, 'Ozzie wasn't exactly what you could call sane, was he?' He shook his head. 'You messed with a Tempest,' he stated, his voice becoming suddenly menacing. 'And as I've already said, you fucked up big time.' He locked eyes with his son then flicked his gaze towards Lenny. 'Do your worst,' he grinned.

Mason didn't need to be told twice and as he charged forward, he plunged the screwdriver deep into Lenny's cheek.

Lenny howled with pain and collapsing to the floor he clutched at the gaping hole in his face, his eyes blazing from a combination of both shock and fury. 'You bastards,' he hissed as blood oozed through his fingers.

Jamie chuckled. 'Compared to what you've got coming, it's a mere scratch.' He flicked his head towards Mason again and as his nephew pulled back his arm, Jamie's expression became hard. 'Stop toying with him,' he demanded, 'and show him what you're really capable of.'

Sonny was beside himself and as he paced up and down the pavement just outside the scrapyard gates, he couldn't help but give the office furtive glances. Jonny had gone too far this time. His stupidity, his carelessness was going to have repercussions for them all. And God only knew he'd be one of the first to hold his hands up and admit that they weren't saints: they committed armed robbery, they'd even murdered in the past, but never had they been so brainless, so stupid that they'd actually killed someone on their own property.

Moments later, Jimmy pulled up beside him, his skin ashen. 'Where is he?' he barked out, his gaze automatically drifting towards the portable cabin.

His face as equally pale, Sonny jerked his head behind him in the direction of the office.

'Right.' Switching off the ignition, Jimmy leaned his elbow on the open window and as he tapped his fingers on the steering wheel, he sighed.

Sonny's forehead furrowed, and as he looked from his elder brother to the office, confusion swept over his face. 'You need to sort him out,' he said. 'He's about to kill Tucker in our fucking office.'

Thinking it over, Jimmy sighed again, then shaking his head he leant across the passenger seat and unlocked the door. 'Get in,' he ordered.

Just as Sonny was about to argue the case, Jimmy lifted his eyebrows. 'Get in, Sonny, please.'

'The thing is,' Jimmy said once Sonny had climbed into the car. 'What kind of message will we be sending out if we go over there and start throwing our weight around?'

Sonny screwed up his face and as he was about to open his mouth and answer, Jimmy continued.

'He's in charge now. He's the boss, so to speak. And as reckless as he might be at times, we can't undermine him, not in front of the Tempests.' He turned to look at Sonny and lifting his eyebrows he sighed again. 'He's got to learn by his own mistakes. We've all been there. Look at the amount of times I've messed up over the years. For a start I trusted Gary when I shouldn't have. And then there's Tommy.' He gave a smile. 'He nearly killed both me and Gary in the office when we were young, he absolutely battered the life out of the pair of us.' He glanced back towards the office, still tapping his finger on the steering wheel. 'Jonny needs to learn how to be the head of the family bruv, and he's not going to be able to do that if we keep stepping in every five minutes to sort him out.'

As he thought over his brother's words, Sonny nodded. 'So what do we do then?'

'We wait,' Jimmy said, making himself comfortable. 'What else can we do. And when it's over we make sure the stupid fucker hasn't left any evidence behind.'

* * *

Jonny blew out his cheeks and as his chest heaved he stared down at the blood covering his hands. He had to give it to him, Tucker had put up a fight, not that he'd stood much of a chance against them. At the end of the day the fact he'd been so heavily outnumbered could have only meant one outcome, and that was death.

'What are we gonna do with him?' Mason asked as he prodded Lenny's body.

Jonny fought the urge to shrug. In truth he didn't know what they were going to do with Tucker's corpse. One thing he did know, was that they couldn't leave him in the office, give it a day or two he'd start stinking the place out and the amount of grief that would cause him didn't bear thinking about. No doubt Sonny would be one of the first to have something to say about the situation.

He chewed thoughtfully on his bottom lip and as he raked his fingers through his hair, he jerked his head in the direction of Lenny Tucker's body. 'I'll get on the blower to my mate, the one who cleaned up the warehouse after we did Frankie Gammon over.'

Ricky glanced up. 'Looks like this is becoming a bit of a habit, eh,' he grinned. 'Four murders in under two years.'

Screwing up his face, Jonny shook his head. In his mind, all four of the murders they'd committed had been warranted. That wasn't to say, however, that he was in a hurry to commit a fifth murder anytime soon.

'Right then.' Jamie stepped over the body. 'Get on the blower to this mate of yours. Oh, and one more thing,' he said, stabbing his finger forward. 'Don't think that we haven't forgotten about you. You're still on our radar and you'll soon get what's coming to you.'

Jonny rolled his eyes. His love-hate relationship with the Tempest brothers was beginning to get on his last nerve. If it wasn't for Terri, he'd happily never lay eyes on them again. As it was, she thought the sun shone out of their arses, even Mason, and he was a bona fide nutcase if ever Jonny had seen one. He pulled his mobile phone out of his pocket, and as the Tempests left the office, not for the first time did it occur to him that they'd left him to deal with the dirty work.

* * *

As Jimmy tapped his thumb on the steering wheel, Sonny nodded towards the office.

'I suppose it's done then?' he said as Ricky, Jamie, and Mason walked across the forecourt.

Sitting beside him in the driver's seat, Jimmy nodded. 'Looks like it.' He glanced at his watch, then opening the car door, he stepped outside. 'It took them long enough.'

At the doorway to the portable cabin Sonny paused and as the unmistakable scent of blood assaulted his nostrils, he wrinkled his nose. Just as he'd expected it would, the office resembled a blood bath. Not only did speckles of blood coat the walls and ceiling but if the condition of the corpse was anything to go by, he had a feeling his brother and the Tempests had gone more than just a little bit overboard.

Jonny turned to look at them and as his shoulders slumped, he ran his hand through his hair. 'Have you been out there this whole time?' he asked.

Sonny ignored the question and blowing out his cheeks he motioned around him. 'This is going to be a bugger to clean,' he said to no one in particular. He shook his head again and as Jonny gave an irritated sigh, he snapped his head towards him. 'It looks like an abattoir,' he hissed. 'And that's putting it mildly.'

Jonny swallowed and as he looked around him, he shrugged. 'It's not that bad. It just needs a bit of a clean up that's all.' He peered closer at the specks of blood sprayed across the wall. 'And if that doesn't work, I'll buy a tin of paint and paint over it.'

Sonny let out an incredulous laugh. 'I've been saying for

months,' he said, tapping his head, 'that you're not right up here, that you've got a screw loose. You've got to be deluded if you think a paint job is going to be able to sort this mess out. It needs...'

'Burning to the ground,' Jimmy suggested.

'It'd be a start,' Sonny agreed.

Jonny sighed. 'I'm not burning it down. There's a lot of history in this old place.'

'Yeah,' Sonny agreed. 'You can say that again.' Over the years every single one of their heists had been planned out in the cabin. It was more to them than just an office, it was their second home. He gave a shake of his head and studied his younger brother. 'Do you feel happy now?' he asked, raising one eyebrow. 'You've got the diamonds, topped Tucker, made an absolute mess of the office, and to top it all off you've only been in charge for two fucking weeks.'

For a moment Jonny thought the question over, and shoving his hands into his pockets, he shook his head. 'No, not really.' And it was true. As much as he'd achieved what he'd set out to do, it had come at a price. All because of him and the decisions he'd made, he'd very nearly lost Terri and his son. At the end of the day, it hadn't been worth it, none of it had.

Relenting, Sonny scooped up the rucksack and shoved it towards his brother. 'I take it you've organised a cleanup?'

Jonny groaned. 'Despite what you might think of me, I'm not entirely stupid.'

'Yeah.' Sonny blew out his cheeks and as his gaze raked over the blood splattered across the walls, he shook his head again. 'If you say so bruv, if you say so.'

EPILOGUE

As far as diamonds went, the ones currently grasped in Jonny's fist were what could only be described as stunning.

'What did I tell you?' Grinning from ear to ear, Jonny uncurled his fist to reveal three glittering, brilliant round-cut diamonds. The larger of the diamonds weighing approximately four carats and boasting fifty-eight facets. 'Didn't I say that they were beauties?'

Albert Warren's rheumy blue eyes widened. Having been in the diamond trade for the majority of his adult life it would be fair to say he knew quality when he saw it. 'They certainly are,' he said, leaning in closer to have a better look. 'And where was it you said you'd sourced them from?'

Testing the waters, Jonny tapped the side of his nose. 'I can't tell you that Albert,' he said, his voice barely louder than a whisper, as though he and Albert were fellow conspirators. 'But what I can tell you is that there are plenty more of them at my disposal.'

'And the workmanship,' peering even closer Albert gave a low whistle, 'is out of this world.' He swept his arm around the shop. 'And far better than anything in my collection.'

Jonny raised his eyebrows and taking note of the shards of light rebounding off the gems in the glass cabinets either side of Albert's shop, he gave a nod. He hadn't needed Albert to tell him that the diamonds were of good quality, in fact if the newspaper reports on the robbery were anything to go by the stones had been highly sought after, with buyers from all over the world interested in purchasing the gems. Out of habit he glanced around him, his eager gaze falling upon each of the security cameras. 'So,' he said, curling his fingers back around the stones, 'can you make me a ring or...' he paused for a moment to let his words sink in, 'do I need to take my custom elsewhere?'

Albert's eyes lit up and gesturing for Jonny to follow him through to the back room, there was a sense of urgency about him, almost as though he were afraid Jonny would change his mind and leave the shop without the business at hand being concluded. 'Of course, I can and let me tell you something else for nothing.' He puffed out his chest with a measure of pride and flashed a wide smile, his thin lips almost disappearing to reveal a set of wide gums and crooked, tobacco-stained teeth. 'I'm the best in the business.'

'I'm sure that you are.' Jonny gave a wink. 'You came highly recommended. In fact,' he paused and lifted his eyebrows, 'it was Danny McKay who recommended you.'

Albert's eyes widened and as his gaze went from Jonny's face to where the diamonds were being held in his fist, he gave a slight shake of his head. 'I take it they aren't above board then.' He gave a wicked grin and lowered his gravelly voice. 'That there's a strong possibility they fell off the back of a lorry.'

Jonny couldn't help but grin. 'Something like that.'

'Well, why didn't you say so earlier?' Albert winked. 'And I trust,' he said, nodding towards the diamonds. 'That the lady in question will also be very happy.'

Jonny gave a light laugh. His Terri would be more than happy, in fact he could have given her a plastic ring from a Christmas cracker and she would have treasured it. Not that he actually would, of course, he may have been many things but tight-fisted certainly wasn't one of them. As Albert pulled out a series of gold and platinum settings, his mind began to wonder. He'd never imagined the day he would want to settle down, let alone get married, and yet here he was. Not only had he recently become a father but he was also about to pop the question.

'What do you think?' Albert grinned. He pointed to one of the platinum settings. 'This one,' he said, 'once set with the diamonds would look quite spectacular.'

Jonny studied the setting. It was a simple, elegant design, and he knew instinctively that Terri would love it. 'It's perfect,' he grinned before glancing at his watch. Terri and his son were due to be discharged from the hospital at any moment. And although it would be fair to say that he was feeling nervous at the prospect of having the baby at home without the aid of the nurses, he couldn't help but feel a ripple of excitement tear through his veins. Both James and Terri needed to be at home, where they belonged, and even more than that, as a family, they needed some normality back in their lives.

As Jonny left the shop, there was a spring in his step and just as he reached the car the distinctive sound of police sirens echoed through the air. For the briefest of moments Jonny froze, and as he glanced back at the jewellers, he cursed under his breath. Had Albert called the filth the moment his back had been turned?

Minutes later two police cars sped past him, and placing his hand on the car roof, Jonny bowed his head, his heart practically beating out of his chest, before he promptly burst out laughing. The Carters may have been what he would call lucky thieves, but it wasn't only down to sheer luck that they had never had so much as a whiff of the old bill on their tail, let alone a capture. They worked hard, put the groundwork in and never left anything to chance. In other words, they covered their tracks well; a stipulation that had been passed down from his eldest brother, Tommy.

Climbing behind the wheel of the car, Jonny started the ignition and as he flicked the indicator, he gave the jewellers one final glance before pulling out onto the road, already thinking of his next target.

The jewellers had been heaving with diamonds and with only three security cameras trained on the premises, it would be the equivalent of taking candy from a baby. Not that Sonny or Mitchell would ever agree to the heist, in fact, if anything, they'd accuse him of not learning his lesson the first time around. And then there was the threat of having Jimmy on his back again. Just the mere thought of his elder brother coming out of retirement for a second time was enough to make him shudder. As it was, Jimmy had given him a swerve and he had a feeling that it was only a matter of time until Jimmy's patience finally ran out. As quickly as the idea sprang to his mind, Jonny hastily discarded it again. Maybe they should stick to robbing banks for a while, if for no other reason than to keep Sonny and Mitchell happy, or at least until his younger nephews had some experience behind them. And speaking of his nephews, Tommy Jr had brought an opportunity to his attention, a heist that he was sure his brothers would happily agree to. After all, they would be fools to pass up the prospect of turning over a van filled with cash, and the fact the said van had once been owned by the Queen wouldn't be enough to deter them. At the end of the day they were experts, robbing banks was their bread and butter so what could possibly go wrong? As for the future, who knew what it held? Maybe one day his son, or perhaps even sons, should he and Terri decide to have more children, would join the family business. With a new generation of Carters on the horizon, the possibilities were endless. The only thing he did know was that he couldn't wait to get stuck in, couldn't wait to teach his boy the way of the world, or rather the Carters' world, and what better teacher than himself, after all, he himself had been taught by the best, a legacy that he was more than happy to pass down.

* * *

Sadie wandered from room to room of his new apartment and as the removal men carried in pieces of furniture, he held his finger to his lip as though deciding where to place his belongings.

'Put it right there,' he said as the men heaved his new sofa, courtesy of the Carter family, into the lounge.

In fact, the entire apartment and its contents had been paid for by the Carters. His compensation, they called it, although in Sadie's mind it was nothing of the sort. He didn't require payment for his actions, neither did he regret what he'd done. And although it had somewhat broken him to extinguish Ozzie's life, he'd had no other choice but to see the grisly murder through.

The Carters had even seen to it that he'd been given employment, and although it didn't pay particularly well, he didn't need much. The apartment had once belonged to Jimmy and just that morning the deeds had been placed into his name. He was a homeowner, something he would never have believed possible.

For the first time in what seemed like decades he was actually free. Never again would a man have control over him; if anything it was time to start living and he had so many plans for the future that he wasn't so sure where to start.

'Where do you want these?'

Sadie glanced up and as he looked from Jake to the box of magazines in his hands, he gave a gentle smile. 'Over there.' He gestured to the floor to ceiling length window that looked out over London. The view was stunning, one that he had a feeling he would never tire of.

Jake placed the box in front of the window then straightening up, he turned to look at Sadie. 'Are you going to be okay?'

'Of course I will.' Sadie beamed. 'Besides, I'll see you at work Monday morning, bright and early.'

Jake laughed. 'I wouldn't get too excited,' he said. 'You'll only be making endless cups of tea.'

'And cleaning,' Sadie added, pursing his lips. 'And from what I've seen of the office, it needs a good spring clean.'

'I suppose so.' Shoving his hands into his pockets, Jake turned back to look at the view. 'I'd better be off then.'

Sadie nodded and as they walked to the front door, Jake paused. 'Thank you.'

Screwing up his face, Sadie waved his hand dismissively. 'No need to thank me,' he sighed then offered a sad smile. 'I did what I thought was best.'

'No.' Jake shook his head. 'I'm not talking about Ozzie Tucker...' He took a deep breath. 'I meant what you did for me.'

Sadie's eyes ever so slightly widened and before he could open his mouth to answer, Jake pulled him into a bear hug.

'I should have said it sooner,' he said, letting go. 'You saved my life.'

A hard lump formed in Sadie's throat preventing him from answering, and as Jake turned to walk away, he glanced over his shoulder and flashed a cheeky grin.

'See you on Monday,' he called out before stepping into the lift.

For several moments Sadie stood motionless, and it wasn't until the removal men heaved the last of his furniture into the flat that he gave a shake of his head and followed after them, a broad smile across his face and his heart light.

* * *

As Carla sat on the edge of the hospital bed, Bernie clasped hold of her hand.

'Thank you for coming to visit me,' he smiled. 'It means more to me than you could ever know.'

Carla returned the smile and as she nodded towards the empty chair beside him, she lifted her eyebrows. 'It's a shame that I missed my mum, I would have come earlier if I'd have known she was here.'

Bernie chuckled at the obvious lie and clutching his hand across his ribs, he gingerly leaned back against the pillows. 'I forget it hurts when I laugh,' he groaned. 'Not that I can say I've had much to laugh about in recent weeks. The house is due to be repossessed any day now, and your mum...' He shook his head. 'Well, you can imagine what she's had to say about the situation.'

Carla patted his hand. 'But you're on the mend?' she asked, lifting an eyebrow.

'Of course I am,' Bernie reassured her. 'Give me a week or two and I'll be as right as rain. I'll bounce back, you just wait and see if I don't.'

Getting to her feet Carla glanced behind her. 'There's someone here to see you.'

Bernie narrowed his eyes.

'But before he comes in, I just wanted to say...' she swallowed and looked away, unshed tears burning her eyes. 'I am so sorry for the way I behaved towards you. I made your life hell when I was growing up.' She lifted her shoulders. 'I wanted someone to blame, I suppose and you were the easy option. I wanted to hate you, really hate you, only you didn't make it easy for me. Even as I was plotting your downfall, I knew it was wrong, that I was targeting the wrong person. If anyone was to blame for all of this then it was my mum.'

'Hey,' Bernie reached out for her hand, his expression one of concern, 'I wasn't entirely faultless. Besides, you weren't that bad.'

Carla let out a laugh. 'I was and you know it.'

'Well, maybe a little,' Bernie smiled and as he turned his head to see Sonny standing in the doorway, his jaw dropped.

'My dad's got something he wants to say to you,' Carla said as she dropped a kiss on Bernie's cheek then made her way over to her father. Giving Sonny's hand a reassuring squeeze she slipped past him then gently pushed him into the room.

Hastily composing himself, Bernie looked up at his old friend.

Awkwardly, Sonny shifted his weight from one foot to the other then clearing his throat he looked Bernie in the eyes. 'I just wanted to say thank you.'

Taken aback, Bernie waved his hand dismissively. 'I didn't do anything,' he protested.

Sonny gave an incredulous laugh and shook his head. 'You warned me about the Tuckers,' he said, lowering his voice a fraction. 'Warned me not to come after the diamonds, and,' he motioned behind him, 'if it hadn't been for you giving me the heads-up, I would have never known that Carla was in danger.'

Bernie nodded. 'I know the feeling isn't exactly mutual, but I love her as though she's my own daughter and I've done my best over the years; I've tried to be there for her.'

'I know.' Sonny gave a small smile, then digging his hands into his pockets, he shrugged. 'Name your price and I'll make sure you've been repaid for helping us out.'

Bernie screwed up his face. 'I don't want your money, Sonny.'

Sonny huffed out a breath. 'I owe you,' he said. 'And considering your money troubles. It's the least I can do.'

'No.' Bernie shook his head, his cheeks flaming red. 'You owe me nothing, not after what I did...' His eyes filled with tears and as he swiped them away, he swallowed down the hard lump in his throat. 'If anything, it's me who owes you.'

For a few moments Sonny studied the man he'd once loved like a brother. They had been so close once, even closer than he and Mitchell were. 'Look,' he said, stepping even further into the room. 'What you did took a lot of bottle.' He gestured to Bernie's injuries. 'Tucker could have killed you.'

Bernie shrugged. He'd risk his life over and over again if it meant saving Sonny and his family.

'So, name your price,' Sonny continued.

About to protest again Bernie paused. 'Anything?' he asked, cocking his head to the side.

'Anything,' Sonny reiterated.

A glint sparkled in Bernie's eyes and as he gave a half-smile, he lifted his left hand in the air and studied the gold band on his wedding finger. 'Can you pass across the details for a divorce lawyer?'

Sonny narrowed his eyes and as he too cocked his head to one side, he spoke. 'Are you being serious?'

'Deadly,' Bernie said as he slipped the ring off and placed it on the bedside table. 'And I know it's too late for us to ever go back to where we were, but I want you to know that I am sorry.' Full of remorse he placed his hand upon his heart. 'I will go to my grave regretting my actions, there aren't enough words to even begin to describe how sorry I am. I ruined our friendship...' He wiped a stray tear from his cheek. 'But believe me when I say this, I never meant to hurt you, Sonny. I would have died for you and if I could, I'd give anything to be able to turn back the clock.'

As he contemplated Bernie's words, Sonny briefly closed his eyes. 'I'll do one better than that,' he finally answered, flashing a grin. 'Not only will I give you the details for a divorce lawyer but I'll also fucking pay for it.'

Collapsing against the pillows Bernie chuckled. 'You always knew exactly how to make me laugh,' he cried, clutching his arm around his broken ribs.

Sonny shrugged. 'Only because you were as fucked up in the head as I was,' he grinned.

As they fell into a familiar camaraderie, Sonny plonked himself on the end of the bed. 'I don't know if I can ever forgive,' he stated. 'Or even forget for that matter, but...' he paused, then offered out his hand, 'I'm willing to give it a try.'

Bernie swallowed deeply, and blinking his eyes several times, his heart began to race. 'I'll take that,' he answered, grasping Sonny's hand. 'In fact, I'll take it with both fucking hands.'

* * *

As Carla stepped out of the hospital room, Rina jumped up from her seat.

'How is it going?' she asked, her expression one of concern as she wrung her hands in front of her.

Glancing behind her, Carla bit down on her lip, then turned back to give both Rina and Logan a weary smile. 'They haven't started tearing chunks out of each other yet, so I'd take that as a good sign.'

Rina nodded. 'They just need some time,' she said, still somewhat unsure.

'I hope so,' Carla answered. She placed her hand on Rina's arm. 'I've been meaning to tell you that I'm glad you and my dad found each other.' She glanced behind her to Bernie's hospital room. 'He deserves to have someone in his life, someone who actually cares about him.'

Rina's face lit up. 'And I do,' she answered. 'Very much so.' She glanced down at her watch. 'I was going to go and get a coffee while I wait for your dad, would you and Logan like one?'

Carla shook her head and as she gripped hold of Logan's hand her gaze drifted down to her engagement ring. Just as she'd hoped he would, Logan had proposed and without even needing a moment to think the question through, she'd flung her arms around him and said yes. 'No thanks, Rina. I promised Terri that we'd pop in on her and the baby before Jonny comes to collect them.'

Moments later both Carla and Logan said their goodbyes and as they headed in the direction of the maternity unit, Carla gave a light laugh. 'You know,' she said. 'I've been thinking about Terri and Jonny's baby.'

'What about him?' Logan frowned.

Carla lifted her eyebrows. 'With Carter and Tempest blood running through his veins, little James could very well be one to watch out for.'

As he shook his head, Logan sucked in his bottom lip. 'You've got a point,' he said, his eyes twinkling. 'But add Murphy blood to the mix and it's going to be nothing short of absolute chaos.'

'Blimey.' Carla's eyes widened. 'I didn't even think of that. I hope the world's ready,' she added with a shake of her head. 'Because if the next generation of Carters is anything like the last, they'll be more than just a force to be reckoned with and God help anyone who stands in their way.'

ACKNOWLEDGEMENTS

A huge thank you to Boldwood Books for your continued support and also a special thank you to my editor Emily Ruston.

I would also like to say to say thank you to Joana Castro for always being there. And also a huge thank you to Elizabeth Tyler. Not only do you know my characters even better than I do, but you also spend endless hours discussing plots with me.

Thank you to each and every member of NotRights Book Club. You have been there from the very beginning and your support means more to me than you could ever know.

And lastly a special thank you to Carla Allison for allowing me to use your name. I hope that you love Carla as much as I do.

ABOUT THE AUTHOR

Kerry Kaya is the hugely popular author of Essex-based gritty gangland thrillers with strong family dynamics. She grew up on one of the largest council estates in the UK, where she sets her novels. She also works full-time in a busy maternity department for the NHS.

Sign up to Kerry Kaya's mailing list for news, competitions and updates on future books.

Follow Kerry on social media here:

 facebook.com/kerry.bryant.58
x.com/KerryKayaWriter
instagram.com/kerry_kaya_writer

ALSO BY KERRY KAYA

Reprisal

The Fletcher Family Series

The Price

The Score

Carter Brothers Series

Under Dog

Top Dog

Scorned

The Reckoning

The Carters: Next Generation Series

Downfall

The Tempests Series

Betrayal

Revenge

Justice

PEAKY READERS

GANG LOYALTIES. DARK SECRETS.
BLOODY REVENGE.

A READER COMMUNITY FOR
GANGLAND CRIME THRILLER FANS!

DISCOVER PAGE-TURNING NOVELS
FROM YOUR FAVOURITE AUTHORS
AND MEET NEW FRIENDS.

JOIN OUR BOOK CLUB
FACEBOOK GROUP

BIT.LY/PEAKYREADERSFB

SIGN UP TO OUR
NEWSLETTER

BIT.LY/PEAKYREADERSNEWS

Boldwœd

Boldwood Books is an award-winning fiction publishing company seeking out the best stories from around the world.

Find out more at www.boldwoodbooks.com

Join our reader community for brilliant books, competitions and offers!

Follow us
@BoldwoodBooks
@TheBoldBookClub

Sign up to our weekly deals newsletter

https://bit.ly/BoldwoodBNewsletter

Printed in Great Britain
by Amazon